PRAISE FOR CH

THE MISREMEMBERED MAN

"Her portrait of rural life is amusing and affectionate, wittily and winningly detailed."

Kirkus Reviews

"Known chiefly as a painter . . . McKenna proves in this, her first novel, to be equally adept at word portraits."

Washington Times

"I love how McKenna combines seemingly effortless comedy with literary truth. She doesn't pull any punches. I literally laughed out loud at several points."

Goodreads reviewer

"Outstanding . . . one of the best novels I have ever read. I did not want it to end. She has a wonderful ear for dialogue and a talent for observing awkward social situations and unspoken intimacies."

Amazon reviewer

THE DISENCHANTED WIDOW

"I've been racking my brain to pounce on at least one minor flaw in . . . Christina McKenna's riveting account of a new widow and her nine-year-old son fleeing the IRA in 1980s Belfast, and all in vain. So I have no recourse but to succumb to the pleasures of her prose."

Free Lance-Star

"There are at least two ways to read this story. One is as an Irish prose version of an Italian opera buff – a tragicomic tale with emphasis on the bumbling comic. The other is as a satire, along the lines . . . of Henry Fielding's classic novel *Tom Jones*."

Washington Independent

"This is the second book I have read from Christina McKenna and I LOVED IT. What characters and plot! Story so well told, I couldn't put it down! I can't wait for the next one."

Goodreads reviewer

"Her characters have such depth, you feel you know them intimately. This is a gem – a literary page-turner."

Amazon reviewer

"McKenna is a master in the great Irish tradition of telling bittersweet tales."

Amazon reviewer

THE GODFORSAKEN DAUGHTER

"*The Godforsaken Daughter* is a perfect complement to the first two books and makes the reader beg for more."

Goodreads reviewer

"Best read for the year. Poignant, romantic, thriller, relationships, love and so many more. How could a book carry so much emotion, and yet flow so fluidly? A compelling read. If there is only one book you have time to read in a year, better make it this one."

Amazon reviewer

The Spinster Wife

ALSO BY CHRISTINA McKENNA

My Mother Wore a Yellow Dress (memoir)
The Dark Sacrament (non-fiction)
Ireland's Haunted Women (non-fiction)

The Misremembered Man (fiction)
The Disenchanted Widow (fiction)
The Godforsaken Daughter (fiction)

The Spinster Wife

CHRISTINA McKENNA

LAKE UNION
PUBLISHING

Text copyright © 2017 Christina McKenna
All rights reserved.

Published by Lake Union Publishing, Seattle

www.apub.com

Amazon, the Amazon logo, and Lake Union Publishing are trademarks of Amazon.com, Inc., or its affiliates.

ISBN-13: 9781612186993
ISBN-10: 1612186998

Cover design by Richard Augustus

Printed in the United States of America

For my sister, Marie-Celine
In memoriam

Nobody heard her tears; the heart is a fountain of weeping water which makes no noise in the world.

Edward Dahlberg (1900–1977)

PROLOGUE

Do you ever ponder how many times you've come close to death? How many times you've met a stranger on the street, not realizing he carried a knife in his pocket and was randomly selecting "the one" whom his voices that day were urging him to kill?

But he liked the way your hair shone in the sunlight. And you smiled at his approach, not knowing that your smile had saved you.

How often have you shared tea with a psychopath? Brushed up against a bomber in the checkout queue? Opened the door to a serial rapist who reads gas meters for a living? Bought fertilizer from a garden centre whose owner killed his wife five years before and sank her deep beneath the patio where you stand to pay your bill?

But you do it all the time: come within touching distance of the Dark Angel. Except . . . except some inner prompting steers you clear and you survive to take in the next breath. And the next one, and the next one. A lifetime dealt out in breathing and heartbeats, and the sheer blood-pumping effort of surviving, dodging the bullets of happenstance, with your hopes and your dreams, your obsessions and fears held tightly inside. Until one day you trip up, fall down, peter out, and the earth finally claims you for itself.

CHAPTER ONE

Portaluce, Antrim Coast

Dorinda Walsh knew she lived in a dangerous world. On the night of 25 January 1986, manifestations of the bleakest kind were invading her dreams, hovering like some great amorphous thing, seeking to engulf her.

Keep breathing! a voice called from the darkness. *Keep breathing. The breath is God, Dorrie. The breath is God.*

Dorrie twitched under the satin quilt of the narrow divan bed but did not awaken. She was caught in a web of terror, haring like a wild creature over a desolate beach, face uplifted, elbows flailing, mouth wide in a voiceless scream. She could feel her heart thudding, sweat coursing down arms and legs, but could not stop.

She was running towards a light. Eyes steady on the beam. She must not lose sight of the light. If she blinked, all would turn to darkness and she'd be gone.

Then, quick as a shutter click, the light became a vision. Dorrie slowed. The image was oval shaped, its outline shimmering with a celestial glow. It dazzled her and she shaded her eyes, transfixed.

Was it the Virgin Mary? Was it an angel?

No, she saw now that within the bright ellipse stood a familiar figure, one gloved hand raised in greeting. The Fatima-blue coat and the fall of white mantilla were unmistakable. It was her mama. But Florence Walsh was on the Other Side. Those were her burial clothes.

"God must see me at my best, Dorrie," she'd said with feeling. "Make sure of that before you put me in the ground."

Dorrie *had* made sure. But now her mother was no longer in the ground. She was very much above ground, standing just fifty yards away, waving. Oh, the joy of touching her again!

"Wait, Mama dear, wait! I'm coming, I'm coming!"

Dorrie's feet gathered pace again, racing over the sand. Death could not touch her in her mother's arms. It was imperative that she reached her.

Bongggggg!

The sound of a bell.

Her legs buckled.

She fell.

Her eyes snapped open. She was lying on her back, gasping for air. Beneath her: the yielding softness of fabric. Not the cold, wet sand of a beach.

She was in bed.

It was only a dream.

Yes, she was in bed. It was only a dream and she was back in the waking world.

But where?

Above her: a woodchip ceiling, a light fitting of dimpled glass. Her whole body tightened. Where was she? She blinked, eased herself up on her elbows.

This was not her room. Light was hazing the window, but those were not her drapes. She took a deeper breath.

The bell tolled again: deep-throated, ominous. Sunday? Sunday bells calling the faithful to prayer. Over the dwindling notes came other sounds: screeching, clamorous. Gulls. Seagulls.

It must be Sunday, Dorinda decided, and I must be at the seaside. But how did I get here?

She sat up, squinted at her watch. Ten past eight. Took in her surroundings: white furniture, cupid-pink decor. The carpet, a deeper shade: raspberry. Yes, raspberry; that's what Mama would have called it. "Colours have personalities, Dorrie. They give us meaning. So they deserve engaging names."

Tears. Quick and hot. She squeezed her eyes tight against them. Saw her mother again, radiant in her Fatima-blue outfit, one gloved hand raised. The almond gloves with pearl trim, buried with her too. "A lady is never fully dressed without gloves, dear."

Consoled. Yes, at that moment she felt consoled. All would be well. When she dreamed of her mother it was always a good sign. She was with her in spirit. She'd always be, but—

Without warning, out in the corridor, there were footfalls on carpet. Floorboards creaking, quietly. Dorrie held her breath. Light treads. A woman's. Yes, a woman's surely. They halted for a moment at her door, passed softly on, gathered pace down a staircase, clipped across hardwood and were gone. It was safe to breathe again.

Gingerly she drew back the covers and sat on the edge of the bed. Something in the footsteps, their urgency across the hallway, told her she must get moving.

Her head ached. She pressed a palm hard against her brow, gazed at the bedside table. On it was an empty bottle of Jameson whiskey and a glass. Did I, she thought, drink *all* that? Alongside the bottle: a brochure lying face down. She turned it over. **WELCOME TO THE OCEAN SPRAY.** Below the greeting, a reproduction of *Under the Wave Off Kanagawa*, its curling wash tinged with gold. She opened it up:

**LOCATED ON THE PROMENADE, PORTALUCE
EXCELLENT ROOMS FACING SEA FRONT
BEST DRINKS IN STOCK
CATERING PAR EXCELLENCE
MODERATE RATES
COMFORT – STYLE – CIVILITY
MRS GLADYS D MILLMAN – PROPRIETRESS**

At last, a clue. Portaluce.

Hard on the heels of this knowledge, a snapshot of her childhood came unbidden. Mama on the beach in a tea dress, frowning. "Uncle Jack" in a gaberdine suit, hands shoved loosely into pockets, staring out to sea. They'd had an argument. Dorrie, standing with bucket and spade between the two, knowing she'd been the cause of it—

No time for that!

She slammed a brake on the memory.

Recent events were what mattered. Events of the evening before. She tried hard to recall them, but they kept slipping from her like elvers on an ebb tide.

"Focus!" she rebuked herself, softly but firmly. Focus on getting dressed and resolving the situation. The owner of those footsteps would surely know what had happened. Dorinda *needed* to know, no matter how embarrassing such an explanation might be.

Emboldened, she stood up and, in one swift movement, slipped out of the nightgown. Only when the baggy thing – two sizes too big in a ghastly shade of yellow – lay on the bed did she realize it did not belong to her.

Her legs went weak. Good Lord, had a stranger put her to bed? She looked down, horrified to see she was still in her underwear. She never slept in her underwear. Someone *had* put her to bed. A woman. Yes, a woman, thank heavens. A man would most likely have removed the lingerie.

Frantically she scanned the room for an overnight bag. If she'd booked in here for a night then surely she'd have packed one. But there was no sign of a bag. Only an untidy jumble of clothes on a chair.

Dorrie, darling, pull yourself together and get dressed! A voice in her head. Mama's voice, warm but chiding. *Get dressed, go downstairs and have a nice cup of Darjeeling. Go with the flow, my dear. Go with the flow.*

Her hands were shaking as she sorted through the clothing: a beige blouse, black skirt and matching velvet jacket. The colours and soft textures were appealing. *Remember, dear, you were born the year Chanel became an adjective. Aim for neutral tints. Bright colours are for prostitutes.*

Oh, how she missed her mother's sage advice on all things con-sumerist and shallow! But there was no time now to dwell on the late Florence Walsh.

Dorrie dressed hurriedly and went to check herself in the wardrobe mirror. Her auburn hair was in disarray, but a comb would sort that out.

Rat-tat-tat. A soft rapping on the door.

She tensed, smoothed down her skirt.

"Yes, what . . . what is it?" Her voice sounded like the rasping of a can opener in the quiet of the room.

"Your breakfast . . . it's ready, ma'am!" The young woman's tone was diffident and for that reason seemed reassuring.

A pause.

Dorrie fought for the right words.

Then: "Miss Gladys wants to finish up, so Cook can get the lunches, you see."

"Yes . . . yes, of course. Sorry. I'll be . . . I'll be down in five minutes."

"Thank you, ma'am."

She waited for the footsteps to fade away down the stairs. Miss Gladys? The "proprietress"?

Immediately she scrambled about for her shoes. The black high heels were lying by the bed. But they were a sight: covered in sand, with fronds of seaweed sticking to the soles.

"I strolled along the beach in my stilettos?" she said aloud. "*Never. I always go for walks in flats. Always.*" Somehow she had to convince herself of that.

Panic gripped her. Dear Lord! But there was no time to cogitate on why she'd done such a crazy thing. *Dorrie, dear, being late for appointments and keeping others waiting is a sign of vulgar breeding.*

"I know, Mama. I know."

Yes, the cook was waiting. Miss Gladys was waiting. She was keeping everyone waiting and it was all her fault because she'd got drunk, lost control and had let a stranger put her to bed. Oh dear, how was she going to get herself out of this one?

Desperately, she rummaged in her handbag, found a comb, teased her hair into shape.

Now: a coat. I must, she told herself, have brought a coat in this weather surely. Puzzling that it wasn't hanging over the chair along with her other things.

She went to the wardrobe and pulled the door wide open. There was no sign of a coat – but there was a shopping bag. It contained a white trench coat.

No sooner was it in her hands than she dropped it in horror.

Down the front of the coat was the ineradicable evidence that something very dire indeed had taken place.

The coat was mottled with bloodstains.

CHAPTER TWO

Samaritan Centre, Killoran

The phone rang. Rita-Mae Ruttle prepared herself. She sat down. Took a deep breath. Picked up the receiver.

"Samaritans. May I help you?" Her voice was warm and calming: the tone she'd been trained to adopt when offering succour to the afflicted.

"I wanna kill meself!" A man's voice, gruff and breathy down the line. "I wanna kill meself and be done with it, so I do."

A heavy sigh.

Rita-Mae sat as still as a waxwork, the telephone receiver pressed tightly to her ear. She was conscious of her breathing – controlled, inaudible, so as not to disturb the client – a list of emergency numbers pinned to the board in front of her, and the thrum of the strip light: a light that filled with brash effulgence the all-too-tiny cubicle.

It was important she remain immobile in these situations. In training sessions they'd told her that if you scratched your nose, doodled on the pad in front of you, even rolled your eyes, the person on the other end of the line could sense it, intuit that you weren't really *listening* – which meant you didn't really care – might cut the call and go out and kill themselves.

And the reason this man was speaking now into Rita-Mae's right ear was because others had stopped listening, stopped caring, and that was *why* he wanted to kill himself. She was his last hope. Hers might be the ultimate voice he'd hear before departing this life. But she hoped not. As a Samaritan it was her business to save him from the rope, the knife or the river – three of the more popular methods used by men to end it all.

"I'm sorry to hear that," she said gently. "I'm Rita, by the way. Would you like to tell me your name?"

A pause.

"Rita, did you say?"

"Yes. Rita."

Stertorous breathing, low-pitched and snuffly.

"You don't have to give your real name if you don't want to . . . and only your first name is necess—"

"Lenny."

"Lenny. I'm sorry, Lenny . . . so sorry to hear that you're not feeling the best." The words slow, careful, a calculated pause. Then: "How long . . . how long have you been feeling this way?"

"Och, now . . ." She heard him suck heavily on a cigarette, exhale the smoke, shift in his chair. Leather or vinyl, judging by the squeak it made. "Been like this a good wee while. That's why I wanna kill meself, 'cos nobody cares what happens tae me no more."

"I'm sorry to hear that, Lenny. But killing yourself is a permanent solution to a temporary problem."

She'd been trained to say that too, with emphasis on the words "permanent" and "temporary".

"I am here to let you know that nothing is ever as bad as it seems, that every state we find ourselves in is a temporary one. That tomorrow is another day and there is always light at the end of the tunnel, even though you may not be able to see it at this precise moment in time."

"Aye, right," the caller said, in a tone that conveyed that he was not at all convinced by Rita-Mae's string of fridge-magnet platitudes, tripped out for his reflection.

He took a swallow of something and Rita-Mae knew, by the greedy guzzling sound he made, it was likely alcohol. She waited. The telltale report of glass on wood confirmed her guess – mugs made a duller sound – and it was five o'clock on a Saturday morning after all.

"Have you got family?" she asked, maintaining that quietly comforting tone.

"Nah."

"So you live alone?"

"Sort of, aye."

Another drag of the cigarette, another gulp of the drink. "She – the wife – left me 'cos of the drink. Crashed the car on a skinful last year and the oul' leg isn't what it used to be . . . have to use crutches to get about. Nothing down there is what it used to be, if you get me drift. She sez tae me: 'I married a useless alcoholic, now I'm married to a bloody crippled alcoholic, so you can just go feck yerself.' That's what she said, if you'll pardon me French."

Rita-Mae had winced at the coarse language. But she must not judge; that was another injunction from the Samaritan rulebook.

"Aye, pardon me French, Rita, but that's what she said, the bitch. And then she fecked off herself, so she did."

"You're in pain then and you're living on your own. That can't be easy, Lenny."

"Nah, not aisey atall. The drink takes me mind off it. I'm drinking even more than afore the accident. So out of it all I've got a shot liver, a dodgy dick, a wrecked leg and a broken heart. Is it any wunder I wanna kill meself?"

Rita-Mae flinched again. She'd better steer him on to more positive ground.

"Hmm . . . I understand, Lenny. Do you . . . do you have any hobbies?"

"Used to play football, but can't kick a ball about no more with me leg."

More drink was sloshed into the glass.

"Nah, can't kick the ball about no more," he sighed.

"Do you . . . do you have any children?"

"Aye. Livin' with me daughter these days."

Another drag of the cigarette. Then: "And would you be married yerself, Rita?"

She hesitated. "That's neither here nor there, Lenny."

Long pause. Pauses were good. Her trainer had assured her that a caller's pauses could speak volumes. That she shouldn't rush into them right away, like a fireman with a hose.

She relaxed her grip on the receiver and waited.

"I know it's neither here nor there," he said at last, "but I just wanna know anyway. 'Cos a married woman would understand better what a man like me's goin' through, like."

"No . . . no, I'm not married," she lied.

Her admission was met with an exhalation of breath. Was that a sigh of relief or . . . ?

Then: "What colour of knickers would you be wearin', Rita?"

She tensed.

"That's . . . that's neither here nor there."

She squeezed her eyes tight. He was one of *those*. TM callers – telephone masturbators in Samaritan-speak. The instructor had warned her about those too. The TM callers shunned sex lines because sex lines cost money. Besides, an automated voice in Belfast demanding one's credit-card details was no match for a soft-voiced woman with a sympathetic ear, alive and breathing in the middle of the night, somewhere in mid-Ulster, completely free of charge. This was the third TM caller she'd had in as many hours. She'd have to terminate the call.

"Aye, I know it's neither here nor there," Lenny was saying, "but are yer knickers big flowery ones, or them nice wee skimpy boys?" Breathing heavier now, more laboured. "I hope they're the wee skimpy type 'cos they'd be aisier to take off you."

She was fighting to control herself. Wanted to scream down the line, "You're wasting my time, you selfish cretin! Someone in *real* need could be trying to get through." But she reined herself in, steadied herself, shifted her tone into pragmatic official-speak and said: "I am sorry, but I am now going to have to terminate this call."

"Aye, so . . ."

She was careful not to use contractions. People listened more attentively when one shunned them in favour of complete words. "It is always best to call the Samaritan helpline when sober. That way, we can discuss all the options that are open to you in a clear and frank manner."

"Aye, so."

"If you have a problem with alcohol you can call the Alcoholics Anonymous helpline, day or night. You will find their number in the front section of the *Yellow Pages*. You can avail of *our* services at any time. If you wish to speak to any of us face to face, you can make an appointment and come into the office. I hope this information has been helpful. Goodnight, Lenny."

"Och, yer no fun atall, Rita. Wait a wee minute—"

Click. She'd put the phone down.

CHAPTER THREE

Rita-Mae took the memory of Lenny all the way back to Willow Close and in through the front door of her rented semi-detached house on the outskirts of Killoran. Yes, in the front door and right through to the kitchen, where she peeled off her gloves, shed her coat, set down her handbag and let out a sigh. She'd been advised about that too during training sessions: taking "emotional baggage" home with her.

"Everything you hear within these walls must *stay* within these walls," the director, Mrs Emmeline Wilton, had said. A retired hospital matron with powdered cheeks and a mouth that resembled the artwork of a toddler. "If you have problems dealing with what you've heard, talk it over with a fellow-volunteer before leaving the Centre. Do not discuss it with family or friends. That is a cardinal rule."

She sighed again. Caught sight of herself in the mirror above the sink. She was thirty-four, and without sleep looked ten years older. Her short hair, bluntly cut, emphasized her elfin features and wide-set eyes. In the playground she'd been nicknamed Pixie-Mae, and as she grew into womanhood, the taunt stuck, resulting in her eschewing adornment of any kind – no cosmetics, no earrings or necklaces that might draw attention. At times, especially when wearing a scarf tucked behind her ears and tied at the back, she bore a passing resemblance to Audrey

Hepburn in *The Nun's Story*. But all that effort to remain inconspicuous only served to spark the interest of the onlooker even more.

It was what had attracted Harry, her husband. He saw in her a child-woman he could bend to his will.

She banished the thought of him and switched her focus to making tea. Snatches of Lenny's conversation came and went as she put the kettle on and prepared a tray. His was not a "serious" case. That was a comfort. He had no desire to kill himself and was most likely sleeping off the incident on his vinyl sofa, oblivious to the fact he'd even made the call. Alcohol did that to a person. Messed with the memory. She never touched the stuff herself, but Harry's binges had shown her more than enough of its diabolical effects. There were mornings when she'd find him fast asleep on the doorstep, clothing in disarray, the car-door wide open. It would have been laughable had he not been such a brute.

In Larne she'd been a Samaritan for over three years. It was the only thing she'd been permitted to do outside the home – apart from shopping, and the occasional stint at the local hairdresser's if one of the girls called in sick. The sole reason Harry had agreed to her becoming a volunteer was because his own brother had committed suicide. In his twisted logic it eased his conscience somewhat to have his wife do penance for this grave wrong.

She'd been happy to learn that Killoran had a Samaritan Centre. She could continue to do the good work she'd committed herself to in Larne. Listening to the many anguished callers gave her perspective on her own life. Made her feel useful. Kept her focused. "No matter how bad you think things are, there's always someone worse off than you." Yes, she'd heard some tragic tales down the helpline.

This thought lifted her momentarily out of the funk that had followed her home. She was doing important work by listening. Nobody really listened any more. They were too busy with their own problems to be bothered. As a Samaritan you stopped the ceaseless chatter in your own head – deliberately so – and tuned into the fears and trials of another human being. Listening attentively and not judging could save lives.

At first she was both surprised and shocked to discover that there were so many women just like her, living at the mercy of abusive husbands. So many men like Harry driving their wives, with breaking voices, to the refuge of the suicide helpline. She imagined shoals of them tossing about on a turbulent sea, their hands grasping for the lifebelt that was her voice. The fearful clung on! Oh, how they clung on!

". . . for the sake of the children."

". . . because he loves me."

"Deep down he's really nice."

"It's the drink, you see."

"Och, he doesn't mean it really."

"When he's not on the tear he's the best in the world."

"It's the cross I have to bear."

"I'll just have tae offer it up, like me mother before me."

All the excuses trotted out to keep them netted, just as Rita-Mae had allowed herself to be kept netted and bound for so long. Trapped in a two-up, two-down council house, accepting the black eyes, the broken ribs, the splintered teeth and jawbones. Better to suffer the beating than find oneself alone. Living life on one's own terms was simply too scary to contemplate.

"Run!" she wanted to tell them all. "Just pack a bag and run. It's never too late." But as a Samaritan she wasn't permitted to dole out advice. Simply listen. Listen and be there for the desperate. Besides, how could she ever tell those women to cut and run when she was too cowardly to do so herself?

Too cowardly, that is, until three weeks ago. Yes, a mere three weeks ago something extraordinary had occurred.

It all started with Harry's scrawled note.

Got job on site in Croydon. Cause we needs the feckin money and your not gonna make nuthin you useless naggin bitch. Ye cut my bloody face. Yer gonna pay for that when I get back. I'll see you before you see me.

As she was reading it, a mix of joy and terror mounting – joy that he was gone, terror because he was accusing her of hitting him, something she'd never dared to do – the local newspaper was pushed through the door. Normally she'd have taken it from the letter box, run an iron over any creases, carried it into the sitting-room and placed it on a table by "his" TV armchair. For that was the way Harry liked things done, and what Harry liked, wanted or demanded, Harry got. It was safer all round. She'd learned that lesson the hard way.

But now he was gone. The newspaper shook in her hands. It was her paper now. *Really hers.* Or was it? She'd never been allowed to read it. The realization caused her to drop it.

Pages fanned out at her feet. In a panic, she scrambled down to gather them up. That was when Fate winked like a precious gem and she found herself staring at the property page and the photo of a house framed in black.

A quaint, Tudor-style semi with bay windows, flowers flourishing in pots either side of the door, and a neat little garden out front. It was the kind of home she'd always dreamed of.

An excitement took hold of her. A tightly folded bud of desire, kept in check for so long – by Harry and the world at large – began to quiver and unfurl as she read through the fine print: one bedroom, box-room, bathroom, kitchen and lounge. A lounge. How lovely that sounded! Newly renovated. Fully furnished with fitted carpets throughout. The best part of all was the price: £30 per month. Cheaper by far than the poky dungeon she called home.

She looked up from the page, sensing that this was a seminal moment. A reckoning point, once glimpsed, that might never come again. Fifteen years of marriage hung in the balance. Fifteen years a drudge, at the mercy of a man who'd never really loved her, had never really cared.

How often had she dreamed of escaping? How often had she summoned the courage, only to waver at the last minute with his voice booming in her ears: "If yeh ever try tae leave me, yeh bitch, yer dead."

She glanced back at the page.

Located on the outskirts of Killoran.
Contact Abraham Hilditch on 082 796282 for details.

She faltered.

Waves of fear rose up. Images quick and terrifying: images of the consequences this action could bring. Harry's hands throttling her. The room spinning round and round. Her world turning black.

She stared at the printed telephone number. Felt her body flood with purpose. Should she? Could she? The tiny numerals lined up in heavy type held the promise of a new life. The advertiser, Abraham Hilditch, held the key to her release – literally.

With trembling fingers she dialled the number.

The phone rang several times. Her heart quivered. Give it up, a niggling voice in her head said. You've never succeeded at anything. Just give it up!

Yes, maybe I—

Then suddenly on the line a man's voice: "Good morning. Abraham Hilditch speaking." The tone was cheery, businesslike.

"Hello . . . I'm . . . er . . . I . . . I . . . was wondering about the . . . er, house . . ."

"You mean the rental?"

"Y-Y-Yes, the rental."

She heard Mr Hilditch rustle through some papers. "Yes, now let me see . . ."

"Is it . . . is it still available?" She hoped he didn't detect the desperation in her voice.

"Indeed it is, Miss . . . er . . . ?"

"Oh, Ruttle . . . Rita Ruttle . . ."

"Miss Ruttle. Anything further you'd like to know?"

"Yes, I'm living in Larne at the moment. Where is it exactly?"

"Outskirts of Killoran . . . just off the Tailorstown road . . . if you know where that is?"

"Killoran, yes. I . . . I've heard of Killoran."

"Excellent. Since you're in County Antrim, you're about . . . let me see . . . I should say a couple of hours at most by car."

Far enough away, she thought: far enough away not to be known by anyone.

Later in the day, that photograph in the newspaper had become a reality, when she found herself pulling up outside 8 Willow Close.

Abraham Hilditch opened the door on the first ring. He was a short man, the shape of a Russian nesting doll, brown hair crenellated across the brow, eyes as blue as a summer sky, inquisitive.

"Miss Ruttle!" He checked his watch approvingly. "You're an excellent timekeeper. I like punctual people. Shows respect." He held out a hand. "I'm Abraham, but everyone calls me Bram. Come in. Come in."

He was dressed impeccably. A grey three-piece suit, white shirt, the toecaps of his black shoes buffed to the gleam of an eight ball.

"Her Grace didn't want me to let this one until I'd redone everything from scratch."

"Who?"

"Sorry, my mother. She gets 'Her Grace' because she's very fussy . . . very particular when it comes to tenants." He was showing her round the house, keeping up a running commentary. "Likes respectable people. No riff-raff. That presents a bit of a problem, since – generally speaking – it's people of limited means who tend to rent." He stopped suddenly. "I'm babbling. I'm so sorry. I didn't mean to imply that you were a lady of limited means. Is it just for yourself?"

"Yes," she said, knowing that she was indeed a lady of limited means. But she had enough to cover the deposit and a couple of months in advance. Money she'd been saving religiously for the "unexpected". Now that "unexpected", which had been no more than a faint hope for so long, was actually happening. She could not quite believe it.

"You're not a married lady then?"

"Er . . . no. No." She was going to follow it up with a "not really" but checked herself in time. She'd removed her wedding-ring before the meeting. That way, she'd no need to explain herself. A single woman in her thirties evoked pity rather than interest.

The disclosure pleased Mr Hilditch. "Good . . . very good," he said, showing a row of perfect teeth. "Ladies of your standing make excellent tenants. Her Grace will be very pleased that you're a spinster."

Spinster! She could barely suppress a grin. Spinster. It was such an old-fashioned word. Last time she'd seen it written down was on her wedding day, when she and Harry had been asked to sign the official form.

She'd wondered at the time if the word had not been some kind of omen. A warning of things to come. That she was entering into a contract whose roots lay in medieval times, when the husband was lord and master. With a stroke of the pen the spinster had become a chattel.

For all his bulk, the landlord was surprisingly light on his feet. He bounced about on his balletic toes, alluding to the finer points of his residence with a flourishing hand. "Carpet: Cyril Lord, very hard-wearing. Bed, curtains: brand new. Walls painted in vinyl satin, so won't stain. And if it does, easily removed with soapy water and cloth."

There was an odour, however. It was one of the first things she'd noticed about the house. Just a note of something unpleasant filtering through the reek of fresh paint and varnish. He saw her wrinkle her nose.

"Drains I'm afraid. Been on to the authorities to come and clear them, but you know what they're like. I'll try again." He adjusted his frameless spectacles, unblinking blue eyes regarding her. "Do you think that will be a problem for you?"

"Oh, no . . . no, not at all. It's so lovely. Really lovely!"

"Excellent. You can always open the windows a little. But don't forget to shut them on leaving the house. That's assuming you wish to rent the place of course. That's not to say the neighbourhood isn't safe . . . but better safe than sorry. You can't be too careful these days."

He led her upstairs. She followed in the waft of his pungent cologne.

On the landing she balked. She stood and stared at an unusual object affixed to the wall. It was a flat, box-like structure containing six butterflies pinned on a black satin ground.

"My lovelies. What do you think?"

Suffocated to death, then trapped for ever behind glass. How could he take pleasure in the destruction of such beauty?

"Y-Yes . . . they're lovely," she managed to say.

"*Cynthia cardui* and *Argynnis paphia*." He tapped the glass lightly and a sovereign ring glinted on his pinkie. "Painted lady and silver-washed fritillary to you. One of my little hobbies: collecting."

He opened the door to the box-room and she got a strong whiff of scent. When she stepped inside she detected another odour underneath it – a not very pleasant one – that several air fresheners and a bowl of potpourri were attempting to mask.

"You won't really be using this one," he said a little too quickly. "Except for storage, as you can see." He pointed to a vacuum cleaner and some brushes. "That's why I didn't really bother much with it."

The room was indeed small with a little sink in one corner. Taking up most of the space was an old trunk.

"The trunk belonged to a great-aunt of mine . . . just some of her effects and family albums. My mother hates clutter so I put it there out of harm's way. You don't mind, do you?"

"No, not at all."

She drew back suddenly at the sight of an animal on the window-sill. Long body, glossy coat the colour of cinnamon, snub nose and beady eyes. It looked so startlingly real.

"Are you a taxi . . . er . . . a taxi—?"

"Taxidermist . . . No, but my father was." He shut the door briskly. "A hobby. Well, it comes with the territory."

He saw her look of puzzlement.

"He was an undertaker. As was I until he passed over. Hilditch and Son, Funeral Directors . . . been the family business for generations. It's a delightful place for the weary and disenchanted . . . death I mean, not undertaking."

Rita-Mae was flummoxed. She'd never met anyone like Bram Hilditch. An eccentric – and an educated one, to judge by the sound of him. That fact unnerved her a little. She was at once conscious of her own rather modest education.

He chuckled to himself. "Just my little joke, Miss Ruttle. Lovely to help people through those pearly gates into the glories of the afterlife. Now I help people through the doors to their new homes, which in some ways is much more satisfying."

He led her through to the main bedroom. Rose-strewn wallpaper, deep-blue carpet, pinewood furniture that didn't overwhelm. A fluffy cream rug by the double bed. It was the kind of room she'd seen in women's magazines. She couldn't have asked for more.

"Oh! This is so lovely, Mr Hil—"

"Bram. Call me Bram . . . Very kind of you to say so, Miss Ruttle." He gave her a beatific smile, rocked on his heels and steepled his fingers, flushing slightly. "Her Grace chooses the colour schemes. She has a very good eye. It's my job to find the right properties . . . So much more rewarding than dealing with . . . Oh, I've told you that already."

◆ ◆ ◆

The kettle whistled, tugging her back to the present. He hadn't even asked for references. It seemed he was only too pleased to rent her the house. Had trusted her completely after such a short meeting. She smiled at her good fortune and wondered about him now: Mr Hilditch, Bram. No, she would not be calling him Bram for a while yet, preferring the formality of Mister. She considered what he might be doing at this present moment on a Sunday morning. Would he be escorting Her Grace to church? The thought reminded her that she might just visit a church herself for appearance's sake. Tomorrow he'd be coming to check out a dripping tap in the bathroom. Perhaps she'd offer him tea. But as she filled the teapot, something worrying caught her eye.

The catch on the window was undone.

She froze.

She secured every window before leaving the house, as Bram Hilditch had instructed.

Always.

The kitchen window especially, because it looked out on a secluded patch of grass, providing the perfect cover for intruders.

Harry's face reared up at her like a ghoul's on a ghost train.

Oh dear God, has he found me?

What if he's lying in wait upstairs?

What if he never went to England? Just fooled me into thinking he had gone, to see what I would do.

Panicked, she found the flick-knife in her handbag. The flick-knife with its pearlized handle, which, out of necessity, had become her protector, bodyguard and friend.

Taking care to make no sound, she stole up the stairs.

The door to the box-room stood open. Tentatively she put her head in. Nothing unusual except for the beady eyes of the ferret regarding her.

Outside her bedroom she readied herself, placed her palm flat against the door and pushed it wide open.

23

There was no one in the room.

But the bed . . . there was something different about the bed.

A slight creasing of the covers. As though . . . as though . . .

Had she sat down before leaving, without being conscious of doing so? She tried to think back. She was in the habit of smoothing the cover as soon as she made the bed. It was one of her many fussy little quirks, like arranging her clothes in the closet: blouses, sweaters, skirts, dresses and coats from left to right, always in that order, always blouses first. And her shoes lined up below: casual and low-heeled on the left, formal high heels on the right. Always in that order. Always!

So how come she'd forgotten to smooth the bed-cover?

How come she'd been so careless?

Terror pulsed through her.

She got down on her knees and checked under the bed.

She crossed to the wardrobe, gripping the knife more tightly.

But everything was as she'd left it, clothes and shoes perfectly ranked. Mocking her.

She slumped down on the bed, relieved.

It wasn't Harry.

Who then? Bram Hilditch? He had a key, but the contract clearly stated he could not enter the property without giving her prior notice.

Mrs Gilhooley, the next-door neighbour? Hardly. She was an elderly lady whom she'd barely spoken to since moving in. Seemed the private sort who kept to herself, which suited Rita-Mae just fine.

Back on the landing she felt more reassured. But, as she turned to go downstairs, she knocked against the landlord's display case of butterflies.

It crashed to the floor.

In a panic she bent down to retrieve it.

Panic turned to relief. The glass was still intact.

However, the impact had dislodged one of the specimens.

Oh dear. He was coming tomorrow to fix the tap.

There was nothing else to do but prise open the back and reaffix the poor dead creature. Distasteful as that operation might be, she could not afford to have Bram Hilditch see that she'd been careless.

Carefully she turned the case over, but to her dismay saw that one side of the rear panel had also come loose. Something was protruding. Part of the mounting card?

She carried the case through to the bedroom and laid it on the bed to take a better look.

No, it didn't look like mounting card. She tugged at it – and drew out an old brown envelope. Had the landlord used it to reinforce the case backing? But it felt as though there was something inside the envelope, and it was sealed. A colourful illustration of a Celtic cross was taking up most of the back.

She turned it over and to her astonishment saw the following words written in a neat hand.

The Truth I Could Not Tell.

Vivian-Bernadette O'meara

CHAPTER FOUR

"'Lord Frederick Evesham entered the parlour in his breeches and morning coat, a glittering sabre at his side.'" Bram Hilditch, erstwhile undertaker and newly installed landlord, was seated in an armchair by his mother's bed, feet resting on a velvet footstool. He was reading from *In the Arms of the Viscount* by Bathsheba Love St John, one of many historical romances favoured by his mother. "'The Countess Fantasia almost swooned at the very sight of him, so dashing did he appear. He—'"

"But what's his *nose* like?" Bram's mother demanded. Octavia Hilditch, pushing the creaking door of 79, was sitting up in bed nursing a sprained wrist, the tail end of influenza and a pair of restless legs. Plumply pink with burgundy hair and a glowing complexion – sun avoidance, rigorous cleansing and expensive lotions from age twenty – she was fighting off old age with the energy and rigour of an Olympic athlete. A gin and Dubonnet – one part gin, two parts Dubonnet – every evening between 9 and 10, during what she termed "my magic hour", was a curative for all ills in Octavia's book, and her son's reading to her served as a prelude to this "medicinal restorative" that rounded off the day.

"What's his nose got to do with anything?" countered Bram, annoyed that she'd interrupted his flow.

"One can tell character from a nose. Its shape can make a prince or a devil of any man. This Evesham person didn't have a nice one, if memory serves, which means he *isn't* handsome."

"The word 'dashing' implies that he *is* handsome, thus obviating the author's need to belabour the point."

"Don't you lecture *me* on the intricacies of the literary narrative! The author described Lord Evesham's nose two pages back. I'm not senile. I've the memory of a nutcracker bird, as you well know." Mrs Hilditch, a retired archivist, was still as sharp as a trephine. Crosswords, bridge and Scrabble kept the old neurons firing at full throttle in spite of the passing years.

"Well, if your memory's that good, how come you don't remember what it said exactly?"

Octavia grimaced, her mouth a croquet hoop of pique. She resented it when her son challenged her. And he was doing it more and more these days. "It's not that I don't *remember*," she shot back imperiously. "I simply need reminding, that's all."

With a sigh, Bram flipped back a couple of pages.

"Yes, here we are. 'Lord Evesham had a face of noble bearing: long and thin with a high-born forehead, deep-set eyes and the aquiline nose of the maternal Dewsbury line.'"

"That's it! I knew it! Aquiline, indeed! *Beaky* is the word. And he's a baldy with sunken eyes to boot. I'd never trust a baldy man with sunken eyes and a beaky nose, and neither should Countess Fanny."

"People can't help their faces, Mother. And anyway, the countess is far more interested in his wherewithal than his nose."

"Where with *who*? What are you saying?"

"*Where-with-al*, Mother. I said *wherewithal*. His money."

"Well, there's no need to be caustic with me. I know what it means. I can't help it if your diction is as fickle as a foreigner's."

"My diction is perfectly clear."

Increasingly, Bram was finding himself caught up in these games of verbal tennis with his mother. He put it down to his having sold off the undertaking business on his father's demise barely a year before. A momentous decision that the matriarch had bitterly opposed, but finally assented to when Bram threatened to leave her altogether and relocate to north Cornwall, where Gregory, his favourite uncle and a keen lepidopterist, lived in a ramshackle manor near a wood of dwarf oaks. As a boy, Bram had spent many delightful summers with his eccentric uncle, who'd introduced him to the wonders of wildlife and given him a lifelong love of winged creatures and the great outdoors.

He eyed her now over his reading glasses. Saw her fumble at the bow of her bed jacket. Untie and redo it. A ploy she used when cornered. But Bram had been bullied enough by his father and was determined that his mother would not be picking up where the old man left off.

"Do you wish me to continue?"

"No." She shook her head vehemently, setting her soufflé of burgundy hair aquiver. "That's enough of Freddie and Fanny for now. We're well into my magic hour, so plump up my pillows and fetch me my cocktail, please. Then you can tell me all about your day."

Bram replaced the satin bookmark and removed his spectacles. He rose from the chair and Octavia leaned forward for the pillow-plumping protocol. He did not like being cast in the role of lackey, and believed his mother pulled rank just to show who was boss. On his father's death, the total assets of the company had passed to her.

He'd managed to persuade her to invest in property. The career of funeral director had never been his choice. He being the elder of two sons, the job had been foisted upon him. No matter that the business had been in the Hilditch family "since time began". Now, having recently turned 40, and feeling all the regret and ruefulness such a milestone age can bring, Bram could finally make a run for the door marked MY LIFE, with emphasis on the "My". He had a keen interest in photography and the natural world, and was finally exploiting those interests to the fullest degree.

He'd spent enough time around dead bodies and wished to join the world of the living. Buying and letting properties was a fine arrangement, for it afforded him the time to indulge his lifelong passion at the same time as meeting new people.

He busied himself with gin and Dubonnet bottles, a permanent feature on the sideboard. Today he noted that the gin, which he'd purchased only three days before, was all but depleted. But best to keep quiet for now.

Yes, having chalked up the sale of three properties and with a couple more in the pipeline, things were going very well for Bram Hilditch. There was always the obstacle that was his younger brother Zac, of course: a "resting poet" who lived in Toronto and did something vague in the import-export trade. Usually he kept himself scarce, which was just as well. Hopefully things would remain that way.

Bram handed over the cocktail.

"Thank you, son. Now, you must tell me all about that new tenant. The spinster. What did you say her name was?"

He returned to his reading chair, and was shocked to see Her Grace throw back her head and down in one the rather healthy measure of gin and Dubonnet he'd poured.

"You're drinking that far too quickly. It will give you heartburn."

"Poppycock!" She held out the glass for a refill, jiggling it with impatience. "Everyone needs their little peccadilloes – most especially a woman at my time of life. If the Queen Mother can have her gin and Dubonnet whenever the mood takes her, I can jolly well have mine too. She goes nowhere without it, you know, 'in case it is needed'. Those are her very words, not mine."

"Don't believe everything you read in the newspapers, Mother," he said, reluctantly refilling her glass. "And stop trying to change the subject. I bought those bottles only three days ago and they're almost finished. Charlie Magee will think *I'm* the one with the drink problem."

"Such a fine lady: Elizabeth, the Queen Mother!" Octavia rhapsodized, ignoring the rebuke. "People say I resemble her, you know, but I should think I'm much slimmer. I'm sure she disapproves of that Sarah Ferguson person . . . far too uncouth for darling Prince Andrew. You'd think he could have done better than a mouthy redhead with freckles and the hips of a Clydesdale horse. A princess should never have freckles or hips. No good will come of it you know."

Octavia, a staunch royalist, had the Hilditch residence bedizened with royal family kitsch. The Windsor clan grinned out of plaques and plates all over the place, even in the bathrooms.

"I *said,* Charlie Magee will think *I* have the drink problem."

"I *don't* have a drink problem. You have an overactive imagination. Charlie Magee knows very well I'm still mourning the loss of dear Nathaniel."

"Yes, but filling oneself with alcohol isn't going to bring him back, now is it?"

For his part, Bram was not missing his father one bit. He'd been bullied relentlessly from childhood, and given nightmares as a boy by being locked in the funeral parlour with corpses if he misbehaved.

Nathaniel Emanuel Hilditch had died on his feet on the sabbath day, as would befit a mortician. He'd found him in the preparation room, collapsed over old Mrs Dobbins from Cedar Haven Mews. He'd been dressing her remains at the time, and Bram was gratified to see that his father had just completed the disagreeable task of embalming her, thus saving him the trouble.

The day he laid out the old man was the happiest of his life. To celebrate, he'd slapped him hard across the face. My, did it feel good to finally do what he'd longed to do when his bullying dad was alive!

"Nat savoured everything," Octavia was saying, a misty look in her eyes. She sipped the drink tearfully. "That's what attracted me to him, you know. His equable temperament. I think it came from working with the dead. Pity some of it didn't rub off on you, Abraham. That impatience of yours is more marked since dear Nat passed away." She took another grateful gulp. "It's not good for your heart – not to speak of the stress you cause me. I need peace in my life."

Bram sighed inwardly. Every evening ended more or less on the same note. Two glasses down the line, Her Grace would play the sympathy card, make a lachrymose declaration, and round off by throwing in a little barb or two, just to remind him who was in charge.

"I'm perfectly equable, Mother. Father did his best to ruffle me. You were too busy shopping and having lunch with your friends to notice how he treated me. But that's all in the past now. You enquired about the new tenant . . ."

Octavia was barely listening, the effects of the gin and Dubonnet giving her a vision of her twenty-year-old self, waltzing about the Lido ballroom in the arms of the handsome Nat. The band playing "Moonlight Serenade" as they twirled around the floor beneath the glittering chandeliers. Oh, what days! Carefree and pain-free, dancing through the first few pages of the story that would become their married life together.

". . . yes, Ruttle. She seems nice enough," Bram was saying.

He thought Rita-Mae very nice indeed, but could not share such a view with his mother. Octavia, ever the matriarch, was very censorious when it came to other women. "Mother, are you listening to me?"

"Y-Yes, sorry. Ruffle, you say."

"Hmm . . . *Ruttle* . . . with two t's. Rita Ruttle."

"Curious name. Is she pretty?"

"Yes, I suppose . . . in her own way."

"What's that supposed to mean? She either *is* pretty or she isn't." Octavia, eyes shooting out rays of suspicion, was sensing a threat to her domain. She had her son down as a confirmed bachelor, had mapped out a path for him from cradle to grave. There'd be no adventuring down byroads so long as she was around. That's the way it had always been and that's the way it would stay.

Bram knew what she was thinking, saw the conflict play across her face, her fingers tighten on the glass. He enjoyed the tiny surge of power such a display afforded him. With his father gone, at last he had some control over his own life.

"It shouldn't matter to you what she looks like, Mother. That's not the important thing here. The important thing is that she's from Larne, on the east coast. So, far enough away not to know what happened with that other—"

"Woman!"

"Exactly."

Octavia searched her son's face, a look of panic taking hold. "She's not . . . she's not the nervous type, is she? We wouldn't want her to just disappear."

Bram shook his head resolutely, leaned forward and fixed her with a steady look.

"No, absolutely not! She seems quite the opposite of Miss O'Meara. Very level-headed, has her feet planted firmly on the ground. Besides, she didn't hesitate over paying the deposit, and not one but two full months in advance. And in cash. So even if she did change her mind, which I think is highly unlikely, she'd forfeit over sixty pounds . . . quite a lot, in anyone's money. So really, Mother, there is nothing at all to worry about."

He saw her relax a little at this news.

"You've told Maud not to say anything?"

"Well of course I have. Mrs Gilhooley won't say a word. She was only too pleased that I'd rented to a respectable single lady as opposed to her biggest nightmare: a noisy young family. No, Maud would be the last one to want to scare Miss Ruttle off. You mark my words, Mother: I have everything under control. Trust me."

Octavia sank back gratefully on the pillows and shut her eyes. "Thank heavens for that, son. Thank heavvv . . ."

Bram was pleased to see her drift off without another word. He rose quietly, eased the glass from her fingers and studied it. Laid a gentle hand on her brow.

"There, there . . ." he soothed, "now you have a good night's sleep. Don't you worry about a thing. I've got everything under control. E-v-e-r-y-t-h-i-n-g . . ."

By the time he exited the bedroom, glass in hand, Her Grace was sound asleep.

CHAPTER FIVE

Portaluce, Antrim Coast

Feeling somewhat calmer, Dorinda Walsh made her way – carefully
– downstairs, and entered the dining-room of the Ocean Spray: a sub-
stantial, light-filled space, gifted with a bay window which gave on to a
spectacular view of the ocean. The sky was overcast with just the faintest
hint of blue seeping up from the horizon.

To the west, she saw a stately white castle jutting out on a headland
of rock overlooking with lofty grace the sweep of sand and sea below.
She wondered briefly about the residents of such a spectacular edifice.
What good fortune to occupy such an exalted position!

The scene was soothing and a feeling of relief swept over her when
she realized she was alone with this view. There were no other guests in
the room. Perhaps she was the only resident? At that time of year it was
likely the case. Encouraged, she relaxed a bit more and made her way
to a small table by the window. It had been set for one.

Images of that bloodstained raincoat kept pushing into her
thoughts. Whose blood? And how had it got there? Images of her
mother, one gloved hand raised in greeting. Or was it a farewell? Was
she saying a final goodbye because of some treacherous act her daughter
had committed? Dear Lord! Dorrie's heart sank.

Maybe she should just run out of the Ocean Spray. Right this minute. Not wait for explanations from whoever owned this lovely place. The urge to flee was strong. But leaving without paying her bill would mean ending up in a police cell, or worse. She wanted to weep. But breaking down in a public place must be fought against at all costs.

Concentrate on this, she urged herself. The present. The here and now. It's the only way to stop the bad thoughts intruding.

She placed her handbag on the floor, folded her hands in her lap and looked about her.

The room's interior had an aquatic theme: muted greens and blues with pictures of shells and marine life on the walls. Potted palms stood in corners. Along the rear wall: a large aquarium glinting with tropical fish probing for their freedom through the glass. Whoever owned the Ocean Spray had good taste, and the money to exploit it with enthusiasm. Her mother would have approved.

She switched her focus to beyond the window: waves pulling their lacy borders over the sand, gulls wheeling like scrunched paper on the breeze, people in their Sunday best making their way to church. The bells a beautiful refrain now, far from the clamorous tumult that had forced her awake.

There were cars parked end to end beside the promenade and, as she watched, a black saloon pulled into a vacant spot and a man emerged. He was rail-thin, dressed in a dark suit and an elegant trilby hat. He carried an air of restiveness, as if to say: I have more important things to be doing than wasting time going through this church-business charade every week.

He opened the rear door briskly and a little girl of about six clambered out. He didn't bother to help her, just stood staring down as she negotiated the challenging step from car to kerb, her tiny legs tested by the steep descent.

Dorrie's heart went out to the little one. She was dressed in a bright green coat and clutching a prayer book. She could sense the child's fear under the lash of the father's impatience. She blinked away a tear, hoping the girl had a more caring mother, but there was no mother to be seen.

The father locked the car and strode ahead, forcing the daughter to run after him. He's always been a bully, Dorrie thought. Has always had women running after him. Always had his own way.

In that moment she hated him – a man she'd probably never get to meet.

Her breathing quickened at the injustice. She wanted to run out and snatch the little girl away from him. Save her. Set her on another life path, where dour men posing as fathers did not exist. She dug her nails into her palms under the protective fall of the tablecloth. Felt powerless that she couldn't give life to the fantasy.

Then: "What is it you'll be wantin', ma'am?"

She flinched. The vision broke, and turning she saw that a young woman was standing close by. How long she'd been there, she'd no idea. She looked like a throwback to Edwardian times, dressed as she was in a black frock and white apron. Dorrie recognized the voice. At last, a familiar link in this strange place. It was the voice that had spoken through her bedroom door earlier.

"Sorry, I . . . ?"

"Breakfast, ma'am. Do you want the full fry?"

The word "fry" made her stomach lurch. She shook her head. "No . . . no, thank you."

"Tea and toast then, ma'am?"

"Yes, tea . . . strong . . . th-that would be lovely. Thank you."

The waitress smiled nervously. Turned to go.

"Sorry . . ."

"Yes, ma'am?"

"What's your name?"

"Maureen, ma'am."

"Maureen. Last night when I . . . when I checked in, were you—"

"Maureen, stop dawdling!" A voice from nowhere. "You've got work to do."

Without another word, the waitress scurried off obediently. An elegant, statuesque woman was advancing across the room. Mid-seventies, Dorrie guessed. Expensively attired in a tailored suit and patent courts, she exuded an air of entitlement founded on serendipitous groundwork and canny decisions made.

The reluctant guest was at once afraid. Her stomach clenched like a fist. This must be the "proprietress". This woman would have witnessed her derangement. Would have removed her clothes. Put her to bed. She could barely meet her eye. How was she going to explain herself?

"Millman . . . Mrs Gladys Millman," the woman announced, a cloud of scent preceding her, strong and cloying. She held out a hand. "We met last night. I trust you had a comfortable night?"

Dorrie, on the verge of tears, felt humiliated. She made an effort to rise.

"Oh please, sit."

"Yes . . . I'm sorry, I . . ." She struggled to explain herself. But the words died. There was no explanation. Her mind was a blank. In her distress she reached into her handbag, found a handkerchief and broke down. There was very little else she could do.

"Oh dear, I'm so sorry," she heard Mrs Millman say. "I didn't mean to upset you."

Dorrie gazed down at the table, the starched white napkin in its silver ring, the cutlery and delicate china fogging and blurring through her tears. How had she come to this? With no memory of who she was except for her name and the dreamlike vision of a woman she knew to be her dead mother. And this lady, this stranger, now drawing up a chair, would she fill in the blanks of her story? A story that had started God-knows-where and brought her to this seaside town, into a room with the number 5 on a brass plate on the door.

"It's just that, I . . ."

"Never mind, dear. Here's Maureen with the tea. We'll get you a nice strong cup and you can tell me all about it."

Dorrie dabbed at her eyes. Tell her all about what? She focused on Gladys Millman's hands as they fluttered over the tea things. Nails perfectly manicured, diamond rings aglitter, a gate bracelet clinking on the left wrist.

"Maureen dear, my cigarettes. And we'll need a cosy for the pot. I'm sure Miss . . . or is it Mrs? Sorry, I . . ."

The waitress scuttled off again.

Dorrie was forced to look up. She met eyes of vivid blue. Mrs Millman had once been beautiful and was still winning the war on ageing with the help of expertly applied make-up. Her bronze hair, swept into a chignon and held in place by a diamanté clip, lent her a regal air; a dowager came to mind. Dorrie at once felt intimidated and small.

"Miss," she said weakly, sensing that the admission was a black mark against her. "Miss Dorinda Walsh."

"Of course, *Miss* Walsh . . . Dorinda. Sugar?" A set of tiny tongs hovered over the sugar bowl; pencilled eyebrows were raised.

Dorrie shook her head. Guided the cup to her lips with both hands, willing them to remain steady.

Gladys Millman watched her keenly. "A little toast perhaps?"

She shook her head.

"Are you quite sure? Toast settles the stomach, don't you know."

Why was she referring to her stomach? Oh God, the implication was clear. Miss Walsh, you were pathetically drunk last night, therefore you *must* have an upset stomach.

"N-N-No, thank you. I'm sorry, Mrs Millman . . . about last night. I—"

"Oh, there's no need to apologize. Cars break down all the time."

What was she saying? She'd come by car? Well, of course she must have done. She felt a real need to tread carefully. Perhaps if she said very little, Gladys Millman would help untangle the events of the previous night by dropping enough clues to explain the drama.

"My car?"

"Yes. Don't you remember?"

Dorrie looked away. The bloodstained raincoat was blocking out the vision of the beautiful view beyond the window. She was facing into the horror of things unknown. Could easily have been standing in the dock waiting for a judge to pass sentence.

"But of course you were distressed at having broken down," Mrs Millman continued, "so I'm not surprised your recall is hazy. It was fortunate it happened so close to the Ocean Spray. Also fortunate that I had not already retired when you rang the bell. You don't mind if I smoke, do you?" She drew a cigarette as long as a pencil from a silver case and lit up. "Sorry, do you want one?"

"No, thank you. I don't smoke."

"Now, where was I?"

"My car. I—"

"Yes, cars. Such tedious things. Even when new they're not dependable. Rather like men, don't you think?" She gave a little laugh, tapped the cigarette in a tiny crystal ashtray. "Teddy Sinclair is a very dependable mechanic. I can vouch for that. Not that my Mercedes gives much trouble, mind you." She shifted her gaze out of the window, raised the cup to her lips.

"Mrs Millman?"

"Yes?"

"When will it be ready d'you think . . . the car?"

"Well, that's the thing, Miss Walsh. Teddy doesn't work on the Lord's Day." She drew leisurely on the cigarette and eyed her victim through a plume of smoke. "A dedicated Methodist. You know what *they're* like."

The guest tried to hide her disappointment at this news. She'd be stuck here another night, and, given the look of the place, how on earth would she pay for the privilege?

"Not to worry. Another night in my little palace is not so bad now, is it?"

"Oh, no, not at all. It's . . . it's . . . beautiful here. Really nice! It's just that I've no overnight bag and—"

The proprietor waved a hand. "That's easily remedied. In the drawer of your bureau there is a toilet bag with all the necessary effects. I make sure that each guest has one. We do things differently here at the Ocean Spray. I keep night-attire as well, just in case a guest might have forgotten to pack theirs. Often people" – she wrinkled her nose derisively – "most especially rural folk, fail to bring the most basic items with them. One would think they were raised in fields as opposed to houses."

"Thank you for the nightdress," Dorrie said, feeling she had to make some kind of contribution to Mrs Millman's monologue. "It's very kind of you to think of such things."

Gladys flashed a pearly smile. "Oh, think nothing of it, my dear. I'm sorry it was a bit on the big side, you being such a slender little thing. But I'm sure it served its purpose. More tea?"

"Very well. Thank you, yes."

Dorrie allowed herself to relax a little. From the way Gladys Millman was acting it seemed nothing untoward had really happened. She'd had a mishap with the car. Booked herself into the nearest guest-house, which happened to be the Ocean Spray. Mrs Millman had checked her in and provided her with a nightdress, because, quite naturally, she didn't have an overnight bag. Once in the room, she'd drunk some whiskey to calm herself. Too tired to remove her underwear, she'd simply pulled on the ghastly yellow garment and collapsed into bed.

The phone rang. Mrs Millman crushed out the cigarette and stood up.

"Excuse me, dear. Back in a mo. Help yourself to more tea, won't you."

Dorrie watched her scissor across the room, head held high, and breathed a sigh of relief. Quickly she dived into the handbag, hoping she'd have enough money to pay for this unexpected seaside break.

She found her purse. But there were only a few pieces of change. What would she do now? Oh, the embarrassment of not being able to pay the lovely Mrs Millman, who'd been so kind! In desperation she dug deeper into the bag. She saw to her delight that there was another purse: a black leather one. But wait, it wasn't exactly a purse. It was a wallet.

A *man's* wallet.

Fear gripped her again. What was she doing with a man's wallet? There were no men in her life.

She looked up nervously to check that the coast was clear. Mrs Millman, out in reception now, could still be heard, all tinkling laughter and exclamatory asides. Maureen was nowhere to be seen.

Under cover of the tablecloth, she cautiously opened the wallet. It was worn and shabby with some stitching undone. To her utter surprise she found it to be stuffed with cash; a thick wad of ten-pound notes fanned under her fingertips. Easily £100 in total, although she'd no desire to count it at that moment.

How on earth had she come by that? She felt tears pricking her eyes. That familiar feeling of shame and helplessness was enveloping her again. Had she stolen it?

From reception came a jaunty "Bye now!" followed by the receiver being clunked back down. The staccato clacking of heels across hardwood meant the proprietor was returning.

Dorrie stuffed the wallet back in her handbag. At least she'd be able to pay her way, but . . . but *who* would actually be footing the bill?

That question, as with the mystery of the bloodstained raincoat, needed answering, but she wasn't sure whether she really wanted to know.

Don't you be brooding, Dorrie, came her mother's voice again. *I'll see to everything. You just smile and go with the flow, my dear.*

"Yes, Mama, I will . . . pretend everything's, yes . . . all right. Yes, I'll go with the flow."

"Excuse me?" A polite cough. "Are you sure you're all right? You appeared to be talking to yourself just now."

Dorrie reddened and stood up. How come she hadn't heard her approach?

"Sorry, I . . . Yes . . . no, I think I've a headache coming on."

"Would you like a painkiller?"

"N-No, thank you . . . I just need the bathroom."

"You poor thing," she heard the proprietor say as she hurried from the breakfast-room, clutching tight the handbag that would surely get her out of this mess and away.

But away where? She did not know where she'd come from; she did not know where she was bound.

Face it, Dorrie, she told herself, you barely even know who you *are*.

CHAPTER SIX

The butterfly display case looked perfect again. No one could have guessed it had been dismantled and put back together over the course of an hour of painstaking labour.

Rita-Mae had delayed assembling it, unable to trust her fingers with the delicate operation. What if the tiny wings fell apart? That would be a disaster. But in the early hours she hit upon an idea. She'd use tweezers to affix it.

It proved to be the perfect solution.

Paying excessive attention to detail was one of many disciplines she imposed upon herself. Living under Harry's cruel reign had heightened such quirks to an insane degree. Everything in the house in Larne – *his* house – had to be absolutely the way he decreed: curtains drawn back precisely eighteen inches either side of each window, stairs climbed and descended left and right, never in the middle (to save wear on the carpet), his tea mug set down exactly six inches from his food plate. Even in her new circumstances Rita-Mae still clung to these same ritualistic habits. They'd become ingrained. Fifteen years of servitude and conditioning were hard to shift. In fact she could not remember it having been any other way. She'd learned early on that it was safer to comply than rebel.

She stood now on the bottom tread of the stairs, gazing up at the butterflies, back on the wall in their proper place. Then, with eyes steady on the target, she mounted the stairs slowly, magnifying glass in hand. This, she told herself, is exactly what Bram Hilditch will be doing in a couple of hours' time: climbing the stairs to the bathroom to mend that dripping tap. There was every chance he'd halt on this very spot and check on his "lovelies", just as he'd done on that first day when showing her around.

She peered closely at the painted lady, its lovely speckled wings of orange and red shimmering like silk under the magnifying glass. Its reattachment to the board had demanded the most delicate touch. The slightest damage to the wings would have been a disaster. He would not have failed to notice. It had not taken her long to decide that her new landlord shared the obsession that had soured her marriage to Harry: an almost fanatical attention to detail.

She'd had to call upon quite a bit of courage to push that tiny pin through the thorax again. But the poor creature was long dead, which was of some consolation. She did not want to think about how it had met its death or why the landlord chose to use butterflies as wall art. The item had been repaired and that was the important thing.

Yes, she was pleased. He'd never know his trophy case had been tampered with.

But the accident had revealed something that had lain hidden, and Rita-Mae had been saving that something until she'd righted the wrong.

She went into the bedroom and took the letter from the top drawer of the bureau where she'd stowed it the night before.

It measured about six inches by four and its thickness suggested there were several pages inside. She gazed again at the mysterious declaration.

The Truth I Could Not Tell.

Vivian-Bernadette O'meara

She'd given it no more than a cursory look before putting it away. A mystery was for delving into with proper care and attention. Mystery-solving should never be rushed. She turned the envelope over to study more carefully the image of the Celtic cross. It took up most of the back. At first she assumed it to be an illustration cut from a magazine, but scrutinizing it through the glass she saw that it was actually hand-painted. Each twist and turn of the intricate design lovingly executed. The mysterious Vivian-Bernadette was quite the artist.

And there was something else, something she hadn't noticed before. On either side of the upright, in tiny lettering, were the words:

I must follow in the footsteps of Catherine of Siena.

Catherine of Siena? Who might *she* be? A saint perhaps? Well, she'd soon find out if she opened it.

But . . .

What to do? She sat down. Should she give it to the landlord? It was his house after all, so by rights it was *his* property. But she could hardly tell him where she'd found it, now could she?

Perhaps she could lie; say she'd found it behind a drawer in the bureau. No, the bureau was new, like everything else in the house. She had to be careful. Bram Hilditch was no fool. His exacting eye and diligent hand had seen to every last facet and feature of the house.

No, she could not risk telling him the truth. But maybe . . . just maybe I was *meant* to find it, she thought. Words from an old school-teacher came back to her: *Nothing in this life happens by accident, Rita. Everything is meant to be.* So, looking at it that way, she was *meant* to bump into the butterfly case, it was *meant* to fall, she was *meant* to open it and make this discovery.

She studied the neat handwriting once more: Vivian-Bernadette O'Meara. What secrets are in here, Vivian? And do you want *me* to know them?

No sooner were the words out than the doorbell rang.

Flustered, she stuffed the mysterious envelope back in the drawer and went downstairs.

Bram Hilditch stood on the doorstep in a boiler suit, a large hold-all in one hand and a paper bag in the other.

"I'm so sorry, Miss Ruttle. I know I said two o'clock—"

"N-No, that's all right . . ." she lied, trying to hide her agitation. "Come in. Come in, won't you."

"It's Her Grace, I'm afraid. Her hairdresser in town has taken poorly." He flushed slightly. "So she thought she'd visit a friend in the vicinity rather than have the outing wasted altogether. She's not especially fond of car journeys I'm afraid. Not even short ones. So we're killing two birds with one stone, you might say."

She could see he was genuinely discomfited.

"Oh, that's all right!" she said breezily. "Perhaps you'd like a cup of tea before you start?"

Bram smiled and inclined his head in the manner of a flunkey before his mistress. "That's very gracious of you, Miss Ruttle, but I will save that lovely treat for after this little operation. Best to get the work out of the way first." He held out the paper bag. "Some date-and-almond scones . . . Her Grace made them. She's an excellent cook."

"Th-That's very kind. Thank you."

"Never visit anyone without bringing an offering. It's one of her little dictums. Mine too, I might add."

"R-Right . . . but you really shouldn't have. I'll put the kettle on."

"Excellent! I won't be long."

He mounted the stairs and she remained standing on the same spot, keeping a tally of his treads until he reached the top: twelve in total. Sure enough, on the landing he halted to examine his "lovelies".

She held her breath, her eye on the wall clock registering the seconds. At the count of seven he moved again.

All was well. Had he noticed anything amiss, he'd have lingered longer. She waited to hear him open the bathroom door, but to her consternation he did not. His footsteps carried on down the corridor and halted.

He was outside her bedroom. She was certain of it.

Sure enough, she heard the door of the bedroom click open. She knew that sound by now.

What on earth was he doing?

She thought of the envelope in the top drawer.

Perturbed, she climbed the stairs as quietly as she could. Found him in the corridor, staring into the bedroom.

"Do you take sugar?"

He turned, startled, hand on chest.

"Oh, dear me! You gave me a fright there, Miss Ruttle. Didn't hear you. Yes . . . yes, indeed. Just noticed the carpet a bit puckered here." He indicated a spot outside the door. "I'll see to that too . . . now that I'm here."

Was he lying? Was it merely a ruse to enter her room? And if so, why? She gripped the banister hard, holding herself in check.

There was an awkward pause.

"I'm sorry, I had to open your door to take a better look," he said, reading her mind. "That was remiss of me. I should have asked your permission first."

"Th-That's all right." She was taken aback by his show of courtesy. "The carpet you say? I . . . I didn't notice anything amiss."

"No, it's a bit dim in this corridor when all the doors are shut . . . that's, er . . . why I needed to open your bedroom door. Do you always do that?"

"Eh, sorry . . . do what?"

"Shut all the doors up here."

"Yes."

"I'd keep them open if I were you. All the better to see where you're going. We wouldn't want you to have a nasty fall, now would we?"

The words "nasty fall" and "we" made her feel queasy.

He's playing games with me, she thought. Just like Harry. He's challenging me because he knows I don't believe him. If I go and check this pucker he'll know I don't trust him. And what if there *is* one and he's right? How will I look then? How will I feel?

All the questions she needed to ask hitting her at once, goading her on to take a stand but then, as ever, backing down, slipping from her, leaving her voiceless. Leaving her powerless.

"Yes," she said. "Perhaps. I'll try to keep that in mind in future."

"Good. Better safe than sorry I always say."

"Indeed."

Reluctantly she left him to it. Going back downstairs again she dwelt on the words *Better safe than sorry.*

Harry used to say that too. Somehow it had just taken on a new shade of meaning.

It took the landlord thirteen minutes and eight seconds to complete the work. She timed him as she quietly laid the table, ears alert for any trespassing in the bedroom. It lay directly above the lounge so she would have known immediately; the creaking ceiling would have betrayed him.

When he finally came downstairs she felt certain that he hadn't been in there.

"Splendid!" he enthused, casting an eye over the beautifully laid table. He'd removed his boiler suit to reveal a white shirt and green trousers. He'd even changed his shoes. "May I?" He pulled out a chair and settled himself. "You shouldn't have gone to so much trouble on my account."

She took the chair opposite and proceeded to pour.

"It's no trouble at all, Mr Hilditch. I always make tea around eleven."

She sensed that he was about to insist on "Bram" but kept her eyes fixed on the stream of tea filling the cup. The formal "Mister" was safer all round, creating a divide between them that kept her out of his reach. No man would ever be allowed to bridge that divide. It would never happen again. Not if she had any say in the matter.

The tactic worked. He backed off. "Yes . . . well, how lovely all this is!" He stirred in one sugar but didn't touch the milk jug, selected a scone and placed it daintily on his side plate. "Nothing too serious, only a loose washer. The carpet outside your bedroom just required a couple of tacks to make it more secure. The sloppy work of the carpet-fitter I fear. It was remiss of me not to have noticed it sooner."

"I hadn't noticed a thing."

"Well, you wouldn't with all those doors shut up there."

She wanted to say: *I feel safer with all the doors shut. You don't know how many times a shut door saved my life, Mr Hilditch. But how could you know that?*

"And how are you finding things generally in Willow Close? Settling in all right?"

"Yes, thank you. I'm very comfortable here."

"I'm so pleased! Doesn't do to have a house vacant for too long . . . dampness and burglars always being a cause for concern." He applied himself to buttering the scone.

She watched him with interest. He'd surprisingly elegant hands for his stature, the fingers tapered and conical like those of a praying saint. She thought briefly of Harry's – square and rough, the spatula-like fingers all the better to squeeze the life out of her. Saw him take her roughly by the chin, thrust her head back against the wall. She flinched. Raised a hand to her throat. Hastily withdrew it again.

". . . and that's good to know," Bram was saying. "Change is difficult for a lot of people . . . and I'm no exception." He reached for the dish of preserves. "Well, given the family business, I had little choice in the matter other than to stay put. You have family still in Larne, Miss Ruttle?"

He'd caught her off guard.

"Er . . . hmm, yes. Some."

"No doubt they'll be coming to visit you?"

"Perhaps . . . Did you find it difficult to rent this house then?" She had the question out before she could stop herself.

He stopped chewing, his expression quizzical. There was the tiniest of pauses. "Difficult to rent? No, why do you say that?"

"It's just that you mentioned having to redo it from scratch. I was thinking the tenants before me weren't very . . . well, tidy . . . didn't perhaps take care of things as they should have."

He gazed out of the window. "Ah . . . yes, well you know how it is. Appearances can be deceptive. Aren't you having a scone? Her Grace will want to know your opinion."

Why was he changing the subject? No, she did not want a scone, but it would be rude to refuse. She took one and broke it into tiny pieces. She never ate anything she hadn't prepared herself. Yet another rule she dared not break.

"And what do you do for a living, Miss Ruttle? If you don't mind my asking."

"I'm a . . ." She very nearly said housewife. ". . . a hairdresser."

"Really!" He paused, reflecting on something. "That's very interesting. Yes, indeed. You see, if you're looking for a job I'm sure Susan would be glad of you to fill in."

"Susan?"

"Yes, she runs the Get Ahead hairdresser's in Killoran. The one my mother goes to. One of her employees has fallen ill, I believe."

She'd never thought about getting a job. She'd rented the house for three months and had just enough money, if she were prudent, to carry her through that period. She couldn't bear to think what would happen after that. But now the landlord was proposing something that would ease her financial situation a little. She had to be careful though. The less the locals knew about her, the better.

"If she's in need then I'd be only too willing to help her out," she said, placing a morsel of scone in her mouth to appear mannerly.

"Excellent! Susan will be pleased." He reached into a pocket and drew out a small notepad. "I'll give you the telephone number. I know it by heart since I make Mother's appointments. She loathes the telephone too I'm afraid. Disembodied voices upset her."

She saw him eye her diced scone and felt the need to distract him immediately. Her Samaritan skills came to the fore. Ask open-ended questions that require more thought and explanation than the simple "yes" or "no" of the closed type.

"Which part of the funeral business did you consider the most important, Mr Hilditch?"

She could see that the question took him aback. "Oh dear, let me think . . ." He slid the phone number across the table, recapped his fountain-pen and returned it to his pocket. "Why do you ask?"

"Just curious. I've never had tea with someone in your profession before."

"Well, for a start I've always had an interest in photography. Portraiture mostly. So the faces of the dead held – and indeed still hold – a certain fascination for me . . ."

She tried to hide her shock, took another sip of tea, sat more rigidly in the chair.

"That fascination came into its own when I was preparing the deceased's faces. Given our tradition of having an open coffin at the wake, you see, the last image of a loved one is the one they'll take away, so the job is a rather delicate one." He smiled. "Plus the fact that I rather pride myself on my memorial photography."

"Memori . . . ?"

"Memorial portraiture. Sometimes called post-mortem portraiture. In short: portraits of the dead."

He saw her look of horror. His face took on an earnestness. He leaned forward.

"Yes, I know, Miss Ruttle. You're reacting the way most people react when I tell them that. But there's really nothing to be frightened of. Nothing at all."

She had difficulty preventing herself choking on the piece of scone. Without a word he reached into a pocket of his green trousers and took out a wallet. She saw him thumb its compartments. He passed across a photograph.

"As they say in the film business, show don't tell. Meet my late father, Miss Ruttle."

With great reluctance, and trying to keep her hand from trembling, she took the picture from him. It was a close-up of an elderly gentleman with a cadaverous face, a rictus grin, eyes just two black slits and hair awry. In short: an image from your worst nightmare.

"I took that not long after he'd passed. Not very pleasant to look at, is it? Now . . . have a look at this one."

He handed her a second picture.

She was deeply regretting having asked him about his former profession. But it would've been rude to show just how revolted she really was. Her duty was to feign interest and be respectful.

She forced herself to look at the second picture. Was surprised to see an altogether more acceptable image. The same visage now sported a pair of ruddy cheeks, eyes and mouth thankfully shut. Hair slicked across the forehead, much in the manner of the man who sat across from her.

"Oh . . . I see. This is your father but . . ."

Bram nodded. "Yes, indeed. Nathaniel Emanuel Hilditch after I'd brought him back to life – in a manner of speaking."

"So how did you manage that?" She felt moved to pose the question, not at all wanting to hear the answer.

"Well, firstly some judicious padding of the cheeks with cotton wool to achieve that fuller look. Then stitching the mouth shut . . . from the inside of course. I stitch the eyelids too, but not before inserting plastic half-moons under the lids to help them hold their shape. The eyeballs fall to the back, you see, so we have to be creative in that area. In essence, bring the face back to how it was in life. That's the difficult part, retaining the likeness. After that it's just a matter of washing the hair and applying make-up. I found Max Factor Ivory Beige gave the most realistic hue, and a little blusher, most especially for the ladies, just to bring back that nice bloom to the cheeks."

She was relieved to see him returning the snapshots to the wallet.

"Y-You make it sound all so . . . all so matter of fact."

He smiled. Lifted his teacup. "Well, I grew up surrounded by dead bodies. Never knew anything else. So death doesn't frighten me like it would the average person." He leaned back in the chair, glanced briefly at the ceiling. "It's the living we should fear more than the dead."

He was more perceptive than she was allowing for. She saw the name Vivian-Bernadette O'Meara written neatly on a brown envelope. Was that last statement connected with her? Had they been lovers? Had he spurned her? Was that why she'd concealed the envelope inside one of his prized possessions? Was it her suicide note, written before she'd taken her own life in the bedroom above? Was that why he'd glanced towards the ceiling? Was that why he'd opened the door and stood on the threshold gazing in?

He sat staring at the butter dish, seemingly lost in thought.

"Your mother bakes a lovely scone," she said, pulling him out of his reverie.

He smiled, his face lighting up with the compliment. She was almost prepared to ignore his eccentricities.

Almost.

"It's kind of you to say so," he said. "I shall tell her that. She'll be pleased." He pushed back his chair, checked his watch. "Now that you mention her, I really must be going. Time and tide wait for no man. Thank you for the tea, Miss Ruttle. We'll meet soon again no doubt."

"No doubt."

"And remember: anything you need, don't hesitate to call me."

"Oh . . . y-yes, there's . . ."

He paused. "Yes, Miss Ruttle?"

"Now that you say it, there is just one thing. The drains."

"Drains?" He looked at her quizzically, causing her to avert her eyes. Her gaze shifted to the floor above – by chance rather than design. He followed her gaze.

"Yes," she said. "The, eh . . . the smell. It's strongest in the box-room. I was wondering . . . didn't you say you'd try and get on to the council again?"

He flushed visibly. "Oh, hasn't anyone been?"

"No . . . no one called."

Then: "But you don't need to use that room much, do you?" He got up and crossed to the door. "I'll get on to them right away. Sorry about that. You can't depend on people these days."

"Thank you, Mr Hilditch. Well, bye now."

Having shown him out, she went at once to the kitchen bin and disposed of the rest of the scones. She felt bad about doing it, but it was the only way to be safe.

Back in the lounge, she heard voices coming from next door. Mrs Gilhooley had a visitor, and that visitor sounded as though she was taking her leave.

Odd.

In Rita-Mae's brief experience her neighbour rarely had callers. Intrigued now, she took up position behind the curtain.

Into view came an elderly lady wearing a bright red hat and a garish, ankle-skimming kaftan. As the woman moved down the path, Rita-Mae was surprised to see Bram Hilditch escorting her. Mrs Gilhooley tottered in their wake, chatting all the while.

So "Her Grace" had been right next door all the time. Funny he hadn't been more specific.

The trio halted at a car – a flashy red Daimler – and turned as one to look towards her window.

They were discussing her, obviously.

She ducked further behind the curtain and waited until the car moved off.

So there was more to Bram Hilditch and his mother than met the eye. And there was more to this house than he was disclosing. How come the rent was so low? Mrs Gilhooley was in on the wheeze also. What was going on?

She thought again of the mysterious envelope. Now more than ever she needed to open it.

She climbed the stairs, conscious of the butterfly case and the boxroom, and the faint odour seeping out from under its shut door.

She shivered slightly. Promised herself she would not go into that room. There was something not right about it, with its ominous trunk and the weird ferret that seemed so real it looked poised to attack her.

Maybe that's why the landlord had placed it there on the windowsill: to frighten her, to repel her.

I'll find another place to store the vacuum cleaner, she told herself, as she entered the bedroom and crossed to the bureau.

She slid open the drawer.

And was immediately pulled up short.

Vivian-Bernadette's letter was gone.

CHAPTER SEVEN

"Lord in heaven, that Maud Gilhooley can be insufferably tedious! Why on earth did you leave me in her company so long?"

Her Grace, seated in the back of the speeding Daimler – the Queen Mother never sat up front, after all – was holding forth as Bram drove home.

"Well, it was *your* suggestion to visit Maud, not mine," he said, slowing for a stop sign.

"That's hardly the point. You should have rescued me earlier. Fixing a tap takes ten minutes at most, not three-quarters of an hour. What on earth were you doing in there?"

Bram sighed. Waited for a car to pass. "Miss Ruttle very kindly offered me tea. It would have been rude to refuse. And *you* were the one who gave me the scones for her, remember? So naturally such a gift prompted the offer of a collation."

"Collation indeed! You simply wanted to be in her company. Don't think I can't read between the lines. You didn't want me to meet her either. Why was that?"

"There is no need to be querulous, Mother. You might have scared her off. She's quite reserved, from what I've seen. You really aren't aware of how you come across sometimes."

The passenger headrest received an almighty slap. "How *dare* you talk to me like that, Abraham Hilditch? Querulous, indeed! If it wasn't for my training you'd still have the manners of a Congolese pygmy. I was the one who instilled good breeding in you and your brother, and don't you forget it. Dear Nat never knew proper etiquette until we met, God rest his soul."

Bram knew he'd gone too far. He slowed for a sharp bend. "Oh, fair enough, I spoke out of turn. I apologize, but we want Miss Ruttle to remain in the house, don't we? So we mustn't impose ourselves on her too much. Better that she stays put and helps pay off the mortgage than have it come out of your own pocket, is it not?"

He eyed her in the rear-view mirror. She sat with head turned away, hat feather aquiver, staring out of the window. From experience he knew that this petulant fit could last well into the evening. There was one sure way to leaven things though. Instead of making his usual left turn at the upcoming junction he turned right. The familiar sign for the Royal Hotel hove into view.

"Fancy luncheon at the Royal?"

"Now, that's the most sensible thing you've said all morning!" She patted his shoulder. "Luncheon would be splendid. I'll redo my lipstick just in case I run into someone important. Major Holloway usually dines in the Oak Room. *Such* a gentleman, the Major."

Fifteen minutes later they were installed at their favourite table in the hotel's restaurant. Lunch had been ordered, and Octavia, sipping from a large glass of Chablis, was in much better form. Bram was relieved to see that there was only a scattering of customers, it being early in the lunch slot. His mother could become quite loud the more she imbibed and he hoped they'd be finished and long gone before the rush started.

"You *did* impress upon Maud the importance of remaining tight-lipped?" he said now, picking up on their conversation in the car. He reached for his glass of Evian.

"Well of course I did. That was the object of the exercise after all. I certainly would not go seeking out Maud Gilhooley's company through choice. She insisted I take tea from a ghastly Pyrex mug and talked non-stop about her bladder complications. A singularly distasteful topic at the best of times. The Lord only knows why she felt such a subject would interest *me*."

"Well, maybe she thought you might have similar experiences, being around the same age."

"There's no need to be coarse."

"I'm not being coarse. So, how *does* she find her new neighbour?"

"Isn't that Mr Barclay-Brown over there? The solicitor." Octavia rearranged her silk scarf, adjusted her hat.

Bram, irked, did not bother to look round. "Hardly, Mother. We buried him last year. You really should wear your glasses. Now, you were saying . . ."

"Did we?"

"We did. Coffin: solid oak with Last Supper decoration, brass fittings, crêpe lining and three-tier raised lid. Most expensive we stocked: fifteen hundred pounds. You got a Tiffany necklace and matching ear-studs out of the profits, so you're either seeing a ghost, a relative of his, or that wine is going to your head already. Most likely the latter."

Octavia pulled a face and took another defiant swig of Chablis.

"Now, what else did Maud say about Miss Ruttle?"

"Keeps herself to herself, which in my book is code for someone who either has no social skills or has something to hide."

He let out a laugh.

The food arrived. Chicken Kiev for Her Grace, a filet mignon for Bram.

Octavia leaned across the table, the outsized feather from the bucket hat nearly brushing his eye. He ducked out of its way, making pointing motions with his fork.

"Do you have to wear that thing while we're eating, Mother?"

"It's not a *thing*," she said a little too loudly. He saw the waitress look their way. She was making a spectacle of herself again. "It's a Christian Dior classic with a rare Astrapia feather. Not that you would recognize quality, even if it stood on its hind legs and sang 'God Save the Queen'. And of *course* I must wear it, most especially since I haven't had my hair done. Now, where was I before you so rudely interrupted me?"

"You were accusing Miss Ruttle of having no social skills or—"

"Hiding something, yes. Well, how would *you* know she wasn't? She could be an IRA bomber, given the times we live in. One of those sleepers, I believe they're called. Sent in to reconnoitre the locale. Killoran is a mixed community after all."

"You have a very vivid imagination," Bram said, his attention on his filet mignon. "Those novels of yours are giving you a specious view of society, if not reality itself."

"Nonsense!" Octavia dropped her voice. "Who in their wildest dreams would have thought that O'Meara woman could've behaved as she did, bringing the house into disrepute?"

If only Her Grace knew the real story behind Miss O'Meara, thought Bram. But he would not be telling her that. Not ever.

"She looked like she belonged in a convent," the mother continued. "And that aunt who delivered her to us . . . just a ruff and cloak away from Mary Maker Ready, or whatever on earth she was called—"

"Mary *Baker Eddy*."

"Yes, that one . . . Straight out of the eighteen fifties—"

"Well, Miss Ruttle is not a religious freak, if that's what you're implying. I didn't see a crucifix or statuette about the place. There's nothing sinister about her. And she is certainly not in the IRA. I've spoken with her twice, so have more to go on than either you or Maud Gilhooley."

Octavia set her cutlery down and dabbed at her mouth with the napkin. She leaned across again, holding the feather out of harm's way.

"If that's the case, why did she leave the house last Saturday night around ten and not return until seven the next morning? Out the entire night."

Bram glanced quickly about him and frowned. "Maud said that?"

"Yes, she was quite adamant with regard to the time. Like your father – God rest him – she's not the best sleeper and so hears a lot through that dividing wall. Always opening and closing doors at all hours . . . what's that all about, one wonders."

Well, he knew Maud Gilhooley was correct on that score. He recalled all doors on the landing being shut when he went upstairs.

"So she's up to something," Octavia declared, a bit too loudly. "She wouldn't be a *prostitute*, would she?"

A woman at a nearby table wearing too much make-up and a low-cut top stopped eating and glared at her. The gentleman sitting across from her turned in his chair with an audible creak and said rather loudly, "Honestly, *some* people!"

Bram grimaced. "Don't be preposterous, Mother! And keep your voice down, for pity's sake. That lady over there thought you were referring to *her*!"

"You're eating too fast," she shot back, reaching for the wine again. "You'll get indigestion."

"And you're *drinking* too fast. We don't have a train to catch. Accusing a woman you've never met of being a . . . a . . ." – he couldn't bring himself to say the word – "is simply ludicrous."

"But how would *you* know? What could possibly take her out on a Saturday night, *all* night? Maud Gilhooley thought as much herself."

"Oh, she *would*. Gossips like her always think the worst! She could have a boyfriend. Haven't you thought of that?"

"That's a disgusting idea . . . spending the night with a man, and her a spinster."

"Less disgusting than your . . . your 'lady of the night' idea? I don't think so."

"If that's the case, why does Maud not see this boyfriend visiting her? Wouldn't that be more in keeping with proper behaviour?"

Bram couldn't answer that one. He barely knew the young woman, yet here he was championing her cause. He saw her now: that lovely elfin face, a face so perfect it needed no adornment. In his mind's eye he'd already framed it in the square viewfinder of his Hasselblad, had decided on a telephoto lens, the 200 mm perhaps, and a wide aperture, in order to render her fittingly serene and detached from the background. He knew that even in death that face would still retain its beauty.

Was that why he was so quick to defend her – because of her appealing face? This mysterious woman he scarcely knew. He thought back to his visit, recalling the way she'd stolen quietly up the stairs, believing that he'd entered her bedroom. He'd simply been standing on the threshold, remembering Vivian O'Meara and all the sleepless nights she must have passed in that very room. Something had compelled him to halt and take stock. He'd have to be careful of that kind of thing on any future visits though. What was past was past.

There was also the way Miss Ruttle had pretended to eat the scone. He'd noticed that too. And the curious manner in which she'd sat at the table: bolt upright, as if ready to make a dash for the door at any moment. He sensed she harboured a sadness locked deep within her, and wondered if he'd ever discover the reason.

Octavia pushed her plate aside, dusted off the bib of her kaftan, bracelets clacking. "It's worrying all the same. What if Willow Close was brought into disrepute for a second time? How would it look for us? More to the point, what would it say about your judgement, Bram?"

He could not but agree with her there. He'd been very quick to rent the house to Miss Ruttle. So quick, in fact, that he hadn't bothered asking for references. That was rather remiss of him he saw now. All he'd gleaned so far was the fact that she was single, came from Larne and worked as a hairdresser. That was about the extent of it.

The waitress pushed past the table, trundling the dessert trolley. At the sight of it, Bram's sweet tooth kicked in and his musings on the new tenant came to an abrupt halt. "Now for pudding. What would you like? And *don't* say another glass of Chablis."

"I'd love another glass and you won't stop me—"

Without warning, the wailing of an infant had filled the room. Octavia's face took on a grave expression. Bram ignored the interruption.

"Another Chablis is out of the question, Mother," he said firmly. "Just so you know." Bitter experience had taught him that a quarter of a litre of wine in the middle of the day was quite sufficient for Octavia. He signalled to the waitress.

When he turned his attention back to Her Grace, however, he grew concerned. She looked sombre and put out.

"Mother, what's the matter? Are you all right?"

"I've just remembered something . . ." She studied her discarded napkin. "Something else Maud said. Something rather odd."

"Really? What was that?"

"You rang the doorbell and I couldn't wait to get away, so it slipped my mind." She glanced across the room at the screaming infant, now being carried out in the arms of an embarrassed young mother. "The crying of that child brought it back to me."

"Crying of the child? Brought what back exactly?"

"What Maud said . . . well, I suppose it's not impossible. But how . . . how could she hide something like that?"

"Hide something like what?" Bram's impatience was getting the better of him. "Look, spit it out, Mother. Tracy's on her way with the puddings."

"One day last week Maud saw baby clothes drying on Miss Ruttle's line . . . Babygros. A pink one and a blue one."

"Now, what'll it be?" the waitress asked, cheerily positioning the trolley of delicious desserts alongside the table.

"Oh, just another glass of Chablis for me, dear," Octavia said airily, unfrowning her look in anticipation of more alcohol.

"Babygros," Bram repeated to himself, feeling nauseous, an image too frightening for words rising in his mind's eye.

"What's that, Mr Hilditch?" he heard Tracy say.

He pushed back the chair, holding his stomach.

"Abraham, what on earth's the matter? You look like you've seen a ghost."

"You'll have to excuse me, Mother. I don't feel at all well. I . . . I need the bathroom."

He rushed to the door, hoping he'd make it to the Gents in time.

CHAPTER EIGHT

The fifth-hand Hillman Avenger throbbed and rattled along the main road to Killoran, Rita-Mae Ruttle at the wheel, knuckles whitening on a sharp bend. She wasn't used to driving. Harry rarely allowed her in the driver's seat. Driving was men's work. She'd worn out many a pair of shoes on the streets of Larne, suffering blistered heels and aching arms to bring him his daily bread.

All that changed with her decision to flee. The car was hers; the road was hers. This life was hers, *finally hers*, for the first time in fifteen long years. That she was unsteady in this new world was no surprise. There'd been no subtlety in the transition. It had happened in a flash, like a lightning bolt that fires up for the briefest time – for seconds, mere seconds – giving her no option but to run. Now, finally outside the darkness of her prison, the blindfold ripped off, chains loosened if not yet broken clean, she must find a way to live life on her own terms.

The outskirts of the town lay ahead. The countryside slid past on either side, fields flung haphazardly like bolts of green cloth, tiny birds fluttering in arcs, a mob of crows pecking at roadkill, the sky sagging, hinting at rain.

But she saw none of it. In her mind's eye, Rita-Mae was searching the rooms of Willow Close for that envelope, the name Vivian-Bernadette O'Meara going round and round in her head. She was checking drawers that were empty. How could they be otherwise? She'd so few possessions that they fitted into two suitcases. No photographs, no mementos, no memories; she'd enough of those. She was opening cupboards. Looking under cushions. Turning up chairs as the landscape flowed past.

Had she imagined it?

The envelope.

No, definitely not.

It was there when the butterfly case fell. There for her to find. There for her to open and become part of the story that was Vivian-Bernadette O'Meara's life. Rita-Mae the Samaritan knew this in her heart, in the very pit of her being. Vivian-Bernadette was a troubled soul who needed the compassionate understanding only she could give. She, Rita-Mae, would be the bearer of her secrets. The emissary who'd reveal her truth if need be.

Nothing in this life happens by accident. Everything is meant to be.

She was hearing yet again that saying from her old schoolteacher.

She tightened her grip on the steering wheel, slowed for an oncoming tractor.

The farmer touched his cap, raised a hand. She returned his wave, smiled, relaxed a bit. Eased the car into gear and moved off again, crunching on the gravelled verge. Here she was, driving through this unfamiliar place, waving at people she didn't know. Making things up as she went along. Where would it take her, this story that she'd begun without her incarcerator, her jail warder?

She pictured him high up on a nondescript construction site, slathering mortar on to bricks, light glancing off a safety helmet, his face contorted with the effort of it. So hard in the bone, his heart silting up rage at the poor hand life had dealt him. On whom would he unleash his ire now? That vicious energy that flared up at the slightest wrong. She and Harry: the pair of them such a bad fit right from the beginning, such an inflammatory match.

She saw herself in the bridal suite of the Strand Hotel. The first offence: pouring his beer too quickly. The liquid frothing over the rim had sealed her fate. How could she have known? She'd never poured a beer in her life. Their honeymoon ended abruptly that night, she being throttled half to death on the balcony, her virginity taken violently and sadistically in the bed. The wedding-ring and vows a wicked con, her married life a war zone from that day on.

She shut her eyes briefly to stop the tears. Envisioned Bram Hilditch standing on the threshold of her bedroom as she neared the centre of Killoran. Could he have crossed to the bureau in such a short space of time, taken the envelope, secreted it in his boiler suit? The boiler suit had several pockets, but he'd removed it before coming downstairs. Why was that? Had he taken it off out of politeness because she'd offered him tea? Or had he . . .

She drove slowly down the main street, eyes alert for the Get Ahead hair salon.

It was late afternoon. There were few people about. She saw a pub called Barney's Bar; Butcher O'Dea's; Gilhooley Greengrocer's with a crudely chalked sign in the window offering KERRIS PINKS FRESH DUG £2 A BAG. Johnston's Purveyors of Ladies' & Gentlemen's Fashions, one mannequin on display in a black cape coat, wan bald head, legs as white as birch sticks.

The hair salon was wedged between the BiteSize cafe and a bakery called For Goodness Cakes. She pulled into a vacant spot and killed the engine.

Nervous? Yes, she was nervous. She'd phoned ahead to the number Bram Hilditch had supplied. Susan Mulvey, the proprietor, said she'd be happy to have "a wee chat".

She pushed the door into the hot fustiness of the salon. Three customers: one lying back having her hair washed, an old lady in curlers reading *Woman's Realm* – the cover showing a smiling Prince Andrew and Sarah Ferguson under the banner ALL YOU NEED TO KNOW ABOUT

THE ROYAL ROMANCE. Another female, smoking a cigarette, was having her long blonde hair blow-dried. She looked pregnant.

"Well, I just told him where to go," the blonde was declaiming above the noise of the dryer, eyes on the stylist in the mirror – a slight woman in a black coverall, feet stuck in flat mules. "Honest tae God, expecting me to still help him with the farm-work and me ready tae pop."

Rita-Mae stood by the reception desk, allaying panic by focusing on her surroundings. It was something she always did, most especially on entering a new place. She was a forensic observer, mentally framing the shots, inner camera clearly focused: six posters of glossy hairstyles, one between each mirror, eight mirrors in all, four on each wall. Three washbasins along the back. An exit door to the right. Chequered floor tiles, blue and white. She was slowly counting them when abruptly the hairdryer was shut off.

An unnatural silence imbued the room, through which she could hear the faint strains of "Manic Monday" playing on the radio.

The stylist looked her way, smiled, excused herself and came forward to greet her.

"You must be Rita?" She held out a hand.

She was attractive: mid-forties with dark hair worn in a feathered style like one of Charlie's Angels, regular features, flawless skin. Only the dark hammock of worry under each eye spoilt the near-perfect effect.

The handshake was firm and confident. "I'm Susan. Just take a seat and I'll be with you in two ticks."

Rita-Mae, nerves easing slightly, sat down on a sofa by the window and watched Susan brush the blonde's hair into shape, blast it with a can of spray and send her on her way.

"Now, Rita." She sat down beside her. "So, what's your experience in this business of ours?"

"Ten years . . . yes, about ten in all—"

"That long? I'm impressed."

"Well, yes, in Larne . . . but not all the time. I mean . . . it was more on a part-time basis . . . or when someone was ill."

"Why was that? Husband and children getting in the way I suppose." She chuckled. "Tell me about it. Have three of my own to contend with. All in their teens now, so you can imagine . . . How many do you have?"

"No, it wasn't that . . . I . . . I'm not married."

"You're not?!" Susan's eyes widened in surprise. "A pretty woman like you? Must be very hard to please then. Not a bad way to be. Wish I'd waited myself. Got hitched at nineteen. Far too young. So what brings you here?"

"Well, I thought . . . I thought you might need help."

"But besides that. Larne . . . a bit out of the way. Why come so far to a little backwater like Killoran?"

She hadn't prepared herself for such questions. Careless of her. Once you set foot in the outside world, she told herself, you need to get your story right. If you get to work here there'll be more questions from the locals. A new face in a new place needs to give an account of itself. No one likes an interloper.

"Er . . . just wanted a fresh start I suppose."

"Do you have references?"

Yes, she did have a reference: from Grace Thorne, the owner of the Eclips salon in Larne. She'd been carrying it around for months in expectation of an opportunity such as this.

Susan read through it. "I'll need to call her. Not that I don't trust you . . ."

No, you don't! She wanted to get up and leave. This whole venture had been a bad idea, not properly thought through. But Grace knew where she was. She was the only person she'd entrusted with the news of her escape. She'd called her from Willow Close as soon as she'd settled. And Grace had promised she'd alert her the moment Harry returned.

"I understand," Rita-Mae said. "Please do."

"Susan, whaddya want me to do now? Will I brush out Mrs Mulhern?"

It was the young girl who'd been washing hair. She was plump with rosy cheeks, pigtails as thick as hemp hanging down her front. She looked as though she should still be in school.

"No, Laura, you just sweep up that hair now, like a good girl."

"All right," Laura said nonchalantly, and slapped away in her rubber clogs to fetch the floor brush.

Susan rolled her eyes. "Work experience I'm afraid. Y'know, between you and me, they're more bother than they're worth at times." She patted Rita-Mae's arm. "Now, back to you. I'm not going to call . . ." She checked the reference again. "Grace . . .'cos I can see you'd be an excellent asset here. Emma's going to be out for the next two Thursday and Friday evenings doing a beauty course. Those evenings okay for you?"

"Yes, indeed, that's fine," Rita-Mae said, conscious that Mrs Mulhern, nose stuck in her *Woman's Realm*, was listening to every word of the conversation.

"It's two pounds fifty an hour – the going rate – but the tips are good and you get to keep them yourself. That sound okay?"

"Fine, yes."

"Great!" Susan gave her widest smile. "Now, just one more thing." She reached under the coffee table and produced a notebook. "All I need is your address and telephone number?"

"Eight Willow Close . . . Killoran, of course."

No sooner were the words out than the room went quiet again. The silence that had fallen when the hairdryer was switched off was nothing compared to this one.

The pen that Susan held froze above the page.

Mrs Mulhern turned in her chair and stared openly.

The brush sweeping up the hair had stopped abruptly.

"Sorry, did I say something wrong?"

Only silence answered her, a silence spreading like a rumour. She swore she could hear her heart beating.

"Now, Laura, that hair won't sweep itself," Susan said, recovering her composure. But she was unable to meet Rita-Mae's eye and scribbled the address down so quickly it was barely legible.

She got up. "See you next week then. It was very nice meeting you."

Mrs Mulhern was following the exchange grim-faced, the magazine discarded.

Rita-Mae, not a little irked, moved towards the door. The warm reception followed by such a chilly dismissal was not at all to her liking.

"Now, Molly," she heard Susan say. "Let's get you out of these rollers."

Hand on the door-handle, she hesitated. Susan hadn't even waited to get her telephone number. She thought about turning back to give it, but prudence stopped her.

Best just to go.

She stepped outside, awkward with urgency and the disquiet of that not-yet-finished moment tumbling into something altogether bigger and more sinister.

The sky had darkened; a last bleed of sun was disappearing in the west. Rain was on its way.

She hurried to the car. Was about to get in when she noticed a folded piece of paper under one of the wipers – a pamphlet advertising some event or other no doubt.

She freed it, opened the car door and slid into the driver's seat, just as the first drops of rain began to spatter the windscreen.

She unfolded the sheet of paper.

No, it was certainly no pamphlet. No invitation to a bring-and-buy sale in the parish hall. No announcement of a bingo evening the following week. No printed matter at all.

It was a handwritten note. The letters large and childlike.

You shouldn't a put the phone
down on me Rita
and you the good samaritan
Nobody does the like a that to me
as you'll soon be finding out you bitch

CHAPTER NINE

Exposed.

Vulnerable.

Helpless.

Hopeless.

Powerless.

Alone.

Alone.

Alone.

Rita-Mae sat in her parked car, fighting the feelings she knew so well. For years she'd fought the enemy right in front of her: Harry, the monster she could *see*. Now another one had entered the fray. One even more menacing because she could not see him.

But she'd *heard* him. Oh, yes.

A lewd, drink-sodden voice down the Samaritan helpline in the middle of the night. A man who complained about his bad leg, his ex-wife, his sorry lot, and called himself Lenny.

He could be watching her right now. Seeing her distress. Relishing the callous game his twisted mind had conjured.

She thought of a winged thing fluttering wildly in a killing jar, put her face in her hands and leaned into the steering wheel, questions hitting her like hail.

What have I done?

Where is he?

How did he know my car?

Did he follow me from the house?

Is it Bram Hilditch playing games?

Is it Harry playing games?

No, no, not Harry. Grace would have warned me.

A sharp rapping on the window made her jump.

She looked up to see Bram Hilditch grinning down at her, tipping the brim of his hat.

She wound down the window.

"Miss Ruttle. I *thought* it was you."

"H-Hello . . . Mr Hilditch. I . . ."

"Are you all right? You look a little pale."

He was impeccably dressed as usual: white shirt, claret waistcoat and matching dicky bow, camel coat. Had an official-looking black bag slung over one shoulder and a newspaper sticking from a side-pocket.

Rita-Mae stared up at him, trying to figure out where he'd sprung from. There was no sign of his car. And she now knew what it looked like.

A red Daimler was hard to miss.

"Yes . . . I . . . I think . . . I think I have a cold coming on, that's all."

"So sorry to hear that!" He threw a look in the direction of the salon. "Get sorted out with Susan then?"

"Yes . . . yes . . ."

He bent down, clutched the window ledge, leaned in. She got the reek of strong cologne and a whiff of peppermints on his breath. "I can recommend half a lemon squeezed in boiling water first thing in the morning, last thing at night. Works wonders . . . detoxifies the system, clears the sinus passages."

"What? Oh . . . yes, I see. Thank you . . . yes, I'll try that."

She reached for the ignition key, eager to get away.

He glanced across the street. Turned back to her with a look of expectation. "Tell you what, I'm going across to the Heavenly Realms for a spot of tea. Would you care to join me? They do delicious cakes."

Her immediate instinct was to refuse, but then a thought struck her. She'd be safe enough with him in a public place. Besides, if this "Lenny" person were watching, the sight of a man accompanying her into a cafe might give the impression that they were a couple, and so have the effect of deterring him completely.

Stalkers liked their women single, living on their own. Defenceless, lonely women: all the better to terrify.

She slipped the note into her pocket. "Yes, that . . . that would be lovely, Mr Hilditch. I'll . . . I'll just get my handbag."

The landlord threaded his way between the grouped tables in the Heavenly Realms – all linen-clad and tinkling china – to a conservatory area at the rear. At the sight of him, a flurry of smiles and greetings broke out amongst the customers – mostly ladies of a certain age.

"Abraham, how do you do?" a plump woman in a shimmering top exclaimed, jowls wobbling, a forkful of pastry poised in mid-air. "And where is Octavia today?" She gave Rita-Mae the once over. "Or is this young lady the secret you keep from her?"

Bram bent his head reverentially, hat clamped to chest.

"Mrs Baldwin-Piggott, you're incorrigible. Her Grace is resting and this is Miss Ruttle, my new tenant."

"Tenant . . . oh, I see." She lowered the fork, interest suddenly piqued. "How do you do, Miss Ruttle. You're the one in Willow—"

"Sorry, Mrs Baldwin-Piggott, we *really* are pushed for time."

"Oh . . . remind Octavia she's coming for cocktails. My chauffeur will collect her at six."

"Yes, indeed. Good day to you, ladies."

The new tenant was conscious of surprised looks and a spirited murmuring in her wake. She caught a snatch. ". . . wonder does Octavia know what he's up to."

". . . wonder does *she* know what *she's* in for."

He halted at a table with a RESERVED sign – she wondered about that too – and pulled out a chair. Had he booked the table in advance, knowing he was going to meet her outside the salon? Had he engineered this whole meeting?

"Everyone seems to know you, Mr Hilditch."

"Yes, that's what comes from living in the same place all one's life." He placed his shoulder-bag on the floor, removed his coat. "That of course, and having officiated at most of their husbands' funerals."

A waitress placed a teapot on the table.

"Thank you, Pauline . . . One builds a special rapport with the bereaved."

Rita-Mae was more unsettled than ever, not only by the threatening note in her pocket, but that RESERVED sign on the table. She clutched her hands tightly in her lap to stop them shaking. She could not trust herself with the teapot, even though it was proper etiquette for the lady to pour.

"Would you mind pouring, Mr Hilditch?" she said, a sudden brain-wave coming to her. "My hands are a little numb from the cold . . . I forgot my gloves you see."

"Why, of course." Bram lifted the lid of the pot and peeked in. "A woman is like a teabag," he said, perfecting an American drawl. "You can't tell how strong she is until you put her in hot water."

What on earth was he saying? And why was he using that odd voice? "Sorry . . . I . . . I don't understand."

"Oh, don't mind me. It's one of Her Grace's little maxims. I believe Eleanor Roosevelt said it but Mother pretends it's hers. Yes, a nice cup of tea is a fine restorative. You'll be right as rain in a minute or two. Would you like a drop of milk?"

She nodded.

"Always the milk in first, to protect the china. I like this little cafe because they know the value of good china in the tea-making process."

He smiled, showing those lovely even teeth.

She envied the deftness of this little performance. His steady hands, the fluid movements, the easy talk. There was no awkwardness. None of the discomfort that was such a feature of her own life. It seemed as though he'd had tea with countless women just like her.

Strangers just like her.

"Do you know how tea was discovered?"

She shook her head, grateful that he wasn't picking up on her distress, allowed herself to be carried along on the tide of words flowing so easily from him.

"Shen Nung, the ancient Chinese emperor, was having his morning drink of hot water when a leaf from the tree *Camellia sinensis*, which he was sitting under, fortuitously fell into his bowl. Instead of discarding the leaf he decided to taste the infusion. And so, Miss Ruttle, that is why you and I can enjoy this wonderful beverage so many millennia later. Fascinating, is it not?"

He passed her the cup and saucer.

"You know so many things." She glanced at the cup, still unable to trust her hands. Instead, she drew a hanky from her pocket and dabbed at her nose.

"Oh, I read a lot. Undertaking could be a slow business, especially in the summer – winters were our busiest period. The bleak weather leading to depression, and so more suicides. The elderly dears succumbing more readily to the cold – so one filled one's time constructively. Her Grace has an extensive library, courtesy of her father . . . a professor of History at Trinity in his day—"

Pauline interrupted his gush of reminiscence and set down a stand of dainty cakes. The sugary confections, so beautifully arranged, looked like a work of art.

"Thank you, Pauline. Almost looks too good to eat, Miss Ruttle," he enthused, seemingly reading her thoughts. "Do you bake cakes yourself? Well, I expect you do." He picked up the silver cake fork and set about cutting up a cherry slice with the utmost care.

"I do from time to time, yes," she said, wondering how she was going to forgo the cakes without causing offence. "They look delicious, but I'm . . . I'm sorry to say on this occasion I can't partake."

"Oh, no!"

"Yes . . . my stomach . . . part of this cold I think."

"That's too bad . . . but I understand completely. You won't mind if I take your portion home to Her Grace then, will you?"

"No, no, not at all. They're all yours."

He smiled again, this time more broadly. The pleasure he took in her assent regarding the cakes was thawing her a little. Perhaps, she thought, he's just lonely and in need of company. Female company. Perhaps the mother is the only woman he's ever been close to. Because from what she'd gathered so far, Octavia Hilditch was quite the domineering sort. And Rita-Mae knew only too well what that felt like. She'd lived under the thumb of a controlling bully long enough. At least they had *that* in common.

For some reason the name Vivian-Bernadette O'Meara came unbidden – the secret letter, the stricken box-room. Should she ask him about his former tenant? She hesitated. Then thought of the perfect pretext.

"By the way, I was just wondering . . . who lived at Willow Close before me?"

He was in the process of lifting his teacup. Decided not to. Placed it back on the saucer. Looked straight at her, all cordiality seemingly gone.

"A young lady. Why is it important?"

"It's just that if post arrived for her I'd like to know where to forward it."

"That won't be an issue," he said crisply. "There'll be no post arriving for her. As landlord, it's my job to take care of such formalities. You need not concern yourself with that, Miss Ruttle." He lifted his cup and smiled. "Now tell me about your family . . . your brothers and sisters."

She did not recall mentioning anything about brothers and sisters. She could tell that her question had hit a nerve.

"Don't have any I'm afraid."

"None at all?"

"Well, I had a twin sister, but she died as a baby, alas." No sooner had she said it than she wondered why she'd shared such an intimacy with him.

"Oh, how awful for you, Miss Ruttle!" He set the teacup back down, voice deepening with concern. "I'm so sorry to hear that."

"Thank you . . . Yes, well, it's in the past . . . And you?"

"One brother . . . younger . . . Zac. Considers himself a poet of sorts. He's in Canada so I don't see much of him." He scanned the room. "We really must do this more often, you know."

"How interesting!"

He gave her a quizzical look.

"Your brother being a poet." She raised the teacup to her lips with just the slightest tremble.

"Oh, that . . . well, yes, I suppose. It's good to get away from Mother. She can be quite a handful at times." He saw her sniff the tea. She took a sip.

"It tastes of flowers," she said, not a little surprised.

"Beautiful, isn't it? Smoky lapsang souchong with just a hint of jasmine. I *thought* you'd like it."

"But how did you know I'd be coming here with you?" She had the words out before she could stop herself. She felt her whole body tense again.

"Oh, you misunderstand, Miss Ruttle. Lapsang is what Her Grace and I always have when we visit the Heavenly Realms. It's just so lovely that I can introduce another lady – and may I say a lady of such refinement as your good self – to the glories of this wonderful brew."

He was either guileless or a very good actor. She couldn't decide which.

Get a grip, she told herself. Bram Hilditch is about the only person you know in this town. If the faceless stalker were to strike, he's the only one you could turn to for help.

She allowed herself a brief smile. "Thank you for the compliment."

"Oh, but it's true." He reached for another cake.

His next question, however, had alarm coursing through her like a riptide.

"I was wondering, Miss Ruttle, have you ever had children?"

She paused.

Set the cup down. Boldly met his piercingly focused eyes.

"No. Being a spinster, how could I?" she reminded him.

"Sorry if I offended you," he said, but she knew he wasn't. He was searching for information because he didn't believe her.

"It's just that you're very pretty and I thought perhaps you might have been married in the past . . . that's all."

She wanted to say, "It's none of your damned business!" But "a lady of such refinement," and a pretty one to boot, needed to act the part he'd cast her in.

"Nice of you to say so, Mr Hilditch, but looks can be deceptive you know." She lifted the teapot without a quiver. "More tea?"

CHAPTER TEN

Rita-Mae drove back home from her unexpected tea date with Bram Hilditch in a state of high agitation. So much had happened in the two hours or so she'd been in Killoran that she now wondered if – all things considered – it might be safer simply to stay put behind the walls of 8 Willow Close and not go out at all. There was a little grocer's shop on the edge of town where she could buy the basics. She baked her own bread and could live quite well on canned food if she had to. But as soon as she had this thought another more urgent one came rushing in. Was she even safe in that house? She saw again the shocked faces of those in the Get Ahead salon at mention of her address. Something terrible *had* happened at number 8. And it appeared that everybody but her was in on the secret.

Arriving in the driveway, she instinctively steered the car round the back and parked it. The alarmed face of Susan Mulvey had been supplanted in her mind's eye by a clear and present danger: that of a faceless man called Lenny. Given the sinister message, which could only be from him, it was best to keep the vehicle out of sight.

She got out of the car, berating herself for not having taken such a precaution earlier. Her number-plate had been there in full view, right out front, for nearly a month. Who was to say this Lenny character wasn't living on the same road? Hadn't been watching her every move and following her back and forth?

She found the house keys—

"Hello, there!" A male voice behind her.

The keys clanked on the ground. She spun round to see a man hunkered down near the garden shed.

Her knees went weak.

"Sorry, I didn't mean tae give yeh a shock," he said, getting up. "Bram sent me to check the drains. Said yeh were complainin' about a bad smell."

"Oh, I . . . h-he . . . he never said you'd be coming *today*."

"Aye, that's Bram . . . a bit forgetful sometimes." He cleaned his hands on his coveralls and came forward.

Was he dragging his left leg? Suddenly, in her head, a voice down the Samaritan helpline: *Crashed the car on a skinful last year and the oul' leg isn't what it used to be.*

She had the urge to dash into the house and bolt the door. Get out of danger as quickly as possible.

"That oul' leg of mine's went to sleep. Been on me knees for a while." He slapped his thigh several times. "You'll be Miss Ruffle, I s'ppose. I'll not shake hands 'cos they're a bit durty, so they are."

She could barely speak.

He bent down and retrieved her keys. Handed them to her.

"Th-Thank you. Y-Yes . . . I'm R-R*utt*le," she managed to say. "Miss *Ruttle*, yes, with two t's."

"Och, aye, Ruttle . . . pardon me. I'm Dan Madden." He was tall with a cadaverous face and wore a cap pulled low over his forehead. Well into his forties she guessed, even though most of his face was in shadow.

"Do odd jobs about the place," he continued, rubbing a hand over his stubble. "Do a bitta mechanic work too." He eyed her car. "So if that wee car gives yeh any bother I'm yer man. Nice wee motor she is too. Aisey on the juice, is she?"

There was that word "aisey". It was a mispronunciation of "easy". The Lenny character had used it too: *They'd be aisier to take off you.*

She nodded. "Thanks. I'll . . . I'll remember that . . . well, I'll let you . . . let you get on, Mr Madden."

"Right yeh be. I'll give yeh a knock when I'm finished up, so I will."

Once inside, she swiftly locked the door. Went to the kitchen sink and gulped down a glass of water.

From her viewpoint she could see him hunkered down again by the garden shed. He had a long stick and was ramming it down the drain hole.

There was only one way to make sure that this Dan Madden was genuine. She'd call Bram Hilditch immediately.

The phone rang out several times and she was on the verge of hanging up when it was finally lifted.

"Good afternoon, the Hilditch residence," came a brusque female voice.

Rita-Mae was immediately on edge, for she realized that the formidable Octavia Hilditch, aka Her Grace, whom she'd glimpsed briefly and heard so much about, was addressing her.

She coughed politely and, adopting her most assuaging Samaritan tone, said, "Might I speak to Mr Bram Hilditch, please?"

"No, you might not!" came the abrupt reply. "And his name is *Abraham*, not Bram."

"Er . . . em . . ."

"And the reason you may *not* speak to him is because he is not *here*. Heaven knows where he's got to. Catering to the needs of that new tenant of his no doubt. She seems to be taking up all his time these days, more's the pity. And who might you be?"

"I . . . I'm Rita Ruttle . . . his new tenant."

There was a pause on the line, which Rita-Mae took to be an embarrassed lull, during which Mrs Hilditch would be preparing the requisite apology.

The reply, however, when finally it came, was anything but apologetic.

"Well, good day to you, Miss Ruttle. At last we get to at least speak, if not meet. Isn't he with *you*?"

"Pardon?"

"Isn't Abraham with *you*?"

"No, but—"

"He said he was seeing to your drains or some fatuous pursuit or other! So when he turns up send him right back home. I wish to speak to him before my engagement with the Baldwin-Piggotts at six."

"Well, I just—"

"Good day to you, Miss Ruttle."

With that, the line went dead and Rita-Mae was left holding a loudly purring receiver.

So much for that!

She dropped it back on to the cradle, irked, returned to the kitchen and peered out of the window.

Madden had disappeared. Come to think of it, where was his van? If he were a maintenance man he should surely have one. She hadn't noticed it on her way in.

She went back to the lounge and checked the front window.

No van.

A sudden scraping sound had her pressing her face against the glass.

She saw him bent down by the drainpipe at the front of the house.

There was no way she was opening the door to him. She simply could not risk it.

She pushed open the window.

"Mr Madden!"

"Aye." He turned round, a length of piping in hand.

"Where's your van . . . just wondering?"

"Didn't bother wi' it, 'cos I live just down the road."

"You do?"

She held tight to the window-handle. Reminded herself that both front and back doors were locked. She was in the dominant position.

"Aye, just down the road." He pointed with the piping. "Madden Motor Repairs . . . me garage's about half a mile down that way. That's why I'm very near yeh, if that wee car of yours gives yeh any bother."

He saw her eyeing the drain hole. Its grating had been removed and a lump of black stuff was lying beside it.

"Aye, that's what was givin' yeh the bad smell." He went over and prodded it with his boot. "Hard tae say with all that durt on it, but I'd say a chaffinch or buntin'."

"A bird?"

"Been lyin' there this while by the looks of it . . . got stuck in the gratin' and rotted. If you've got a plastic bag I'll take it away with me."

She went through to the kitchen, found one.

"Well, thanks for that, Mr Madden," she said, handing him the bag through the window.

"No bother. As I say, if yeh have any other wee jobs that need doin' just give me a call." He proffered a grubby piece of notepaper. "Save yeh the bother of ringin' Bram. 'Cos, as I say, I'm just down the road, like. Me name and number's on that, so it is."

Gingerly she took the paper from him and placed it on the sill. "Thanks, Mr Madden. I'll remember that. Now, if you'll excuse me."

"Right yeh be." He touched the peak of his cap and went to deal with the bird.

She waited behind the curtain, watched him bag the bird, put the grating back in place.

Would he drag his leg as he went down the garden path?

Didn't seem to. But he did have an odd, shambling step.

He fastened the gate, looked towards the window, raised a hand and went on his way.

It was safe to breathe again.

The folded note lay on the sill.

The scrunched-up note from "Lenny" was still in her pocket.

She smoothed it out on the table. Unfolded Madden's and laid it alongside.

MADDEN MOTOR REPAIRS was written in a surprisingly neat, right-slanting hand, as was his telephone number underneath. The sets of writing could not have been more different.

So maybe he *was* on the level after all.

She consigned both notes to the table drawer, and was about to remove her coat when a thought struck her. That explanation about a dead bird didn't quite ring true somehow. After all, the smell was *inside* the house and mostly in the box-room.

There was a distinct chill in the air as she stepped out.

She pulled her coat around her and bent down to inspect the drain.

There was no way a bird could have flown in there. The grating would have to be removed first. And she doubted that even the most dexterous bird could manage that.

She returned indoors, flopped down on the sofa, leaned back and shut her eyes.

It had been quite an afternoon. She'd met Susan Mulvey, her new employer and salon owner, and found the menacing note on her wind-screen. She'd had that unexpected tea date with Bram Hilditch, followed by the rebuff on the phone from his very rude mother. Finally, she'd arrived home to find a stranger claiming to be a handyman on the premises. Curious how Bram had never mentioned him over tea.

Am I, she asked herself, being too mistrustful? I'm new here. These people have their way of doing things and I have mine.

She cast her mind back to that conversation in the Heavenly Realms.

A cryptic statement delivered in a fake American drawl boomed in her head. *A woman is like a teabag. You can't tell how strong she is until you put her in hot water.*

What on earth had he meant by that?

And he was good at accents.

She heard a slurred drunken cadence – the voice of someone calling himself Lenny breathing down a telephone line.

Mimicry such as that would be a cinch . . . a doddle for . . . for . . .

For someone like Abraham Hilditch.

CHAPTER ELEVEN

Portaluce, Antrim Coast

After breakfast and the chat with Gladys Millman, Dorinda felt herself on firmer ground. She had money to pay her way, a bed for the night, and a car which – when repaired the following day – would take her home. She did not know exactly where "home" was, but she trusted Mama would help her out on that score. Florence Walsh always showed up on awkward occasions to deal with the practicalities and guide her through the maze. That's how it had been and always would be.

"A bracing walk on the promenade would do you the world of good." Gladys Millman's voice broke in on Dorrie's musings as she mounted the stairs back to her room.

She turned to see the proprietor regarding her from behind the bulwark of the ornate reception desk.

"Yes . . . yes, I'd love to . . . I mean, go for a walk. But I don't have a coat you see."

"You came out without a coat? In this weather?" The sound of the wind seething at the windows, and buffeting the flags out front, lent weight to the incredulity in Mrs Millman's voice. "I have to say, I *did* wonder last night about that."

"Yes – I mean, no. I . . . I mean to say I *do* have a coat, but I spilled tea down the front, so c-can't really wear it."

"Oh, that's easily remedied, Miss Walsh. We can launder it for you. Maureen will see to it right away."

Dorrie dithered. How would she get out of this one? The stained trench coat in all its gory detail flashed before her.

Tell her you've washed out the stain. It's drying in your room.

"That's very kind, but . . . but I . . . I washed it in . . . in the sink. It's drying on the radiator."

"Oh, you shouldn't have gone to such trouble." Mrs Millman had moved from behind the desk and stood at the bottom of the stairs gazing up at her.

Dorrie was fearful of what might come next. She needed a diversion. It came in the form of the white fortress she'd caught sight of earlier. She had a clear view of it from her vantage point on the stair.

"Who lives in the castle?"

Mrs Millman frowned. "Sorry, what castle?" She followed Dorrie's pointing finger. "Oh, the convent you mean. The Daughters of Divine Healing occupy it."

She turned back, slightly irked. "Now, where was I? Yes, the coat. Now, for next time, just leave laundry in the basket in your room and Maureen will take care of it. After all, that's what we're here for. I can lend you a coat."

"Thank you, Mrs Millman, but I'd just as soon—"

"Nonsense. The sea air will do you the world of good. Besides, Maureen has to tidy your room."

The statement set alarm bells ringing. But she knew it would be futile to protest. Mrs Millman was sovereign in this domain. The stained raincoat would have to be well hidden before the maid set to.

Without further ado, the proprietor ducked through a door behind the desk. She re-emerged holding out what appeared to be the pelt of some endangered species.

"Here," she said.

There was little Dorrie could do but submit herself to the other's will.

The bell coat of red fox was a little on the big side, but it felt beautiful and Dorrie regarded herself oddly privileged to be wearing it. It smelt of cigarette smoke and Mrs Millman's musky scent: an expensive aroma redolent of Garbo and Dietrich, those Hollywood dames who'd flitted across the movie screens of her childhood.

She wrapped it tightly about her as she made her way down the promenade, pulling the collar taut against the crisp northerly breeze.

Although loath to leave her room and take this walk, she was glad now to be out, and away from the surge and fall of emotions that meeting the proprietor had triggered. Perhaps being free of the Ocean Spray for a little while would jog her memory and bring some order to things. Perhaps this is how the dead feel, she thought now, when they first move into spirit. The wires of the memory box suddenly disconnect and they find themselves in a mysterious world, trying to recover the links and relatedness of things that will take them back to their old life and the face they once knew in the mirror.

A perverse thought stuck her. What if I can't find my way back? What if I'm stuck here like a wandering ghost? What if the car's beyond repair and I'm stranded here in this seaside town with nowhere to go?

That slurry of dread, as dangerous as held breath, was threatening to pull her under again.

Mama, you must help me; you simply must!

It's all right, Dorrie. You worry far too much. Everything will be just fine. You'll see. Just go with the flow, my dear. Go with the flow.

An empty beer can rattled into her path and she sidestepped it immediately. But the intrusion, tiny and trivial though it was, brought back memories of the whiskey bottle in her bedside table.

"I hope I've concealed it well enough!"

An elderly man wearing an outsized hearing aid threw her a look of mild reproach as he passed. Dorrie averted her eyes, vexed she'd been caught talking to herself for a second time that morning.

Yes, she *had* secreted the bottle. In her mind's eye she saw herself wrap it in a hand towel and push it to the back of the bottom drawer of the bedside table. And, more importantly, she *had* made sure to hide the trench coat too, in a place where the maid would not see it. It was flattened out on top of the wardrobe, well out of sight. Maureen was not likely to clean up there. The layer of dust Dorrie had found was evidence enough that the girl's duties didn't extend to being *that* thorough with the cleaning cloth.

Reassured, she brought her mind back to the present and her lovely surroundings.

The little town of Portaluce appeared to be sitting at the very edge of the world, its row of shops and houses bravely facing down the roar and vigour of that vast stretch of ocean, which seemed poised to lash out at any moment and swallow them whole.

The sea frightened Dorrie. And she knew it had something to do with the only memory she'd been able to summon thus far: that snapshot of Mama in a floral dress drawn at the waist, her hair the colour of wheat taking on the light, and Uncle Jack standing on the beach, the air between them thrumming with tension and mistrust.

She forced herself to glance back at the beach now, a ribbon of foreshore the colour of mustard lying far beyond the white castle she now knew to be a convent. Was that the same stretch of sand she'd raced along last night in her dream? It must be. That childhood memory and the dream both featured the beach *and* her mother. Somehow they were connected, and were the reason she'd been drawn to this coastal town. If only she could figure out why. But she had the feeling that perhaps it was best not to know.

Everything would be just fine, Mama had assured her, and she must trust her good counsel. Just because she was in the spirit world didn't mean she was any less real.

Dorrie continued on her way. Made a half-hearted resolution not to puzzle any more over her circumstances. She'd be out of Portaluce tomorrow and would look back on this crazy episode, and laugh at how easily she'd got herself worked up over nothing.

She dug her hands deeper into the pockets of the beautiful borrowed coat and tried to focus on the specialness of this lovely little place: the smell of the ocean, the squawk and shriek of the herring gulls, the sound of her stilettos striking the pavement. The high heels made her feel special and in control, qualities she imagined came easily to the likes of Mrs Millman. Oh, how she wished she could be more like her! Settled and resolute in her beautiful guesthouse, which looked like a frosted wedding cake of piped and fluted loveliness.

A sudden gust of wind blew her into the path of a mother trundling a pushchair, and all at once she found herself bending over a chubby infant behind a hood of protective plastic.

The baby woke up and gave out an ear-splitting squeal.

"I'm so sorry," Dorrie said, regaining her balance. The mother scowled, regarding her through tired eyes, ropes of ash-blonde hair blowing about her face. She looked poor and burdened and no more than eighteen.

"All right for some," she muttered, eyeing the expensive coat.

The coat's not mine, Dorrie wanted to say, but before she knew it, mother and baby had taken off, the peals of the child adding to the soundtrack of ravening gulls shrieking for scraps at the water's edge.

Dismayed by the event, and with the wind increasing, she spotted a cafe called Marcella's across the road and headed towards it.

After the wide-open chill of the promenade the little cafe felt as warm and cosy as a gloved hand, and she was glad of her decision to take cover.

It was a simple, L-shaped room, with a long glass counter running down one wall facing a row of curved banquettes twinned with tables on the opposite side.

There was only one other customer, an old gentleman intent on the pages of the *Sunday News*. Unfortunately, he was seated at the table she would have chosen, the one nearest the window. He lowered the newspaper and eyed her for longer than was polite.

"Good morning," she said. But her greeting was met with a grudging *harrumph* before he went back to his reading.

Behind the counter a young waitress was carefully topping up a row of glass sugar bowls.

"Good morning!" she said brightly, setting the bag aside and giving her full attention to the new customer. "What can I get you?"

Dorrie approached the counter. A nametag on the waitress's lapel read JANE.

"A pot of tea would be lovely, please."

"That everything? I can recommend the lemon meringue. It's very good. My mum made it, so I'm a bit biased I have to say."

Sweet food was the last thing she wanted but the expectant look in Jane's pretty brown eyes had her caving in.

"Very well . . . just a little slice then."

"Breezy today . . . more so than yesterday," Jane declared, transferring a slice of the pie to a plate. "The boss says it comes with the winter tide. Are you up for the weekend?"

"Yes, just . . . just for the weekend. How much do I owe you?" She made a pretence of looking for her purse.

"That's okay. Sure you can pay me when you're finished." She nodded at one of the booths. "Just take a seat there and I'll bring—"

The waitress's voice was suddenly cut short by a loud bout of coughing. They turned to see the old man enveloped in a cloud of blue smoke.

"All right, Mr Donnelly?" Jane called out.

He raised a hand without looking up.

"It's the cigarettes. He's a sixty-a-day man I'm afraid."

With the coughing fit over, the atmosphere of calm returned.

Dorrie settled into a booth with her tea and lemon meringue pie. Jane went back to her duty with the sugar bag.

The pie was surprisingly good, and after the first mouthful she discovered she was indeed quite hungry. She had no wish to engage in small talk with Jane, charming though she was, and hoped more customers would enter and occupy her.

Very soon her wish was granted. Two women of pensionable age surged in, talking loudly and incessantly.

". . . *sure didn't she find him out for the count in the bed when she got herself home from work and it only four o'clock.*"

"*Get away! And there was me thinkin' he was over beyond with the Daughters of Divine Healing, gettin' himself dried out—*"

"Morning, Irene . . . Brigid. Usual, is it?"

"Thanks, Jane love. *Dried out, me arse. The day Charlie Deakin dries himself out he'll be six foot under, wearing the wooden overcoat, you mark my words.*"

They installed themselves in the booth next to Dorrie. At the sight of them, the gentleman by the window frowned, folded his newspaper and prepared to leave. It was only when he turned his head and adjusted a large hearing aid that Dorrie realized he was the man on the promenade who'd heard her talking to herself.

". . . *that's too bad, and there was me thinkin' he was off the booze completely . . .*"

"*He has wee Mary's heart broke. That's a nice dress yer wearin', Brigid. It's only now that you've got your coat off yeh I can see it right.*"

"Och, there was another one with blue in it far nicer. Would of fitted me lovely if only I could of got into it."

Taking her cue from the old man and not wanting to be a party to any more of Irene and Brigid's gossip, Dorrie decided it was time she shifted too, that favoured seat by the window now being free. She hastily took another forkful of the delicious pie, but in her haste dropped a dollop of it on her blouse.

"Oh, fiddlesticks!"

The door opened again.

She glanced up and saw a man enter.

His appearance immediately created a flaw in the room and straightaway left her fretful.

He was the tall, rangy individual she'd seen earlier: the one wearing the trilby and getting out of the black saloon car with the little girl. There she was, the little one: following behind him in her bright green coat. He pointed to the vacant seat by the window and watched impatiently as the child clambered on to it.

"Now stay there," she heard him say.

The sadness of the little one was all too painfully apparent. She sat at the table, hands folded in her lap, staring forlornly at the centrepiece: three paper daisies in a vase.

Dorrie felt an urgent need to go and comfort her. But the stain had to be removed first, otherwise the silk blouse would be ruined.

She saw the father approach the counter.

Guessed that, yes, she would have time.

She rushed to the Ladies.

It took her less than a minute to clean the blouse.

Still panicked, but feeling more assured, she re-entered the cafe.

But . . .

Frantically she scoped the room.

The man and child were nowhere to be seen.

How could that be? Could they really have exited so quickly?

She ran to the window and looked left and right.

Nothing.

"Everything all right?"

She turned to see Jane's concerned face.

"Yes . . . yes. I . . ."

"Can I get you more tea? That pot's bound to be a little cold by now."

"Yes . . . sorry, I mean no . . . I don't want any more tea." Nervously, she approached the counter, trying her best to suppress the alarm that was welling up inside her. "Jane . . . th-that man with the little girl . . . Have they . . . have they left already?"

"*What* man and little girl?"

"The tall man in the hat and . . . and the little girl . . . in . . . in the green coat . . . They were . . . they were there by the window. You . . . you were taking his order when I went to the Ladies."

Jane looked at her oddly. "Nobody came in, miss."

"But I *saw* them." Why was the waitress lying? What kind of crazy town was this? Why was nothing making sense? She wrung her hands in despair.

". . . then I went to the Ladies to clean my blouse," she forged on. "I-It was only a couple of minutes ago. Y-You must have . . . *must have . . . seen them?*"

The gossips had stopped talking. They were staring at Dorrie.

Jane broke the silence. "Brigid, Irene, was there a man in here just now? Tall, with a little girl?"

The women shook their heads. "No, we didn't see nobody," one volunteered, before returning to her chinwag.

Jane leaned closer to Dorrie. "Those two talk so much they wouldn't notice a bomb dropping between them. How was the meringue?"

"Good . . . very good . . . yes." Oh, why did I have to let that piece of it fall on my blouse? How clumsy of me! Her eyes were drawn to where it had landed.

"Are you sure you're okay? That'll be one pound fifty, when you're ready."

"Quite sure." But when she handed over the £5 note, Dorrie could not stop her hand from shaking.

There was only one way to stop this nightmare, only one sure way.

Her mind made up, she rushed to the door.

"M-Miss, you forgot your change! Miss—"

She banged the door shut on the voice and fled back the way she'd come.

CHAPTER TWELVE

Samaritan Centre, Killoran

The Centre occupied a three-storey corner house down a quiet side street off the main square in the town. Its unremarkable appearance – bookending a terrace of similar houses – belied the important work that went on behind its modest front door.

Only the orange-and-black sign over the lintel, and restated on the gable wall, set the building apart. It had been left to the charity by a war veteran, Samuel McCann, whose life had been saved from the suspension bridge at Rosnacarna by the wise counsel of a volunteer some decades before. The sympathetic words he'd heard down the telephone line had enabled him to reappraise his life and given him the strength to carry on breathing the good air he realized was his gift.

On this occasion Rita-Mae felt slightly more anxious when turning the key in the door to the Centre. She looked about nervously. Could the stalker be out there watching her right now? She'd taken the precaution of parking well out of sight behind the building. Perhaps the move would throw him off.

She pushed open the door quickly, comforting herself with the thought that at 4 p.m. on a weekday she was less likely to encounter many drunks or TM callers the likes of Lenny. They were generally a phenomenon of the later hours at weekends.

She went through to the cloakroom and hung up her coat, catching the whiff of cooking as she went. Odd, she thought; must be the people next door, and continued on down the corridor.

But the aroma of brewed tea and baking only intensified. It was clearly not coming from outside but from inside the Centre and from the upstairs kitchen. Someone was up there and they were singing: a female voice, trilling out the words to a familiar air.

How very curious! There were only two other volunteers at the Centre: Linda and Henry. She'd met them briefly at the beginning and they'd exchanged phone numbers, but she'd not seen them since. They were so short-staffed that the three of them were timetabled to do separate shifts and on different days. In between times the phone lines were switched over to the bigger centres in Belfast and elsewhere to pick up the slack.

"Hello there!" she called out.

But the singing continued unabated, to the accompanying sounds of crockery being set down and cupboard doors opening and shutting.

There are three lovely lassies in Bannion,
Bannion, Bannion.

She climbed the stairs, not a little perturbed.

There are three lovely lassies in Bannion,
And I am the best of them all.

The door to the kitchen was slightly ajar and she was taken aback to see a woman in a floral-print overall bent over the cooker, retrieving something from the oven.

"Hello there!"

"Good heavens!" the woman cried, twirling to face her.

She was clutching a tray of cupcakes between a pair of oven mitts. Mid-fifties, Rita-Mae reckoned, a little on the heavy side. Kindly face all pinked from the stove heat. Brown hair cut into an unflattering bowl shape.

"Sorry, I didn't mean to startle you," Rita-Mae said.

"Oh, that's all right," the woman flustered, smiling shyly and setting down the tray. "I'm Blossom Magee." She removed the gloves and proffered a hand. "You must be Miss Ruttle? Pleased to meet you."

"And you . . . you're a volunteer too, Mrs Magee?"

"Oh, no, I'm only the cleaning lady and I keep the tea things stocked," Blossom said meekly.

She pulled out a chair and checked the clock.

"You'll have time for a wee cuppa tea, won't you, Miss Ruttle? There's still plenty in the pot. For when you're cold it warms you. When you're warm it cools you. When you're depressed it cheers you, and when you're a wee bit anxious it calms you down."

She flushed some more when she saw the new recruit's bemusement.

"Oh, don't mind me, dear. It's an old saying of my father's . . . and call me Blossom. Everyone that knows me calls me that."

Rita-Mae sat down, not a little surprised by the congenial Blossom bustling about the simple kitchenette, filling it with homely smells and the lilt of her cheerful voice. Her normal reserve, so rigidly held when meeting someone new, was beginning to thaw.

She eyed the cupcakes nervously. No, she didn't really want to have tea. How was she going to eschew the cakes without offending the lovely lady though? That was the question. Because she had the impression that Blossom's primary function in life was looking after others and performing selfless acts.

"Just the tea would be fine, Blossom. The cakes look lovely but I've already eaten. Later, perhaps."

"That's a pity," Blossom said, setting a cup and saucer before her. "I'll put them in the tin when they're cooled, and yous can have them whenever. I know Henry and Linda love a bun now and again."

The cleaning lady wasn't the persistent type when it came to food. Rita-Mae was glad of that. She seemed so easy-going and she envied that a little.

"What a lovely name you have! And call me Rita, please."

Blossom smiled her endearing smile and sat down.

"Now, it isn't what I was christened, Rita. My mother loved flowers, y'see, and I was an only child, so she used to always call me her little blossom."

Her cheeks dimpled with the reminiscence and she dipped her chin briefly in reflection.

I'm sure you had a lovely mother, thought Rita-Mae; a kind woman who loved you and didn't call you names. She regretted that she couldn't have had someone like that in her own childhood – someone with open arms and an open heart who really cared. A spurt of envy flamed briefly in her when she thought of the heartless mother who'd raised *her*. But she doused it swiftly; looking back was a dangerous thing.

"Have you worked here long?" she asked gently, drawing Blossom out of her beautiful memories.

"Nearly three years now. After my Arnold passed I had to get out of the house. The loneliness was terrible, Rita."

"I'm sorry."

"Thank you, dear. But y'know, God doesn't give us burdens unless He knows we can carry them," she added, stroking a little gold cross she wore. "Now tell me this: where d'you live, Rita?"

"Willow Close." She was interested to see how the news would be received.

A flicker of concern passed across Blossom's features.

"You're a tenant of Bram Hilditch then?"

"Yes . . . I'm renting number eight."

Blossom considered this.

Rita-Mae thought of a ruse to draw her out. In fact, she reasoned that Blossom's cupcakes would be quite acceptable, given what she'd seen of the lovely lady so far.

"D'you know, Blossom, perhaps I'll have one of those nice cakes of yours after all."

Blossom's eyes lit up. "I'm so glad," she said, proffering the plate.

"By the way, did you know the woman who was renting number eight before me?" She paused. "Just in case I get post for her."

"Oh, Vivian . . . she was a lovely young woman. Very religious. Always praying in the church. That's why it makes no sense what happened to her."

"Oh . . . What happened exactly?"

"Well, she just disappeared one day, y'see. No one knows where she went. Bram couldn't understand it. None of us could. She didn't leave a note or anything." She sighed. "But you never know what's going on in someone's life, do you? Maybe she was running away from something and just couldn't confide in anyone."

Rita-Mae could understand that. "That's awful. Did they never find her?"

Blossom shook her head. "The strange thing is, her relatives in Sligo didn't seem too concerned. Said she was adult enough to live her own life. But you've no worries on that score, Rita. And Bram's a good man . . . a gentleman, just like his father . . . so good to me after Arnold passed. You can depend on him."

You can depend on him . . . I wonder. She took a tentative bite of the cupcake.

"Yes, he seems so," she said. "These cakes are very good by the way."

"I'm glad you like them, Rita! Here, have another one."

"Okay, just one more then."

Something occurred to her at that moment. She was recalling that peculiar sentence written on the outside of Vivian-Bernadette's letter. Blossom, being religious herself, would probably know the answer.

"Does the name Catherine of Siena mean anything to you?"

Blossom's countenance took on a look of reverence. "Oh, she's one of my favourite saints! Italian she was. I pray to her all the time, Rita. Why d'you ask?"

"Just wondered . . . came across the name recently, that's all."

"She's the patron saint against illness and miscarriages. My mother was a great believer in her, God rest her soul. She nearly lost me when she was expecting, y'see. I'll bring you a wee book about her next time. Now, I'll get us more tea."

Rita wanted to say "no thanks" to the book, but had no wish to disappoint the lovely Mrs Magee. She could decline the tea though, with a good excuse. "Gosh, is that the time? Duty calls I'm afraid."

Blossom returned the teapot to the stove and smoothed down her apron.

"I understand. You're doing the Lord's work, Rita, and He'll reward you for it, God bless you. I'll just tidy up here and be on my way." She held out her hand again. "It was lovely meeting you, and we'll meet again soon I'm sure."

"Thank you . . . I'm sure we will."

Rita-Mae turned to go.

"Oh, Rita?"

"Yes."

"On the notice board in the office you'll find my telephone number."

"R-Right."

"Just . . . just in case you need . . . you need someone to talk to," she explained, blushing slightly. "It can be difficult settling into a new place."

"That's kind of you, Blossom," she said, finally taking her leave.

But as she went down the stairs she wondered whether Blossom's offer stemmed from Christian charity or from concerns about her occupancy of 8 Willow Close.

She rather suspected it was the latter.

CHAPTER THIRTEEN

Samaritan Centre, Killoran

"Samaritans. May I help you?"

No answer. Rapid breathing down the line.

Oh dear God! Let it not be him – Lenny.

"In your own time . . . when you're ready . . ."

"This bloody life's pointless." A male voice, sudden and belligerent, in her ear. A young man.

She palmed the mouthpiece for a moment to steady herself, uncovered it again and said as calmly as she could: "I'm sorry you feel that way. I—"

"No, yer not. You're just trained like a monkey to say that. Yer as sorry as Hitler in his bunker. Only sorry for yerself, that's all."

It was going to be one of *those* evenings. Mondays invariably brought a raft of desperate young men to the helpline. The boozy weekend was over. They'd squandered a week's pay in two nights. Now penniless, depressed and suffering the mother of all hangovers, they wanted to offload to somebody or kill themselves.

"Would you like to give me your name? I'm Rita. It doesn't have to be your real name—"

"Kevin!"

"Kevin. Hello . . . and why are you feeling so down right now?"

She heard his breathing quicken with irritation. In the background: cars swishing past in the rain. Guessed he was calling from a public phone. Then:

"'Cos this life's bloody pointless, like I . . . like I told you at the start. That's why I'm feeling down *right now*, if you must know."

"When did you start to feel this way, Kevin? Did something go wrong today? I need to know, so we can talk it through."

"I've always felt this way," he said in a flat voice, "from the bloody minute I was born."

"I'm sorry to hear that. You're no doubt dwelling on the past. We cannot live in the past or . . . or the future for that matter. The present is the safest place for all of us. You had the courage to make this call . . . to reach out for help . . . so in that respect you are being very positive, and we can take things from here."

"Rubbish! How can I *not* live in the past? The past is who I am. If we didn't have pasts we wouldn't exist. That's why your comment is rubbish, and that's why this life is shite, and I'm sick of do-gooders like you trying to tell me different."

"I'm sorry you—"

"And stop sayin' yer bloody sorry. No, yer *not* sorry . . . Yer . . ." She heard him grope for the right obscenity to hurl back. Pictured him trapped behind the breath-fogged glass of the phone booth. Launched into life from a dark place, trapped and lonely, just like herself. Like so many.

He sighed.

"May I ask how old you are, Kevin?"

"What's it to you?"

"I'm interested . . . And you sound . . . well . . . young."

"What age d'ye think I am?"

"Gosh, let me see . . . Late teens, early twenties perhaps."

"Twenty-two last Friday."

"See? I'm not as rubbish as you think."

"No big deal. I know what age *you* are. Don't have to guess neither 'cos you sound like an oul' doll."

She suppressed a chuckle. "Yes, I suppose you could say that, Kevin. What did you do for your birthday?"

"Got smashed."

"Kevin, you're only twenty-two. You've got your whole life ahead of you."

"Yeah, right. And you think that's something to celebrate? Well, I *don't*! I've no job. No money. No bloody hope! Me dad's a violent bastard . . . me ma's a nervous wreck. The bastard kicked me outta the house 'cos I was tryin' to save her from his bloody fists. I've nowhere to go. That's my life! So when you say I've got my whole life ahead of me, that's what I see and I don't want any of it. And no matter what you say it won't change the facts. Yer just full of senseless talk . . . That's all any of you are good for. You don't know nuthin' about anything."

"Perhaps," Rita-Mae said carefully, "perhaps nothing makes sense because you're just in a bad place right now. But life changes from moment to moment, hour to hour. We shouldn't look back because we see so much we regret doing . . . so many things we believe we did wrong. It's dwelling on the past that makes us depressed."

She felt such a fraud saying those words because she could not live by them herself. The past was an ever-present spectre in *her* life and in so many lives. There were few perfect parents, so few perfect childhoods.

"How do *you* know I do that?" Kevin was saying.

"Sorry, Kevin, do what?"

"That I *dwell* on the bleedin' past."

"Well, you've just said as much, and you wouldn't be calling the Samaritans if you didn't. All negative thoughts are about the past, or indeed the future. But more often the past, and so they make us feel bad about ourselves."

She tried not to sound too assertive. But sometimes assertiveness, or rather firmness, was necessary to make people understand where they were in their stories. Mrs Emmeline Wilton used to say as much, in training sessions. *Your job is to lead them out of the dark chapter where they're stuck, and give them hope so they can begin a new one.*

The caller made no answer.

"Kevin . . . are you still with me?"

She heard the sound of him slumping down.

"Kevin, are you all right?"

Nothing.

"Kevin, can you hear me?"

Then: "Yes," he said calmly. "I'm still here . . . but not . . . not for much longer. Wh-What did . . . wh-what did yer say your n-a-m-e . . . w-a-s?"

Emmeline Wilton's voice came again. *Sometimes they will die with you on the phone. They will have already overdosed and just need someone to be with them as they pass. Yours will be the last voice they hear.*

She knew she was dealing with just such a situation.

"My name's Rita, Kevin . . . *Kevin*, what have you taken?"

"Does-ent . . . m-a-t-t-e-r . . ."

"Kevin, where *are* you? I can get an ambulance to you right away. Please, Kevin, tell me where you are. I can come immediately and be with you." She knew she was breaking the rules with her plea. But sometimes you simply have to forgo rules when the heart demands.

"N-o-o-o, Rita. There's . . . there's no . . . no point any . . . more. N-o-b-o-d-y cares . . . They n-e-v-e-r did . . ."

"That's not true. *I* care! I can get an ambulance and get you to the hospital. I'll stay with you and be your friend. I promise. *Please*, Kevin, *please* just tell me where you are."

She heard his breathing slowing, pictured him slouched down in the cold telephone box with the rain lashing the windowpanes, the desolation of the scene making her weep. There was a kiosk at the end of the street. Maybe he was there. Should she run out and check? But she'd promised him she'd stay on the line.

"I care, Kevin. Believe me, *I care.*"

"Then . . . just . . . s-t-a-y wi-with me, R-i-t-a. Don't . . . leave . . . me. I . . . I don't . . . don't want to die . . . a-l-o-n-e."

"I'm here, Kevin," she said, trying not to weep, "I'm here. No, I won't leave you. You're doing fine. Everything's going to be all right. I promise."

"Thank . . . *thaaank youuu.*" His voice was barely audible. "It's . . . it's so . . . so c-cold in . . . here . . . *soooo* . . ."

His voice faded.

His breathing ceased abruptly.

She heard the receiver fall.

"Kevin, Kevin . . . hold on."

But her appeal went unheeded, filled instead by an eerie quiet where Kevin used to be.

"I love you, Kevin!" she cried down the line, knowing that she'd lost him. "You were always loved by people like me, even if you never realized it."

She put the phone down, sobbing quietly, for both Kevin and herself; for she knew what it was like to live life as a victim and pass the days unlauded and unloved.

Brrrring brrrring . . . Brrrring brrring . . .

The phone was ringing again. No time to mourn. She wiped her tears. Picked up the receiver.

"Samaritans. May I help you?"

The sound of weeping. Female. A young girl, she guessed.

"It's okay . . . I'm here to help . . . When you're ready you can tell me all about—"

"H-He hit me."

"I'm very sorry to hear that. Who hit you?"

"Stephen."

Pause.

"Is Stephen your boyfriend?"

"No, he's . . . he's Mammy's new boyfriend . . . H-He's always hit-tin' me."

"That's too bad . . . My name's Rita. What's your name?"

"V-Viola."

"That's a lovely name! How old are you, Viola?"

"Th-Thirteen . . ."

"And why does Stephen hit you, Viola?"

"'Cos . . .'cos he's angry."

"Is he angry often?"

"Aye . . ."

"So what happened this evening to make him angry?"

"I burnt his dinner. I . . . I wanna run away b-but I've nowhere tae go."

In the background she heard a door slamming and a man's voice raised in anger.

"Oh God, he's comin' back!"

"Viola, Viola, don't hang up!"

"He's gonna kill me!"

The line went dead.

Rita-Mae put her head in her hands. She'd failed another one.

Less than a minute later the phone rang a third time. She snatched it up immediately, hoping it was Viola calling back.

"Samaritans. May I help you?"

"How you?" a man asked.

"My name's—"

"Rita . . . Oh, I know who yeh are."

She heard the squeak of a sofa: the sound of a glass being placed on wood.

Lenny!

"Did you like that wee note I left for yeh, Rita?"

She gripped the receiver more tightly to stop it trembling.

"Look, I'm going to have to termin—"

"If you hang up on me you'll pay for it, Rita." Irritated.

"Enjoy that wee tea with the undertaker, did you? Yer wastin' yer time with him . . . bit of a mammy's boy. Not your type at all. No, you need a real man . . . like me. A woman like you shouldn't be livin' on her own."

"I don't *live alone!*"

Sniggering. "Hmph . . ." She heard him drag on a cigarette. Wanted to drop the phone and just run. "Nah, you don't live alone 'cos you've got me."

"I don't know what you're talking about. Now, if you don't—"

"The one before you, she thought she was on her own too. And look what happened tae her . . . not much luck in that house, yeh see. Would be better if yeh just left it."

She was dumbstruck. Had she heard him correctly? Dear God, he knows where I live!

She heard him gulp more of the drink.

"But then, where would you go, Rita?"

She slammed the phone down, distraught.

CHAPTER FOURTEEN

Bram let himself into the Hilditch residence at 9.30 p.m. precisely. Her Grace had spent the evening in the company of Edwina Baldwin-Piggott, tucking into cocktails, canapés, and no doubt putting the world to rights on all matters royal. Going on past form, such an evening usually meant that when Edwina's chauffeur dropped her off, Octavia, too addled for her "magic hour", would simply collapse into bed and snore till morning, thus leaving her son a peaceful evening all to himself.

He was quietly removing his shoes and contemplating getting stuck into part two of *Memorial Photography: A Study in the Still Life* when the unthinkable happened.

"Where on *earth* have you been?" bellowed his mother from above. "I'm well into my magic hour. Come up here at once!"

Bram's spirits drooped. He let out a sigh.

"Are you still awake, Mother?" he shouted up the stairs in a voice replete with impatience. "I expected you to be asleep by now."

"Do not raise your voice to me! If you can't address me in a civilized manner I'll . . ."

He sprinted up the stairs.

To his chagrin he found her in her crimson night-attire, sitting atop the bed-covers, right leg heavily bandaged and resting on a pile of cushions. A glossy supplement featuring the royals lay open beside her.

"My goodness, what happened?"

"I tripped on Edwina Baldwin-Piggott's Serapi Persian, more's the pity."

"Pardon my ignorance but is that a cat or a rug?"

"Both, if you must know. The silly woman has the rug in her entrance hall and her peke-face was sleeping under it. I fell over both of them on my way out."

"How awful!" He went over to inspect the injury. "In the circumstances, I expect her cocktails didn't help matters. She does make them rather strong, if memory serves."

"I was *not* intoxicated, Abraham! Her hallway is badly lit and she failed to mention the feline's propensity for napping under the blessed rug."

"Can you walk on it? Looks a bit swollen."

"I can. With difficulty."

"Then how did you get upstairs?"

"Melrose, her chauffeur. How else?"

"Sorry I wasn't around. Had a lot to do today. It's just that I assumed you'd forgo your magic hour as you usually do when you've been to Edwina's, and that's why I'm a bit late."

"Oh, I know very well what you assumed. You assumed you'd be able to slip in at this hour without my noticing. You assumed I'd be asleep. Well, as you can see I'm very much awake. I have a bone to pick with you – a rather large bone, I might add – before I can rest this evening. And I'll *have* my gin and Dubonnet as usual, thank you very much. If anything, it will help ease the pain of this."

Bram went to the drinks tray and busied himself.

"I expect you'll be wanting a double in that case?" he said, aiming for appeasement, feeling a little guilty but consoling himself that, going on appearances, the fall didn't seem to have fazed her overmuch.

He'd committed quite a few transgressions in recent days, aside from having tea with Miss Ruttle. There was also the small matter of having signed the lease on a little premises in town, which he planned on turning into a photography studio. The idea had presented itself only the previous week. J.P. Rooney, the pharmacist, had very kindly offered him a couple of rooms over the shop at very reasonable rates. The opportunity was simply too good to pass up.

The only problem was informing Her Grace that he'd conducted the business deal without consulting her first. Maybe after a couple of stiff gin and Dubonnets she'd be more amenable and he could broach the subject.

"What on earth were you doing in the Heavenly Realms with that spinster tenant of yours? Edwina wondered if you and she were 'an item', as she called it. And I have to say I'm beginning to wonder myself."

He handed her the drink. "Never mind, Mother, we'll get the doctor to have a look at you in the morning. Better he checks it, just to make sure nothing's broken."

"I said—"

"Yes, I know very well what you said. I spoke with Edwina in passing. I guessed she'd report back to you. Who needs the BBC when we've got Mrs Baldwin-Piggott? She certainly missed her vocation as a jobbing journalist."

"Oh, very droll. So why didn't you tell me you were going to have tea with this Ruttle person?"

He did not answer immediately. Went and poured himself a large brandy. Felt he was going to need it.

"Because," he began, sitting down slowly in his reading chair, ". . . because firstly, I don't need to tell you *everything* I do in the course of a day, no longer being ten years old." He held up the brandy glass, feigning appreciation of the lead crystal to buy time. "Secondly, I just happened to see Miss Ruttle parked outside the hair salon. She looked rather lost and . . . well, shall we say . . . lonely. I thought it might be nice to give her an unexpected treat. And in so doing get to know her a little better. So you see, I hadn't planned anything, Mother dear."

He toasted her. "Chin chin! Life can be full of little surprises when you don't make plans. So here's to adventure!"

"*Adventure*, indeed! I don't understand any of this. She rang around four o'clock, looking for *you*. Weren't you supposed to be checking her drains? And why was she calling you *Bram*? I had to correct her. What's this bowdlerizing your name all about? You were christened *Abraham*."

He shut his eyes briefly, making a mental note to apologize to Miss Ruttle at his earliest convenience. How very embarrassing that she be subjected to a harangue down the telephone line!

"I think you mean truncation of one's name, Mother," he said, going off-topic just to annoy her. "Dr Thomas Bowdler published an expurgated edition of Shakespeare in the eighteen-hundreds, hence the term 'to bowdlerize', which in essence means to clean up or sanitize, *not* abbreviate, which is the word you were looking for."

Octavia shot him a withering look. "People who *think* they know everything are of great annoyance to those of us who actually do. I know very well what it means. You're dodging the issue as usual. So, where *were* you and why weren't you checking her drains as you said you would?"

"I sent Dan Madden to do it as I'm no expert on plumbing."

He felt bad about using Dan Madden to make the drain story more plausible, but what else could he do in the circumstances? Madden wasn't the sharpest knife in the block so wouldn't give it a second thought.

"Dan Madden! Why on earth are you involving him? You know the fewer people she gets to know, the better."

"Dan's a specialist."

"Specialist my eye! *Daniel* Madden, to give him his full appellation, is nothing more than a trailer-dwelling car-salvage man from the boglands of Donegal. And a gasbag to boot." She took a sip of gin and Dubonnet. "There are rumours about him, you know."

"Yes, I dare say there are rumours about everyone in these parts."

"Not very pleasant ones either! I wouldn't trust Mr Madden with the silver. What if he blabs about that O'Meara woman?"

"I *trust* him because I warned him not to. Also I've given him the job of cleaning the windows and tending the garden. I also intimated to Maud Gilhooley that she could be a bit more neighbourly and win Miss Ruttle's trust a little more. That way, she'd be more usefully employed than watching soaps and talking to that budgie of hers."

"But—"

"*And* by the way, Dan is *not* a trailer-dweller. He's in a mobile home on a temporary basis while he does repairs to the roof of his house."

"If you say so." Octavia rested back on the pillows. "Well, I suppose you're making some kind of sense. And this little tea you had with her: I hope it yielded something of interest. Did you learn anything new about her?"

"Yes. Apparently she had a twin sister who died at birth."

"Really? Would that explain the baby clothes Maud saw on the clothesline?"

"Hardly. She's thirty-four after all. I doubt baby clothes would survive that length of time. Besides, I asked her if she had children."

"You did *what*? How utterly impertinent of you! It's a wonder you didn't ask why she stayed out all night too. You need to be careful, you know, or she could have you up for stalking."

Bram had his reasons for asking such a direct question of Miss Ruttle. Reasons his mother would never be privy to.

"Now who's being preposterous? Give me some credit. No, sometimes the direct approach is called for. I wouldn't like to think she was harbouring a baby in there without my knowledge."

"Well . . . I suppose you have a point. But I'm sure she was rather taken aback by your forthrightness?"

"You'd expect so, but it didn't seem that way . . . It's just . . ." Bram studied the contents of his glass.

"Just what? Stop keeping me in suspense! I've had enough to cope with for one day."

"Okay. It was the way she answered me. She didn't seem to be shocked at all by 'my impertinence' as you put it. Calmly said 'no' and reminded me she was a spinster. I think there's more to her than meets the eye. You just never know what's going on with someone, do you?"

"Or indeed what they're up to."

Octavia drained her glass. Rested her hand on her chest.

"This gin and Dubonnet tastes funny."

Bram shifted in his chair. "Oh . . . perhaps the glass wasn't rinsed properly . . . washing-up liquid . . . a little residue can mar the taste. What's that you're reading about the royals?"

"Since when did you become interested in the royal family? And I *always* rinse my glassware thoroughly, thank you very much."

He shrugged. "I could arrange for Blossom Magee to come in."

"No, you certainly will not. I'm not a helpless infant and I will not tolerate Mrs Magee – pleasant and all as she is – handling my things and telling me how I can be saved by the Lord. She has that dead husband of hers on a pedestal, but everyone knows he was nothing more than a layabout with a drink problem who collapsed between the Gents and the cigarette machine in the Bull and Pig bar. Heart attack indeed! Liver failure in anybody's book. He was as yellow as my grandmother's churned butter."

He wished Octavia would not be so critical of the poor woman, but then she was critical of most people she deemed to be of the "inferior classes". In other words, people who weren't as educated or well off as herself.

"Abraham, are you listening to me?"

He flinched.

"Sorry, Mother, I was miles away there."

"I could see that. You're up to something."

"Certainly not."

He saw that she was still examining the glass. Time to change the subject. He eyed a photo of Sarah Ferguson.

"Miss Ferguson not to your liking then?"

Octavia yawned. "No, she certainly isn't. Her mother ran off with a polo player to live on the Argentine pampas. With a mother like that, one can see there'll only be trouble ahead for lovely Prince Andrew. Besides which, she's barely . . . she's barely . . . edu . . . educated."

She stifled a yawn for the second time.

"In that case she's perfectly suited to marry royalty," Bram said. "As far as I can gather no scholar's ever become the consort of any of them. Who needs an education to dress up and eat lavish dinners, I say."

Octavia covered her mouth with her free hand and yawned.

"Oh, I feel . . . I feel very drowsy of a sudden."

"That's not so surprising . . . you've had a nasty fall."

He got up, took the glass and placed the magazine to one side.

"You need to rest now, Mother," he said, pulling up the eiderdown. "Tomorrow's another day. I'll have the doctor look at that leg in the morning."

Without another word, Her Grace fell asleep.

He lifted the glass, scrutinized it. Sat down again.

Well, his mother might think he wouldn't be hiring Mrs Magee, but on this matter he'd be overruling her whether she liked it or not. He'd brought the subject of Blossom up because he'd met her by chance that very day and she'd imparted some rather interesting bits of information. He reflected on the exchange now as Octavia's slumber deepened.

"How are you, Bram, and how's your lovely mother?" Blossom had said, ambushing him in the doorway of J.P. Rooney's shop. "Hope she's keeping well."

"Oh, she's fine, Blossom, but between you and me she could use some extra help. I can't always be around . . . now with the property business to run."

"I understand, Bram. With your poor father gone, God rest him, it isn't easy. I miss my Arnold so much and he's three years gone. But I could maybe help your mother out."

"You could?"

"Yes, I'm a 'home help' these days . . . it's parish work I do with the Senior Citizens' Outreach Club. Do three days a week . . . visiting the sick and people living on their own . . . do cleaning and run the messages for them and the like. People only pay if they want to or can afford it. All the money we get goes to charity, so it's all in a good cause."

J.P. had interrupted at that point. "The bunion pads and knee-high compression supports have come in for Miss Scullion, Blossom, if you want to take them away with you now."

"Good enough, J.P."

Bram had found himself wondering what on earth knee-high compression supports actually were.

"That's very interesting, Blossom. I'll certainly run the idea past Mother. I'm sure she'd appreciate your help."

"No bother at-all, Bram . . . anything to help out. You have my phone number, haven't you?"

They'd said their goodbyes at that point, but Blossom turned back to him.

"I was talking to that lovely lady who's renting from you earlier."

"R-Right . . ."

"Yes, wee Rita. We had a lovely chat."

"Oh."

He'd wanted to ask where they'd met, but hadn't wished to appear nosy.

"Yes, she's a lovely lady . . . so nice-looking and with such a good heart too. Well, cheerio, Bram. Let me know when you need me."

With that she'd taken off, leaving him wondering what exactly she'd meant by Miss Ruttle having such "a good heart".

It was hardly the kind of thing you said of a complete stranger. So how come Miss Ruttle had made such a favourable impression?

Her Grace stirred in her slumber and let out a low moan. Bram looked at the glass still in his hand. Well, she wouldn't be waking up any time soon. He was sure of that.

Time to retire too.

He got to his feet and quietly left the room.

CHAPTER FIFTEEN

There is little difference between a verbal fist and a human fist. Harry was an expert at wielding both. Ugly scenes from Rita-Mae's marriage spun forward without pause, like footage from a war zone.

The Lenny call and the suicide of Kevin on the Samaritan helpline were forcing her down a dark path she was powerless to steer clear of. Harry had said she was useless often enough, and now his slurs and charges were booming in her head so loudly that he could have been standing right there in the bathroom where she was brushing her teeth . . .

"You stupid, useless bitch. Can't do nothin' right, can yeh? I *said* that bath is *not* clean!"

She stopped brushing and stared at the toothbrush, helpless in the face of the memory pulling her back.

"But I scrubbed it thoroughly after you left for work . . . and I . . . I haven't used the bath—"

"How *dare* yeh contradict me?" His face was in hers, the stench of alcohol on his breath nauseating. He wrenched the toothbrush from her, rinsed it under the tap. Put the plug in the bath. Found a tin of scouring powder.

"Now, sprinkle that in there and start scrubbin'."

She did as she was told. "All right, I'll do it again." Trying to pacify. Always trying to pacify. "You go on to bed, Harry. You must be tired."

It was well past midnight.

"Don't you fuckin' tell me how I feel or what I'm to do in my own house."

He snatched the brush from her. Thrust the toothbrush at her. "I'm stayin' right here and you're gonna use this *tooth*brush to do the cleanin', not that *scrubbin'* brush. Oh, no, yeh don't get away that easy."

He pulled a chair into the bathroom, produced a six-pack of beer. "But, before yeh start, get me a glass and pour that."

She'd learned from her honeymoon how to pour a beer "properly". Half in first, slowly, with glass tilted. Wait for froth to settle. Remainder in slowly while easing glass upright. He watched her very carefully as she went through this ritual, waiting for the traitorous bead of liquid to escape down the side and so seal her fate.

She handed him the beer – hoping she could get through this episode without being hit – and started on the bath rim with the toothbrush, mentally imprinting that she'd need to buy herself a new toothbrush the following day.

"Fuckin' kneel down when yer doin' it," he roared, kicking her hard on the shin. "I like tae see a woman on her knees. If I had my way they'd never be off their bloody knees."

She tried not to cry because that would make him worse. Maybe he'd fall asleep on the chair and she could just go and lock herself in the spare room. Often when he woke up the next morning he'd no memory of what he'd put her through. Unless of course there was evidence: a split lip, bruised eye, puffy face.

"Have you been knockin' into doors again, Rita?" he'd say, tut-tutting in mock sympathy. "Yeh'll have tae watch that, yeh know. What if yeh were to lose an eye, what would you do then? Even worse, if you were to hit yer head so hard you knocked yourself out, and I wasn't here to get you an ambulance. You'd just die here on your own. So I'd watch that if I were you."

"Yer not doin' that quick enough," he bellowed now, bringing his boot down hard on her coccyx as she leaned over the bath.

She yelled out in pain, collapsing.

He was on his feet, bearing down on her. "Shut the fuck up, d'yeh hear?" He pulled her up by the hair, shoved her against the wall, gripping her throat.

"P-P-Please, Harry, I . . . I'm sor . . . sorr-y. I . . . I did-n't . . ."

The ceiling was spinning, her legs going numb, every nerve and muscle on strike. She shut her eyes tight to block out the horror of his face and stop the tears he hated so much to see.

"What's wrong with yeh now, Rita?" he said in a mocking voice, loosening his hold slightly so she could breathe.

"I . . . I . . . I'm sorry . . ." she stammered.

"Good! That's more like it."

But in spite of her best efforts, the tears she was trying so hard to hold back came anyway.

"Don't fuckin' whinge! I don't like it when you whinge, Rita . . . yeh should know that by now."

He threw her back against the bath. "Now, get on with it."

In Willow Close the toothbrush trembled in her hand. She stared at it, threw it into the sink, went into the bedroom, switched off the light and got into bed. But the memories followed her in there like vengeful ghosts. Ganging up on her as she pulled up the bed-covers. The spectre of Harry on top of her now, pinning her down . . .

"Now yer gonna do yer duty as a wife."

She shut her eyes, reliving the pain of the many rapes all over again, the horrors bursting back like sewage through the manhole covers of self. The post-drinking aftermath of sexual violence was a given. But then she'd got used to it all. Could leave her body – actually leave it – and make this mental leap, which would see her floating out of her physical self, up to the ceiling where it was safer – much safer – than being that poor, defenceless woman suffering down there on the bed.

It was scary the first time it happened, this disconnect from self, but the more she had to do it the easier it became. She'd just hover up there till sleep overtook him then return to consciousness and the painful fallout, roll his weight off her, go into the bathroom and wash him away.

Several months into the marriage it had become the norm. Harry had never wanted a wife, but a slave, a chattel, and Rita-Mae fitted the bill perfectly: pliant, biddable, reserved.

It was pointless to resist him. Physically she could never fight back, being as fragile as a twig. "I could snap you in two if I wanted to," he used to say. "Aye, snap you in two and bury yeh out there in the garden. Nobody would be the wiser. I'd say yeh'd just left me for another man."

And she knew he meant it. He really meant it, for she had no one to turn to. What few friends she'd had he'd insulted early on, so they stopped calling. She'd no family to speak of. Her mother, a harridan who hated the sight of her, was only too pleased when Harry came along, passing her over to him like some unwanted parcel. How often she'd longed for the company of her twin! Her mother told her that she'd died at birth, but one day in a temper said that she'd given her away. Couldn't afford the two of them. How different Rita's life might have been had that not been the case!

He kept a knife by the bed, just in case she got "uppity".

Yes, he'd stitched her well into the warp and weft of his life over those few heady months of courtship. Played the loving, attentive boy-friend she'd always dreamed of.

But all too soon Harry was deciding everything. How she was supposed to think and feel. When she would eat and sleep. If she didn't understand something he made fun of her, because Harry knew everything and never got anything wrong. His sole aim seemed to be to bolster his ego by sapping her self-esteem. It was easier to go along with it all, because to unpick the pattern that he'd set seemed too risky an undertaking.

The insults, the beatings, came almost as soon as the wedding band was on. And she had to accept those too because the alternative was worse. Much worse.

It was going to be one of those nights. Recalling the dark past, dwelling on it, reliving it, suffering it again and again and again stopped Rita-Mae from thinking about Lenny the stalker, the new ogre in her life.

He knew where she lived. Or did he? If he knew where Vivian-Bernadette had lived, he knew where *she* was living.

That thought made her switch the light on, to dispel the implications of what she could not face.

It was 2 a.m. She'd go downstairs and make a nightcap.

It was cold in the room. The heating had turned itself off hours before.

She crossed to the bureau to fetch a cardigan.

Pulled out the top drawer. The action sent something flying out at her.

She stepped back, and was astonished to see that at her feet lay the mysterious letter she'd thought was missing. There was a long crease running across it. Aha, thought Rita. *That's* why I couldn't find it. It was wedged there all along.

So Bram Hilditch had not taken it.

Vivian-Bernadette had returned.

Whether for good or ill, the new tenant would now learn the truth the former tenant could not tell.

CHAPTER SIXTEEN

Bram the photographer was in his studio above the pharmacy for the first time, enjoying a lazy afternoon. He was not a little chuffed with himself that he'd managed to achieve a long-cherished ambition without interference from Her Grace.

He knew he could never have managed to create such a workspace in the family home, roomy as it was with four bedrooms in disuse. She would never have allowed such "disfigurement of my ancestral residence". She'd used the phrase often enough when his father had proposed creating his taxidermy workshop indoors.

"I'll not have dead animals in this house. What sort of a hobby is that? Isn't dealing with dead *people* enough for you?"

Well, she did have a point, Bram reflected now, as he poured developer into a film tank. Father had finally ended up in a shed in the garden, which was perhaps the best place for him, given his weird pursuit.

He set his stopwatch. It would take half an hour to develop the film. And for every minute of that time he'd have to agitate the tank for ten seconds. A tedious process, but well worth the effort.

He sat down by the window, which looked out on the backs of some houses facing on to a minor street called Master's Avenue. It was not such an inspiring sight and the attic of Lucerne House would have been much more pleasing to look out from, especially now in early spring: rolling pastures, plumply garnished hedges, fat snowy clouds advancing over sheep-dotted hills. That's the view he'd have preferred. But with the mother's hearing 100 hertz above that of the average bat, he had no desire to tiptoe, quite literally, around up there in order to keep his hobby secret.

And it had to be a secret for the time being. Octavia was highly suspicious of anything new entering the established order of her days. Most especially now, when that established order had been so effectively thwarted by the fall at Mrs Baldwin-Piggott's house only the previous week. Dr Sweeney had ordered a week's bed rest – putting a brake on her hair appointments, her chiropodist's appointment, her bridge, her parish council meetings, Women's Institute get-togethers and cocktail parties with various widows just like herself.

He agitated the tank again, checked the stopwatch. Almost wished his father were still alive to keep *her* distracted. The fall and subsequent confinement were making her even more cantankerous and demanding.

It was just as well Blossom Magee was waiting in the wings.

He'd telephoned her in desperation, to beg for her help.

"That's no problem at all, Bram. I'll be there tomorrow afternoon. Could come earlier if you want."

"No, that's fine! There's just one thing, Blossom . . ."

He was uncertain about how to put the next bit. Had to be a trifle delicate about it because he knew that Her Grace would have a fit at the sight of Mrs Magee.

"Yes, Bram. What's that?"

"I wonder, would you mind not mentioning to Mother that I hired you? It's just that she likes to be in control and doesn't like being over-ruled. Being indisposed has disheartened her somewhat. You know how it is."

"I understand that sure enough, Bram. People get down when they have to stay in bed for a while, God love them. And your mammy being such an active woman! I know it must be hard for her."

"Yes, indeed. It's just that . . ."

"You want me to say I was sent by the doctor or the Friendship Club, do you?"

He was amazed at Blossom's prescience.

"Something like that, yes."

"That's no trouble, Bram. Whether *you* sent me or *they* sent me, it doesn't really matter. It's all in God's plan."

"Excellent, Blossom! You are most understanding. Until tomorrow then."

Yes, Blossom would be making her inaugural visit on Thursday. He was in no doubt that sparks would fly, with a bonfire of words erupting from the bedroom at the sight of her. No way would he be hanging around for that little pantomime!

He sighed and agitated the tank once more.

Down below he could hear the faint murmur of voices where J.P. was conducting the business he'd been doing for decades. Pharmacies were always such busy places, and by rights the proprietor should have retired long ago. He was in poor health, wheezing his way towards seventy with a dicky heart and smoker's cough. One wondered why he bothered getting out of bed at all. But he was a bachelor, and if he didn't have the shop and the townspeople to blather to about their haemorrhoids and hip problems, what purpose would his life indeed have?

Old J.P. made Bram feel a little sad. For he represented what Bram could become if he didn't succeed in finding himself a wife. If only Mother were out of the picture he'd be totally free to pursue such a notion. Marriage could only be countenanced upon her passing. She would not tolerate another woman on her patch.

The face of Miss Ruttle rose before him – a beauty, and one with "a good heart" according to Blossom Magee. Perhaps Blossom could pave the way for him. Get to know her better. Make things easier because at present, his new tenant, like a quadratic equation, was very hard to figure out.

She was far more interesting than his former tenant, Miss O'Meara. Vivian was one of life's eternal victims. Was it any wonder things ended so badly?

It wasn't for the want of trying to get to know her, he reflected.

She'd no car. Had to walk everywhere. Was an ardent church-goer. And the church was a good three miles distant. So on one particular Sunday morning, when the sky looked promisingly overcast, he'd attended Mass, in the hope of offering her a lift home.

He'd offered her a lift several times before, but the weather always seemed fine and she told him she enjoyed the fresh air, and sure wouldn't the walk do her good anyway?

Fair enough. He could hardly argue with that, or insist she got into his swanky red Daimler. But fortunately, on that particular morning, as he'd been hoping, a storm broke out during the Prayers of the Faithful. Thunder rumbling so loudly you'd think the Devil himself was doing a clog-dance on the roof. Rain battering so fiercely, Father Moriarty's words could scarce be heard.

"You can't walk home in this, Miss O'Meara," Bram had said, catching up with her as she hurried towards the gates.

She turned, long dress flapping in the wind. Face wet with rain.

No hat. No umbrella.

She could hardly refuse him. The courteous landlord – whom she now saw was a Mass-goer.

"Oh, Mr . . . Mr Hilditch, it's . . . it's you."

He was conscious of the fear in those haunted green eyes. Ready excuses dying on those pretty red lips.

"You could catch your death, Miss O'Meara," he said with concern. "Come, I'll give you a lift."

"Y-Yes. Maybe . . . maybe you're right. Thank you, Mr Hilditch."

And he escorted her to his car. Ever the gentleman, springing to open the passenger door for her. Anything to ease her obvious anxiety.

She hadn't given much away throughout the journey. Sat tightly wedged up against the door. All his attempts to draw her out were met with noncommittal replies.

On their arrival at number 8 he thought – really thought – she'd invite him in for tea by way of a "thank you", but she hurried from the car. Couldn't wait to get away from him – or so it seemed.

He still had nightmares about her. And they'd become depressingly more frequent since Miss Ruttle's move to Willow Close. It was as if Vivian-Bernadette were trying to tell him something. Or did she resent the house being occupied again?

Always the same dream and in the same sequence. He, Bram, on the threshold of the box-room, unable to move, and she there in the corner, just a handful of fragments suddenly rising up, reconstituting, taking shape from the bloodstained mappings on the floor. Her face an eyeless orb, the lips mouthing something from behind the tawny tumble of her hair, then a hand reaching out to clasp him.

Sometimes he'd wake with a start, believing she'd touched him. And at such times, sweat-soaked and shaking, he'd rise and dress, pick up his camera, creep down the stairs and out into the broad, silent safety of early morning.

Oh, the freedom of it: the light, the sky, the immensity of being outside and away from that grotesquery!

Last night had been such a night. The latter part of the film in the tank was a record of what he'd seen as he tramped the fields, crunching over the bracken of Crocus Wood with only the bird-song and breeze and the sound of his softly pounding heart.

What was it she was trying to tell him? She, Vivian-Bernadette, or the spirit of what once was her? He had an idea, but . . .

He could not share these ordeals with anyone, least of all his mother. Father Moriarty, the parish priest, perhaps. Priests knew things about the afterlife – or believed they did. He and the clergyman, collaborators over so many coffins slowly lowered into the clay of St Clement's grave-yard at the sorry end.

Maybe Father Moriarty held secrets about the dead that only his sort were privy to.

But could Bram trust another human being with the secret he was carrying?

That was the question.

CHAPTER SEVENTEEN

Portaluce, Antrim Coast

Dorinda Walsh was a little calmer now, aided by the fact that the wind blowing in off the ocean had lessened considerably.

A safe distance from Marcella's Cafe, she turned and looked back, not really knowing what she was expecting to see; a man in a black trilby and a little girl in a bright green coat, perhaps. Could they still be in there? Hiding from her.

She *had* seen them, hadn't she? Yes, as clear as day. She wasn't going mad. She wasn't.

You're not going mad, Dorrie. You're not. Those two gossiping women and that girl Jane are the mad ones, not you. But soon all this will stop. Very soon you will find the means to stop, look back and laugh at them all.

"Yes, Mama, you're right. You're always right, Mama."

She turned again to resume her walk – and collided with another pedestrian.

"Oh God, I'm sorry!" she blurted. "So dreadfully sorry."

A knobbly old hand shot out and clasped her wrist. She looked up into the rheumy eyes of an elderly woman, dressed in black.

"What are you saying, dear?"

"W-What?"

"You were talking out loud, dear," the woman said, her gaunt face creasing with concern. "Weren't you aware of that?"

Dorrie swallowed hard. "Y-Yes, maybe . . . erm, sometimes I forget myself."

Her eyes were taking in the woman's strange attire. And it *was* strange. She saw now that she wasn't wearing a coat – odd, given the time of year – but a black dress of layered lace with a woollen shawl. Her grey hair was woven into a thick plait and wound about her head in a kind of halo. Her neck was all but obscured by a choker of bright turquoise stones.

She resembled a gypsy woman from another era, but a sophisticated gypsy woman. Not a peasant.

Was she seeing things again?

"Are you feeling all right, dear?" the woman enquired. "You look like you've seen a ghost."

I could very well have seen one or two, thought Dorrie, but dared not give voice to such a notion.

"I . . . I feel . . . feel a little dizzy, that's all."

The strange lady was still holding her wrist and her touch felt oddly comforting. For some reason Dorrie did not want her to let go. Someone in this alien town, with its shrieking gulls and brooding sea, was concerned for her welfare.

"Who . . . who are you?" she asked a little hesitantly. "Do I know you?"

The woman shook her head. "I'm Edith LeVeck. Would you like to come to my house for a cup of tea? I can give you a tincture for the dizziness."

It was a gentle, soothing voice. The voice of a woman accustomed to reassuring those in crisis. It was Mama come to life again – or somebody very much like her.

She pointed in the direction of the white convent. "I live just over there. It's not far."

"Y-You live in the convent?"

"Good heavens, no. My house is just behind it. Come."

She set off at a steady pace without saying another word. Dorrie was amazed at the elderly woman's agility and found it hard to keep up.

Finally, they reached a row of tall Georgian houses.

"Here we are," Mrs LeVeck said, opening the gate of the third house down.

She ushered Dorrie across the threshold of her front door and into a gloomy hallway.

Dorrie's heart fluttered. She didn't like dark, enclosed spaces. They'd always frightened her. But now the old woman was bolting the door behind her, locking out the escape route that was the wide promenade, and there was really nothing she could do about it.

"I always lock the door," Mrs LeVeck said, as if reading her thoughts. "You can't be too careful these days. We'll sit in the parlour. It's warmer in there."

She pushed open the door into a cluttered room where a fire was burning. A strong smell of turf-smoke hung on the air and under it Dorrie detected another smell: some kind of sweet incense. She was minded to cover her nose because it was hardly pleasant. But decided it might seem rude. This old lady was showing her a kindness and she needed to be obliging.

"Please take a seat," Mrs LeVeck said, indicating one of the arm-chairs that flanked the fireplace. "You take milk and sugar?"

"Just milk, thank you. But don't go to any trouble on my account, Mrs LeVeck."

She smiled. "Call me Edith, please." She removed her shawl and draped it over a chair. Stood with her hands clasped together, gazing down upon her. "It's no trouble at all. You haven't told me *your* name."

"I'm Dorinda . . . Dorinda Walsh, but everyone calls me Dorrie."

"Dorrie it is then."

Dorrie saw her eye the expensive coat and felt a little ashamed.

"Your coat is beautiful," Edith said, "but I don't approve of defenceless animals being slaughtered to clothe the well off."

"But it's not *mine*. I . . . I was given a loan, you see. I . . . er, stained mine."

Edith smiled. "That's all right then. Make yourself at home, Dorrie, won't you. I shan't be long."

She withdrew quietly, leaving the new guest to take in her surroundings.

Dorrie glanced about her, with mounting unease, because she could see that she was in a very curious room. It looked more like an ancient museum than a parlour.

All the furniture was made of latticed wood, stretched over with tobacco-coloured skins and garish embroidery. They were the kind of things more suited to a log cabin than an old lady's sitting-room.

A large glass-fronted cabinet near her contained a variety of hideous-looking masks. They had inscriptions carved into them, but not in a language she knew. They frightened her a little and she quickly shifted her attention to the walls.

Each wall was adorned with a variety of crudely made objects, all brightly painted. She saw angels, demons, lizards, cherubs, butterflies, birds, several grinning skulls and more masks. There were crosses too, a great many of them, all gem-encrusted, forming heart-shapes in different places.

Over the fireplace hung a huge mirror with a frame composed of bits of broken delft and bones. And more frames, crowding a sideboard, were fashioned in a similar way, but bizarrely they contained no pictures.

Dorrie didn't know what to think. She'd never seen so many peculiar things gathered together in one place. Perhaps Mrs LeVeck was an artist or a collector of some kind.

She turned in her chair to see what was behind her – and nearly fainted. For in the corner stood a skeleton with a ghastly grin, fully attired in an elegant Victorian-style gown and wide-brimmed hat. She'd never seen anything like it.

"My God, what *is* this place?"

She looked frantically about for an escape route, but there was no way out save the door through which she'd entered.

Maybe she should just make a run for it. If she were quiet enough Edith LeVeck wouldn't hear her, she being occupied in the kitchen.

She got up.

But no sooner was she on her feet than footsteps in the hallway forced her to sit back down again.

The lady of the house pushed into the room with a tray.

"Here we are," she said, placing it on a coffee table between them.

Dorrie saw that it was beautifully set with silverware and china. There was a plate of dainty little cakes and another plate of biscuits, which looked home-made.

"You've gone to so much trouble, Edith," she said, as evenly as she could.

Edith smiled as she poured the tea. She handed her the cup and saucer. "No trouble, dear. It's nice to have someone to talk to – apart from Catrina."

"Catrina?"

"I hope she didn't scare you too much." She threw a glance in the direction of the corner where the skeleton lady stood.

Dorrie dared not look round again. "Well, she *did* give me a fright. Why's she called Catrina? Is she a relative?"

"Good heavens, no! I bought the skeleton and dressed it up."

"But why . . . why dress a skeleton?"

"We travelled a lot in Latin America, you see, when I was younger. My husband was a missionary." She waved a hand. "All the artefacts here we collected on our travels. Catrina is known in the Mexican tradition as 'La Calavera Catrina' or 'The Lady of the Dead', and we saw her everywhere. She's always dressed like that, as a comment on women who think that finery and dressing up the body is more important than their inner lives."

Dorrie didn't like the sound of that at all. She didn't really want to hear about the dead from this strange old lady with the soothing voice. She took a sip of the tea, wincing at the slightly bitter aftertaste.

"It's got valerian to help calm your dizziness. You can put a little sugar in to help the taste."

"Yes . . . perhaps I will."

"You see, in those cultures, they don't mourn the dead like we do here. There is no pain associated with death. They celebrate it."

"They do?"

Dorrie saw her gaze across at the skeleton again, her eyes wistful.

"Yes, Catrina is a reminder that death is democratic. Doesn't matter what colour your skin is or whether you're rich or poor, we all end up as skeletons. But our souls live on. That's the important thing. The spirits of the dead are all around us, dear."

Dorrie stirred anxiously in the chair. She thought about the man in the hat and the little girl in the bright green coat, and took another gulp of tea. If Mrs LeVeck was right – that the brew would calm her – then she surely needed it. Her hostess seemed very calm indeed; perhaps she drank this valerian infusion all the time.

"Can you . . . can you see them?" she asked uneasily. "The dead I mean."

"If they're troubled, yes."

She spoke so matter-of-factly that Dorrie didn't doubt for a minute she was speaking the truth.

Mrs LeVeck looked at her again, but this time in a sad, pitying kind of way.

"You're troubled, my dear, aren't you? I can feel it."

"I . . . I'm . . . erm, yes. My car broke down, you see, and I have to stay here until tomorrow . . . until it's fixed."

"That's good."

Dorrie thought it an odd response. "Well, it isn't really good for me, to be honest. I'm . . . I'm trapped here."

"But you've always felt trapped, have you not?"

"What? I . . . I don't know what you mean."

"It's a sense I'm getting. Do you have a sister?"

Dorrie didn't like the drift of Mrs LeVeck's conversation. She felt distinctly uncomfortable, but intrigued at the same time.

"No, I never had a sister," she said, putting the cup down. "Can you see into a person's soul . . . like a . . . like a psychic?"

"I wouldn't call myself a psychic. I have the gift of discernment. That's strange: I'm getting the very strong feeling that there are two of you."

"But I'm an only child."

"Are you sure about that?"

"Y-Yes."

She got up and drew on her gloves, stomach churning. "I'm sorry, Edith, I really must be going now." The urge to flee this weird old woman and her frightening room of strange ornaments was getting stronger and stronger.

"But your mama would like you to stay."

"What? Y-You mean *my* mama?" Dorrie found herself slowly sitting down again. "You . . . you can see my . . . see my mama?"

Edith LeVeck nodded. "She'd like you to stay a little while longer. Now let's have more tea, dear."

CHAPTER EIGHTEEN

Rita-Mae sat at the breakfast table, staring at the contents of Vivian-Bernadette's letter.

I must follow in the footsteps of Catherine of Siena.

I must follow in the footsteps of Catherine of Siena.

I must follow in the footsteps of Catherine of Siena.

The first page contained thirty-two numbered lines, each repeating the curious reference to Catherine of Siena she'd read on the outside of the envelope. It reminded her of writing lines at school as a punishment, usually one hundred at a time: "I must always remember to do my homework." She'd been given that chastisement often enough.

She sifted through the rest of the pages and counted eighteen in all. Each followed the same pattern: pages written on both sides in the same rounded hand. Halfway, however, she noticed something peculiar. The orderly contours of the writing, so precisely executed in the beginning, began to loosen and wander off course, so that by the last pages things were barely decipherable.

Contemplating this, she grew uneasy. It could only mean one thing: that the hand holding the pen had grown steadily weaker. That very possibly Vivian-Bernadette was very ill before she disappeared.

There must surely be more than eighteen pages of meaningless lines.

She looked inside the envelope again.

Sure enough, there *was* something else: a smaller, white envelope.

Should she open it?

Did she really want to know what had happened to the tenant before her? Had she not enough to contend with? But she was intrigued. Unusual circumstances had drawn her to the letter, therefore she felt strongly that she had some kind of obligation to the writer.

She sat there, curiosity tugging at her like a child at its mother's apron strings. Sighed.

Turned it over.

Saw then that the writer had sealed it with Sellotape. That was an important detail because it meant she could safely ease the tape off and reseal it with a fresh strip – if indeed she judged the contents to be too confidential.

She set about the delicate task, her fingernails working it carefully, bit by bit.

Several minutes later it was done.

She withdrew several folded pages.

To her surprise, three snapshots fell onto the table; all the same size, all in black and white.

Her hands were shaking as she spread them out.

Each featured a woman in a cardigan and long skirt. Her waist-length hair was pulled back from her face by a head covering.

She looked like someone from a bygone era. Could easily have passed for a nun, had it not been for the abundance of hair.

Was this Vivian-Bernadette? If her identity was uncertain there was no doubting the setting: 8 Willow Close featured in all three. And all the shots showed the rear of the house.

It was obvious also that they'd been taken without the subject's knowledge.

The first showed her standing on the back step, one hand shading her eyes.

In the second she was hanging washing on the line.

The third – the most intrusive of the three – had her seated at the box-room window combing her hair. The stuffed ferret clearly visible on the sill.

With trembling hands Rita-Mae set the pictures aside, and against her better judgement, opened the letter.

> *To whom it concerns,*
> *I had to conceal this in the butterfly case. If you are read-*
> *ing this you were meant to find it and learn my truth.*
> *Part of me wants you to find it, whilst another part does*
> *not. I'm afraid that if I put it someplace else, he would*
> *find it and destroy it. That way you'd never know.*

The word "he" jumped out at her. She looked up from the page, anxiety mounting. A tightening sensation gripping her forehead.

She was back on the Samaritan helpline:

The one before you, she thought she was on her own too. And look at what happened tae her.

She really didn't want to read any more, but was powerless not to.

> *I had to stop answering the door. People thought I*
> *just wanted to be left alone and that was true but only*
> *because of him. I was just too afraid. He pesters me all*
> *the time. This man whom I cannot see. But he is watch-*
> *ing me. Oh, yes, he is always watching me. He and his*
> *camera are watching me.*

Camera. Two memorial photographs flashed into her head. She saw herself take them from the hand of Bram Hilditch. She felt sick.

From the minute I moved in here he's been watching me. I thought it was my imagination at first, but then the photos came which proved I was right. Later the threats down the phone so I had to stop answering it.

She felt her throat go dry. The pain in her head was increasing. Her stomach was churning. She shut her eyes again, massaged her temples. In spite of herself she looked back at the page.

Every time I went out I was afraid, and every time I returned I felt even more afraid because I knew there was no escaping him—

She'd stopped reading at the sound of her garden gate being unlatched. To her consternation she saw her next-door neighbour, Maud Gilhooley, pink raincoat billowing, shopping bag flung over one arm, bobbing up the path.

Why was she calling?

In a panic she gathered everything up, shoved the lot into the table drawer and went to answer the door.

"Morning, Rita! Lovely, isn't it? Settling in all right, are you?"

"Yes, Mrs Gilhooley, thank you very much."

The last time they'd spoken was the day she moved in. Mrs Gilhooley had appeared on her doorstep with the gift of a cake.

"Oh, call me Maud. 'Missus' is far too formal when we're neighbours."

She resembled a busy little bird, head twitching, bright eyes probing her. Her pull-down hat matched the coat exactly; hair the colour of corn fizzed out from the brim and curled round her ears.

"Yes, indeed . . . Maud it is, of course."

"You look a bit peaky, dear . . . sure you're all right?" She gave her a sidelong glance.

"Quite sure . . . yes. Just a headache. Nothing a good sleep won't cure."

"Yes, I thought I heard you moving about in the early hours."

Unnerved, Rita-Mae tried to gather herself, her headache intensifying. Mrs Gilhooley was angling for information. She needed to tread carefully.

"Really? Perhaps . . . perhaps I got up to visit the bathroom a couple of times. It's . . . it's the coffee. Sorry if I disturbed you."

"Coffee?" Maud squinted at her as she would the small print on a medicine bottle.

"Yes, it's the caffeine. I shouldn't drink it after six. I'm very sorry if I woke you."

"No, dear. I'm such a light sleeper anyway. It comes with age I'm afraid. Edward was the same, God rest him, before the dementia took him. And that's what I worry about too. The less you sleep the more chance you have of suffering it you know. Now, there was something I needed to ask you, but it's gone completely out of my head." She studied the doorstep, nodding. "Oh, it'll come to me. That comes with age too I'm afraid . . . forgetfulness."

"R-Right. Well, I'm always here," Rita-Mae said, glancing back into the hallway by way of hinting she was busy. "I would invite you in but—"

"No, not at all, dear. Me and Polly were just on our way to the shops." She held up her shopping bag as evidence. It was made of hessian with a brightly coloured budgerigar embroidered on the front.

"Oh . . . who's Polly?"

"That's her, my budgie. She's the spit image of my own Polly. I keep her in a little cage in the parlour. I got her after Edward died . . . for company. Just wondered if you needed anything?"

"No . . . it's very kind of you, but I'll be going out later, so . . ."

Maud turned to go. "Cheerio then!"

Rita sighed and shut the door. Stood for a while gripping the sides of her head and seeing the dreaded zigzags of light that presaged a migraine attack.

The doorbell sounded again. She thought of not answering, but guessed it was Maud.

"Sorry, Rita, it's only me again. I just remembered what I forgot." Her little face grew concerned. "Are you sure you're all right, dear?"

"Yes, I was on my way to take a painkiller for my headache."

"You poor thing! I won't keep you. It's just the tin, y'see."

"Sorry, what tin?"

"The one I gave you with the sponge cake when you moved in. I wouldn't ask for it back, but . . ."

"Oh . . . the tin." Alarmed, she recalled consigning it to the waste bin. It was most likely scrunched up as landfill by now.

"I'll leave it round later," she heard herself say, wondering how on earth she'd make good the promise.

"Right you be," trilled Maud before flying off down the path again, pink coat twitching in the breeze.

She shut the door gratefully. Her head was aching more than ever. She dared not return to the drawer and the letter. Fresh air was what she needed, and fast.

She stepped out the back.

The afternoon was pleasant with that lovely pearly glow heralding spring. Already the gorse was putting forth. Tiny bursts of yellow thrusting through the greenery that fenced off her garden from Maud's. Not that you could call the forlorn patch of balding grass on her side an actual garden. It was more a space to accommodate the clothesline and shed. Only the stone cherub in the right-hand corner added interest.

She often wondered who'd placed it there. Bram Hilditch or the former owners?

Knowing now that Maud was definitely not at home, she crossed over to the hedge to have a peek.

It was a joy to the eye, as she'd expected: a neat lawn braided on all sides by tiny clusters of pink and white flowers with a rockery at the far end. Grouped in front of the rockery was a set of garden gnomes. How lovely if she could have the same on her side! But the landlord clearly wasn't that interested in horticulture.

Her gaze travelled to the rear of Maud's house. At either side of the door were knee-high plaster spaniels standing guard. But to her consternation she saw now that the back-door was slightly ajar.

Well, Maud had mentioned her forgetfulness.

I really need to shut it, Rita-Mae thought, even though I might be trespassing. It's the neighbourly thing to do.

She made a mental note to do it before going back inside and continued down to the shed. At her approach, a tiny bird shot up suddenly, settled on the apex of the roof, inspected her briefly, decided she wasn't so interesting and flew off.

She smiled at the beauty of such an unexpected little moment, leaned back against the shed and shut her eyes.

After a few breaths of clean air her migraine began easing. The quiet and the pleasing tweets of bird-song were a balm to her senses.

But very soon her thoughts were turning back to the letter and the photographs.

He could be watching me right now.

The very idea made a fist of itself and struck her hard, setting off a metronomic thudding in her head.

It took enormous strength for her to resist screaming out.

She opened her eyes and in desperation looked about.

The thudding sound, she realized, was not in her head. It was coming from somewhere behind her.

Thud . . . thud . . . thud!

It was growing louder and more persistent by the second.

Frustrated, she decided to investigate. She unlatched the back-gate and crossed the lane.

On the opposite side was a line of dilapidated terraced houses. All had back-gardens mostly uncared for, much like her own. One, however, was paved over with concrete and it was in this one that she saw movement. A young boy was hunkered down tying his shoelace. When he stood up, she saw the source of the irritating noise. He had a football and began kicking it against the wall of the house. Back and forth, back and forth. *Thud . . . thud.*

She picked her steps across the grassy verge to his fence.

"Excuse me!"

He caught the ball and spun round.

Nine or ten years old. Angelic face. Curly hair. Scruffy-looking, in soiled shorts and T-shirt.

"Can I have a word?"

He glanced about him, wondering what to do, then approached her warily, clasping the ball in both hands as if he'd hit her with it if he had to.

"What's your name?" she asked kindly.

"R-Ryan . . . Ryan Glacken."

"Ryan, I wonder would you mind not kicking your ball? I've got a sore head you see, and the noise is making it worse."

Ryan stared up at her, bottom lip curled out in dismay. He looked so sad and innocent. Rita-Mae felt bad because now he was going to cry. But then:

"I don't give a shite about yer oul' head!" he spat.

"I *beg* your pardon?"

"I'm gonna tell me ma on you!"

Before she could speak he ran off screaming into the house.

Such insolence! But at least she'd got him to stop his annoying ball game. She was about to retrace her steps when she heard a woman's voice.

"Hi, you there!"

She turned back to see a dumpy woman in a blue smock shuffling over to the yard, cigarette in hand.

"Hello, Mrs Glacken, I'm—"

"Is this *her*, Ryan?"

"Aye, Ma."

"Who d'ya think you are? Tellin' my son whadda do in his own back-yard!"

"Well, I'm sorry, but I have a dreadful headache, you see, and . . . and the noise of your son kicking the ball was making it worse."

The woman inspected her through tiny eyes buried in a doughy face. She sucked on the cigarette, spewing smoke through her nostrils like a cartoon dragon. Rita-Mae noted that she wasn't wearing a wedding ring.

"Stay in yer house and shut the windee then. Where d'you live anyway? Never seen you round here afore."

Rita-Mae, trying hard to remain calm, pointed feebly in the direction of Willow Close, sensing she'd be getting little understanding from Mrs Glacken.

"Number eight over there," she said.

"Ma, Ma!" Ryan shouted gleefully. "That's the madwoman's house!" He clutched his belly, doubling in two, hooting with laughter.

"So it is, Ryan. Well, no surprises there."

The boy continued his hysterics. At which point the mother grabbed him by the arm and pulled him to her. "Cut it out, Ryan, or I'll rip yer face off."

Rita-Mae began backing away, appalled by the rough language.

"That Hillitch man should turn it into a bloody asylum the way things is lookin'. Never know what sort of nutter's livin' beside us, do we, son?"

"Nah, Ma."

"I *beg* your pardon!"

She threw down the cigarette and stamped on it angrily. "Beg all you like," she snapped, resting her hands on her hips and thrusting her chin out. "Just so you know, Mrs—"

"*Miss*, actually." The Good Samaritan's headache was getting as bad as the situation. All her training, emphasizing remaining neutral and non-judgemental in the face of conflict, was suddenly deserting her.

"*Miss*, aye, I thought you might be . . . if yeh had a wain in yer life you wouldn't be a miserable oul' maid complainin' about nathin', so you wouldn't. The last one was a miserable oul' maid too, just like you."

"Well, I can see where your rude son gets it from. There is no point in trying to be civil to the likes of you."

"Och, buzz off and leave us alone!" She tugged at the boy. "Come on, Ryan. Yer tea's ready. We're not safe around this nutter."

Rita-Mae staggered back across the lane, head throbbing. She really needed to take a pill and lie down. Behind her she heard the neighbour-from-hell hurl one last missile: "You haven't seen the last of us, you screwball!" It was followed by a door being banged shut.

Mortified and confused, she was glad to reach the safety of her garden once more. But as she was locking her own gate she remembered she must shut Mrs Gilhooley's back-door.

Quickly she doubled back and went to do her neighbourly duty.

CHAPTER NINETEEN

Some hours later the sound of a car door banging disturbed Rita-Mae from slumber. After her contretemps with Mrs Glacken she'd taken a pill for the worsening migraine, which had tipped her over into a deep sleep.

Groggy but heedful, she stumbled now to the window and peered out.

Bram Hilditch was going in next door. At the sight of him her whole body tensed in warning. There was something about him that indicated it was not a social call.

All was not well at Mrs Gilhooley's.

Alert to the idea he might be calling on her too, she pulled on her clothes and dashed downstairs.

But when she reached the bottom step a shocking sight confronted her.

The lounge was a mess.

Plant pots toppled, the cushions of the settee overturned. Cutlery tossed everywhere.

Oh dear God!

The stalker.

Terrified, she moved slowly into the lounge. Saw that the back-door was ajar.

But I locked the door. I must have done.

Oh God, what if he's standing out there waiting for me? Just waiting to laugh in my face.

She edged her way into the kitchen and peeked through the window.

Nothing.

But he could be standing *just outside the door*.

No time to get the flick-knife. It was upstairs under her pillow. She eyed the knife block – saw that the paring-knife was missing.

Had he taken it? Was he standing there just outside, waiting to pounce, drag her inside and slit her throat? The paring-knife was very sharp. She knew that from washing up the previous evening. Could still feel the nick in her forefinger, the blood from it turning the water crimson in the kitchen sink.

She drew out the chef's knife, heart thudding like a jackhammer, and flung the door wide.

No one.

She put one foot over the doorstep, heard the gravel crunch quietly.

Nothing stirred. The shed, the clothesline, the cherub, the gorse frozen like stage props, waiting. Was it all a calculated illusion just to trick her? Had *he* done this? Set it all up. Arranged things to coax her out into the open, so he could aim his lens and shoot her – click-click-click. Like he'd done with Vivian-Bernadette.

She tightened her grip on the knife.

Then:

"Hi, there!"

Oh, Christ!

She spun round, knife aloft.

Dan Madden was standing in Mrs Gilhooley's garden, staring at her over the fence.

Their eyes locked.

He took a step back.

It took her several seconds to register why he looked so shocked.

She lowered the knife and opened her mouth to explain, but the words would not come; the sheer relief of seeing *him* instead of . . . instead of the dreaded, deadly stranger had rendered her speechless. She dashed inside, slamming the door shut, all thoughts returning to the ransacked lounge.

Her handbag?

Her money?

But her bag was in the usual place by the armchair. When she looked inside, her purse was there, the money untouched.

What savings she had were under her mattress, so they were safe too.

She went back to the kitchen and examined the door.

There was no evidence it had been forced.

How come she'd forgotten to lock it?

You haven't seen the last of us, you screwball!

The voice of Mrs Glacken, loud in her head.

Of course: that harridan's behind all this. She sent the son over to wreak havoc and get her revenge.

She surveyed the lounge again.

Yes, it looked like the work of a child. No valuables stolen. No really heavy items disturbed: the plant pots, cushions, cutlery all pointed to the work of a naughty little boy playing a silly prank.

Quickly she began tidying up, relieved.

It was important to right things before Bram Hilditch came a-calling. Something told her it was better not to tell him anything. She could not admit to being so lax in forgetting to lock her back-door. Nor could she risk getting pulled into something bigger involving her next-door neighbour.

She gathered up the cutlery and put it in the sink.

How come she hadn't *heard* him, though? Ryan Glacken. But she'd taken that pill and knew from experience how deeply they could make her sleep.

When the last of the cutlery was soaking, the doorbell sounded.

She took a deep breath, adjusted herself in the mirror and went to answer it.

"Mr Hilditch! I thought I saw your car."

"So sorry to bother you, Miss Ruttle."

He appeared agitated, not his usual ebullient self.

"May I come in, just for a moment?"

"Of course. Is . . . is anything wrong?"

He took his usual chair at the table and removed his hat. "Oh, it's a terrible business . . . a terrible business altogether, Miss Ruttle."

"I'll make some tea, shall I?"

"No . . . no tea, thank you." He scanned the room, wiping sweat from his brow.

"Are you all right, Miss Ruttle?"

"Me . . . ? Yes, I . . . I'm fine, thank you . . . just a little tired, that's all."

She took the chair opposite, sitting down slowly, eyes steady on him, so many desperate thoughts seething in her head.

"What's the matter, Mr Hilditch? You . . . you look put out."

"It's Mrs Gilhooley, I'm afraid. She's been taken to hospital. Someone broke in and robbed her."

"Oh, dear!"

"But that's not the worst of it."

He removed his spectacles and pinched the bridge of his nose, as if what he was about to say was just too painful to put into words.

"My goodness me . . . was she assaulted?"

He shook his head. "No, not as bad as that. They killed Polly."

"Y-You mean h-her *budgie*?"

"Yes, cut . . ." He cast his eyes briefly at the ceiling then studied the floor. ". . . cut its little head off and threw it back in the cage. She arrived home to find blood and feathers all over the place and her jewellery stolen."

He gazed at her in earnest. "Who would *do* a thing like that?"

She tried to take in what he was saying, but could not bring herself to imagine such a horror. Was the man who was stalking her stalking Maud as well? She too lived alone, but she was elderly and stalkers generally liked their prey young.

"That . . . that's so awful! So very, very awful! The poor woman."

"She fainted with the shock of it. Only for Dan Madden . . ."

At the mention of Madden's name a terrible image presented itself, sharply focused.

She with knife raised, turning to face him.

The alarm in Madden's eyes at the sight of her.

Had he told Bram Hilditch what he'd witnessed?

". . . yes, only for Dan coming to do her garden," Bram Hilditch was saying, fixing her with that earnest look again, "heaven knows what might have happened. He found her collapsed on the floor. She has a weak heart you see."

"My goodness me, that is *so* shocking! Who on earth would do a thing like that?" She was quaking inside. "Is she . . . is she going to be all right?"

"We sincerely hope so."

"I'm so sorry. I was just chatting to her before she went to the shops."

"You were?"

"Yes, just for a little while. She very kindly asked me if I needed anything."

"She's the salt of the earth, Maud. That is why this is so dreadful. You didn't notice anyone acting suspiciously, did you?"

She hesitated. Thought of Ryan Glacken, but couldn't afford to tell him that. Not now. Less said the better for now.

"No . . . well, the thing is, I was lying down for a couple of hours."

"Oh!"

"Yes, with a headache. I only woke up at the sound of your car."

"I'm sorry."

She wasn't sure if he was sympathizing for the headache, her lack of awareness at a crucial moment or the fact that he'd woken her.

"Well, hopefully the police will be able to catch the ruffian," he said, getting up.

The word "police" had her heart shifting up a gear.

He turned to her. "They'll want to have a word with you, being her nearest neighbour. You'll be all right with that, won't you?"

She saw her whole life unravelling right there with his question.

Her secret would be out. He'd learn she was not who she said she was. That she was not the lonely spinster deserving of his attention and respect. That in fact she was a liar and a fraud.

"Yes, I'll only . . . only be too glad to assist them," she heard herself say, marvelling at the ease with which the words slipped from her.

At the door he patted her arm. A gesture she found comforting in the circumstances. "You mind yourself, Miss Ruttle. Make sure you lock all windows and doors. I'm only a phone call away. You know that, don't you?"

"Yes . . . thank you." She made to shut the door, but he turned back.

"By the way, Miss Ruttle, have you ever visited Portaluce?"

"Erm . . . no, but I've heard it's lovely."

"It's just that . . ." He adjusted his glasses. "I need to go there soon to book my mother's next little break. She stays at a lovely guesthouse there every summer, you see. Would be nice to have your company on the journey."

"Maybe . . . yes . . . that would be nice."

"When this ghastly business with Maud's cleared up. Would be a day out for us both."

She forced a smile and nodded.

He touched his hat. Made to go. "Oh, just one more thing before I forget, Miss Ruttle."

He reached into an inside pocket. Drew out an envelope.

"Your receipt for the deposit. I totally overlooked it. Sorry about that. It was a little remiss of me."

"That's all right. There's no need to apologize."

"Well, good day to you, Miss Ruttle. See you again soon."

She shut the door on him with a heavy heart. Gazed down at the envelope, thoughts spinning out of control. Went through to the kitchen and pulled out a drawer. It contained all the receipts she'd accumulated so far since coming to Killoran.

Why, she asked herself, am I keeping these?

But in seconds she was back there in the past, remembering the abuses another had inflicted.

Sadly, she knew no other way to be.

CHAPTER TWENTY

"Receipts," Harry demanded, "and make it quick. Haven't got all day."

It had just gone 6 p.m. on a typical weekday. A year or two into Rita-Mae's marriage and already Harry had moulded her, shaped the clay, which, over the years, would set and harden into the object that would be his alone.

She'd just set down his dinner-plate and was halfway to the table with the teapot when he'd asked her for them.

"The receipts. I'll get them for you as soon as I've poured the tea," she said.

"I said *now!*"

She turned back to the stove.

"Where the fuck d'you think yer goin' with that tay?"

"You said you wanted to see the receipts."

"After yeh pour the bloody tay. Are you thick or what? Do I have to spell everything out for you, do I?"

She could have remonstrated. Could have said, "I thought you wanted to see the receipts *now* and the word 'now' usually means immediately." But she was too afraid to say anything. Was already, in the time she'd known him, planning moves, editing thoughts, censoring speech, just to keep his temper at bay. It was the best she could do – tiptoe carefully on the thinnest of ice, dreading that sudden cracking sound, which might propel her into casualty – or the morgue.

It was Friday. On Thursday evenings, when he got his wages, he'd give her £20 for the week's groceries. He needed to see receipts for everything, just in case she'd frittered some of it away on herself. In Harry's book anything apart from the basics – food, drink, toiletries and cleaning agents – was unnecessary. Money spent on nonsense "upset" him. She could never have imagined how something as innocuous as a receipt would hold such terror for her. They were the evidence Harry needed to keep track of her when he wasn't around, giving the how, when and where she'd spent *his* precious money. She'd had no idea that receipts contained not only date-stamps but *time*-stamps as well. Until of course those times of purchase became weapons in his war against her.

"Sorry," she said, pouring the tea. "I'll get them now."

He thrust into the food without a word. She found the receipts in her purse and laid them by his plate.

"From now on," he said, gesturing with the knife, "I wanna see them sittin' out here on the table when I get home. That way I don't need-a keep lookin' them off you."

"Yes, I'll do that," she said meekly, sitting down at the other end of the table to her own meagre ration. Baked beans on toast. Just the one slice of bread and a half can of beans. It was the safest food she could eat.

One evening, after finishing a bowl of stew, he told her he'd put rat poison in it when her back was turned. She was immediately sick in the toilet bowl and he laughed at her for being so stupid as to believe him.

But following that incident she never again left her food unattended. Every morsel she ate had to be protected, from sealed packet to mouth. That was the only way she could be sure.

"How was your day, Harry?" she asked now, trying to lighten the atmosphere.

"My day?" He loured at her. "Why are yeh tryin' to change the subject?"

"It's just that it's Friday and you're usually in a good mood because it's the weekend, that's all."

"Aye, right. That fucker George was called away today and I'd to fill in for him, if you must know. Missus havin' another wain, so he had to go down the hospital. But tell me, was that *my* fault? Why did I have to do his work on top of my own?"

She could have asked why he hadn't complained to his boss. Why he hadn't just refused to do it. But she knew better. Harry never questioned those above him. Like most abusers he was unable to challenge authority and hated his own impotence in that regard. The cuts and bruises his wife took were his most expedient way of expressing such frustration.

"No, it wasn't your fault," she said, trying to mollify him, "but you'll get paid overtime? The extra money will come in handy."

"That's *not* the point, is it? The point is that they used me to clear up after him, and I don't like being anyone's dogsbody. Nobody uses Harry Ruttle. Anyway, why are you so interested in my mood all of a sudden?"

He'd almost cleared his plate, bolting his food greedily as if it was the last meal he'd ever see.

"Just wondered. That's all."

She had no appetite. Asked herself if she'd get through the evening unscathed. The morning-sickness was getting worse, but he was never a witness to that, thank God. Up and away by 7 a.m. with the lunch-pack she'd prepared the night before.

"There must be something," he growled, "something in these receipts . . . something you know I won't be too happy about."

"No," she said, shaking her head. "Nothing like that."

But she could see he wasn't convinced.

She watched him tear a slice of bread in two, a muscle beating in his right cheek. Tension was building, the very air around him vibrating.

Yes, there was something: she'd been to the doctor and he'd confirmed what she'd already suspected. She was pregnant. Well past the first trimester.

Harry snorkelled from the mug of tea, eyes as cold as ice chips. A predator's eyes.

"I *said* there must be something you don't want me to know about."

She sliced into the toast, feigning concentration, measuring the lines, corner to corner, so that each quarter looked exactly the same. Aware of the silence and what words she might safely place into it. Forming them in her head. Choosing carefully, like a Scrabble player.

"I hate the bloody way you do that!" There was a sharpening edge to his voice, her timidity and way of eating serving as a whetstone.

No, the evening would not end well.

"Do what?" she asked, trying to stall the inevitable.

"The way you toy about with your bloody food. It's for eatin', not playin' with."

"Oh, that. Well, it's just the way I eat." She glanced at his empty plate. "Do you want some more? There's more in the oven if you want."

"Me ma used to eat like you. Me da called her The Mouse. Aye, Mary Mouse. You remind me of her y'know. Thin as a rake, nervous as a bloody rabbit, mad as a friggin' hatter. But she was easy to run, like yerself. That's what Da used to say. 'Mary Mouse's easy to run.' That's about the only good thing I can say about you too. The less you eat, the less I have to spend."

She got up. "I'll get you some more."

"Aye, that's a good idea, Rita. You just do that and I'll take a wee look at these, 'cos from where I'm sittin' I think you're hidin' something from me."

She reached for his plate.

"Why are you wearin' that loose thing?" He was staring at her belly. "Can't be 'cos you're puttin' on weight, since you eat fuck all."

She'd taken to wearing a dress one size bigger, because she was beginning to "show" and needed to deflect his attention. She'd found it in a St Vincent de Paul charity shop for the paltry sum of £1.50. Hardly an extravagance.

"Don't think so," she said, lifting the plate. "It's this dress. It's a bit on the big side."

He grabbed her wrist. His rough hand a manacle.

"Then why did you buy it, if it was too big for you?"

She had to think fast. "There was . . . no changin' room . . . it being a charity shop, and I only realized when I got it home. It . . . it looked all right on the hanger. The dinner's getting cold, Harry."

His grip grew tighter. "Looks like a bloody *maternity* smock to me. Hope yer not pregnant, Rita, 'cos if yeh are you'll just have to get rid of it. The last thing I want in my life is a screamin' brat disturbin' my peace. D'yeh understand me?"

"I know."

He released her. Dropped her arm like it was a diseased thing.

"Now, get me the rest of that dinner. And make it quick."

He took the calculator from the window-sill as she went through to the kitchen.

She never thought herself capable of having a child, but now that it was happening she was amazed. A little one quickening inside her that was hers – all hers, because she was the one nurturing it, not him. Maybe if she broke it to him gently he'd have a change of heart. Now, however, was clearly not the best time.

A week before they married he'd sent her to the doctor for the contraceptive pill. And she'd gone along with it because she was in love with him – or thought she was. But she'd stopped taking it on purpose. Her one act of defiance because she wanted a baby so much. She had so much love to give – love that Harry clearly had no need of – and what better way to feel complete and useful in the miserable situation that was her marriage? Becoming a mother seemed the only way of remaining sane in the circumstances.

Slowly she refilled the plate, hunkering down at the oven. Everything was accounted for. But unfortunately there was a half-hour gap between the supermarket and her visit to the butcher's. The time she'd spent at the doctor's surgery.

"What the hell's *this*?"

She heard his voice detonate in the dining-room.

Immediately she got up and shut the oven door.

"What's what?" she said, returning with the food. "I'll get you more tea."

He shot up off the chair, slapping the receipts with the back of his hand.

"Don't you come the innocent with *me*. How come there's a half hour between yeh buying stuff in the supermarket and the roast in the butcher's? They're right next door."

There was no way she could broach the subject of that visit to the doctor. Not now. But she had already thought of an excuse. Had braced herself against this very sort of confrontation.

"I . . . I met Grace outside O'Mahony's a-and we chatted for a while. That's all."

Grace Thorne, the hair-stylist she did stints for. The only person she was allowed to talk to. The only person she knew would defend her.

"We'll see about that," he barked, heading for the phone in the hallway.

She rushed after him.

He lifted the receiver.

"Look . . . Harry, don't do that. Grace is at her tea now and your food's getting' cold and . . ."

"Right, what's it to be?" Fingers poised over the dial, anger pouring from him like steam from a boiling kettle. "Am I gonna ring Mrs Thorne or not? 'Cos if I ring her and she says you didn't have that wee conversation, that's gonna make me look stupid. Now, what's it to be?"

"Go ahead," she said, knowing she could depend on Grace.

He dialled the number. Rita-Mae heard it being answered almost at once.

"Hi, Norman. It's only me. Is Grace there by any chance? Just need a wee word."

She left him in the hallway. Sat down at the table again. Stared at the congealing beans on the toast, heart beating wildly against her ribs like a caged thing.

Then: "Oh, she's in Galway, is she? Och, well, it wasn't important. Sure I'll see her when she gets back."

Her whole body went limp.

The telephone receiver was crashed back on the cradle.

She shot off the chair, backing into a corner as he blazed towards her.

"Sorry, Harry, I—"

"I *knew* yeh were fuckin' lyin'! Grace Thorne's in Galway these couple of days."

"B-But I can explain, Harry. Really Harry. *P-l-e-a-s-e!*"

He lunged at her. "*Where the hell were you for that half hour?*"

She ducked, missing the swipe of his fist.

Ran upstairs, screaming.

She was quicker and lighter than Harry. The only advantage she had over him: the gazelle fleeing the lion into the refuge of the bedroom – the only space in the house that guaranteed a soft landing with the first blow.

She made it, got inside, slid the bolt in the lock. But not for long.

She shoved her back against the door as his fists rained down. Every thump on the thin plywood a prelude to the beating her body would be taking very soon.

"If I have to break down this fuckin' door I'm gonna have to break yer fuckin' neck. You're pregnant, yeh bitch. Think I haven't noticed them monthly rags not on the receipts this past while? Eh? Eh?"

"Please, Harry, I can explain. Just let me explain. Don't hit me. Please don't hit me."

She pressed herself against the shuddering door, pleading, shielding her abdomen with both hands to protect the life inside her because she knew he was in the mood for murder.

"I *said,* open this fuckin' door. You start actin' up on me again I'll be lockin' you in the shed and you can bloody well stay there. Now, open the fuckin' door!"

"No, I can't, Harry. Until you calm down, I can't open it."

The thumping ceased.

"By Christ, if yeh don't open this door now yer really gonna pay for it, and far worse than the last time. D'yeh *hear* me?"

The last time she'd waited before opening the door he'd put his boot through it. She'd taken three broken ribs and a fractured arm against the cost of a new one.

It was useless to resist.

There was no escape.

She opened the door, offering herself up like a saintly martyr.

"*Come out here!*" he roared.

She fell to her knees, crying, pleading. "Stop, Harry, please, Harry! I . . . I can explain. It'll be all right. The baby'll make us happier. You'll be a father. Things will be different between us. I promise."

But Harry wasn't listening. Harry was no longer *himself*, but the monster of her nightmares.

He pulled her up off her knees by the hair. Dragged her across the landing.

Held her chin in a vice-like grip and spat in her face.

"I'll teach you not to bloody lie to me, and *I'll* decide if I want a wain or not. *Not you.*"

"Please don't hurt *us*, Harry, please. I'm begging you."

"See that beggin' of yours? The more yeh beg the more annoyed that makes me! So shut the fuck up."

He punched her hard in the face.

"As I was sayin', *Rita*, at this present moment in time I don't want a fuckin' wain in this house. Is that clear?"

She nodded, terrified, feeling the metallic taste of blood in her mouth. Knowing that this time, *this time*, she really could be a few short breaths away from death. And she didn't much care. Maybe it was best that it ended now. All the suffering. All the pain.

"What was *that*? I didn't *hear* a bloody answer!"

"Y-Y-Yes . . . I . . . I . . . I understand."

"*Good*. I'm glad we got that sorted."

The last thing she remembered was the world tumbling in on itself from the blow to her back that sent her flying headlong down the stairs.

CHAPTER
TWENTY-ONE

Rita did not know how long she stood there in the aftermath of Bram Hilditch's words, staring down at the drawer of receipts, thinking about Harry and how he'd put paid to her dream of becoming a mother. The Babygros were in her case upstairs – one pink, one blue. She'd bought them in expectation, and commemorated the tragedy each year with the ritual of washing and airing them on the day she lost the baby.

She gazed out of the kitchen window. Saw that darkness was falling. So she must have been standing there a while, remembering. Looking back through the tangled, addled mess of memories, in a feeble attempt to block out the reality of the danger she was now facing. A real and present danger that had been visited upon her so suddenly.

Well, hopefully the police will be able to catch the ruffian, she heard the landlord say again. *They'll want to have a word with you, being her nearest neighbour. You'll be all right with that, won't you?*

No, she certainly would *not* be all right with that. The last people she wanted to come into contact with were the police.

She slammed the drawer shut on the receipts. Went through to the hall and switched on the light.

The universe that had given her the courage to escape from the prison of her marriage was now forcing her back the way she'd come, throwing up roadblocks, erecting walls, cutting her off from sight. She heard doors slam behind her, sensed with a gut-dissolving terror that she was cornered in a drama of her own making.

Battered Rita, spineless Rita, cowardly Rita. Soon Bram Hilditch would know she was all of those things. All of those things she'd worked so hard at masking. Oh, the shame! The respectable spinster with her good manners and modest needs. All a sham.

Wearily, she climbed the stairs, all steadiness of thought gone. Halted at the butterfly case. Counted the specimens for no good reason. Glanced at the door of the box-room. The unpleasant smell had been strongest in there. It was there still. It was not the drains, as the landlord would have her believe. The dead bird that Madden had taken away was another ruse. Something terrible had happened in that room. She saw Vivian-Bernadette innocently combing her hair by the window.

He photographed her, at the window, combing her hair: the faceless man. Her tormentor. The stalker.

The shut door mocked her.

He'd photographed her. Had *Hilditch* photographed her? Now he was suggesting she get in his car and accompany him to the seaside. How would she get out of that one?

She backed away from it, down the corridor, fearful, acutely aware of the creaking floorboards. Silence was a terrible thing, deepening her aloneness. All the old feelings were coming back, taking up residence like unwanted guests she didn't have the strength to order out.

The bedroom seemed the only refuge for now.

As soon as she put her foot over the threshold the phone rang.

Police?

She let it ring out.

A couple of minutes later, it started up again, quivering like a shiny black toad on the bedside table.

If it *is* the police and if I don't answer it *they'll come in person to the door and that will be worse.*

She lifted the receiver.

"Yes . . ."

"Hello, Rita. Susan Mulvey here."

"Who?"

"Susan, at the Get Ahead hair salon. Did you forget?"

"Er . . . Susan." She paused, embarrassed, not knowing what to say.

"Am I speaking to Rita Ruttle?"

"Yes, that's me."

"You said you'd be here at seven to do the evening shift for Emma. Don't you remember?"

No, she hadn't remembered. So much had happened since that innocent little interview with Mrs Mulvey that its relevance in the scheme of things had taken flight. And now the last thing she wanted to do was stand in that salon at the mercy of the locals. At the mercy of *him.* He'd known she was in there that day. Had put the note on her windscreen *while she was in there.*

"I'm so sorry," she began. "It's just th-that I've . . . er . . . I've come down with a stomach bug. I . . . I meant to ring you but it went completely out of my head."

"*What?*"

"Yes, sorry—"

"But—"

She hung up, hating herself for being so cowardly, but relieved she'd got it over with.

Maybe it would be best to simply pack her things now and leave.

Bram Hilditch already had her rent money, so she'd not be doing a runner. She could write him a note, leave with her good name intact.

I'm sorry, Mr Hilditch, but due to unforeseen circumstances I've had to leave earlier than expected.

Isn't that what departing notes usually said? "Unforeseen circumstances". It was a phrase that covered quite a lot.

Where to go? Larne seemed the only option. Harry wasn't back yet. Grace Thorne had assured her she'd let her know as soon as he showed up. Construction jobs in England could last months, so he wouldn't even know she'd been away. At the end of the day, which was worse? Negotiating a war zone whose terrain you knew well, with an enemy whose moves you could sometimes predict and so outmanoeuvre, or continue stumbling round in a no man's land, not knowing where the next faceless foe would spring from—?

Her brooding stalled at the sound of a vehicle drawing up.

The police?

"Dear God, no! Let it not be *them*!"

She slid on to her knees, crouching down at the side of the bed. Curled into a ball on the floor, trying to disappear.

If it is the police I'll have to face them. The light's on downstairs. My car's parked outside. Signs that I'm at home.

All of a sudden: the chatter of male voices punctuated by an electronic squawking.

She held her breath. Squeezed her arms more tightly about her.

Maybe . . . maybe it's the ambulance. Maybe they're bringing Mrs Gilhooley home. Yes, paramedics also use two-way radios. That's it . . . the ambulance bringing Mrs Gilhooley home from the hospital.

The gate latch lifted.

The squawking grew louder.

All at once, a brusque rapping on the door.

Her door.

She dared not move. Legs like granite. Heart thudding so loudly she felt sure *they* could hear it; the *strangers on the doorstep*.

She'd have to answer it. Because if she didn't they'd know she'd something to hide. The next day they'd be back for certain, suspicions aroused. For sure!

She took a deep breath. Uncurled herself, crept out of the room on all fours to the head of the stairs.

Through the frosted glass of the door she could make out two figures. Even in the distortion their uniformed silhouettes were unmistakable, the blue glare of electronic gadgets glimmering in breast pockets.

Yes, *they* had arrived.

The police.

She'd *have* to face them.

There was no way out.

She gathered herself. Stood up and – to steady her nerves and buy herself more time – slowly descended the stairs, counting each step as she went.

She pulled the door open mid-rap.

Two men of average build wearing the regulation dark green garb of the Royal Ulster Constabulary stood facing her.

"Sorry, officers. I was taking a nap."

She did not know why she said that. They looked so forbidding that some explanation for her tardiness in answering their call seemed necessary.

"Evening, miss," the older man said. "Sorry we disturbed you then. Just need to ask a few questions about your neighbour, Maud Gilhooley . . . just routine. D'you mind if we come in?"

"No . . . no, not at all. Please. It's through here."

She led them into the lounge, channelling her calmest persona.

Look them in the eye when you're answering their questions. Don't waver. You were asleep. You saw nothing. You heard nothing.

They waded into the lounge, bringing the cold air of evening with them, and doffed their peaked caps in unison.

"Won't you sit down," she said.

"No, thank you all the same." The taller one had spoken again. He was the more important of the two. The cap had given him gravitas.

Without it he looked less menacing: late fifties; gaunt face, thinning hair, weary eyes simply longing for the armchair of retirement.

"I'm Sergeant Taylor and this here's Constable Barry."

Barry, early thirties, nondescript, flicked his eyes over her and nodded.

He took out a notepad.

Taylor began. "You're new to these parts, Miss . . . eh?"

"Ruttle . . . Rita. Yes, I am."

"And you came from—"

"Larne."

"Larne, right . . . nice wee spot. Needed a change, did you?"

"Something like that."

"Any form of ID?"

She found her driving licence and handed it to him. He glanced at it and passed it to Barry.

"Married, are you?"

"No."

Taylor stared at her. "Says 'Mrs' on your licence here, miss."

What an oversight! But she'd never had to produce the licence for anyone since taking flight. Not even for Bram Hilditch.

How bloody stupid of yeh! she heard Harry say.

"Sorry . . . separated now," she said. "Is . . . is she going to be all right? Maud . . . I mean Mrs Gilhooley."

Barry looked up from his note-taking.

"We hope so, Miss Ruttle," Taylor said, putting his cap down carefully on the table.

She felt her knees go weak. "Yes . . . what . . . what a shame! Such a . . . sweet lady. I'll . . . I'll just sit, if you don't mind."

She took her usual chair, resting her hands on the table. Thought they would sit down too, but to her dismay they remained standing, making her feel even more vulnerable.

"When did you last see her?" Taylor continued. "Your neighbour."

"Around half past three . . . she was going to the shops and very kindly asked if I needed anything."

"Then what did you do?"

"I lay down because I—"

"You do a lot of that, do you?"

"Sorry?"

"Well, you were lyin' down just now at . . ." He checked his watch. "A quarter by seven."

"Sometimes . . . sometimes if I've had a bad night, yes. But this afternoon I had a migraine attack and the only remedy is to take medication, which unfortunately makes me very drowsy . . . s-so it's best to sleep."

"Hmph . . . so you saw off Mrs Gilhooley at half three then you took to your bed. Is that right?"

She was vexed by his tone. But she must remain calm! After all, only a budgie had died. It was hardly a hanging offence. And hadn't this pair more serious crimes to involve themselves with, given the political climate?

"Miss Ruttle . . . ?"

"Yes, that's right. I didn't see anything or hear anything out of the ordinary. I'm sorry I can't be of more help."

"Maybe I'll have this wee seat after all," Taylor said, taking the chair opposite her. He threw a look at Barry, who remained grim-faced, pen poised over notebook.

The joints of the chair creaked as he canted forward, fixing her with his watery eyes, which now at close range looked inflamed and cruel.

"You see, that's very odd, Miss Ruttle, 'cos we have it on good authority – me and the constable here – that you were seen at Maud Gilhooley's back-door."

Her throat constricted. She knew immediately that the Glacken woman was their informant. That spiteful, vengeful harridan was trying to frame her.

"Yes, well, I forgot to mention . . . I went out the back to get some fresh air . . . hoping it would help my headache and . . . I . . . I noticed . . . happened to notice that Maud had forgotten to shut her door. Naturally I did the neighbourly thing and shut it, in case . . ."

"In case what, Miss Ruttle?"

"Well, in case she was robbed of course."

"Which she was."

"Erm . . . sadly, yes . . ."

Taylor continued his unblinking regard, forcing her to add, "I didn't have a key to lock it for her. She never gave me one, alas."

"And you didn't think to mention that important detail before now? Being in Mrs Gilhooley's house, like you say."

"But I wasn't *in* her house. I just shut her door. That's all."

He's playing with me, she thought. Trying to get me to admit to something I didn't do, so he can tick a box in his COMPLETED file.

"You didn't enter her house then?"

"No."

He threw another glance at his colleague, who shrugged and sighed.

"Look, I've got nothing to hide. I really don't know what you're suggesting, officer. I could never hurt a fly, let alone a bird. How could you even think I'd do such a thing?"

"Right, then. In light of what you've just stated . . . that you've got nothing to hide. In light of that statement, Miss Ruttle, you'll have no objection to Constable Barry here having a wee look round upstairs."

Two sets of eyes held her. She felt as trapped as one of the landlord's butterflies.

"Well . . . no," she said, feeling very much invaded. "I've . . . I mean that's . . . that's all right. Go ahead."

Taylor nodded at Barry. "Won't be long, miss," Barry said, before sprinting up the stairs, taking two steps at a time. She heard him go down the corridor to her bedroom.

Taylor remained seated, drumming his fingers on the table, whistling softly.

"Like it here, do you, Miss . . . er . . . Mrs Ruttle?" He didn't look her way but scanned the room, his eyes taking in everything, whistling his tuneless tune.

"Yes . . . it's very pleasant, thank you."

She thought about folding her arms. Quickly changed her mind. He'd know she was being defensive. Cops were trained in reading the signs. She'd read it in a magazine once. He might be sitting a few feet away pretending not to notice her but she knew he was still tuning into her every move and breath.

She heard Barry slide open the shower door. Shut it again. Then move across to the box-room.

He opened the door. "*What the—*" An exclamation of surprise.

"Abraham Hilditch owns this place, doesn't he?" Taylor said.

She heard the constable moving about in the box-room. Felt herself tense. He was invading her space and she wanted to race upstairs and order him out. How dare he do that! Why were these two treating her like a criminal? Why?

Because you're a woman on your own, and they resent that.

"Miss Ruttle?"

She looked up from her lap to see Taylor scrutinizing her.

"Sorry . . . I didn't hear that."

"Abraham Hilditch your landlord?"

"Yes . . . yes, he is." A thought struck her: "Have you visited this house before, Sergeant?"

The drumming fingers stopped.

"Why do you ask that?"

"Just wondered . . . Constable Barry seems to know his way about."

"You don't need house plans to negotiate the upstairs of a two-bed semi, Miss Ruttle."

She didn't like this man at all. He was a sarcastic bully. Liked making her feel small. Just like Harry.

Suddenly the constable was coming down the stairs again.

Taylor got up.

Barry looked at Taylor. Then turned to her. "That wee room at the top of the stairs. Have you been in there since you got up, miss?"

"No . . . why?"

Barry eyed his boss again. "It's just that . . . just that it looks like it's been done over, miss. Not unless . . . not unless it's always like that."

"*What?*"

Taylor drew himself up to his full height. "In that case, Miss Ruttle, you'd be the best judge of that."

He gestured towards the stairs. "If you'd like to go up ahead of us and we'll all have a look?"

Nervously, Rita-Mae mounted the stairs, Taylor close on her heels.

Even more nervously, she pushed open the door to the box-room.

She gaped in disbelief, only with difficulty holding herself in check.

The place was a mess: window wide open, the beady-eyed ferret knocked on its side, a chair upturned, vase broken, the rug kicked over, air fresheners and potpourri strewn across the floor.

"Well, Miss Ruttle," Taylor said over her shoulder, "is this always the way yeh keep this wee room?"

She turned on him defiantly, a thought occurring to her. "Given that I never use this room, Sergeant, I can only assume the wind blew the window open and caused all this."

Taylor unclasped his hands from behind his back. "If that's what you want to believe, Miss Ruttle, then who are we to say different?"

CHAPTER
TWENTY-TWO

"Are you sure she's not in?" Bram said, unlatching the gate to number 8, not a little irked.

An employee from the electricity board had called him while he was filing his tax-return – interrupting him at a most inconvenient time – and was insisting he be admitted to read Miss Ruttle's meter.

"I *say*, are you sure she's *not in*?" he repeated, coming up the garden path.

The man, loitering on the doorstep, pivoted round and straightened.

"Oh, are *you* Mr Hilditch? No, she isn't in. That's why I rang you."

Bram didn't like the look of him. Thirtyish, he reckoned, shifty, unkempt, the type that would be better suited to holding up a bar, or indeed a street-corner, shouting obscenities at passers-by. He peered pointedly at the ID card on his lapel.

"No worries. I'm bona fide, Mr Hilditch. You can ring the boss if you want."

"Seamus Rafferty, NIEB. Well, one can't be too careful these days, Mr Rafferty. The board usually sends Carl to read the meters round here, and he always gives notice well in advance."

"Carl's on leave, so you've got me. As I said on the phone, Miss . . ."

He checked his clipboard.

"Ruttle," Bram provided.

"Yes, Miss Ruttle would've got notification in the post. We always send them out a week in advance."

"Well, she forgot, obviously. Mind you, it's not like Miss Ruttle to forget such things. She's an excellent tenant."

"That's as may be, but I need to get in."

He pulled irritably on the last of his cigarette and squinted at him.

"I get paid for three meters an hour and I've wasted a good half hour on this doorstep, with two more waiting out in the sticks."

Bram pushed the doorbell and rapped loudly on the glass.

"Look, I've done all that."

"Done all what?"

"Rung and knocked. D'you think I've been standing here all this time admirin' the paintwork? Just let me in, please."

"Indeed! Have you checked round the back if her car's there?"

"Have and it isn't," Rafferty said curtly, carelessly flicking away the spent cigarette and checking his watch. "So, if you wouldn't mind."

"Well, I would mind, as a matter of fact. My tenant's contract states I have to give advance notice if I, or anyone else, wishes to enter the property when she isn't present. So, I'm transgressing contractual rules to satisfy your impatience."

Bram saw him tussle with the idea of clocking him one and losing his job, or being mindful that this pompous twit of a landlord might well report him for being rude.

"Look, I won't tell her if you won't," he said, backing down. "I'm running late as it is, so *please*, Mr Hilditch. She'll never know. It's your house after all."

"I'm quite aware of that, thank you, Mr Rafferty."

With a sense of resignation, he took a bunch of keys from his pocket and rifled through them. "But being a reasonable man and a very busy one . . . having better things to do than stand here and parley with you, I'm prepared to make an exception on this one occasion . . . and I mean *one* occasion."

"Thank you, Mr Hilditch."

Bram opened the door and admitted him.

Rita-Mae sat in the waiting-room of Killoran surgery, trying to alleviate her anxiety by scanning the pages of a glossy magazine. She hadn't foreseen this situation when making her escape from Larne – that things would fall apart so quickly and drive her to seek out the local GP as a matter of some urgency.

The unthinkable run of events the previous day – the set-to with the Glackens, the horrible events next door, culminating with that visit from the police and the discovery that the box-room had likewise been done over – meant that she couldn't even bring herself to go in there again, let alone tidy up the mess.

In such a situation, upping her medication seemed the only answer to deaden the many questions raining down on her.

Who's behind all this?

The Glackens?

The landlord?

The handyman, Madden?

The stalker?

Is the stalker Madden?

Is the stalker Hilditch?

Is the stalker Harry? Oh God, no! Let it not be Harry. Grace would have *warned* her. She could depend on Grace for sure. Yes, *for sure*.

In the waiting-room of Killoran surgery she squeezed her eyes tight against the endless questions. Blinked to wash them away, and tried to concentrate on a feature in the magazine: the recent engagement of Sarah Ferguson to Prince Andrew.

She was conscious that she needed to feign interest in the printed words to steady herself and deflect the attention of the two others in the room: the receptionist, a flinty, matron-type in a starched blouse behind the desk, and an elderly lady sitting across from her, hugging a bag of groceries on her lap.

Prince Andrew chose an outstanding Garrard engagement ring for his future bride. The centrepiece is an exquisite example of the Burmese ruby, whose fluorescence is legendary. It's surrounded by ten drop diamonds, the whole seated on 18-carat white and yellow gold. The effect is stunning and echoes Sarah's lush hair colouring to perfection.

The old lady stirred, dipped into her shopper and produced a bag of sweets. Rita-Mae eyed her covertly from behind the pages of the magazine.

"Would you like a barley sugar?" the woman asked, rustling the bag at her.

"No, thanks."

The offer was simply a ruse to engage in small-talk. These local folk love to sound out a stranger. And she was in no mood to be interrogated. The doctor would no doubt be doing a good deal of that pretty soon.

The phone rang. The pensioner shut the bag and pricked up her ears.

"Hello, Killoran surgery. Miss Devlin speaking . . .

"Well, I'm sorry but Dr Sweeney won't be able to see you today, Barney. He's full up I'm afraid . . . I said, Dr Sweeney won't be able to see you today, Barney. He's full up I'm afraid . . . Hmm . . . and where did you say you had the pain . . . ? Oh, yer knees again . . . Hmm . . . well maybe you shouldn't kneel down to say the rosary then . . . Aye, I know . . . Hmm . . . Hmm . . . In that case the best I can do, Barney, is send a nurse . . . No, not a *hearse,* Barney, a *nurse* . . . Okay, I'll get on to it right away. Bye now."

She put the phone down and let out a sigh.

"Suppose that was Barney Todd complainin' about his knees again?" the old lady piped up.

Rita-Mae waited to hear a curt "Mind your own business" from the redoubtable Miss Devlin, but was surprised by: "Aye, Aggie, that was him. Deaf as a post . . . never stops tormentin' me. He's got the arthritis and insists on prayin' on the sore knees."

"I know. Sure my Albert does the same for tae get the plenary indulgence."

Miss Devlin picked up the phone again and began dialling with her pen.

Aggie retrieved her bag of barley sugars once more and directed her attention back to the stranger sitting opposite.

Rita-Mae dived further into the royal engagement story to discourage another sweet offer.

Sarah Ferguson, known to her friends as Fergie, has a vibrant personality and is clearly to the manor born. In short, she's a made-to-measure sister-in-law for Diana, being horsey, bouncy, with an unchallenging IQ.

All at once the outside door burst open.

"Thank heavens to be out of that wretched wind!" a female voice was heard to declaim brusquely before the door was banged shut again.

Rita-Mae dared not look round. She thought she recognized that voice and hoped against hope that it was not who she thought it was.

Then: "Oh, good morning, Mrs Hilditch. Didn't expect to see you today."

Her fears were confirmed. She raised the magazine a little higher to try and shield herself.

"Well, I dare say you didn't expect to see me, Miss Devlin. More's the pity that I have to see *you* because it can only mean that I'm poorly. I hope you can fit me in."

"Och, I'm sorry to hear that, Mrs Hilditch. But your leg must be a bit better now that you can get about on it. Of course I can fit you in. As you can see, we're not so busy."

"Thank you, Miss Devlin. My leg is slowly improving I'm glad to say. I expect it's that novice Dr Sweeney, as opposed to the excellent Dr Doyle?"

"Afraid so, Mrs Hilditch."

"I thought as much. Hence the reason you're not so busy. Oh well, he'll have to do I suppose. I don't trust youth, as you well know. It's wasted on the young, as Oscar Wilde so sagely put it."

She let out a sigh and moved with a show of exaggerated slowness, aided by a walking-stick, to the bench seat opposite. From behind the screen of the magazine, Rita-Mae observed her: green suit, expensive-looking tan brogues, a capacious handbag that matched the shoes exactly. The room seemed to shrink a little with her daunting presence. She understood now why Bram used the term "Her Grace".

Aggie quickly put away her bag of sweets and hastened to make more room for her.

"Mrs Hilditch. Keepin' all right, are yeh?" she asked sheepishly.

"Thank you for your concern, Mrs McCusker, but I'd hardly be all right if I'm here, now would I? I had a fall – if you must know – and want the doctor to check on things."

"Och, that's too bad. The damp weather won't be helpin' yeh neither."

"I daresay it isn't helping matters, no."

At that moment the intercom at reception sounded. Miss Devlin listened then spoke quietly. She raised her head. "Aggie, the doctor wants to see you now too."

Aggie gathered herself and departed.

Rita-Mae kept her eyes firmly focused on the royal engagement piece, acutely aware that she was now the sole object of interest for Octavia Hilditch.

It might be said that Diana picked her sister-in-law well. Sarah is pretty but not in quite the same league as Lady Diana Spencer. In fairness though, five years ago the former nursery-school teacher was worlds away from the idolized royal personage gracing our TV screens and magazine covers—

"You're new here, aren't you?"

She glanced up to see a pair of brown, toad-like eyes regarding her from a plump, round face. There was nothing of Bram that she could discern, apart from the snub nose and healthy complexion. The mouth was generous but downturned, giving the impression that its owner was permanently displeased with the world around her and life in general.

"Er, yes, that's right," Rita-Mae said, dropping her gaze back to the magazine.

She heard Mrs Hilditch open her handbag, draw out a hanky and blow lightly into it. Snap the bag shut again. Please, she thought, let Aggie and her husband finish soon so I can escape this. But the mumbling on the other side of the door signalled that the doctor was taking his time. No, she'd just have to brazen it out.

Then: "I expect you're Miss Ruttle, the new tenant. Would I be correct?"

"Erm, yes . . . as a matter of fact I am. And y-you must be Bram's – sorry I mean Abraham's – mother."

"Indeed. Octavia Hilditch. I thought it was you. Not many strangers happen along the way of Killoran, and you tally with all my son has told me about you so far."

All my son has told me about you so far. What on earth *had* he told her? For Rita-Mae had made doubly certain to impart as little as possible about herself to anyone – and most especially to Bram Hilditch.

"Nice to meet you, Mrs Hilditch," she said, attempting a conciliatory tone. "We spoke on the phone."

"We did indeed." The matriarch cast a glance at the receptionist and immediately Miss Devlin took her cue, busying herself at a filing cabinet.

"Yes . . . now that I've got you here, Miss Ruttle, there are a couple of things I need to say to you."

The large accusatory eyes were fixed upon her once more. Rita-Mae wanted to bolt out the door. But she could hardly do that; she needed her medication.

"Oh . . . ?"

"Yes, I believe in being direct. It saves a lot of time and misunderstanding further down the line, so I'll come straight to the point."

Mercifully, the phone rang, halting her momentarily. Miss Devlin answered straightaway, turning her back on them and speaking in a low tone.

The door to the surgery remained tightly shut, alas.

There'd be no escape for the present.

"Now, the first thing you need to know, Miss Ruttle, is that my son Abraham is *not* available. He may be well-off and eligible – an attractive prospect for many a woman down on her luck – but is most certainly *not* the marrying kind. So if you have designs in that area you'd do well to put them from your head completely."

Rita-Mae felt her face redden at the audacity and bluntness of the dreadful Octavia. Her polite reserve was failing.

She put aside the magazine, mentally loading another kind of magazine – a more combative one.

"I can assure you, *Mrs Hilditch*, that I have absolutely no interest in your son," she fired back. "I wonder where you got such a notion. I am a tenant of his and that's the extent of it."

She saw Octavia flinch slightly, wobble momentarily on her pedestal. The toad eyes blinked rapidly. Her right hand sought the reassurance of her gold necklace.

There was a tense little pause. But Rita-Mae stood her ground. She had nothing to apologize for. She was not the one who'd started this little clash.

"Well . . . just so you know, Miss Ruttle," Mrs Hilditch sniffed. "It's just that . . . well, it's just that I can't afford to have further trouble during your tenancy of number eight. The last spinster who lived there caused Abraham quite a bit of upset you see. Discomfited not only him, but me—"

Fortunately, at that point the door to the surgery had opened, cutting Octavia short. Aggie and her husband tottered forth.

Rita-Mae rose gratefully, and Dr Sweeney beckoned her in.

It didn't take the electrician long to record the meter reading. He was in and out in less than a minute and offered a grudging thanks to the landlord.

Bram scribbled a note of explanation for Miss Ruttle and apologized for the fact that he couldn't reach her.

He placed it on the mat and was about to take his leave when a thought struck him.

There was something he needed: an album of nature photographs belonging to his Uncle Gregory, which he couldn't locate in Lucerne House. He considered now that it was most likely in the trunk in the box-room of number 8. Octavia had dumped quite a lot of stuff in there during her last "decluttering" spree.

Should he nip up now and do a quick check?

He dithered on the doorstep. What if Miss Ruttle were to appear suddenly? That would be a disaster.

He nipped down the path to make sure the coast was clear.

All was quiet. Not a sinner in sight.

Yes, he'd take the chance.

Dr Sweeney was not what Rita-Mae was expecting. She recalled Mrs Hilditch's dismissal of him as a young "novice". For that reason she'd certainly not envisaged a dusty old codger the like of Dr Wilson, her GP in Larne – a man who simply went through the motions of writing prescriptions and didn't ask too many questions. This one, with his neat hair and handsome features, nattily dressed in a linen suit and white shirt, was a world away from Wilson. He gave off an air of competent professionalism.

The type who'd most likely be all too thorough and ask far too many questions.

"Take a seat," he said, shutting the door and going behind his desk. "I'm Dr Sweeney."

He sat down and glanced at a register. "And you must be . . ."

"Ruttle, Doctor . . . Rita Ruttle."

She hoped he'd concentrate on taking notes, relieve her of the burden of being inspected. The run-in with Octavia Hilditch had unsettled her and she needed time to recover. But to her dismay he leaned back in the chair. It was going to be an interview.

"And you're from Larne?"

"L-Larne . . . yes."

A beam of sunlight stole through the window and settled across the desk. She wished she could be outside, away from the stuffy room. Not sitting here in front of this stranger and requesting the false friends, the pills that she'd come to depend on so much, for sleeping, for anxiety, for migraines. Because without them life would be intolerable.

"Hmm . . . rare name, Ruttle. Haven't come across it before," Sweeney was saying. "So, what brings you all the way from lovely Larne?"

"Just . . . just felt like a change of scene, Doctor."

"And your former GP was Dr Wilson I see."

How did he know that? Then she remembered Miss Devlin had requested the information earlier when she'd rung to book the appointment.

"I spoke with him earlier, naturally, to acquaint myself with your medical history."

She could feel her face redden.

"Oh, it's just routine, Miss Ruttle . . . nothing to worry about."

There was no way she could make a fiction out of this. How much had Wilson disclosed? Had he told him about the beatings, the hospitalizations, the multiple breakdowns, the suicide attempts? Had he filled Sweeney in on every detail of her life with Harry? The life she was so ashamed of; that she dragged around like a dead beast, leaving a murky trail of clues.

"Miss Ruttle . . . ?"

She was forced to look up. "Yes . . . sorry, I . . ."

He rested a hand on the desk, pushed himself forward in the chair. She avoided his eye. Caught the glint of a wedding band. Wanted to bolt from the room.

First the police, now the doctor. They were ganging up on her.

But she needed the medication. The pills that would keep her from falling into despair. The pills that would never cure, only numb her to the reality of the long nights and days.

"And what seems to be the problem on this occasion, Miss Ruttle?"

"Migraines, Doctor. I . . . I take pills for them and I'm having trouble sleeping, so I need something for insomnia as well, and . . ."

"How long have you suffered with the migraines?"

"Quite a while . . . a few years now."

"How often do they occur?"

"Not often . . . I can go for months. Then . . ."

"Do you remember what caused the first episode?"

Why was he grilling her so much?

Harry smashing her head against the floor had caused the first episode, but she could hardly tell him that.

"No . . . just stress I suppose."

"And the most recent attack, when was that?"

"Yesterday . . . and I . . . I took the last one . . . I meant to get more from Dr Wilson, but I . . . I forgot."

"So, the change of scene isn't working."

"Sorry?"

"The move to Killoran. I'm just wondering what event triggered the attack *here*."

"Don't know . . . it just came on, Doctor."

"What about blackouts?"

"No."

"You look very thin. Are you eating?"

"I . . . I'm a very small eater and . . . well, when I'm under stress I don't feel like eating . . . very much, Doctor."

He made up his mind about something. Leaned forward and flicked through a notebook. She saw him frown and look at her quizzically. But he recovered almost at once, smiled, and reached for his prescription pad.

Bram, with a pained reluctance, placed a hand on the handle of the box-room door. He had very good reasons for not wanting to venture in there alone. The memories made him nauseous.

He eased open the door – and was at once stunned.

"What on earth!"

His eyes took in the scene with disbelief. The place was a mess: his father's precious ferret knocked on its side, a chair upturned, vase broken, the rug kicked over, air fresheners and potpourri strewn across the floor.

His immediate instinct was to right everything, but he reminded himself that *he* was the trespasser.

The album of photographs. That's what he'd come for. He needed to get them, and fast.

He opened the trunk.

Dug down through a history of papers and ancient bric-a-brac. Found the album. Was about to shut the lid when something caught his eye, jutting out from beneath a folder.

An object he'd seen before but definitely *not* in this setting.

He drew it out.

The jewellery box of black lacquer with gold engravings was distinctive. Maud Gilhooley had one just like it in her china cabinet.

Could Miss Ruttle have one exactly the same?

Was it possible?

Or . . .

With trembling hands he opened the lid.

Stared in dismay.

There in the box, nestling in all their glinting glory, were Maud Gilhooley's precious little pieces of jewellery: her cameo brooch, her Claddagh ring with the emerald stone, a bracelet of gold-and-silver charms. She'd described the items to him through tears at the hospital.

What on earth was going on?

What kind of woman was Rita Ruttle that she'd rob a poor old lady of her jewellery and kill her beloved little pet?

But there was no time to ponder such a conundrum.

It was imperative that he leave. And fast.

He shut the box. Stuffed it into his coat pocket.

Would the dark history of 8 Willow Close never let him be?

He grabbed the photo album and swiftly left the house.

CHAPTER
TWENTY-THREE

Portaluce, Antrim Coast

In Edith LeVeck's curious parlour Dorrie sat stunned at what she'd just heard.

"Y-You can really *see* my mama, Edith? I . . . I mean *really* see her?"

"Yes . . . she's here in the room."

"But where?" Dorrie clasped her hands together. She was overjoyed. "Can I see her too?"

"She's standing near Catrina," Edith said, holding Dorrie's gaze. "I'm sorry, dear, but only those with the gift of discernment can see the dead. So it's best you don't look."

Dorrie didn't really want to look back in the direction of the awful skeleton woman again anyway. If she did, she'd only see Catrina, not her lovely mama, and that would be far too scary and far too sad.

"Oh, I'm so glad I met you, Edith. It was meant to be, so you could bring me so close to Mama."

"All meetings are meant to be, Dorrie. No one is where they are by accident. Would you like to ask your mama something?"

All at once Dorrie's face clouded over. She was remembering Edith LeVeck's words of only moments before.

"But you said . . . you said you only see those spirits that are troubled. That can only mean . . ." She felt tears welling. "Th-That can only mean that Mama is troubled . . . that she's in a bad place on the Other Side."

"There are no bad places on the Other Side, Dorrie dear. Your mama is simply concerned for your welfare and that's why she's troubled. She says she wants to see you settled and happy. She wants nothing more than that you find peace here on the earthly plane."

Dorrie took a hanky from her handbag, unable to stop the tears. "I'm sorry," she said. "I must be such a disappointment to her."

"Your mama loves you, Dorrie. She was never disappointed in you. And don't feel ashamed of crying. Crying is not a sign of weakness. It's a sign that you've been strong for too long. It's time to let go."

"It's . . . it's just that I . . . I miss her so much. And I blame myself because if I . . ."

"I know. She's sorry she had to leave you so soon. But she says you must stop blaming yourself for what happened. It was not your fault. Everyone passes from this earthly plane at precisely the right moment. The length of time we get to spend here is preordained by God. We humans have no say in the matter. So you see, dear, you cannot take the blame for your mother's death. No one is to blame."

Dorrie mopped her tears, feeling a little better as she listened to the wise words and gentle voice of Mrs LeVeck.

"Tell me about her, dear. You were talking to her when we met, weren't you?"

Dorrie felt her cheeks grow hot.

"Oh, don't feel guilty. It's good to talk to those who've passed over. I talk to my late husband all the time."

"You do?"

"Yes, but I make sure I don't do it in public. People might think I was losing my mind, which mightn't be so surprising at my age."

She laughed and Dorrie laughed too. Edith offered the plate of cakes.

"Here, take one. I sense you haven't talked about your mama for a long time. Now might be the time to start."

Mrs LeVeck was right about that. Dorrie couldn't remember mentioning her mother to anyone throughout her whole adult life.

"You think it is?" she asked selecting another cake, uncertain. "It's just that . . . just that I'm afraid if I talk about her something terrible will befall me."

Edith shook her head. "No harm will come to you. Believe me. You must keep her memory alive. It strengthens the bond between you."

That sounded reasonable. She knew she could trust this woman, despite sitting in such weird surroundings with the skeleton Catrina looking on. If Mama could be in this room with the two of them it meant that she, Dorrie, was safe and in good hands too.

"I could never talk about Mama because I was too afraid," she began, not really wanting to touch on those memories she'd locked away for so long.

"And why was that, dear?"

"When . . . when I was little I was warned never to mention her or *he'd* . . ."

"It's all right, Dorrie. He's not here now. You're safe."

"Or he'd . . . he'd beat me. And lock me in a dark room." Dorrie broke down again. "After she died I'd call out for Mama, thinking she'd come back. I . . . I didn't understand death you see. Oh dear, I cried so very much. She was always there to protect me from him but then it was only him and me. One time I screamed out for Mama so much in the night I thought I'd die . . . a-and . . . h-he beat me so badly I never . . . never said the word 'Mama' again."

"Was there no one else to take care of you but him?"

Dorrie shook her head. "No . . . no one. His sister would come to clean the house, but sh-she was no better than him."

"You poor, poor thing," Edith said. "You suffered as a child, Dorrie, but you don't have to suffer now. You're an adult now. The past is over."

"That's so easy to say, Edith, but the past is never over. It haunts me everywhere I go. I . . . I try to get away from it but . . . but it follows me."

"Tell me about the good times . . . when it was just you and your mama?"

Dorrie brightened a little.

"Oh, she was so, so beautiful, Mama. She had hair like silk and skin like roses and cream. I loved it when it was just the two of us. She used to read me stories and tuck me in at night and play games with me. Best times we had were at the seaside. I loved looking at the waves, but I was too afraid to go in. Mama was never afraid. She loved swimming . . . was a very good swimmer. That's why, when . . ."

"Yes, when?" Edith coaxed.

"When he came along . . . he ruined everything." Dorrie wrung her hands in despair, face hardening with pain. "I *hate* him for what he did to Mama and me. *Really hate him.*" She got up suddenly. "I can't talk any more. I'm sorry. I really need to go now."

"So soon?"

She looked at her watch. "Yes. It's coming lunch-hour at the guest-house and I don't like being late."

Edith got up too. "As you wish, my dear."

She led her back down the dim hallway and unbolted the front door. "Perhaps you'll come again, now you know where I live."

"Y-Yes."

Dorrie stepped out into the cold daylight, taking in a welcome gulp of the fresh sea air.

"Yes, perhaps I will," she lied. "Thank you for the tea, Mrs LeVeck . . . I mean Edith."

Edith made no reply. Simply smiled her placid, enigmatic smile.

"Mind how you go, dear," she said, resting a hand on Dorrie's wrist again. "Be like the tree in winter, Dorrie. It sheds its leaves . . . lets go of the past. Be like the tree. Let go . . . make way for the new . . . make way for love. It's not as difficult as you suppose. You'll never experience the beauty of life until you let go of the hate you carry for your abuser. Don't let him win. He's taken enough away from you. Forgive him and set yourself free. God bless you now." With that she shut the door.

Dorrie practically ran from the house, more anxious than ever. She desperately needed to escape the panic building inside her.

She dashed down the promenade, looking wildly about her for the means to end this nightmare.

Then, at last, she saw it. A sign that read THE SAILOR'S ARMS.

Soon her troubles would be over. Soon she could forget everything.

She hurried towards the sign and the door of the public house. Once inside those walls she'd find the means of her release.

CHAPTER TWENTY-FOUR

Samaritan Centre, Killoran

Rita-Mae drew her car to a halt outside the Centre for her afternoon shift, wound-up and anxious. The sleeping pills from Dr Sweeney had given her the "death sleep" she'd craved, keeping the black thoughts well outside the pen. But come morning, when she opened her eyes, they were back, like a swarm of bats battering their black wings against her, berating, admonishing, chiding her relentlessly, making her heart thump more loudly and the blood drain from her face.

The notion that Bram Hilditch had been in the house while she was out was uppermost.

The electrician's date she'd forgotten. How had that happened? How could she have been so careless? When the notice arrived she'd pinned it in plain sight on the fridge door, *so she wouldn't forget.*

You needed the medication and you needed to see the doctor that morning, the little voice of reason called out to her, striving to be heard. But that voice was fading, disappearing like sand down an hourglass, leaving only the empty, clamorous noise of rebuke.

The oversight with the meter reading had opened another door, and through it she could see that Bram Hilditch had not simply admitted the electrician, written her the note and left. No, he'd climbed the stairs – for whatever reason – and entered the box-room.

Why?

This question, now flashing like a danger signal, demanded an answer.

The sound of a far-off siren brought her back to reality and, of a sudden, she was conscious of the fact that she was sitting outside the Samaritan Centre with her car engine still running. She switched it off, checked the time, saw that she still had a quarter of an hour to go, and went back to her thoughts.

On her return from the doctor she'd found a clue.

A glaring, unmistakable clue.

At the top of the stairs on the first tread: a piece of potpourri, a bright pink petal simply lying there.

The intruder had dumped the bowl of dried petals on the box-room floor.

I did not go into that room after the police left because I was too afraid, she told herself, therefore *I* did not track it out.

The cops did not track it out either because I would have seen it after they left.

I would have seen it because it was of such a bright colour.

And had I seen it, I'd have lifted it and disposed of it right away.

I know I'd have done that, because I like things to be clean and in order.

Therefore, Bram Hilditch was in that room.

He was in that room.

What must he be thinking now?

What must he be thinking of *me* now?

He must think I'm mad . . . that *I* wrecked the room in a fit of rage. That I'm not the person he thought I was.

But he can't ask me why outright because I would know he'd trespassed and then he'd lose face.

Oh God, what am I going to do?

She clasped her head, trying to stop the sludge of dark thoughts from pulling her under.

She tried not to weep. But the tears came anyway – the tears Harry hated so much to see. She couldn't afford to break down. Not now. Not here. Not when she needed to remain strong for all the dear souls who'd presently be calling her via the Samaritan helpline.

Desperately, she rummaged in her handbag for a pill to calm her nerves, found one and swallowed it down.

Thought briefly about just driving off. Not doing her duty at all. Perhaps no one would phone in, and her absence wouldn't be noticed. She could simply sign the register and leave. Nobody would be the wiser.

But she couldn't do that, no matter how much she wanted to. Her volunteer work was the only thing that made her feel useful in this frightening world.

And, even if she were to drive away, where would she go?

There was a little wood she'd noticed on the outskirts of the town. Maybe she'd go there and sit with the squirrels and the bird-song, forget all the terrible thoughts multiplying in her head like wort weed.

But inevitably she'd have to return to the house she'd thought was a haven. Back to the house that was tainted now, whether by young Ryan Glacken or the stalker.

Back to a house she no longer felt safe in.

The less time she spent there, the better.

She saw Vivian-Bernadette's letter in the drawer of the kitchen table. She saw the photographs the stalker had taken of her: the one that showed her combing her long tresses by the window of the box-room.

She wished now she'd never found that letter.

She wished she'd never opened it.

Curiosity killed the cat . . . but . . . but satisfaction brought it back.

She saw herself gather the pages together and shove them back in the drawer at the sound of Maud Gilhooley bobbing up her garden path that day.

Before . . . before . . . Maud was robbed and her budgie killed and her jewellery stolen . . . and . . . and before the awful Glackens had entered her life.

Oh, why did I have to go over there when I heard the sound of that football?

Why?

If . . . if I'd just ignored it and gone back into the house, none of this would have happened and I wouldn't be in this terrible mess now.

All at once, through the snarl of recrimination, the sound of a door opening.

She peeped through her fingers and saw Blossom Magee emerging from the Samaritan Centre in her hat and coat.

I don't want her to see me. Not now. She'll see I've been crying and I'll have to explain myself.

She tried to duck further behind the steering wheel.

She mopped her eyes and pretended to be fetching something from under the passenger seat.

Then: heels on paving, a tapping on the window and she was forced to look up.

There was Blossom's pleasant face, bright as a flower, at the glass.

She wound down the window.

"Hello, Rita! I thought it was you." A pause. "Are you all right, dear? You look upset."

"Er . . . erm . . . Blossom . . . no, j-just a touch of a cold. Makes my eyes water."

"I'm sorry. Maybe it's best you go inside then. I've set out the tea things for you and some more of those cupcakes you like."

"Y-Yes . . . maybe. Thanks, Blossom."

She got out of the car, thinking Mrs Magee would take the hint and leave her to it, but . . .

"I'm so glad I caught you, Rita," she said, dipping into her handbag. "Now, I brought this, like I promised. *The Life of Saint Catherine of Siena.*"

She passed her a booklet. On the cover was the image of a dolorous woman clutching a crucifix and a lily.

"That's very kind of you, Blossom! Thank you. I look forward to reading it."

"Oh, she was a wonderful woman, Saint Catherine. She spent her life giving to the poor and fasting." Blossom gazed up at the sky. "I do not want food. There is a table laid for me in heaven with my real family."

"Sorry?"

"Oh, not me, dear . . . that's what Saint Catherine used to say."

A few minutes later Rita-Mae was glad to be inside the Centre, having made her excuses to Blossom. The poor lady was under the impression that everyone believed in God as resolutely as she did. How could she know about the years of abuse that she, the Good Samaritan, had endured? A suffering so relentless that it had all but destroyed her faith in the Almighty.

She slipped the booklet into her pocket and hung up her coat, trying to focus on the work ahead.

There was something she'd forgotten to do at the end of her last shift: fill out a comment sheet for Viola – the thirteen-year-old who'd complained about being hit by her mother's new boyfriend. The suicide of Kevin and the shock of the stalker calling her a *second* time that evening had overshadowed everything.

At the end of each shift members were required to record details of conversations they'd had with clients, so that other volunteers could cross-check their situation.

She went to the filing cabinet and pulled out the drawer to its fullest extent, going right to the back section. The folders in that part were thin, due to the rarity of first names beginning with the final letters of the alphabet.

In the folder marked V there were only a few entries. The first was marked VALERIE, the second one VINCENT. No sign of Viola. It must have been her first call. She'd have to start a new report.

But just as she was about to shut the folder she saw there was another set of notes inside a plastic pocket.

She drew them out.

It took her a while to appreciate what she was staring at. What was making her feel so faint she wanted to drop the papers, get in her car and go.

Across the top, a date written in green ink: *12 July 1985*, and underneath it, a name weighted with so much portent it made her shudder.

Vivian-B.

CHAPTER
TWENTY-FIVE

Bram was heartened to see the lounge of the Royal Hotel deserted. At that hour, just after two, with the luncheon guests seen off and a lull before afternoon tea, it was the perfect time to be alone with his thoughts.

He made his way to a club chair by the window, having ordered an uncharacteristic Coffee Royale. Felt he needed that shot of brandy, given what he'd discovered in the box-room.

The view through the ceiling-high windows was a sight to behold – soft swathes of green outspread like velvet, flowing and eddying into rockeries of brightly coloured blooms. He always liked to sit in that chair and contemplate whenever his mind was troubled. Since the discovery of Maud's jewellery box in Miss Ruttle's possession – not to mention the issue of his mother's health – his mind was very troubled indeed.

He noted a slight breeze teasing clumps of cat's foot in the nearest rockery bed. They resembled invisible fingers sifting amongst the shrubbery, in search of something.

The image of Rita Ruttle searching through her next-door neighbour's china cabinet, finding the jewellery box and stealing it was something he found very hard to accept – so hard in fact that it had kept him awake for most of the night. He'd have to confront her with the evidence. He dreaded having to do that. But there really was no other way around the matter.

The waitress interrupted and set down the coffee.

"Always nice to see you, Mr Hilditch!" she said.

"Thank you, Millie. This is not a leisure break, alas." He tapped his camera bag, which sat on the adjacent chair, to quell her curiosity. "It's work related, you understand."

"Of course." She smiled. "Your mother won't be joining you then?"

"No, not today."

He knew his single status and financial standing in the community put him in the category marked "eligible bachelor" and so made him an object of interest. But Millie was half his age, with a rather pushy mother who couldn't wait to get her married off. At least with Her Grace in tow the waitress would never have had the nerve to be so forward.

He picked up his newspaper to give her a hint.

"Well, if you need anything else just say, Mr Hilditch."

"I will indeed, Millie."

The front page of the paper was dominated by a shocking photograph. It showed a dead man lying by the roadside, hands tied behind his back, head covered by a black binbag. Above it ran the headline: **IRA CLAIM RESPONSIBILITY FOR "INFORMER'S" MURDER.**

Bram sighed heavily. The Irish Republican Army. Would the horrors wreaked by that terrorist organization ever end? Fortunately, Killoran had been spared much of the bombing and shooting that had been engulfing the province since the early seventies. But there was a family – the Glackens – living not far from Willow Close, who had IRA affiliations. He'd never had dealings with them and hoped things would remain that way.

When he knew the waitress was out of sight he cast the paper aside, not wanting to be further depressed, and checked his watch.

Blossom Magee would now be seeing to Octavia. He was apprehensive about what lay in store for that kind lady and equally what was in store for *him* when he got home. But he'd no plans for returning just yet. Blossom said she'd be there for at least a couple of hours.

He pondered the doctor's words now, delivered well out of earshot of the patient when he'd made the house call.

"It's not just the fall I'm concerned about," he'd said, as they returned downstairs. "That bluish colour, together with the numbness she says she's feeling, would indicate the onset of PAD – Peripheral Arterial Disease."

"Is that serious?"

"Yes, for a woman of advanced years like your mother the risk of heart attack and stroke is considerably higher, due to the likelihood of blood-clots. Not to mention the possibility of gangrene. I'm prescribing anti-clotting medication and digoxin to regulate the heart, but she needs to take extra care. You'll have to get her to exercise more and drink less."

Easier said than done, Bram thought, taking another sip of his Coffee Royale. His mother rarely listened to anyone. Had already dismissed the new locum as "far too young and inexperienced to speak with authority on medical matters. Ink barely dry on his degree no doubt." Exercise of any kind was abhorrent to her. Walking to and from the car was the extent of her physical exertions in the course of any given day. As for relinquishing her "magic hour", that was as likely as her scaling Mount Everest any time soon.

His thoughts turned again to 8 Willow Close as he tried to come to terms with the fact that he was having trouble for the second time with a tenant residing there. Was there a hex on the place? It had belonged to a Mr Henderson, a respectable elderly gentleman and former accountant, who'd gone to live with his son in Scotland. Not likely that Mr Henderson had encountered much trouble while there. He was a chipper fellow, who'd been very sad to have to sell it and move elsewhere.

Then: "Gad, George, maybe I'll ask them to do eggs Benedict tomorrow," he heard a woman exclaim in a throaty American accent. "That toast they serve is goddamn awful!"

He turned to see a couple entering the lounge – casually attired, proprietorial air.

"Honey, you're on vacation," the man replied. "We gotta go native. That's the charm of this part of the ol' country."

Bram decided he'd make a move. He drained the last of his coffee and got up.

"Hope we ain't scaring you off," the woman said, sitting down at a table near him, waving a gold cigarette case. She was wearing a neon-pink trouser suit, matching ballerina pumps, and more glitter than a Christmas tree.

"Vulgar" was what Her Grace might have termed her.

"No, on the contrary, I was just going," Bram said politely, trying to avoid the sight of her igniting a cigarette the length of a knitting needle and releasing puffs of vile smoke into the room. "Now you can have this beautiful view all to yourself."

"The view, hah!" she said dismissively.

He took his leave.

"What a quaint little guy," he heard her squawk to her husband.

"Lower the tone a bit, Verna," the husband said – and Bram mused that the wife's brashness in the modest hotel lounge had most certainly done that already.

He left them to it, focusing on the disagreeable task that lay ahead of him: confronting Rita Ruttle with the theft of Maud Gilhooley's jewellery case.

It was certainly not going to be an easy encounter.

CHAPTER
TWENTY-SIX

Samaritan Centre, Killoran

Rita-Mae sat transfixed by the discovery of the folder.

Vivian-B.

Vivian-Bernadette!

With a name like that, it *had* to be the former tenant of 8 Willow Close.

Her story lay right there at her fingertips. Her truth. And now Rita-Mae was privy to that truth – to the innermost secrets of what had gone on in the house she now occupied. The facts the locals wanted to keep from her and which Bram Hilditch wished would remain hidden.

Could she afford to know them?

Curiosity killed the cat . . .

It was the second time in an hour that the saying had run through her head. Inquisitiveness can lead to dangerous situations. Isn't that what it meant?

I'm being warned, she thought.

But satisfaction brought it back.

The latter part of the adage – being forewarned is forearmed – that's what it meant too.

The satisfaction of knowing what happened to Vivian-Bernadette would arm her against further assault; would let her know who the *real enemy* was. Would let her know that, perhaps, returning to Larne was preferable to being . . . to being . . .

She shut the filing cabinet and, whether for good or ill, carried the folder into the phone cubicle.

She'd read it between calls. That way, if Blossom were to reappear – she lived only a few doors down, so it was always a possibility – she'd have time to conceal it.

DATE: 12/7/85
FIRST CALL: DURATION: FIVE MINUTES APPROX.

VIVIAN-B – SAYS THAT'S HER BIRTH NAME. THE B STANDS FOR BERNADETTE.

It *was* her.

20 YEARS OLD.
RECENTLY MOVED FROM SLIGO. IS RENTING SOME-WHERE IN THE AREA. FRIGHTENED OF LIVING ALONE, HENCE THE CALL TO US. WHEN I ASKED WHY SHE'D MOVED HERE, SHE SAID SOMETHING ABOUT BEING "BAN-ISHED" (HER WORD) FROM THE FAMILY HOME BY HER FATHER. SHE WOULD NOT SAY WHY, ONLY THAT SHE HAD TO ATONE FOR HER SINS THROUGH FASTING AND PRAYER.

Rita-Mae thought back to Blossom's words: *Oh, she was a wonderful woman, Saint Catherine. She spent her life giving to the poor and fasting.* And the pages of lines Vivian-Bernadette had written.

I must follow in the footsteps of Catherine of Siena.

Had Blossom given Vivian-Bernadette a booklet too? Perturbed, she went back to the notes.

SHE TRAVELLED HERE BY BUS WITH AN AUNT. SAYS THE AUNT GAVE HER MONEY TO LIVE ON BUT NOT MUCH. THE AUNT PAID THE LANDLORD AND WENT BACK TO SLIGO. SHE WAS UPSET BECAUSE WHEN THE LITTLE MONEY SHE WAS GIVEN RUNS OUT SHE DOESN'T KNOW WHAT SHE'LL DO.

I TOLD HER WE WOULD HELP AND ASKED HER TO CALL IN AT THE CENTRE FOR A CHAT. SHE HUNG UP.

SUICIDAL: NO – WHEN ASKED THE QUESTION SHE SAID THAT SUICIDE WAS A SIN AND SHE WOULD NEVER TAKE HER OWN LIFE NO MATTER HOW DESPERATE THINGS BECAME.

SIGNED: LINDA.

She eyed the phone. Hoped it wouldn't ring. Turned to the next entry.

DATE: 23/7/85

DURATION: 1 MINUTE APPROX.

WHEN SHE HEARD MY VOICE SHE ASKED TO SPEAK WITH A WOMAN. I TOLD HER THERE WERE NO WOMEN ON DUTY. SHE BECAME AGITATED. I TOLD HER THE TIMES LINDA WAS ON DUTY. SHE AGREED SHE WOULD CALL BACK.

SIGNED, HENRY

Date: 15/8/85

Duration: 10 minutes approx.

Very agitated. Said she was being watched. Feels someone is following her. She mentioned a "reliquary" (her word), a box that she keeps her rosary beads, medals and novena tracts in, had been disturbed. Felt someone had been going through it when she got back from the shop.

Ryan Glacken came to mind. Had *he* been in, disturbing her stuff? She thought of the small top window in the toilet downstairs: so small, she sometimes left it open just a crack. But a little boy of his build could easily climb up and wriggle through it. She saw again the boy chortling, the face of his frightful mother twisted in scorn, and wondered how a woman such as she could be so heartless and cruel to complete strangers simply trying to live in peace.

I tried to reason with her, that she might have upset it herself without thinking . . . that we all can be forgetful at times, but she wouldn't accept that. She says she is very anxious and can't sleep. Then says, it is "the cross she has to bear for her great sin."

When pressed about the nature of the sin, she says she can never tell anyone. Only the priest in the confessional knows and her father, her aunt and God. She says she is praying and fasting to atone for it and when the time comes, only God will know what to do.

SHE SEEMS DELUSIONAL AND IN A FRAGILE STATE. I PRESSED HER TO TELL ME WHERE SHE LIVES, BUT SHE WOULD NOT SAY.

SHE ENDED THE CALL BY SAYING SHE WAS TOO TIRED TO TALK ANY MORE.

SIGNED: LINDA

There was just one more entry.

DATE: 28/9/85

DURATION: 20 MINUTES.

SEEMED CALMER ON THIS OCCASION BUT VERY TIRED. SAID SHE'D MADE A DECISION THAT WOULD END ALL HER SUFFERING, BUT ASSURED ME IT WAS NOT SUICIDE. TOLD ME HE'D LEFT A DEAD BIRD ON THE DOORSTEP . . .

Dead bird! The words jumped out at her. Maud's dead bird. Madden's dead bird in the grating.

She forced herself back to the page.

. . . THIS PERSON SHE TALKED OF BEFORE, THE ONE WATCHING HER EVERY MOVE. ACCORDING TO HER, THE DEAD BIRD IS A BAD OMEN. A WARNING THAT THIS PERSON'S PLANNING TO KILL HER OR "INVADE" HER (HER WORD). WHEN I ASKED HER WHAT SHE MEANT, SHE WOULDN'T SAY. I TOLD HER SHE MUST RING THE POLICE, BUT SHE SAID HER RELIGION FORBIDS HER TO SPEAK TO STRANGE MEN AND ANYWAY, SHE DOESN'T TRUST THEM BECAUSE THEY'RE PROTESTANT.

SHE HAS LOCKED HERSELF IN AND DRAWN ALL THE
BLINDS. SAYS SHE HAS SOME FOOD THAT WILL LAST AND
THAT GOD WILL PROVIDE FOR ALL HER NEEDS. SHE
QUOTES SCRIPTURE. SEEMS OBSESSED WITH A SAINT
CALLED CATHERINE. SAYS THAT SHE'S THE PATRON
SAINT AGAINST BODILY ILLS AND SEXUAL TEMPTATION
AND SHE PRAYS CONSTANTLY TO BE GUIDED BY HER.

I FEAR FOR HER SAFETY AND ASKED FOR HER NUM-
BER, WHICH SHE GAVE AFTER SOME PERSUADING.

Rita-Mae stared at the phone number, which was now *hers*: 082
423586. She was about to shut the folder when she noticed PTO written
in the bottom corner. She turned the page over.

FORGOT TO SAY, SHE TALKED ABOUT A LITTLE
BOY WHO THROWS STONES INTO HER BACK GARDEN
AND CALLS HER NAMES – "NUTTER", "SCREWBALL".
I THOUGHT THIS WAS ANOTHER DELUSION OF HERS,
BUT SHE WAS QUITE ADAMANT THAT HE LIVED ACROSS
THE WAY WITH HIS MOTHER AND SHE'D TRIED TO TALK
TO HIM ON SEVERAL OCCASIONS. SAID HIS NAME WAS
RYAN. WORTH LOOKING INTO I THINK. THERE CAN'T
BE TOO MANY RYANS IN THE LOCAL SCHOOL.

Her hands shook.
She shut the folder, unable to breathe.
Stared down at the phone and willed it *not* to ring.

CHAPTER
TWENTY-SEVEN

Sleep would not come for Rita. The discovery of the notes concerning Vivian-Bernadette at the Samaritan Centre and the knowledge that she'd likewise been harassed by the Glacken boy were opening up another kind of pain. She dreaded what might lie ahead of her.

She felt powerless to extricate herself from the present danger, a danger that was unclear and unpredictable. Better, she thought, to go back to the past. She could fathom the past, the past that was as real as yesterday, the past where Harry reigned supreme and she knew the rules so well.

Although she turned over in her bed in Willow Close, in her thoughts she was coming-to in a hospital bed. To learn of the horror of her greatest loss . . .

Harry was holding her hand. A nurse was hovering somewhere out of sight.

She couldn't remember a thing.

"You fell down the stairs and we lost it, Rita," Harry said, tears in his eyes.

It?

"Aye, we lost the baby."

She tried to form a word but her mouth wouldn't work. There was something stretched around her head, something holding together the scaffolding of her face – a broken face that no longer felt like hers.

"Don't try to talk, love. It's best just to rest."

He squeezed her hand more tightly. "Yeh need to stay in hospital a few days, that's all. I brought yeh flowers. See?"

She moved her head carefully and saw red roses, like so many wounded hearts, crammed into a vase on the bedside table.

Blood.

She remembered blood . . . the bitter tang of it in her mouth. An image swift and brutal in her head: the pair of them at the top of the stairs, his boot in her back, her arm flung wide then crashing down, the floor coming up to meet her.

Oblivion.

The baby!

Her baby!

Memories surging back.

She tried to free her hand, but he gripped it tighter still. She tried to move away from him, but her bones locked, her whole body useless with pain. Tears were the only words she had and they slid freely down her cheeks. Tears for the baby that would never be, cast out so cruelly by the murderer beside her, his hand on hers, his breath in hers.

The nurse hove into view, whey-faced and smiling.

"Just wasn't to be, Mrs Ruttle," she said, dabbing at her tears. "It's a terrible thing, a miscarriage. But sure you're young. You can always try again."

She wanted to howl, to rend the air with such screams she'd wake up the whole world and send *him* and the pale nurse and all the nurses and doctors and patients tumbling into the abyss. But she stayed quiet. Shut her eyes and prayed that death might take her.

◆　◆　◆

After she lost the baby Harry changed.

Back home, he helped her heal, became a proper carer and wept so hard she felt sorry for *him*. He begged forgiveness for all the pain he'd caused her. Said it wasn't right and from then on he'd be a better man.

He kept his word too. Took time off from work to be a house-husband while she recovered.

Pre-honeymoon Harry was back. Shattered Rita-Mae returned to herself. Found her smile and feet again, but her right knee hurt every time she walked, and the arm that broke her fall would ache every time she combed her hair. But they were a small price to pay for the peace that prevailed. The blessed peace she'd known so briefly in the past but which maybe, just maybe, might last.

That summer he took her on a long weekend to Donegal – to a little hotel on the west coast amongst the hills and the heather, where the ocean met the sky and oddlings waved at them as they strolled the foot-worn roads. He held her hand and bought her gifts, told her she looked nice. And she dared gaze into a better future. But, in time, that thought would come back to mock her, throwing up its hands and laughing like a harlequin.

She still laid out the receipts every day for him on his return from work, and he still inspected them, each and every one. He still kept a knife under the bed and told her what to wear and asked whom she'd spoken to at the shops, noting down their names so he could cross-check. And he still inspected the phone bill, looking for numbers she might have called.

But she could cope with that, so long as he didn't hit her.

For a time, this new situation held.

But a niggling voice kept telling her that this new incarnation of Harry's was covering something deeper. Something he didn't wish her to know. The signs were there. The trace of perfume on his shirt. The stray long hair, fair and silken, on his lapel. Out late every Wednesday night and Friday night, and not forcing himself upon her as much.

"Who's Patricia?" she asked one evening at the supper table, feeling brave. She'd found a telephone number in his pocket with the name.

He didn't look up immediately from the plate.

"What?" he said into the food, fork poised.

"I found her phone number in your trouser-pocket when I was clearing them out for the wash."

"New girl in the office."

"You didn't mention her before."

"Why should I? None of yer damned business."

Well, it *was* her damned business. He'd killed her baby. Now he was using her as his slave to cook and wash while he cheated on her with another woman. No, *he would not do that to her.*

He'd done enough.

She'd had enough.

"Well, it *is* my business if you're having an affair."

He threw the cutlery down. Stood up. Fists clenched for combat.

"Aye, and what's it to you? What are yeh gonna do about it, eh?"

The air bristled.

She didn't answer him. Stiffened herself against the assault, but didn't move from the chair. Didn't cower or run upstairs like she'd always done. After this beating she'd call the police, something she'd never dared do before, and they'd see the bruises and the blood, haul him in and charge him with assault and she'd be free.

But he didn't attack her. She was convinced he could read her mind. Could see her plan. Always one step ahead of her was Harry.

The moment passed.

He backed down.

"I'm outta here," he spat, grabbing his coat. "Tricia's more of a woman than you'll ever be . . . whingeing, nagging bitch."

In the aftermath, she sat staring out of the window as he got in the car and tore off. She was feeling jubilant and exhilarated. She'd challenged him. He'd admitted to the affair. One small victory in the war against him. Now it was time to fight back in earnest.

On the window-sill sat a model ship – RMS Titanic Olympic Class 1912 printed on the plinth. Every sill in the house had a replica of an oceangoing vessel he'd constructed over many painstaking hours.

Harry's favourite pastime, carried through from boyhood.

He'd amassed quite a collection throughout the years.

She studied the workmanship of the miniature *Titanic*, marvelling at how gentle-fingered he was for a man who used so much brute force against her. The intricate details of the funnels and decks, the mastheads and lifeboats demanded the most delicate touch.

Upstairs, the small back-room was given over to his workshop. She wasn't allowed to touch anything, and when she cleaned in there, had to be very, very careful. Lifting and replacing hundreds of tiny pieces to clean underneath them took a good hour, week in, week out.

She knew what she had to do.

She went to the garden shed and found a hammer.

His prized *Titanic*, sitting there so proudly, was the first to go, falling to pieces exquisitely under the first blow. Afterwards she progressed from room to room, pulverizing his many specimens of craftsmanship that crowded the window-sills: British Navy Q-Ship Hunter, gone. Dutch Golden Yacht, gone. Mayflower English Galleon, gone. Chinese Pirate Junk, gone.

On and on and on she went, taking revenge the only way she knew. Making up for all the suffering – a tidal wave of hatred gushing through the hammer-head, pulping the very essence of the traitorous, brutal, uncompromising, inflexible, evil, lying, cheating, impossible-to-live-with man she thought she once loved.

Lastly, she opened the door to his workshop.

In a glass case he kept his special collection of model warships. She turned the key and lifted out the ancient vessels with their frail white sails and beautiful shining timbers. Oh so elaborate and ornate in design! So cherished they needed a special cabinet all to themselves to keep the dust away.

Pity.

HMS *Unicorn* gone, splinters flying everywhere. Then *Victory*, *Resolution*, *Neptune* and *Moth*. My, did it feel good!

She smashed them all. Swept the debris into a bin. Kicked over his workbench. Slammed the door on the chaos.

Her arm aching, energy spent, she finally threw the hammer down. Carried the bin of fragments down the stairs and scattered the contents over the hallway floor.

Returned to the supper table, calmly poured herself another cup of tea and sat waiting in the darkness.

Ready and waiting with a flick-knife in her pocket and murder on her mind.

Harry's car arrived back at 2 a.m., the headlights gliding through the kitchen like an oil spill on the walls.

Rita remained immobile, ears pricked for every sound he made. Sitting upright at the table, feeling the weapon in her pocket – the smooth horn handle resting so snugly in her palm.

She heard the car door open.

Heard his feet striking the gravel.

The key turning in the front door.

His shoes crunching over the rubble of her wrecking spree.

"What the *fuck*?"

The light went on.

She'd left the door to the kitchen ajar. From her vantage point she could see him standing there, staring down.

Hunkering down.

Then: "Oh, *Jesus Christ*!" he moaned, falling on his knees, scooping up the pieces in his hands.

He would never guess she was still up. Normally she'd be in bed, cowering under the covers, waiting, wondering what kind of mood he'd be in. What kind of vileness she'd have to suffer.

She drew the knife from her pocket under cover of the table, but did not move. Released the blade.

"Harry," she said softly.

He swung his head in her direction, startled.

"What's the matter now, Harry?" Her tone was mock-bullying. "Did somebody break your toys?"

"Yeh *bitch*, yeh *fuckin' crazy bitch!*"

He was on his feet, lunging at her.

She shot up, brandishing the knife.

He halted.

"Come another inch and I'll kill you."

She held it out in front of her, poised for combat. "I'll kill you and gladly go to prison for it. 'Cos y'know what, Harry? Since marrying you I've *been* in a damned prison."

He made a grab for the knife, missed and crashed against the table, sending the tea-things flying.

She rushed him, thrusting at his chest, but he seized her wrist and they both collapsed on the floor.

"Drop that fuckin' knife!" he roared, holding fast to her wrist.

But she was on top of him, blade trembling perilously, just inches from his throat. Here was her chance.

"Now it's your turn, you cheating, lying bastard!"

With all her might, she forced the blade down. Saw the tip making contact with his flesh.

Blood trickled out.

"Arrr . . . agh!"

He tightened his grip on her wrist, crushing it and causing her to scream. She tried to drive the knife deeper, but he bit hard into her free arm and the weapon slipped from her grasp, lying just out of reach.

She fell to the floor, desperately straining to retrieve it. But Harry was on top, straddling her. He flipped her over.

She yelled for her life as he clasped her head in both hands, shaking it savagely.

"You'll never fuckin' try that again! Yeh hear me?"

He smashed her head against the floor.

She passed out.

She came to, lying in the garden shed. Somewhere outside a light was flashing, sending its blue rays across the darkened timbers of the ceiling.

A walkie-talkie squawked somewhere. People talking.

Men's voices.

She tried to get up but a pain shot through her, so blinding that she went limp again.

The voices were getting closer.

"She's in here." Harry's voice.

The bolt on the shed door was drawn back.

She shut her eyes.

The door creaked open.

They entered on a cold rush of air.

"Aye, I had to put her in here for her own safety, Doctor," Harry said. "As I say, she was trying to kill me."

The touch of fingers on her wrist, feeling for a pulse. A man's touch, soft and gentle.

"Rita . . . can you hear me, Rita?" he said. She got the smell of antiseptic – a hospital smell.

She was too afraid to answer. Felt it was safer that way.

"As I say, she knocked herself out when she fell. I was trying to take the knife off her."

"Hmm . . ."

Her eyelids were pulled up and a light shone into each one.

She heard the doctor stand up.

"She needs to go to the hospital right away."

"Why?" Harry said. "Is it serious?"

"She's badly concussed. There could be bleeding on the brain."

Memories of those initial days in the hospital were hazy.

She lost track of time, slept a lot. Sometimes she saw the sun at the window, sometimes the moon. The medication they were giving her induced long periods of slumber. Which perhaps was just as well.

Once, after admission, she awoke suddenly, her whole body in spasm, as if some callous deity was standing there, striking her down with sudden paralysis for the grave sin of having tried to kill Harry.

They increased the painkillers and she didn't suffer one again.

Harry played the caring husband, as before. Visiting every day, holding her hand, the gifts of flowers multiplying on the bedside table and window-sill.

She was in a room by herself, with an en-suite bathroom, which she was grateful for, but wondered why she'd been afforded the privilege.

Did it mean she was very ill?

Did it mean she was going to die?

Did it mean she was a danger to others?

"Wish my husband was as attentive as yours, Mrs Ruttle," a nurse commented one evening, tucking in the sheets and plumping her pillows before lights out. "Take a lot for him to buy *me* flowers. Every birthday and anniversary I have to give him a nudge."

The patient gave a weak smile.

"Nurse, how much longer will I stay here?"

"Oh, only a few more weeks."

"*Weeks!*"

"Yes, the doctor will tell you on his rounds in the morning."

The nurse checked the IV bag. Injected more solution into the drip chamber.

"What's that for?"

"It'll help with the pain. Now, I'll just strap you in."

"Strap?" A fret of panic ran through her. "What strap? Why are you doing that?"

"Now, now, Mrs Ruttle, don't upset yourself. It's for your own safety. We don't want you to fall."

At sight of the two sturdy straps being secured over her arms she started to scream.

"What is this place? Where the hell am I?"

She thrashed her leg up and down, yelling at the top of her voice: "Let me out of here! Let me out!"

The door flew open and a man entered, bearing down upon her, pinning her to the bed.

"I *told* you nurse; don't do the straps up until she's asleep."

Through her screams she felt the sudden stab of a needle in her hip. Her body flopped back on to the bed.

In seconds all was calm again. Someone switched off the lights.

And she was left to the numbing darkness of another night.

CHAPTER
TWENTY-EIGHT

Portaluce, Antrim Coast

Back behind the door of room number 5, Dorinda Walsh threw the bolt and turned the key. She was glad she'd made it to the Ocean Spray and up the stairs without being seen. Mrs Millman wouldn't have registered her return. When she tiptoed past the dining-room an animated exchange over clinking glasses had told her that the proprietor had company. Male company.

"Gladys Millman, you're incorrigible. And it the Lord's Day."

"Oh, Victor dear, I only drink champagne on two occasions: when I'm happy and when I'm sad."

Dorrie stood against the bedroom door, still enveloped in the fox fur, feeling faint. She'd stolen up the stairs with the stealth of a Persian blue and the effort had drained her. She might have escaped the house of Edith LeVeck, but she now had a desperate need to escape the torturous memories the strange woman of "discernment" had unwittingly dredged up.

It's all right, Dorrie. You're safe now. Listen to the silence.

"Yes, Mama. I know."

She held her breath and listened.

All was quiet. Then a thought struck her.

The raincoat.

Had the maid been in?

Uneasy, she let her eyes drift slowly about the room.

Yes, Maureen had been in. The bed-covers were smoothed, pillows plumped. A set of fresh towels sat folded on the washstand.

She grabbed a chair, crossed to the closet and climbed up.

The trench coat was still in place, just as she'd left it. She decided to leave it up there. Couldn't bear to look at it again. Tomorrow morning she'd be departing and would see to it then.

Settle down now and have a drink, Dorrie. Mama's voice. Oh, dear sweet Mama, always ready to reassure and comfort in times of need. Where would she be without her? *There is nothing to worry about. You've earned it after all.*

The tension in her body eased immediately. Yes, she certainly had earned a drink or two after that courageous foray into the outside world. A sense of relief swept over her when she realized she was safely back, away from all those prying eyes.

It was approaching 2 p.m. Had she been absent for so long?

With reluctance she shed the coat and laid it carefully over the chair, sat down on the bed and opened her handbag. Wedged inside was the only purchase she'd made: a ten-glass bottle of whiskey.

The transaction had been awkward and her stomach tightened at the memory of it. Sunday, no bars open, but she'd tried her luck at the back-door of the Sailor's Arms, and was surprised when a man appeared and swiftly admitted her.

"I suppose it's for your grandma who's come down with the flu," he said sarcastically, gangstery face all glassed over with bifocals.

An old woman in a baggy coat and cracked shoes leaning against the counter sniggered. "A wee drop of the grog'll do you the world of good, daughter. Just visitin', are you?"

"Yes, just visiting."

"Odd time of the year tae be comin' here."

She heard them titter as she pulled the door shut.

I should never have gone out, she thought now, pouring a generous measure of whiskey and gulping it down. But the bottle of spirits was well worth the inconvenience.

The outside world was far too scary; too many strangers probing her with reproachful eyes. She saw their faces staring out at her like criminals in a police identity parade: the pensioner with the outsize hearing aid, the fraught mother pushing the baby, the gaunt man in the trilby with the little girl. Edith LeVeck in her black clothes. The grinning skull of the skeleton lady, Catrina. Were they ghosts, all of them? Ghosts she'd conjured up to shadow and menace her for all eternity because she'd done something terrible?

She bent down and removed her shoes, poured herself another full glass of whiskey and sat back on the pillows. No, she would not be leaving the room again. Not until tomorrow morning when the car was roadworthy.

Several glasses later the turbulent sea of inhibitions and worry she'd been riding since waking up began to steady. Soon she was floating up, up and away into the endless sky above the clouds, where Mama dwelt in a land that was full of happiness and light. Oh, how she wished she could join her up there!

The lyrics of a song came to her and she began to sing.

I'm a single girl trying to live the single life,
I'm a single girl who's got no wish to be somebody's wife,
Not unless I meet the right kind of man,
Who'll give me all the love that he can.

Her eyelids grew heavy and her vision faded. With "other" eyes she found herself gazing upon a scene: a beach scene. There was a little girl kneeling on a rug, digging into the sand with a yellow plastic spade. It was a windless summer's day and the searing hand of the sun was pressing down on her back, the rough fabric of the rug chafing her knees. Filling the bucket was an endless task. There was so much sand, and the little spade trembled under the weight of each golden heap.

A woman was lying beside her in sunglasses and a bright red swimsuit, milky arms spread wide, hair spilling like honey over the towel.

"Aren't you going in?" a male voice intruded. "Not much point in coming to the sea just to lie beside it."

The voice belonged to a man who was sitting half in, half out of the passenger seat of a black car, one foot resting on the sill, the suspenders of his grey socks showing. He had a glass of whiskey in one hand and a lit cigarette in the other.

"All in good time, Jack," the woman answered. "All in good time. Let me soak up this heavenly sun first."

"Did we have to bring *her* along?"

The little girl felt scared. She wanted to run away from the man called Jack and hide. But the beach went on and on; the sand dunes seemed so very far away.

"Well, of course. I could hardly leave her alone in the house. Now don't be beastly! She's only a child."

"She's in the way."

"In the way of what?"

"Of *us*. What d'you think?"

Tears pricked the little girl's eyes, but she must not let the adults see her sadness. It was dangerous to be sad when Uncle Jack was around. And he was around more often these days; now in their home at night in her mother's bedroom, and in the morning at the breakfast table in pyjamas, his hair in disarray.

She put the spade down and moved into the protective curve of her mother's arm.

"You mollycoddle her like she's a baby."

"She *is* a baby."

"She's six, for God's sake."

"Oh, stop complaining, Jack. Can't you just enjoy being here?"

"Go in and have your bloody swim. You've got a customer at three, remember? It's why I drove you here, for Christ's sake. For if you don't I'll—"

Darkness fell . . .

Dorrie slid down on the bed. Dead to the outside world, she was pushing further and further into a past that could only be accessed through the dream state . . .

Back on the beach the child became conscious that her mother was no longer beside her on the rug, but standing by the water's edge, staring out to sea.

She dropped the spade and ran to her, slipping her hand into hers. The feel of her mother's hand was reassuring, along with the silky touch of the little waves tickling her toes.

She gazed up at her, shading her eyes. There was something different about her. The long, flowing hair was all gone and her head was covered in the most beautiful flowers – daisies, blue and yellow daisies – all growing out of a tight white cap. It was the prettiest sight she'd ever seen.

Her mother bent down to her.

"Now, sweetie, I'm going for a little swim, but you can't come with me. Go back and stay on the rug with Uncle Jack. I won't be long. There's a good girl."

"But I don't *want* to stay with Uncle Jack. I want to stay with *you*."

The mother gripped her shoulders and pulled her close, the red lips a sudden pout of pain in her lovely face.

221

"Now *stop* that at once! Don't be a crybaby. Go sit on the rug with Jack, there's a good girl. I won't be long."

The sea yowled.

The gulls keened.

In the pit of the child's stomach something dark and dangerous twisted into life. She tried her best not to weep. Dug her heels deeper into the sand. Clenched her tiny fists. Refused to budge.

"I *said*, go sit on the rug with Jack. I won't be long."

Without warning, hands were lifting her. Big hands grasping her about the waist. She kicked wildly to get away from them.

"Be careful with her!" the mother called out.

But the more the child screamed and kicked the tighter and more painful Uncle Jack's grip became.

"You're a pesky little bitch!" he spat, dumping her back on the rug.

She tried to sit up. Saw her mother cleaving the waves, pale arms plunging in and out of the water. She screamed, but a boot on her chest took her breath away and forced her back down again.

He bent over her, the pressure of his boot increasing. "If you move from there I'll knock your feckin' brains out. D'you *hear* me?"

Terrified, she nodded vigorously.

"Understand me?"

"What *on earth* are you doing to that child?" From somewhere above: a female voice, sudden and strident.

The foot was swiftly lifted. The terrified child turned to see a woman, dressed in dark blue robes, standing close by.

She saw Uncle Jack raise his hat. "Good day to you, Sister. Didn't see you there."

"Obviously not."

"She was misbehavin'. You know how kids are."

The strange woman ignored him, hunkered down, her blue robes spilling over the rug like an ink stain. Gently she cradled the little girl in her arms and helped her sit up.

"Now, my child, are you all right?"

She had a kindly, soft face, framed in stiff white cloth, like the Queen of Diamonds in her mama's playing cards. The child gazed up at her, suddenly afraid. For the eyes were unsettling, the left one bright blue, the other much darker.

"Are you all right, little angel? I'm Sister Clare." She took a hanky from her sleeve. "Now, let's wipe away all of these muddy old tears, so we can see how pretty you are."

The little girl offered up her face, no longer scared of the woman in blue with the queer eyes. She sensed that, as long as she was near, Uncle Jack wouldn't touch her.

He'd moved away from them and was standing by the water's edge, looking out to sea, smoking another cigarette.

"There you are," Sister Clare soothed, her serious features softening into a sweet smile. "Now you're like a princess."

She returned the hanky to a fold in her robes, took the child's hand in hers.

"Now, I've got a little gift for you," she said, and put a small shiny object into her palm.

The child stared at it, eyes wide with wonder. "Is it a fairy?"

The nun leaned close and whispered. "No, dear, it's an angel . . . your guardian angel, and she'll protect you from all danger wherever you go. So don't be afraid. Here, put her in the pocket of your frock, so no one will know about her but you and me."

The little girl did as she was bidden.

"There, that's better. No more tears, my little one. I'll pray that God will keep you safe."

Without warning, she was on her feet, striding away in her laced-up boots and flapping robes, over to the spot where Uncle Jack was standing.

She said something to him then moved off swiftly.

He threw the cigarette down and caught up with her.

"What was that, Sister?"

She stopped abruptly, turned to face him.

"I *said:* this beach is my back-yard. From my cell window I see *everything.* You'd do well to remember that."

A frenetic rapping wrenched Dorrie out of the dream state.

"Ma'am, are you in there? Ma'am . . . ma'am, can you hear me?"

Her head felt like lead. She tried to lift it off the pillow but the effort was too much.

"Y-Yes . . . Who-who is it?"

"Maureen, ma'am. Breakfast's ready, ma'am."

Breakfast?

She turned and stared in disbelief at the clock. It was 8 a.m.

"I'll . . . I'll . . . be down in . . . in five minutes."

"All right, ma'am."

She heard the maid go down the stairs.

She shut her eyes, too afraid to sit up. Heard the rain rap its bony knuckles on the window, the sizzle of car tyres, the screeching of gulls.

Seaside.

Fragments came at her like snowflakes at a windscreen, some sticking, some spiralling off into blackness. Words, pictures, voices, pulling her back to consciousness:

Ocean

Jane

Edith . . . Edith LeVeck

"Lady of the Dead . . . death."

"Death is democratic."

"I could hardly leave her alone in the house."

Sailor's Arms

Millman

"You're a pesky little bitch!"

old man

"Be like the tree . . ."

"From my cell window I see *everything*. You'd do well to remember that."

coat . . . coat

COAT, blood . . .

BLOOD-STAINED RAINCOAT

She shot up, wide awake, heart pounding.

The room swam, floated, then steadied itself as complete conscious-ness returned.

She was still fully dressed.

The room was a mess: bedside table toppled, towels scattered, a red fur coat lying by the door and near it an empty whiskey bottle.

She staggered to the mirror, and nearly wept at the wreckage her drunken night had wrought: blotchy face, swollen eyelids, hair a mess.

It doesn't matter, Dorrie dear. Today you're leaving. Remember? Now get yourself downstairs and get your car. You need to get yourself out of here. Just go! Go with the flow, my dear.

"Yes, Mama, my car . . . yes, yes, *I must get my car*. Must get my car and leave."

Girded by this thought, she grabbed her handbag, flung the fur coat over her arm and left the room.

The stairs swayed as she negotiated her way down, step by careful step.

Nearing the last few treads, she heard a voice, high-pitched and sudden.

"Miss Walsh, there you are . . . *finally!*"

Gladys Millman was standing in front of her baroque desk, strik-ing an imperious pose in a dress of startling mauve and a look of acid reproof.

Dorrie wobbled, teetered, caught the balustrade to steady herself.

"Eh . . . oh, em . . . Mrs . . . Mrs Milkman . . . em . . ."

"*Mill*man . . . *Mill*man. Are you all right, Miss Walsh? You look unwell."

"Yes . . . yes, I'm . . . I'm . . . em . . . Y-Your coat."

She held out the fox fur, hoping the offering would divert attention and soothe matters a little. "Th-Thank you . . . for the loan. I . . . I . . ."

Of a sudden, Mrs Millman stepped forward.

The brisk movement gave Dorrie such a fright that she missed her footing and toppled. Her head struck the polished terrazzo with a sickening thud. Before passing out she was aware of a pair of mauve suede peep-toes and a voice raised in alarm.

"Oh, my heavens! Maureen, Maureen, come quickly! We have an *emergency*."

CHAPTER
TWENTY-NINE

Rita-Mae sat on a boulder under a linden tree in Crocus Wood on the edge of Killoran, trying to find peace. Better there, out in the middle of nowhere with the mist and rising sun, than inside number 8 with the secrets of its afflicted room.

All those bitter memories hauling her back there into her darkest days with Harry! Better to dwell on them than face the new threat: that she was occupying a house that had driven a young woman insane. And that she, Rita-Mae Ruttle, could very well be the next victim.

The boulder was part of a stone circle, a sacred relic from ancient times. They were all over Ireland, these circles, and perhaps she was committing a grave sin by actually sitting on one, but given her plight she didn't much care.

The beauty of the little spot was its location – far enough off the main road for her not to be bothered by the sound of traffic, isolated enough not to be discovered at that hour.

She'd had a restless night. Harry's assaults, a vivid montage mixed in with snatches from that Samaritan file on Vivian-B, prodding her awake at every turn.

SAID SHE WAS BEING WATCHED.

TOLD ME HE'D LEFT A DEAD BIRD ON THE DOORSTEP . . . A BAD OMEN.

Once in the night she could have sworn she'd heard a bird pecking at the window-pane. Got up to look, but the only thing that startled her was her own reflection – wan face and pale gown making a ghost of *her* in the glass.

There was no sign of a bird. But maybe it was the dead one come back to life. The one *he'd* left on the doorstep – the bad omen.

A magpie swooped down on the bracken near her – one for sorrow – and strutted about proudly as if it owned the place.

OBSESSED WITH A SAINT CALLED CATHERINE . . .

She took Blossom's booklet on St Catherine from her bag and flicked idly through it.

Each page was edged with little pink roses. A quotation in ornate script along the top.

PROCLAIM THE TRUTH, one read. DO NOT BE SILENT THROUGH FEAR.

She turned to another one:

START TO BE BRAVE ABOUT EVERYTHING. DRIVE OUT DARKNESS AND SPREAD LIGHT.

And yet another, longer this time:

WE'VE HAD ENOUGH EXHORTATIONS TO BE SILENT. CRY OUT WITH A HUNDRED THOUSAND TONGUES – I SEE THE WORLD IS ROTTEN BECAUSE OF SILENCE.

She stared at the last line. I SEE THE WORLD IS ROTTEN BECAUSE OF SILENCE.

All through her years of marriage she'd been silent. A silence that had brought her nothing but pain.

She heard her tormentor's voice: "If yeh tell anybody, I'll kill you. If you leave me, I'll kill you." With each threat she died a little more inside, until . . .

Until she'd finally had enough of those exhortations to be silent and made her escape. She couldn't fix Harry. He was a project, not a person – not a real person with empathy and understanding. But she could maybe, just maybe, fix herself. Make a life for herself without him.

The magpie moved closer, assertive on its bold black legs, bill probing the earth. She could easily have been just an outcrop of the stone she sat on, for all the notice it took of her.

At close quarters, its wings were a mesmerizing sweep of blues and greens, glossy and iridescent in the light. She felt like reaching out and stroking them.

A beautiful creature, yet so maligned – considered to be one of nature's villains.

All at once it flapped away, making her flinch. The booklet slipped to the ground. She picked it up, disappointed to see that one of the pages was soiled. Wiped away the detritus. Saw that it was the first quote she'd read.

PROCLAIM THE TRUTH. DO NOT BE SILENT THROUGH FEAR.

In her mind's eye she saw a little boy jeering:

Ma, Ma, that's the madwoman's house!

Close by him a woman:

You haven't seen the last of us, you screwball!

Thought again of the line in the case notes:

CALLS HER NAMES – "NUTTER", "SCREWBALL" . . . SAID HIS NAME WAS RYAN.

"No, they will not drive *me* out," she said aloud, seized suddenly by an audacious need, emboldened by the quote. "They drove one woman out or to her death, but not this one. I will not be silent. I will proclaim my truth to Bram Hilditch about the Glacken woman, and the sooner the better."

Her voice rang out in the silence, echoing through the glade.

The sky dimmed. A soft rain began to fall.

Perhaps it was time to go.

Crack . . . crack . . . crack.

What was that?

Something stirring . . .

Some*one* stirring?

She froze.

Someone, *behind* her, watching her. She could *feel* them, *him*. Her spine tingled. Her hand closed on the flick-knife in her pocket.

Yes, she'd come prepared.

She got up.

Slowly turned.

"Who's there?"

A shuffling sound.

To her alarm, Dan Madden the handyman stepped out from behind a tree.

At the sight of him fear turned to anger.

"What are *you* doing here?"

He removed the baseball cap. She saw his face properly for the first time. Features off-kilter. Shifty eyes. Balding.

Guilt-ridden. Yes, she could see he was guilt-ridden. It was the way he stood, kneading the cap, not meeting her eye.

"Sorry if I disturbed yeh, Miss Ruttle—"

"Why are you following me? Why are you watching me?"

"But I . . . I'm . . . I'm not f-following you," he stammered.

"Then what are you doing here, this hour of the morning?"

He shifted from one foot to the other.

"Your, eh . . . your car, parked out there on the road." He glanced over his shoulder. "Noticed it had a flat . . . thought I'd come and tell yeh, 'cos . . ."

Should she believe him? It sounded plausible. She'd never changed a flat tyre in her life. Now she needed him.

"'Cos I could change it for yeh, if yeh want?"

230

He continued to knead the cap, staring over her right shoulder, self-conscious. Was he wall-eyed? Perhaps that's why he wore the bill of the baseball cap pulled so low. Had he taken the cap off out of respect? And if so, why hadn't he removed it back at the house on their first meeting? The time he removed a "dead bird". Oh, God, there it was again – the dead bird.

She braced herself. "How do I know, Mr Madden, that you didn't let the air out of my tyre on purpose?"

"*What?*"

"I *said* how do I know *you* didn't let the air out of that tyre *yourself?*"

He gave her a hard look. Took a step closer.

She took a step back.

"Stay away from me!"

"Don't unnerstan yeh. Why . . . why would I do the like-a that?"

"Because you told me a story about a dead bird blocking a drain at number eight. That was several weeks ago and the smell in the house – and most especially in the box-room – is as strong as ever. So the dead bird was just a story, wasn't it?"

His face darkened.

Her grip on the knife grew tighter.

"Well, I could ask you why yeh were out the back with a knife in yer hand after Maud's budgie was kilt. Didn't make *you* look too good."

She swallowed hard.

"I niver tolt nobody about that," he continued, "not even Bram. And I could-a tolt him and the police as well, but I didn't, 'cos I didn't wanna get yeh into any trouble, like."

"I'd . . . I'd nothing to do with Mrs Gilhooley's bird. Th-That burglar could've come into my house too. I was only protecting myself."

"That's what yeh say! But how did yeh know Maud'd been burgled? It'd only just happened . . . that's the thing."

She knew the answer to that one, but wouldn't be telling Madden. Bram Hilditch would be hearing the explanation about the Glacken boy and her own break-in very soon. The sooner the better. But he'd be the first one and likely the only one.

"Believe what you like, Mr Madden, but my conscience is clear."

"That's as may be, Miss Ruttle, but I'll not be tellin' nobody . . . not unless . . . not unless I have to."

He was threatening her. Trying to blackmail her.

"I'll be telling Mr Hilditch myself."

"Yeh will? Strange yeh haven't tolt him afore now."

"My reasons for not doing that are none of your business, Mr Madden."

"Aye."

He scuffed the earth with his right foot, dug his hands into his pockets, glanced back in the direction of the road again.

"Now d'yeh want me to change that tyre or not?" He checked his watch. Replaced his cap. "I've another run tae do in half an hour and time's goin' on, so it is."

If she said no she'd be stuck, and would have to walk to his garage for his help anyway.

"Yes, Mr Madden," she said, evenly. "I'd appreciate that."

Relaxing her hold on the knife, she took a deep breath and followed him out of the clearing.

CHAPTER THIRTY

Back at the roadside she opened the boot, located the jack and showed him the spare.

"I'll only be a minute or two," he assured her.

"Right." She turned her back on him. She didn't trust Madden and had no wish to make small-talk. She took out the booklet again and pretended to read, ears alert to his every move.

Then: "Miss Ruttle."

She saw him hunkered down, inspecting the spare.

"Yes?"

"That spare of yours is flat too."

She didn't believe him.

"It couldn't be!" she said sharply.

"Well, it is . . . see."

She felt for the knife again. Went over to him.

"There . . . a nail stuck in her."

How the hell did that happen? Did he drive in that nail when my back was turned? Why did I turn my back on him? Why? He's playing games because he knows he can.

She felt powerless. Wanted to lash out at him, but had to hold herself steady, remembering his threat. She couldn't afford to get on the wrong side of him.

The sight of his hands on the tyre repelled her. Crude hands like Harry's. Dangerous hands.

She'd have to play safe. But she was good at that.

"Whoever driv this car afore you had a flat," he went on. "Aye, had a flat and didn't bother tae get it fixed or maybe just forgot."

Harry then. If it wasn't Madden it must have been Harry. He prized the car. The car was his business. He cherished it more than he did her. But he'd been drinking heavily before he took off, which would explain the oversight.

"That's too bad," she conceded.

"I'll need tae take it back to me garage and patch it," Madden said, straightening up and slapping his right leg. "Might take a while. But if you stay there I'll get the van and run yeh home."

There was no way she was going to get into his van.

"No, thank you all the same," she said crisply. "I'll walk . . . it isn't far and it's a nice morning."

He squinted at her. "But, it's rainin', Miss Ruttle."

She hadn't noticed how wet it had become, so preoccupied had she been with safeguarding herself. Her hair was damp. A raindrop splashed against her cheek. She felt her feet clammy in her shoes.

"That's okay, I don't mind the rain," she lied.

"Maybe yeh have an umbrella in the car."

She shook her head. "No, it's all right. Really."

"Aye . . . well, suit yerself. Might take me the hour. I'll drop it off with yeh when it's ready."

She opened the passenger door and took her bag off the seat.

"Thanks again, Mr Madden," she said, giving him a grudging smile, hefting her shoulder-bag. "An hour you say?"

"About that, aye."

She hurried away, leaving him there, not daring to glance back. Sensed him looking after her. Yes, standing there watching her until she rounded a bend and was lost from his view.

As she approached the house she saw Bram Hilditch on the front step, black umbrella raised, hold-all in hand.

She opened the gate.

"Miss Ruttle . . . my goodness me . . . you're drenched to the skin. Are you all right?"

"Yes, I'm quite fine, thanks." She fished in her handbag for the door-key. "My car broke down, that's all. Mr Madden's fixing it."

"But couldn't he have given you a lift?"

"I didn't want one. What did you want?"

She opened the door.

In the lounge, he took his usual seat at the table. Glanced about the room, uneasily.

"Tea," she said, going through to the kitchen.

"I'm afraid it's not a social call, Miss Ruttle, more's the pity. I've a rather delicate matter to discuss with you I'm afraid."

She hung up her coat. Found a towel and ran it over her hair. Patted her face dry, checking herself in the mirror by the back-door.

"Oh . . . ?" she said to her reflection, feeling safer out of sight.

"Yes, I feel it best to clear the air."

She was losing weight. Cheekbones jutting sharply from her tired face. Eyes more prominent. Was it any wonder? Food was the last thing on her mind. She flattened her hair back into place, not really caring how she looked.

"About trespassing in the box-room?" she said flatly, coming back into the lounge and sitting down. *Proclaim the truth. Do not be silent through fear.*

She could see that her words unnerved him. He blushed.

"Yes, I'm so sorry about that. But I can explain."

"Please do, Mr Hilditch. I'm listening."

He looked at her askance. "Are you sure you're all right, Miss Ruttle?"

"Quite all right, thank you. Why wouldn't I be?"

He likes me submissive, she thought. But she'd been submissive for years and it had got her nowhere. Time to fight back. She saw the bold magpie stalk through the bracken. The image gave her courage. She'd be like the magpie. Brazen. Unabashed. Madden, and now Hilditch, would see she couldn't be messed with.

"You were saying?"

He touched the bag by his feet. "Yes . . . I . . . I mean to say. The trunk in the box-room . . . I mislaid a photo album and believed it was there and I just nipped up to get it and . . . discovered it *was* there. It was wrong of me, I know, and I do apologize."

"That's disappointing. I thought you were a man of honour."

"But I *am*, Miss Ruttle. It's just that . . ."

She saw him adjust his spectacles. That gesture she'd seen before – his pushing up the bridge with his middle finger. She was making him uncomfortable.

She knew he wouldn't mention the mess in the box-room. Not now. He was embarrassed enough as things stood.

"You were saying?"

He clasped his kneecaps, gazed at the floor. Made up his mind about something. "This isn't at all easy, Miss Ruttle, but I have to be direct."

He leaned over, undid the hold-all, drew something out and set it carefully on the table.

She saw that it was a shiny black box with decorative designs on the lid.

"What's that?" She wondered what he was playing at.

He canted forward, turned it towards her and opened it.

She saw some pieces of jewellery inside.

He waited.

"Well," he said pointedly. "Do you recognize it?"

"No, it's not mine – if that's what you're asking, Mr Hilditch."

He shook his head. "Are you saying you haven't seen it before?"

"No, I certainly have not! Look, what's this all about?"

"I found it in the trunk in the box-room. It does not belong to me or my late aunt. It belongs to Maud Gilhooley and was stolen by the person who beheaded her little budgie."

"*What!*"

"Yes, Miss Ruttle, I think you have a lot of explaining to do."

"I *beg* your pardon. Are you accusing me of robbing that poor old lady and killing her little bird? How could you think such a thing?"

She got up quickly, her mind in turmoil.

"Well, what am I supposed to think, Miss Ruttle?"

Proclaim the truth. Do not be silent through fear.

"Now let me tell you, Mr Hilditch, the police searched that room when they called. How come they didn't find it? So how do I know *you* didn't put it there when you were getting your album, just to . . . just to put the blame on *me*."

"That's preposterous!"

She turned on him, anger making her bold.

"Oh, so it's all right to accuse *me* with no evidence whatsoever!"

"I have the evidence right here. The police didn't do a very thorough search, obviously. And maybe it's just as well they didn't, Miss Ruttle, or you might be up in court. Now if you have any idea how the jewellery got there I need to know. I could have gone to the police immediately, but I wanted to protect you . . . give you a chance to explain. If you can't tell me how it got there I'll have no option but to report you—"

"Oh, another *man* in the course of a morning, trying to *protect* me. Madden, now you. *Blackmail* me more like."

"What on earth are you talking about?"

She realized she'd overstepped the mark. Where was her Samaritan training now? Get a grip, she told herself.

"I'm sorry," she sighed. "It's Ryan Glacken . . . that young boy across the road, if you must know. Him and his malicious mother – they are the ones who're doing this. *They* did this to me. Trying to blacken me . . . to drive me crazy like they did the woman before me."

"I don't understand. Why would they do something like this? They don't even know you."

"Ask *them* that. I asked the boy politely to stop kicking his ball because I had a headache that day and the mother came out and verbally abused me."

She could feel a migraine hovering. The upset was bringing it on. She paced the room, fuming at the injustice of it all.

"And . . . afterwards I . . . I saw that Maud had forgotten to shut her back-door . . . and I went to shut it, naturally . . . and then . . ."

She was getting dizzy. Groped for the door-jamb to steady herself.

"I feel faint."

"Here," she heard him say, and allowed herself to be guided towards the settee.

"Just sit there. I'll get you a glass of water."

"Thank you . . . yes, I need . . . I need to take a pill. In . . . in my handbag."

He gave her the bag. Sat down on the sofa beside her and handed her the glass of water.

"Are you all right, Rita?"

He'd used her first name. Crossing the bridge that kept him at arm's length. Given the circumstances, she didn't mind. But he was invading her space. She didn't trust him. Shifted away from him. Returned the glass.

"Yes, I'll be all right now. But . . . but the pills make me very drowsy. Any kind of upset can bring an attack on."

"Well, perhaps it's best you rest now. I'm sorry I upset you, but I had to know. I can call later?"

She shook her head. Needed to finish her story. *He needed to know the truth.*

"No, it's best I explain. That day . . . that day, the young Glacken boy was kicking his ball, I had a headache. Then when the mother told me off it got worse and I . . . I had to take a pill. I . . . I lay down and that's . . . that's when he came in."

"Who came in?"

"Ryan Glacken."

"But how do you know *he* came in?"

"When I woke up this room was trashed too."

"What! But, but why didn't you say this before . . . when I called that day?"

She couldn't give him the honest answer – that she was running away from a violent husband and didn't want to be found. Could not afford to get involved with the police and the repercussions of an investigation.

"Was anything stolen?" he asked carefully.

"N-No . . . but don't you see . . . he didn't need to take anything. He just threw things about to let me know it was him. Then he planted the jewellery box so I'd get the blame. The last thing the mother said to me was, 'You haven't seen the last of us, you nutter.' Or words to that effect."

"Goodness gracious me! She said that to you?"

"Sorry . . . Mr Hilditch . . . I lie down . . . have to, please."

She was getting her words mixed up. Could feel the numbness coming into the side of her head and face. He had to go.

"Please . . . go . . . *now*."

He looked alarmed. "Of course," he said, getting up.

He stowed the jewellery box in the hold-all.

"What . . . do . . . what now?" she managed to say, for she *needed* to know.

"I'll drive round there now and have a word with the Glacken boy. This is a very serious matter and has to be sorted . . . the sooner the better. Maud is due out of hospital soon. Are you sure you're all right? Shall I help you up the stairs?"

She shook her head, grateful that he was leaving and that she'd finally unburdened herself.

"Well, you mind yourself now."

He picked up the bag.

"There's just one odd thing," he said. "I was of the impression that Beryl Glacken and Maud got on well enough. Just goes to show, you never really know what's going on with some people."

Rita-Mae Ruttle knew all about that. Perhaps only *too* well.

CHAPTER THIRTY-ONE

Through a drab net curtain Bram observed Beryl Glacken slouched in an armchair, face lit by the electronic glow from a TV screen.

He'd rung the doorbell, but she hadn't heard. Either that or she was purposely ignoring it, hoping the caller would go away. The soap or game show being far more important than the visitor.

But he'd no intention of going away. He was furious at what Miss Ruttle had told him and was determined to have it out with her.

This time it was gloves off. The ill-starred Vivian-Bernadette O'Meara had complained about Ryan too. But he'd brushed it aside, thinking she was delusional, rather than involve himself with the Glacken clan.

Miss Glacken's father was a "high-up" in the IRA and you didn't trifle with people like that. God knows you ran the risk of being knee-capped – or worse – if you looked crooked at any of them. That photograph of the dead "informer" he'd recently seen in the newspaper, shot through the head and dumped in a ditch, was an example of their ruthlessness. Sometimes they used the "informer" ploy as an excuse to eliminate people who crossed them.

The last Bram heard, Glacken senior – or "the Enforcer", as he was known locally – was behind bars for what was euphemistically known as "directing terrorist activities". So he felt safe enough challenging the daughter, knowing he wasn't around.

He rapped on the glass again and finally saw her rouse herself, point the remote control at the screen, toss it aside and leave the room.

It took a while before she answered and he was becoming impatient. She no doubt knew he was there to confront her and was priming the son. Getting their stories straight. Either that or the journey from armchair to door was proving a struggle.

Finally the door was pulled open.

"Whaddya want?" she carped, blinking up at him. "I'm in the middle of Cor'nation Street, so it better be good and you better be quick."

"I'm so sorry to interrupt your very important viewing, Miss Glacken, but I have something of the utmost gravity to discuss with you."

"Gravee-what?" She studied him, mouth agape, hands behind her back, cigarette smoke spiralling up behind her as if part of her was on fire.

"May I come in for a few minutes, please? It won't take long."

"Better not take long . . . c'mon in then."

She led the way down the hallway, which reeked of chip fat, and into the living-room.

Ryan the bird-slayer was lying on his belly on the sofa, sucking a lollipop, head stuck in a comic. He didn't bother to acknowledge the visitor.

"Ryan, get up the hell-a that and let the man sit down!"

Ryan didn't move.

"*Ryan*, did you effin' hear me, did you?"

Bram winced at the crude language, sensing that this meeting would probably not go too well.

The boy slid off the sofa and sidled to the door.

"Perhaps it's best you stay, Ryan," Bram said, sitting down gingerly, trying to ignore the stray hairs from the moulting mutt in the corner.

"Och, whaddya want *me* for?" he griped.

"Shut yer bake, son, and come here and sit down when the man tells you. Where's yer effin' manners?"

He hung back in the doorway, sticking the lolly back into his mouth. Pulling faces at the mother.

"It's all right, Miss Glacken. Ryan can stand there so long as he listens to what I have to say. It's about my new tenant, Miss Ruttle."

"The nutter, Ma!"

She glared at him. "Shut your trap an' let the man have his spake." Bram pressed on.

"Well, Miss Ruttle says you were both very rude to her . . . shouted at her . . . called her names and made threats."

"Aye, and what if we did?"

She swung her gaze back to the TV set. A male character was shouting at another man behind the bar of the Rover's Return, fists raised.

"Aye, knock the shite outta him, Davy!" she bellowed at the set. "He bloody well deserves it—"

"So you don't deny it then?"

"Wha'?"

"Being rude to Miss Ruttle."

"Nah, why should I? Tryin' tae stop my Ryan playin' in his own back-yard. Who doz she think she is, Miss High-Mighty-Muck?"

She sucked on the cigarette and gazed at him dumbly.

Ryan, still sulking, went over to the dog and started feeding it the rest of the lollipop.

Bram really didn't know how he was going to phrase the next question. But, he thought, better just get it out and over with.

"Ryan, why did you trash Miss Ruttle's house and put Maud Gilhooley's jewellery box in her upstairs room?"

All of a sudden, Beryl exploded with a coughing fit, deep and pulmonary, her face turning puce. She patted her bosom, gasping.

"I *didn't*," Ryan protested, seeing the mother indisposed. "We saw *her* goin' in there."

Yes, you would say that, you little ruffian, thought Bram.

He looked back at the mother.

"So that's what's she tellin' yeh?" Beryl snapped, recovering herself. "Well, she's gonna pay for lyin' about my Ryan. We saw *her* at Maud's back-door, me and Ryan did. So she cut the head off that wee burd and stole the jewellery, the psycho."

"Yes, but she was shutting the door because Maud'd forgotten to."

"Aye, that's what she's tellin' *you*."

Beryl clambered to her feet, stabbing a finger at him. "And you're a one to believe *her* side of things. Aye, you think she's so hoity-toity that butter wouldn't melt, and we're just muck, so yeh do—"

"Look, Miss Glacken, I'm only trying to establish the truth, that's all. Miss Ruttle said you called her a 'screwball' and you threatened her. Something about not having seen the last of you. Now, is that true?"

"Aye, and what if it is? Whadda *you* gonna do about it?"

She stood over him, face ablaze.

He got up, feeling intimidated. He was dearly regretting his decision, but forged on.

"Now look here, Miss Glacken, you bullied my last tenant and if you persist in annoying Miss Ruttle I'll have no choice but to report you to the authorities. You are bad for my business and I simply will not stand for such behaviour. Have you nothing better to do than annoy innocent women trying to live in peace?"

"So you think she's innocent, do you? The only feckin' reason we didn't tell the peelers is because we hate the bloody RUC. Pack a black Prod bastards. Wouldn't spit on them if they were on fire, loyalist shites."

She stubbed out the cigarette, elbow going like a piston.

All at once, from above their heads, came a loud creaking noise. It was followed by the thud of a door being banged shut.

Bram, unnerved, had thought there was just the three of them. He hoped – really hoped – it wasn't who he thought it was.

Heavy footsteps could be heard coming down the stairs.

"Ma, there's Granda!" Ryan cried.

Bram's worst fears were confirmed.

"Da'll fix you," Beryl piped triumphantly. "Comin' over here causin' bother."

The door flew open.

"What's goin' on here?"

Glacken senior, "the Enforcer", stood framed in the doorway, sending a pall of umbrage into the room.

He was an intimidating sight – tall, muscular, with the mean face and hardened eyes of the career psychopath.

Bram had never been formally introduced to him and, given his reputation, had no desire to be. Due to his rank within the IRA you crossed him at your peril. His various prison terms for "directing terrorist activities" were at an end, obviously. Either that or he was on the run . . .

"This Hillitch man's accusin' our Ryan of stealin' from Maud and killin' her wee burd over there, Da."

"Is he now?" the Enforcer growled, eyes laser beams of hatred boring through Bram.

"Aye, Granda," Ryan chimed in. "The nutter woman said it was me, just like the other one blamed me for everything too."

"Did she now?"

He'd forced the phrase through clenched teeth, staring at the accuser, feet planted firmly, blocking Bram's only escape route.

There was a dangerous pause.

Ryan went to his mother, taking cover under her wing. Both stared up at the terrorist, alarm in their eyes, wondering what he was going to do with the interloper in their midst.

Bram could feel his legs going numb.

The Enforcer remained still as a panther, ready and waiting for his chance to pounce.

Then he took a step forward – the swiftness of the move making all three of them jump.

"Comin' over here till do her durty work for her, are you, Hilditch?"

He was chewing on a matchstick.

"Look, I'm only trying to establish the truth," Bram explained. "That's all, Mr Glacken."

"You pair: make yerselves scarce," he ordered, eyes steady on Bram. "Leave this boy tae *me*."

"Come on, Ryan," Bram heard the mother whisper.

They hightailed it out and shut the door, leaving host and visitor to it.

Bram could hear his heart thudding in his ears.

He had not come prepared for this. Wondered how in God's name he was going to get away unscathed.

Glacken was standing so close he could smell him – the sweat, the rage, malevolence rising off him like heat off a stove iron.

His whole appearance conspired to terrorize: shaved head, bull neck, medallion of skull and crossbones. Spider tattoos on each shoulder, their webs radiating over the biceps, trapping a fly at the crease of each elbow.

He was wearing a tight-fitting vest, black track-suit bottoms and a pair of white trainers.

Bram cleared his throat, tried to stand more erect. He began in a voice he hoped sounded as equable as possible in the circumstances.

"As I was saying to your daughter and grandson, I was only trying to establish the truth. There is no need to think badly of my new tenant. She's sorry she checked the boy."

The last was a lie but, in a way, if Miss Ruttle were to know what she was truly dealing with she would indeed be sorry. Bram knew, for both their sakes, it was vital he "contain" the situation and not cross this lunatic.

"She had a headache you see," he continued, "and Ryan was kicking his ball, making it worse . . . the headache I mean. So naturally she asked if he would mind stopping."

As an afterthought he added. "Asked him . . . erm . . . asked him as politely as possible of course."

The Enforcer said not a word. He listened intently, like a therapist, head tilted to one side, chewing leisurely on the matchstick.

Bram blinked, pushed his spectacles up on his nose.

Waited.

The silence was killing. He was forced to say more.

"That's . . . that's really all there is to it, Mr Glacken. Just a . . . just a simple misunderstanding. That's all."

Suddenly the Enforcer thrust his head forward, arms akimbo, and spat full in Bram's face, matchstick and all.

Bram stumbled, outraged. Fumbled for a handkerchief.

"How dare you behave in that way towards me! How *dare* you? I'm calling the police immediately. *You'll* be facing an assault charge, *Mister* Glacken."

He had the statement out before realizing what he'd done.

That word "police" was the spark that lit the touch-paper, sending a fist shooting out, hitting him square in the chest.

He fell back on the sofa, gasping.

Glacken stood over him, watching.

He tried to get up, but a boot was pressed down hard on his belly.

He was pinned in place.

"Get off me!" he shouted, trying to move the leg. But the monster's foothold was as firm as granite.

He leaned over his victim, causing him even more pain.

"Now . . . you . . . listen . . . tae me," he said, enunciating the words slowly and deliberately. "My grandson had bother with the other crazy bitch you rented that house tae before, and look what happened tae her. You seem to have a thing for crazy bitches. Understand where I'm comin' from, do yeh?"

Bram nodded, speechless.

The foot was pressed down harder.

"Aarrgh!"

Glacken eased off a little.

"What was that? Didn't hear you right?"

"Y-Y-Y-yes . . . I . . . I under . . . understand . . . yes. Please . . . please let me go. I won't . . . won't say another . . . another word about it . . . and I won't tell the police."

"That's more like it. Yer larnin', son. You go near the RUC and my boys'll have you trussed up in a ditch before you can say, 'Mammy, where's my knickers?' So, I'm warnin' you, if I hear so much as a cheep out of that nutter Ruttle over there, I'll not be responsible for my actions. You tell her that from me."

He released the foot, stood back and hauled Bram up by the ears, so that he was at eye-level.

The pain was excruciating. Bram yelled long and loud. He tried to wriggle free, but Glacken caught him in an arm-lock.

"Wanna run cryin' tae Mammy, do you? Or maybe that oul' spinster Ruttle over there . . . shoulder tae cry on, eh? Maybe you'd get more sympathy from her, seein' as the pair of yiz are as odd as two left feet."

"I . . . I won't s-say anything. I . . . I promise. Please . . . just let me go!"

Glacken released his hold on the arm. Took him by the scruff of the neck and frogmarched him to the back-door.

"Now stay the fuck away from this house!" he roared, pitching him out across the yard and slamming the door.

Bram stumbled in the yard, tripped over a bucket and went headlong, glasses flying off. Lay a minute trying to get his breath back, seeing only the blurry outline of a red bucket and a football: the ball that had caused all the trouble and brought him to this sorry state of affairs.

He was half-blind without the glasses and groped about on his hands and knees in desperation.

The back-door opened again.

He halted, petrified.

The psychopath was back.

He tried to get away, but . . .

"There's yer specs, Mister," Ryan said, smirking, down at him.

He handed them to him and without another word disappeared back inside. Bram struggled to his feet, his whole body aching. He put on the glasses, grateful to see the world spring back into focus.

He lurched to his car, which was parked on the other side of the lane, reeling from the shock. His clothes were a mess and his arm hurt badly. Maybe it was broken, or damaged irreparably. He'd just suffered a serious assault at the hands of a maniac and there was nothing he could do about it, except go to the doctor and pretend he'd had an accident.

The cruel injustice of it nearly made him weep.

He glanced briefly at Miss Ruttle's bedroom window.

The curtains were drawn, as he'd been hoping. She was still lying down then. At least she wouldn't have to witness his distress and have him suffer even more embarrassment.

He was thankful for small mercies and asked himself how long it would take for her to sleep off the migraine.

He eased himself behind the wheel. Wondered how he was going to drive with one hand. But it was the left arm that was damaged and the Daimler was an automatic. So, all in all, he'd manage.

As he manoeuvred the car off the grass verge, he glanced into the Glacken yard.

Mother and son were standing by the fence.

He pretended not to notice the series of rude gestures being enacted by the pair for his benefit as he drove off.

CHAPTER
THIRTY-TWO

Rita-Mae was glad Bram Hilditch had left Willow Close. That Ryan's mother had made the boy plant the jewellery box in that room, to frame her as the perpetrator of such awful deeds carried out against poor Mrs Gilhooley, was beyond belief.

In such circumstances she'd had no choice but to tell the landlord about her run-in with the pair of them. She peeped through the curtains. Saw that his car was gone. God knows what lies the bold Beryl had told him!

She sat down on the bed in the darkened room, staring at the Babygros that were spread out on the counterpane. I must have forgotten to put them away, she thought. That's not like me.

But then, given the upheavals so suddenly visited upon her, it was always possible. She could hardly blame the Glacken boy for that. She kept the little garments locked in a case. Wore the key on a chain round her neck at all times.

She picked up the blue one. Blue for a boy.

Had the baby survived, and had it been a boy, he'd only be a couple of years older than Ryan now. Would he have turned out as badly? Given his father's volatile nature there was every possibility – any son of Harry Ruttle's would have the odds stacked against him. Yet she was confident that her love for the child – the child she'd wanted so very much – would have conquered all.

She lay down on the bed, holding the Babygro to her heart, grieving for the lost boy, remembering all the suffering she'd endured so that Harry could have his way. Even going so far as having her committed to a mental institution.

A mental institution! It was an experience she would never forget, a memory that haunted her still.

She shut her eyes tight against the steadily worsening migraine, but was powerless to block out the scenes from that awful time replaying in her head . . .

"Mrs Ruttle . . . Rita . . . wake up!"

She opened her eyes to see a young woman – a girl – in a blue tunic standing over her.

She felt she'd been asleep for ever. Waking now from some kind of medieval curse, brought back to life by the voice and touch of this . . . this girl with the wide eyes and blonde hair tied up in a topknot.

She couldn't figure out where she was. There was a bright light above her, and beyond the closed door she could hear the smack of heels. Some heavy and striding – men's heels; some lighter, quicker – women's heels, pacing and rushing back and forth.

Busy, busy people moving quickly, but she was going nowhere. Through a fog of unknowing she knew that with certainty.

"Mrs Ruttle," the girl said again. "It's all right. Everything's all right."

Where was she? Who was she – the girl in blue? A drift of questions, banking up in her tired brain, but no answers.

She'd have to search for the answers herself.

Maybe . . . maybe it's all a bad dream, she decided. Yes, maybe I'm dreaming.

"Rita . . . Mrs Ruttle, wakey-wakey, it's nearly visiting time," the girl said cheerily. "Your husband will be coming."

The word "husband" gave her a jolt.

She didn't understand.

What, she thought, suddenly realizing she was not in bed, but sitting in a wheelchair.

"You're in hospital, Rita. Don't you remember? You had a wee bit of a breakdown, that's all."

The word "breakdown" gave her another jolt. She shook her head wildly, saliva all dried up, lips clamped together, as though someone had sewn them shut.

"Now, it's all right," the girl said again, pouring a glass of water. "You fell and hit your head and you're resting here for a while till you get your strength back."

She couldn't hold the glass. Her hands were trembling so much the girl had to help her.

"Now, that's better, isn't it, Mrs Ruttle?"

Something didn't add up. Why was she in a wheelchair? Afraid now. Really afraid.

Were her legs broken?

She needed to ask the question, but the words wouldn't come. They were all jumbled up in her mind, as though someone had dumped a whole bucket of them in there and left them scattered everywhere, for her to seek out and arrange in order.

Now she needed to ask the question: Are my legs broken?

She knew the words. In her head, got down on her knees to find them. Put them in the right order. But they wouldn't line up the way she wanted them to.

My broken are legs

Are legs my broken

Legs my broken are

She gave up, exhausted. It was such a labour and she was so very, very tired. She looked at the words lying there – the useless words – and wept.

"It's all right, Mrs Ruttle . . . Rita," the girl said, turning the wheel-chair round to the window. "Look at that lovely view. Such a beautiful evening, isn't it?"

The sky was dimming. The sun bronzing the trees, casting bogey-men shadows over the lawn. A man in a dressing-gown was wandering aimlessly among the flowerbeds, throwing his head back, arms jerking wildly up and down.

"There's Jimmy conducting his orchestra again . . . you remember Jimmy from yesterday, don't you? He wheeled you round the garden."

She couldn't answer. Couldn't figure out who Jimmy was. Couldn't figure *anything* out.

She shook her head again, speechless, helpless.

The girl continued to gaze out of the window.

"Oh, Jimmy's been here for ever," she said. "Part of the furniture now, poor thing. They've all deserted him . . . his family."

She looked down at her in the chair.

"But you won't be abandoned like him, Rita. You're one of the lucky ones. Your husband looks in on you every day. Maybe you can sit outside instead of the day-room when Harry – I mean Mr Ruttle – comes?"

Harry!

There was that name again. Why did it frighten her? The sound of that name in the mouth of this innocent was like an obscenity.

Her stomach lurched. She began to feel sick.

"Oh, God, I shouldn't have said his name," the girl upbraided her-self, thrusting a dish under the patient's chin in the nick of time.

"It's the medication that does that," Rita-Mae heard her say. "But all in a good cause. You have to get worse before you get better."

The dish was borne away.

Through the window she saw the conductor in the dressing-gown fall to his knees and draw his hands together. Heard his frenzied applause, before the girl drew the curtains and turned the wheelchair round.

A damp cloth found her mouth and wiped around it swiftly. The feel of the moisture was a relief on her cracked lips: the lips that had forgotten how to speak, to smile, to laugh, to shout, to sing, to scream – most especially scream.

The things she longed to do, but could not, locked as she was in this limbo. This hell.

The girl in blue was Betty and she was a carer and this was an institution for the mentally ill.

"That's you all cleaned up," Betty was saying.

She watched her dumbly as she opened a vanity-case and drew out a make-up bag.

"Now, let's get you all nice for your husband. You've got a lovely face you know. He's very lucky to have you."

"But, I . . ."

"What, love?"

"I . . . I don't wear . . ." she said, finally finding her voice, ". . . wear make-up."

"I know, but you should."

A powder-puff was patted round her nose and cheeks.

"And you're very lucky to have him. So handsome, Rita, your husband . . . everyone says so."

Rita-Mae just let her do her bit. No point in protesting. Offering up her face to be made nice. Unable to stop her. Whatever they injected into her, night and morning, made her numb and pliable, just the way Harry had made her, except now she couldn't defend herself. She couldn't fight back or run away. She was trapped in a wheelchair. And her legs weren't broken. They were simply too weak to carry her. She didn't have the strength to put one foot in front of the other.

Harry had her right where *he* wanted her – in an asylum amongst the living dead. The mad wife who'd tried to kill him.

Put long enough away so he could conduct his affair with Tricia.

Face all done, Betty wheeled her out the door.

"My sister," Rita-Mae said suddenly, remembering.

"Your sister?" Betty said in surprise.

"I was . . . dreaming . . . dreaming about her."

"I didn't know you had a sister, Rita. That's nice."

CHAPTER THIRTY-THREE

Portaluce, Antrim Coast

Dorrie found herself in a white room.

In a white room, in an iron bed, tucked in tightly on all sides by a white bed-cover stretched firmly across her chest.

Too afraid to sit up, she cast her eyes downward. Saw that she was wearing a regulation gown with the number F-32 embroidered on the breast-pocket.

Where was she?

Tentatively, she raised her head and peered about.

Directly in front of her was a door with an inset of glass high up.

Above the door hung a crucifix.

On the wall to the left: a narrow window filled up with sky, fog-laden and bleak, a seam of ocean as grey as granite at its base.

Nearby was a wooden chair. And, laid over it, her clothes.

Aside from the bed and the chair there was no other furniture in the room, save for a bedside table with a decanter of water and a tumbler.

It was a spartan and functional space.

Was it a cell?

Was it a ward?

Was she in prison or in hospital?

She tried to think, but her recall was as hazy as the view through the window.

Sounds. Somewhere in the heart of the building a door opened, and shut again.

Her head ached. Her right arm hurt.

Carefully she freed it from under the bed-covers. There was a sticking-plaster on her inner elbow. She ran her fingers lightly over her forehead, felt a lump above her right eye.

Strange!

I need a mirror, she thought. But there was no mirror in the room.

Handbag? In her handbag was her compact mirror. In her handbag was her money. *Where was her handbag?* Thoughts came back to her, frantic thoughts tripping like dominoes, one on top of the other.

She pushed herself upright, wildly scoping the room.

The bedside table?

She leaned across and wrenched the door open. Sighed with relief. There was her handbag, tucked safely inside.

She found the compact and checked her forehead. Saw that a large bruise was developing above her right eye. When she pressed on it, it hurt.

How had she come by that?

She tried to think. Then she remembered: Mrs Millman.

Oh God, I collapsed in front of her! She saw a fur coat lying outspread on the floor. The appalled expression on the proprietor's face. Heard the words, "Maureen, come quickly . . ."

I collapsed in front of her, hit my head and she got me into hospital.

It's all right, Dorrie. You're safe now.

"Mama!"

She called out the word, heard it resound faintly off the walls.

"Yes, Mama, I'm safe now. Everything's fine." She murmured the words to reassure herself. "But where am I?"

She felt like the only person alive in the whole world. The lazy washing of the waves and the sighing of the wind were making her feel melancholy and desperately sad.

Maybe if she looked through the door-pane she might recall where she was.

She threw back the covers, stumbled to the door and tried the handle.

It was locked.

"Hello . . . is anyone there?"

She stood on tiptoe and peered through the glass. Found herself staring at a similar door on the opposite side. From her limited vantage point she could make out a long corridor of such doors. Leading into rooms just like this one, she guessed. There was no sign of life. No nurses. No doctors.

This is not a hospital, she thought. A hospital does not lock patients in. Not unless . . . not unless it's a . . . a . . . an *asylum*.

She rushed over to the window. There were *bars* on it.

Frantically she undid the catch, but the sturdy grill allowed the window to open just a crack. There'd be no escaping this place.

She was about to yell out when she caught sight of the view through the bars, and a memory unfurled itself, absorbing her into the reality of a dream not long left behind . . .

Sun beating down.

A little girl down there on the beach, casting aside her bucket and spade to join her mother at the water's edge.

The mother in a daisy-patterned bathing-cap, wading into the waves.

Fear.

Terrible fear.

Rough hands grabbing her.

Screams.

A man dumping her on to a rug.

A woman in long blue clothes.

Good day to you, Sister. Didn't see you there.

I said: this beach is my back-yard. From my cell window I see every-thing. You'd do well to . . .

Cell window? She said "from my cell window".

Was it *this* window? This cell?

Keys jangling in a lock had Dorrie pivoting sharply to face the door.

She waited, every nerve and sinew pulled taut.

The door was pushed open. A woman entered, dressed in a white uniform. On her head she wore a white coif. She looked like a nun, but could equally have been a nurse.

"Oh, there you are!" the woman said in surprise, looking from the empty bed to where Dorrie stood. "You shouldn't really be out of bed you know."

"What is this place? Where am I?"

"I'm Sister Magdalena. You are in our convent. We're the Daughters of Divine Healing. Mrs Millman thought it best that you rest with us for a little. Until you get back to yourself."

She spoke quietly but firmly. The kind of voice you couldn't oppose. All Dorrie's angst-ridden questions fell away and she allowed herself to be escorted back to the bed.

The nun drew back the covers and helped her lie down. "There. Now, that's better, isn't it?"

She tucked her back in and took her pulse, timing it with her fob-watch.

"Are you a nun?"

"Yes."

"And a nurse?"

"Yes."

"So . . . this must be a hospital?"

"A sort of hospital, yes. But we cater more to people with addiction problems. Mostly alcohol. People who have lost their way. We help them find their path back to God. All addiction is an avoidance of God. When you separate yourself from Him you suffer. When you unite with Him you are healed."

"But, I'm . . . I'm not ill. I'm . . . not a . . . not an alcoholic."

"Let us be the judge of that. You had a fall." She drew a bunch of keys from her pocket and selected one. "We minister both to the mind and the soul. It's all God's work. When suffering comes we yearn for some sign from God, not knowing that the suffering itself is a sign."

She unlocked the top drawer of the bedside table. Put two pills into a medicine cup and poured a glass of water.

"Now, God has given you a sign. Nothing but good will flow from it. He brought you to us. Be grateful and thank Him. We are here to make you whole again."

She handed her the pill cup and glass of water.

"B-But what . . . what are they for?"

"They will ease your withdrawal symptoms and help you sleep."

She stood and waited, watching Dorrie closely.

It was clear that refusing to take the medication was not an option. Dorrie swallowed the pills, took a gulp of water.

"It's best to drink all of the water."

"But . . . when can I . . . can I go home?"

The nun did not answer. Instead she crossed to the far wall and slid back a partition to reveal a closet – the patient wondered why she hadn't noticed it – lifted her clothes from the chair, put them carefully on hangers and hung them up.

Each action was performed with a slow and measured grace. It seemed that Sister Magdalena inhabited a world free from earthly concerns. Her calmness was reassuring. I'm safer here with her, Dorrie reflected, than in Mrs Millman's "little palace". She thought of the haughty proprietor with her disparaging looks and polished airs, and trembled a little. She and this humble nun lived on different planes.

With the clothes safely stowed, Sister Magdalena drew the chair up to the bed and sat down. Folded her hands in her lap. They were slim hands, pale and delicate. Her face was long and narrow, the eyelids heavy, the face of some saintly martyr in a church painting. It was difficult to tell her age, even though her brown hair was just visible under the coif.

"When can you go home?" she said, repeating Dorrie's question back at her. "Well, where do you live?"

"I . . . I . . . live in . . . in . . ."

"You don't remember?"

Dorrie, on the verge of tears, shook her head.

"Alcohol does that. But your memory will come back. That is when you'll be well enough to return home. So it's important you rest here for a little while and take the medication. In no time you'll be back to yourself and this episode will be far behind you."

"My car." Suddenly Dorrie remembered Mrs Millman's mechanic. "Is it fixed?"

"Yes. It is fixed and parked in the grounds."

"When can I drive it?"

"When you are recovered and the alcohol has left your system."

"Al-co-hol . . . but I . . . I don't have a problem with—"

"That's what *all* alcoholics say. It's why Mrs Millman had you admitted here. You had consumed a whole bottle of whiskey. There was evidence of it in your room. The medication will aid your recovery."

Dorrie was about to remonstrate when, in her mind's eye, she saw a ten-glass bottle of Jameson whiskey lying empty beside a red fox fur on the floor of her Ocean Spray guestroom. The memory brought a flood of humiliation and shame. She could not meet the nun's eye.

"It's best to rest now," Sister Magdalena said, slowly and quietly getting to her feet. She returned the chair to its place by the window with barely a sound.

"Please don't lock me in!" Dorrie pleaded.

"It's for your own safety."

"But I . . . I . . ."

"Now, now. It's all right." She came forward, smiled down at her and laid a hand over hers. "There is nothing to be afraid of here. Just rest and ask God for guidance. I'm praying for your speedy recovery. God is good. Relief will come; have no doubt of that."

The last thing Dorrie heard was the sound of the door shutting and the jangle of keys locking her in *again*.

CHAPTER THIRTY-FOUR

"You've dislocated your shoulder," Dr Sweeney said, examining Bram's swollen arm. "Just as well it's the left one. You're right-handed I take it?"

Bram nodded, sweating and feeling faint through the pain.

He was in the GP's consulting room, having driven there with difficulty after his "fall".

"But the good news is that the humeral head doesn't seem to have been put out completely."

He pressed down hard on the joint and it made a loud cracking noise.

The patient yelled out.

"That's it! Sounds like it's back in place again."

"Is it?" Bram asked, breathless, shoulder throbbing afresh.

"Yes. Worst part over."

Dr Sweeney helped him back into his shirt and sat down at his desk again.

"You'll need to wear a sling for a few days until the swelling subsides. And I'll give you painkillers." He began writing. "Good that you came as soon as you could, otherwise the muscles would have gone into spasm, making it far more painful to put back in place."

Bram watched him dumbly: the handsome profile, the film-star looks, oozing such poise and confidence he could have been testing for a screen role.

He finished writing with a flourish and handed over the prescription. "Painful business. How did it happen?"

"I . . . I erm . . . tripped over a football." In a way it wasn't a lie.

"Goodness me! Hadn't you down as a player."

He didn't care for Sweeney's implication – you're middle-aged and overweight so I can't see you following a ball about a pitch somehow – but let it pass.

"No, I don't play," he said, sighing inwardly at the first of many lies he'd have to parrot to all and sundry over the coming days. "It was in the road and I didn't see it."

"Right . . . and your mother . . . how's she coming along?"

He lounged back in the chair, hands clasped behind his head: the picture of relaxation.

"Very well, thank you, Doctor. She's taken to Mrs Magee's ministrations very well, I'm happy to say . . . speaks very highly of her."

Bram was indeed amazed that Octavia liked Blossom so much. Seemed as if they'd become quite close – so much so, that he found himself surplus to requirements on the days Mrs Magee was around. He'd noticed extra bottles of gin and vermouth appearing on the sideboard, and guessed that the reason his mother was so comfortable with Blossom was that she was using the good lady to run errands to the off-licence. He'd decided to overlook this because, as a welcome consequence, the installation of the home help had given him more freedom to pursue his own affairs.

Sweeney grinned. "Blossom missed her vocation as a nurse. Such a fine lady! Hope she's taking the necessary exercise, your mother?"

No, she certainly was not, but he could hardly tell Sweeney that.

"Stairs . . . erm . . . they're a bit of a problem," he parried. "Says she's afraid of falling down them. And she refuses to move from her boudoir to the ground floor, alas."

"Well, you could always install a stairlift. Very important that she gets a good walk in the fresh air every day. We don't want paralysis to set in."

"No, doctor. I agree completely. I hadn't thought of a stairlift, but now that you mention it I'll certainly look into it."

At the pharmacy he got the sling and medication, giving J.P. Rooney the same explanation he'd given the doctor, then mounted the stairs to his studio.

He was grateful he had the studio to go to, not wanting to return home to Her Grace immediately and go through the third degree of questioning as to how exactly he'd acquired the injured arm.

He needed to get his story straight.

Safely behind the studio door, he knocked back two of the painkillers and sat down wearily in his swivel-chair. He'd go over the mother's interrogation, imagining how it might unfold . . .

"Abraham, what on earth have you done to yourself?"

"It's nothing, Mother. I tripped over a football."

"A football! Since when did you start playing football of all things?"

"I wasn't playing. It was lying on the road and I didn't see it."

"Weren't you wearing your glasses?"

"Yes, I was. I just didn't see it, that's all."

"Perhaps you need new ones then?"

"New whats?"

"Why, glasses of course. What road?"

"What do you mean, what road?"

Yes, knowing her, she would pin him down for accuracy concerning the road.

"Thatcher's Row, if you must know."

"There are no young boys living there. It's a row of thatched cottages – hence the name – peopled by geriatrics."

"Well, they must have had grandchildren visiting, which was unfortunate for me . . ."

He gave up, exhausted by real and imagined scenarios. What was happening to him? Bad enough that Vivian O'Meara had caused him so much trouble. Now Rita Ruttle seemed to be picking up where she left off.

What would be the end of it? Perhaps he should have stuck with undertaking after all. The dead didn't demand much.

He thought back to their encounter and Miss Ruttle's rather unexpected forthrightness. Then the confusion she displayed, her language thrown into disorder. Was that all part of the migraine or did it point to something more serious? He was sorry he'd upset her, but what choice did he have?

He really needed to tell her that he'd sorted things out with the Glackens. Fix it so she wouldn't go over there again. The sooner he did that the better. He'd give it a couple of hours. Go and visit her again. By that time she'd be up and about – hopefully.

The very thought of what the Enforcer was capable of scared him. What he might do to Miss Ruttle if she wasn't careful.

She was unaware of the real danger she was in.

His thoughts went back to Vivian O'Meara and the terrible discovery he'd made.

The memory of it made his stomach churn.

The pain in his shoulder started up again. He couldn't afford to go back to that dark place in his head. Not during the daylight hours. The nightmares were bad enough.

No, he would not wait until Rita Ruttle had woken up. He'd write her a note and put it through the letterbox.

Something told him it was imperative he act now, and fast.

CHAPTER THIRTY-FIVE

Rita-Mae was awakened in her Willow Close bed by the sound of pecking. The room was in semi-darkness and it took her a while to figure out where she was and where the noises were coming from.

Had she imagined them?

Her head still hurt and she was reluctant to move. Saw that she was still clutching the blue Babygro.

Slowly her memory righted itself and she recalled Bram Hilditch's visit earlier with the jewellery box and the subsequent migraine attack.

The migraine hadn't fully lifted though.

The pecking noises had drawn her from sleep too early.

Peck-peck-peck.

There they were again.

Was it a bird?

She raised herself up on her elbows.

Listened hard.

Then: *Rat-a-tat-tat-tat-tat-tat-tat.*

A blizzard of raps, more forceful now, against the window.

No, it definitely wasn't a bird!

Fearful, she climbed out of bed and peeped through a crack in the curtains.

Couldn't believe her eyes.

Ryan Glacken was standing *inside her back-gate* with a bucket – a red bucket. As she watched, he reached into it and drew out a handful of . . .

She ducked down as a hail of pebbles hit the window.

Enraged, she pulled on a robe and raced down the stairs.

Through the kitchen she could see him bent over the bucket again, selecting the right-sized missiles.

Seizing her chance, she slipped out the door, unnoticed, hunkering for cover behind the oil-tank.

More pebbles were fired.

Ryan had no idea she was there.

He bent over the bucket again.

She'd kept her bed-slippers on – for a reason. The reason: to take the little rascal by surprise.

With the furtiveness of a cat she crept past the stone cherub and around behind the garden shed. Now his back was in full view, a couple of feet away.

She sneaked right up behind him.

Poised at the ready, she waited for him to raise his arm.

"Gotcha!" she shouted, pouncing on him, gripping him round the wrist and squeezing hard.

Ryan yelled out. She clamped a hand over his mouth. The pebbles fell.

"Not so funny now, you little hooligan!"

Ryan stared up at her, eyes wild with fright, struggling to break free.

But she was stronger. Much stronger.

She hauled him back up the path.

The ground below her window was littered with pebbles.

"Now, Ryan," she said very calmly into his right ear. "I'm going to remove my hand and I'm warning you, if you scream, I'll take you inside and phone the police. I'll be telling them you were trying to break my windows. And you could go to jail for that. Do you understand what I'm saying, Ryan?"

He nodded, terrified.

"Good boy."

She removed her hand very slowly, still holding on to his wrist. The boy was speechless.

"Now, get down on your knees and pick up all of those stones at once. You've caused me enough trouble to be going on with, and this has to stop."

He started to cry, softly.

"Do it *now!*"

He dropped to his knees immediately.

She fetched the bucket and stood over him, blocking any escape route.

"Now, every last one back in that bucket and you can carry them back to your spiteful mother. And you can tell her from me, if she troubles me again she'll be very, very sorry. *Understand* me, Ryan?"

The weeping Ryan nodded, and started picking up the pebbles.

Bram Hilditch decided to walk from town to Willow Close to deliver the note to Miss Ruttle. It would only take twenty minutes and he needed to clear his head. With his arm now in a sling, driving was awkward.

He really hoped his tenant would be over the worst of the migraine and be up and about. Much better that he tell her in person that he'd sorted everything with the Glacken clan, difficult as that might be.

He resented having to be underhand with her. But in the circumstances it was the best thing to do. Rita Ruttle needed to be protected.

The less involvement she had with the neighbours-from-hell, the better for everyone.

He strode along the road at a steady pace.

The showers of early morning had ceased. The sky was rinsed out and luminous, making the journey a little more pleasant.

He tried to put his troubles from him, and switched on his photographer's eye as he proceeded along, questing for those frame-shots you tend to miss while driving. A stream at the edge of the road, which he'd never seen before, drew his attention. Brimful with the recent rain, its gentle gurgling as it sped along was a joy to both eye and ear. And he saw a catch of sheep's wool on the rails of an iron gate, waving in the breeze. It looked as though an Old Testament prophet had climbed through the bars, unaware that he'd left half his beard behind. A few hundred yards from his destination he spotted a white van powering in his direction. Dan Madden.

Bram prepared himself. First the handyman would ask why he was walking, not driving.

Second, what had happened to the arm?

Presently Madden was drawing up and rolling down the window, engine idling.

"God, what happened yer arm, Bram? Not often I see yeh walkin'. The car isn't broke down is it? 'Cos if it is I'm yer man."

"No . . . erm . . . no, Dan, nothing like that. Had a bit of a fall, that's all."

"Aye . . . not broke is it?"

"No, just dislocated, but it's fixed now."

"I meant the car," the mechanic bleated without irony.

"Car's fine, Dan. Well, best get going then."

"And where would yeh be goin'?"

None of your business, he wanted to say, but held himself in check.

"To visit Miss Ruttle, if you must know. Is her car ready yet, by the way?"

"Nah, that's what I was gonna tell you. She's got two baldies at the front . . . flat as bust balloons, begod . . . a blow-out waitin' tae happen. These wimmin check nathin', so they don't. Never think of wear an' tear on a motor. Drive thim till they fall apart then wunder why it happened."

Bram could have done without the lecture regarding women's general lack of car-maintenance skills, but he let him run on anyway. There'd be a point to the story soon, he hoped.

"Aye, on me way in tae Donnelly now," Madden prattled on, "for tae get her a pair-a new ones."

"Well, I'm sure Miss Ruttle will appreciate that."

"Aye so, but what I was gonna say was, seein' you'll be seein' her now, would you tell her she'll get the car the morra mornin'? Save me the bother of tellin' her meself. Wouldn't want tae get on the wrong side of her. Tongue as sharp as a bloody switchblade."

Bram was taken aback by the remark, but was aware that Madden wanted to draw him into some tittle-tattle just for the sake of it. He'd no time for gossip with the locals.

"On the contrary I find her most pleasant. But we're all entitled to our opinions, whether well-founded or spurious."

There was a pause.

"Aye, sure enough . . . whatever yeh say," Dan said, peeved, shifting the van into gear. "Right yeh be, then. Be seein' yeh."

"Thanks, Dan."

He roared off, leaving landlord and landscape in peace once more.

Several minutes later Bram arrived at number 8 Willow Close.

His intention was to go round the back and check if Miss Ruttle was up – fervently hoping that she would be.

He made his way around the side of the house and glanced up at the bedroom window. To his dismay, he saw that the curtains were drawn. She was still lying down.

Too bad. A note through the letterbox it would have to be then.

He fumbled the piece of paper out of his pocket, but in his haste a breeze took it and it ended up on the back doorstep.

"Dearie, dearie me!" He stooped down to fetch it.

To his dismay he saw now that the back-door was slightly ajar.

Concerned, he quietly pushed it open and stepped into the kitchen. "Miss Ruttle, are you in?"

He tiptoed into the lounge. But there was no sign of anyone.

Terrible thoughts assailed him.

Had he delayed too long?

Had the IRA enforcer taken her?

Oh, dear God, let that not be the case!

He moved to the foot of the stairs, too afraid to go up there.

What would he find in the bedroom?

An empty bed – or worse?

The prospect had him reaching for the banister to steady himself.

He'd try one last time before going up. This time more loudly.

"Miss Ruttle, are you up there?"

To his relief, he heard a door open.

Then: "Oh, it's *you*," an abrupt-sounding voice said.

Miss Ruttle stepped out of the box-room. She was in her nightgown.

Her irritation at being interrupted was palpable.

Immediately, Bram was on edge.

"Why, there . . . there you are . . . Miss Ruttle. Yes . . . I er . . . erm . . . I mean, your back-door was open and I . . . well, I thought you'd forgotten to—"

He'd stopped at the sound of someone sobbing – someone inside the box-room, sobbing.

"Wh-What's going on, Rita? Who's with you?"

She stood back from the open door, gesturing into the room with a thumb.

"Well, why don't you come and see for yourself, Mr Hilditch."

Bram mounted the stairs, feeling like Detective Arbogast mounting the stairs of the Bates home in *Psycho*.

Who *was* in that benighted room?

He reached the landing and forced himself to look in.

"That's who's with me," she fumed. "The bold Ryan Glacken."

Bram nearly fainted at the sight. He was indeed too late – far, far too late.

Ryan was on his hands and knees, picking up the scatterings of potpourri, snivelling and shaking.

At the sight of Bram, he wailed, "I wanna go home tae me mammy! I wanna go home tae Mammy, Mr H-H-Hillrich, but she won't let meeeeee!"

Bram was aghast.

Miss Ruttle stood with arms folded, triumphant.

"See? That's what the little vandal deserves. He and his mother will not be bothering me again."

Bram was speechless. He saw his tenant's world crumble before his very eyes. She could not have committed a worse crime than chastising the grandson of Glacken the Enforcer.

"What have you done, Rita? What on earth have you done?"

"What have *I* done?" she said bitterly, staring at him in disbelief. "What have *I* done? I'm teaching this boy a lesson, that's what I'm doing. Whose side are you on, *Mister* Hilditch?"

Ryan's blubbering intensified.

"It's all right now, Ryan," Bram said, going to him and helping him to his feet with his good arm. "You don't need to pick any more of that up." He handed him a tissue.

"What the *hell* are you doing?" Miss Ruttle was ablaze, shouting, waving her arms wildly. She advanced on Bram. "He's not leaving here till everything in this room he wrecked is put right. Do you *hear* me? You're taking that little rascal's side after what he's done to *me* . . . *To meeee!* After what him and his awful mother have accused *me* of." She beat a fist against her chest to hammer home the point. "Do you understand what you're saying? I caught him firing stones at my window when I was trying to sleep."

She threw her arms up in exasperation. "He could have broken *your* window. And *you're* okay with that?"

"Is-Is . . . is th-that true, Ryan?" Bram stammered, uncertain.

The boy nodded sheepishly, drying his eyes. "Aye," he squeaked.

"See . . . you wouldn't . . . me . . . wouldn't . . . believe me." She was gripping the sides of her head. Swaying. Screaming the words out in what seemed like frustration.

"Look, Miss Ruttle, don't . . . don't upset yourself. I'll . . . I'll clear this room up and Ryan . . . Ryan here can go home—"

"*Oh G-o-d! The p-a-i-n . . . my . . . h-e-a-d—*"

Bram caught her arm.

"Rita? Rita, can you hear me?"

But she couldn't hear him. She couldn't see him, or anything else. She collapsed on the floor, whole body convulsing.

"*Go, Ryan!*" Bram shouted. "Go home now!"

The boy jumped to his feet and fled down the stairs.

Bram dashed to the phone and dialled the doctor.

CHAPTER
THIRTY-SIX

Rita-Mae was in bed for three days following the Ryan episode.

Lying curled up in her darkened bedroom, unable to tell night from day. The hours like the darkest clouds pressing in upon her, going nowhere, pushing her in and out of sleep, her head pounding without pause.

A doctor charted her progress. Appearing through the gloom with his stethoscope and pills.

Sometimes another man looked in on her – she could smell his musky scent – his face a picture of sympathy and concern.

More often a kindly woman in a pussy-bow blouse and pearls was in attendance, her soft hands raising Rita up on the pillows with a soothing, "There, there, dear. We'll have you right as rain in no time." Helping her take the medication which made her so drowsy she sometimes forgot where she was, and sent her in search of the scream inside that no one but she could hear.

At times snatches of conversations between the three of them would catch in her mind like a thread-bound needle. And she'd try to follow its journey, dipping in and out, in and out of the dark fabric, swathing her in that alien world.

"Does she have next of kin you could contact?"

"She never mentioned anyone, Doctor. Is she very ill?"

"Hopefully not. She's suffered hemiplegic migraine and epilepsy for some time . . . survived so far . . . the sporadic kind, that is, and—"

The thread of the conversation snapped abruptly, and she drifted back to sleep.

On another occasion it was the man who wore the musky scent and the woman, their hazy outlines just visible at the foot of the bed, speaking in hushed tones.

"It's very important she's not left alone, Blossom. I'll stay at night and we can do shifts during the day."

"That's no bother, Bram. Sure I can work round your mother."

Finally she woke up one morning, alone in the quiet house, headache gone.

Darkness gone.

Sun blooming at the window.

She got up and drew back the curtains, for a moment expecting to see the drab view of the estate in Larne.

But the sight of the little back-garden with the wooden shed, circular clothesline and that stone cherub in the corner brought her back to reality. She was in another house in another town.

Away from danger.

Safe.

Then: of a sudden she heard footfalls on the stairs.

No, she was *not* safe.

Surging fear.

The clock read 6.30 a.m. She was *not* alone. There was *someone else* in the house *at that hour*.

She dashed to lock the door against them.

Key? *There was no key!*

"Rita!" a male voice called out. "It's all right . . . it's only me: Bram. Glad to hear you up and about. I'll . . . I'll make us some breakfast. Come down when . . . whenever you're ready."

Bram?

She pressed herself hard against the door.

Bram Hilditch! The landlord of course.

But what was *he* doing in *her house* at that hour?

"Erm . . . er . . . I'll . . . I'll be down in a minute," she said.

"Feeling better?" he asked when she appeared at the foot of the stairs.

This situation did not feel right. Did not look right. Bram Hilditch – an injured Bram Hilditch with his arm in a sling – was in her house at this early hour, with the table set and breakfast made. The scene looked so inviting: lacy tablecloth, a bunch of flowers in a vase, her chair pulled out, ready to receive her.

Nothing was making sense.

He turned and beckoned her forward.

"It's all right, Rita. You're over the worst of it now: the migraine." He gestured to her chair. "Please, have a seat."

She moved with caution and sat down, feeling as frail as a feather. No doubt he'd be explaining the reason for this odd set-up very soon.

"What happened to your arm?" she asked, wondering idly where he'd got the flowers.

"Oh, it's nothing . . . just a sprain."

He lifted the teapot. "Peonies," he said. "Her Grace sent them. She keeps a beautiful garden. Sends her best wishes, naturally."

"Her Grace?"

"Sorry, my mother."

"Oh." She'd forgotten that he called her that.

Had he stayed all night?

"Er . . . how long . . . how long have I been . . . been in bed?"

"Three days. You had a fall. Blossom and I've been taking care of you. Dr Sweeney's been looking in on you too."

She noticed a blanket folded on the sofa. Cushions moved elsewhere.

"Yes, I stayed nights and we both did shifts during the day."

"You mean . . . y-you stayed . . . stayed h-here all night with . . . with me while I was . . ."

"Recovering? Yes."

"B-But why?"

She knew that her migraines were not life-threatening. What was all the fuss about? Saw that he wasn't touching any of the toast so perfectly arranged in the toast rack. Wondered if he'd done something with it. She wouldn't be touching it either. Had he planned all this?

"I was concerned for you, Rita . . . didn't want to leave you alone. Dr Sweeney was of the same mind. You ran the risk of getting up in the night and well . . . being sedated you might've fallen . . . perhaps down the stairs. When you took ill I wanted to call a relative of yours, but you never gave me a next of kin and . . ."

He gazed out of the window, flushing slightly. "And I . . . I couldn't afford to leave you unattended."

A memory snapped back into place.

Harry!

Harry's face!

Harry's hands!

Had the doctor tried to contact *Harry*? Had he told the landlord about Harry? Was her secret finally out?

She heard the tick-tock of the clock, portentous and loud in the silence. Realized she needed to be careful. There was *no* Harry. She was a spinster – not the spinster wife she knew herself to be, but the lonely spinster of the landlord's imagination. How much did he know, *really know*, about her now? How much had Sweeney told him?

"But, I've always . . . always managed on my own," she said.

"You don't have to any more." He brought his gaze back to meet hers. "Manage on your own I mean . . . I'm here for you, Rita."

She didn't know what to say. Why was he calling her Rita? Why was he being so kind? So concerned for her well-being all of a sudden?

"Where was I when it happened? The attack . . . I mean."

Her memories were vague. She could not get a handle on them. Could not remember anything about the collapse or what had preceded it. What had brought it on? Must have been something very upsetting.

"You were in . . . in the box-room . . . cleaning up and I . . . called with a note."

She noticed his hand quiver slightly as he lifted the cup.

"I knocked, but you didn't hear . . . then I saw that your back-door was open and became concerned."

She heard a car pass and followed the tempo of its lilts and shifts until it faded away. Heard the birds have their say once more, the beauty of their singing making her feel desperately sad.

The landlord was looking at her again. That probing look she saw so often in the faces of those who did not understand her. Who never took the time to understand her. So caught up in their own little worlds. Orbiting her like planets, out of reach.

"Are you sure you're all right now?"

"What was the note about?"

"Nothing really. Just . . . just something from the Water Board. I was out for a stroll and thought I'd pop it through the door. That's all."

She sighed.

"Don't concern yourself, Rita. It's all in the past now. Perhaps you should go away for a few days. Just for a rest . . . away from here. Portaluce. I mentioned it before. Lovely little place. There's a guest-house . . . the Ocean Spray. I'll drive you there."

Portaluce? She recalled him referring to it.

"I don't want to go anywhere. I want to stay here."

She saw that her reaction disappointed him.

"Then I'll call in on you more often . . . whatever time of day suits you best. You don't have to decide now . . . about Portaluce I mean."

"You don't need to call on me. You've been too kind already and I can manage quite well on my own, thank you. I'm fine now . . . really."

She didn't *feel* fine, but sipped the tea to please him and show him she was capable. Capable and functioning again.

"Rita, I need to say something . . ."

He was looking at her solemnly, pushing his spectacles up on his nose. He was nervous again. She could tell.

"Yes?"

"I've sorted things out with your neighbours over there."

"Neighbours?"

"The Glackens, young Ryan and his mother. Y-You don't need to go over there again. Best leave things be . . . let the hare sit, as they say."

Ryan!

The name went off in her head like a rocket flare, lighting up images, sparking snapshots revealing the reasons for her collapse.

Ryan kicking a ball.

Ryan throwing pebbles.

Ryan crying.

Ryan on his knees in the box-room picking up the potpourri!

Ryan, Ryan, Ryan! The cause of all her pain. The cause of all her difficulties.

Ryan Glacken. Ryan Glacken and his awful mother.

She was on her feet, temper-needle shooting wildly into the red.

"You, *you*, you took *his* side. I remember now. You sent him away. Told him to stop . . . stop clearing up the mess that he'd made up there. You traitor. Get out of here *now*!"

"Look, Rita, I can explain."

"Out, *now*!"

He gathered himself quickly, a look of fright in his eyes.

She took a step towards him.

"Please, Rita, they are dangerous people. Keep well away."

"That little *brat* will apologize to *me*. I ended up in bed for three days because of him. How *dare* you tell me what to do? I've had enough of others telling me what to do. Have spent my whole life doing what others wanted me to do. *Not any more.* Now, *get out* and let me live my life by *my* rules. I'm not a child and you're not my father."

Her rant had the desired effect. He couldn't speak. Simply stared at her as if she'd gone mad, backing towards the door.

She congratulated herself. Finally he was listening to *her*. Finally she'd got through to him.

On the step he turned. Opened his mouth to say something further. But she banged the door shut, not wishing to hear any more excuses from him.

She stood triumphant by the window, watching him go, feeling free and light and totally in control.

Victor at last.

Victim no more.

CHAPTER THIRTY-SEVEN

Know when to speak, for many times it brings danger. The fearful are caught as often as the bold.

Rita-Mae was on a mission.

On a mission to get justice.

The Glackens would not drive her out. She'd stand her ground. She'd fight.

The boy needed to be taught a lesson. Made an example of. The sooner he learned, the better.

She pulled on her coat and stepped out the back with purpose.

Crossed the lane and opened their gate. Marched up to the back-door and rapped loudly on the glass.

Waited. Counting down the seconds to the beat of her heart.

Heartbeats quickening with fury, not fear. She was through with being afraid.

A minute passed.

No one answered.

Not to be thwarted, she went round to the front.

Rang the doorbell. Rapped again.

Waited some more.

The curtains on the windows were drawn upstairs and down. Perhaps mother and son were asleep.

She checked her watch. It had just gone 7 a.m.

Of course they'd still be in bed. It was far too early. In her haste to confront them she'd lost sight of the hour.

Not to worry, she'd call back later.

She retraced her steps to the rear of the house. Scanned the upper windows. The curtains were drawn.

Felt let down that her plan of action had been derailed by a slip in time.

Reluctant to leave with nothing accomplished, she scoped the backyard. There must be something she could do.

Then she spotted it – the ball.

The ball – the football that had brought her so much grief – was lying under a wheelbarrow. The red plastic bucket he'd used to carry the pebbles was sitting alongside it. Ball and bucket: the weapons he'd used against her. Well, he wouldn't get the chance again.

There was one way to frustrate his little games and get her revenge at the same time.

She picked up the bucket. Threw the ball into it. She'd take them with her.

She tiptoed out of the yard, mindful that the theft must go unnoticed, and quietly bolted the gate.

The sound of a window shutting behind her made her start.

She turned. Scanned the upper storey again.

Nothing stirred.

The curtains remained drawn, giving no evidence – a pull on the fabric, a gap of light – that they'd recently been disturbed.

She was good at that. Observing the details. Eyesight perfect. Always had been. But the curtains were drawn exactly as before. Orange ones on the larger window drawn properly together. Blue ones on the smaller window – the boy's room – pulled carelessly, one overlapping the other.

Had she imagined it then? The sound?

She let her gaze travel over the roof, slowly, carefully, like a searchlight over a prison yard.

Stopped.

There *was* something she hadn't noticed before – something glinting. A skylight. How come she'd missed it? But it was flush with the roof tiles and hard to see.

The Glacken house was the only dwelling that had one.

Was *that* the window that had just been shut? The window in the attic?

Was someone watching from *that* window?

Please, Rita, they're dangerous people. Stay well away!

She heard the landlord's voice. Saw his shocked face. The alarm in his eyes. Why had he said that? They were hardly dangerous – a little boy and his stupid mother. So what had he meant by that?

Suddenly her courage was on the wane. She felt the urge to flee, and quickly.

She hid the bucket and ball under her coat, hurried back across the lane to the safety of her own place.

Back in the lounge she surveyed the remains of the breakfast table, so hastily abandoned just a few minutes earlier. Wondered what Bram Hilditch was doing. What impression was he carrying of her as he drove back home? Whom would he be telling about her outburst? His mother most likely: the woman who'd been so rude to her for no good reason.

Well, she didn't much care whom he told. She owed them nothing. Had paid her rent in advance and so deserved to be left in peace without meddling from either of them.

The breakfast things would wait.

There was no time to clear up. It was against her principles to leave things untidy, but there simply was no time to squander. She needed to get rid of the ball and bucket before Mrs Glacken came a-calling. The minute the boy found them missing the finger of blame would point at her.

Well, he'd have to apologize to her, before he'd get them back.

She found a binbag and stuffed the items into it. Found her handbag and rummaged for the car keys.

But . . . but the keys were *not in her bag*.

The car. They'll be in the car.

She unlocked the back-door. Stepped outside.

But there was no car.

Had someone stolen it in the night?

"What the *hell's* going on?"

Frantic now. Without the car she'd be lost.

She paced the room, restless, thoughts spinning out of control.

Went out the back, checked again.

Vroom . . . vroom vroom . . . vroom.

Someone was coming.

She dashed round to the front. Couldn't believe her eyes. Someone was driving *her* car.

She touched the flick-knife in her coat pocket.

The car thief cut the ignition and got out.

She waited. Knife at the ready.

Then it dawned on her. Madden. Dan Madden. It was *him*! The man who'd followed her into the wood. The man who . . .

"What are you doing driving *my* car?"

He removed the baseball cap. Fixed her with a harsh look.

"*What?* That's a nice way tae thank me for gettin' yeh a new set of tyres and fixin' yer spare, Miss Ruttle."

"Don't know what you're talking about, *Mister* Madden!"

"Yeh don't. Did Bram not tell yeh? I tolt him tae tell yeh I needed the extra day or two for tae get them from Donnelly in the town. Seein' as you wuz sick and in the bed I didn't think yeh'd be needin' a car till yeh were better anyway."

Now she remembered. The flat tyre. The flat spare. She leaving him at the roadside and walking home in the rain because she wouldn't get into his van. Wouldn't get into his van because she didn't trust him. Didn't believe he was telling the truth.

"I see," she said, sharply.

Something didn't add up.

"How did you know I was well again? That I'd be up?" She checked her watch. "It's twenty past seven."

"Saw Bram's car leavin' yer house, so I did."

"Oh, so you waited till he left. Till I was alone. Why was that? Do you watch my every move, *Mister* Madden?"

She watched a series of contortions pull at his features. He scuffed the ground. Stared at her.

"Why would I be doin' the like of that? I was only tryin' tae help yeh out."

"I don't know. *You* tell *me*."

"Beats me what yer gettin' at, Miss Ruttle," he said, all innocent. "It'll be twenty-five pounds by the way . . . that's for the tyres. I'll not charge yeh for me time."

That was big of him. Playing the I'm-decent-like-that tactic to get her on board again. He was clever, this one. A manipulator of the first order. She didn't have that kind of money to spare.

"Yes, well . . . I'll pay you when . . . when I get to the bank."

"Aye . . . r-right . . . right yeh be, no worries," he said, preparing to go.

She thought of something.

"Oh, by the way, Mr Madden . . ."

"Aye."

"Bram Hilditch knows all about why I was merely protecting myself with the knife on the day of Maud's break-in. So you don't have to hold that petty threat over me any more, d'you hear?"

He didn't answer. Just shook his head, gestured with both hands and walked away.

CHAPTER THIRTY-EIGHT

Bram was in a pickle.

Rita's outburst was the last thing he'd expected. Ordering him out like that! He'd never have dreamed she could behave in such a way.

He drove back home, hoping against hope that she wouldn't go over to the Glacken house. God knows what Lenny the Enforcer might do. Perhaps his parting words about how dangerous the family were would make her think twice.

The sight of the Enforcer reared up: the bulging biceps, the spider tattoos, dead eyes and clenched mouth. The essence of evil darkening the small room where Bram had had the great misfortune to run across him. His painful shoulder a sorry reminder of their encounter.

It was imperative now that he get Rita out of there. That outing to Portaluce he'd mentioned to her seemed the best solution. Far enough away for her to be safe. And far enough away for him to fulfil an obligation to Vivian O'Meara, which now seemed more urgent than ever.

How could he persuade her? That was the question. The Ryan incident and her confinement to bed had caused a major setback in their friendship.

He'd give her time to calm down then go back and try again.

He eased the car round the back of Lucerne House, exiting the vehicle as quietly as possible, just to be on the safe side.

Quietly let himself in by the kitchen-door.

Her Grace had no idea that he'd spent the last three nights at Willow Close. He'd slipped out well after eleven when she was asleep and was back before she awoke at eight.

One thing he could count on with the mother was her sleep pattern. Nine hours every night. You could set your watch by her. Never troubled by insomnia. She'd sleep through an earthquake, as his father used to say.

He stood in the quiet of the hallway, thinking.

All the things happening at Willow Close and the nightmares about Vivian-Bernadette O'Meara pointed to the fact that he needed finally to close at least part of a chapter concerning her.

It would not be easy sharing her secret, but he needed to act. He knew the very man he could trust.

He went into the study. Found Father Moriarty's number and dialled the parochial house.

Rita made her way past the stone circle and followed a path that cut deep into Crocus Wood. In her hand: the binbag containing the Glacken boy's "toys".

There was an urgency now to get the job done. Finish what she'd started. She needed to find a good hiding-place. Somewhere the items wouldn't be discovered. Even though she doubted the boy ever made it out this far, she needed to conceal them well. There was always the possibility of Dan Madden coming across them, returning them to Ryan, and the little brat's tyranny of her would start all over again.

No, that would definitely *not* be happening. She'd make sure of it.

She followed the small path, her passage muted by a carpet of moss and bracken, savouring how pleasant the wood was at that hour of the morning. The air: light with spring and heavy with bird-song. The sun: making a valiant effort through the leaf-choked trees and mist.

She tramped on, feeling good that she was putting paid to things, and safe because she carried the knife in her pocket – a necessary precaution against the unexpected. Now more than ever she needed to protect herself.

She let her gaze shift from the path, surveying the way ahead. Noticed how, some two hundred yards farther along, the track veered sharply and disappeared.

The stone circle was her guide. She could not afford to lose sight of it or she'd get hopelessly lost. The last thing she needed to happen.

She set the bag down. Turned, scanning through the wall of trees.

Yes, there they were! Just barely visible, shining like bits of broken china, bone-white in the distance.

Better not go any farther. She'd have to find someplace here.

She turned round again. Reached down for the bag—

Schklikt, klikt.

She froze at the sound of a shotgun being racked for action.

Fell to her knees, terrified.

Oh, Christ, he's found me! He's trying to kill me!

She clamped a hand to her mouth to stifle a scream.

Bam!

A dead pigeon fell like a stone right in front of her.

Oh, Jesus!

She scrambled to her feet.

Ran into the bushes.

Her right shoe flew off. No way could she stop to retrieve it.

Hide the bag, she told herself. Hide the bag and go.

In her mind's eye she saw Ryan's smug little face, laughing at her. It was as if he and the bird and the stalker – *the stalker that lived in their attic* – were in it together.

She quested frantically about. Spotted a tree-stump not too far into the thicket.

It would have to do.

She hopped across. Parted the bracken. Stuffed the bag behind it, pushed it out of sight and ran like a sprinter back the way she'd come, bloodied foot and all.

"Bram . . . good to see you," Father Moriarty said. "Come in, come in."

"So sorry to impose at this hour, Father, but—" He saw him eye the sling. "Nothing serious, just a sprain. Could be worse."

The priest – a tall, pale man in his mid-seventies – waved a hand.

"That's good to hear, and always good to see you, Bram . . . more than ever these days since you're not in the guise of undertaker. I'm sure you're glad to have that grave business all behind you."

He chuckled at his own witticism and led the way through to the sitting-room – a gloomy, green room full of sombre furniture, redolent of the cloister. A fire was crackling in the grate.

"I'd offer you tea, but Marjorie doesn't turn up till nine."

"That's all right," Bram said, sitting down nervously in an armchair. "Alas, it's not a social call, Father. Oh that it were!"

"Yes, you said on the phone. Mother okay?"

He took the chair opposite.

"No, nothing like that. She's doing fine. Had a little fall recently, but nothing too serious. Improving well, I'm glad to say, and looking forward to the royal wedding."

The priest grinned. "Like a good many ladies up and down the country I dare say."

"Indeed . . ."

Bram cleared his throat and stared at the floor, wondering how he was going to confide the secret he could carry no longer.

"I need to tell you something, Father . . . something I haven't been able to tell anyone up to now, because . . . well . . ."

The priest said nothing, adopting what Bram imagined was his *persona Christi* role.

Then: "Do you wish to make a confession?"

Bram was not prepared for such a question. The last time he'd engaged in that archaic ritual – the Sacrament of Penance – was during his schooldays when it was obligatory. His mother didn't go in for the protocols of Catholicism, thankfully. She made an effort at Christmastime and Easter, as did his father. Undertaking meant that the Church was a constant feature in their lives, so avoiding it outside the business whenever they could seemed eminently sensible.

"Not so much a confession, Father. It's just that I haven't been able to confide in anyone, least of all my mother about . . . about my last tenant—"

"Vivian O'Meara?"

He nodded.

"Has she been found?"

"Alas, no . . . it's just that I'm having strange dreams about her of late . . . terrible dreams. It's . . . well, it's as if she's trying to tell me something and I believe I know what it might be . . ."

Bram stopped, wondering how he was going to continue. Father Moriarty, conscious of his predicament, filled the pause.

"Poor Vivian . . . such a strange affair! A harmless soul . . . she used to visit the church and just sit for hours in contemplation you know. I tried to talk to her on a few occasions, but she seemed very withdrawn." He shook his head. "Perhaps I should have tried harder, but you can't really help someone if they're not willing to accept the hand of friendship. So really, Bram, you can't blame yourself for her disappearance."

"Her disappearance isn't the full story, Father."

"No?"

"It's not . . . not that she didn't want help, Father. It's just that she was too ashamed you see."

"Ashamed? I don't understand."

"She was . . . she was pregnant I'm afraid."

"*What!*" The priest was aghast. "What on earth are you saying?"

Bram knew what he was thinking.

"N-No, it wasn't me, Father. I had no idea either. She wore those long clothes to conceal it. And she concealed it well."

"So how do you know all this? Did she tell you?"

Bram shook his head ruefully. "Sadly, no . . . she told me nothing. I found out in the most awful way imaginable."

"Go on."

"She stopped answering the door you see . . . and all the window-blinds were drawn. Her aunt lives in Sligo, so naturally . . . naturally, I assumed she'd gone to visit her. Then, after three weeks I thought it odd she hadn't contacted me, so I . . . so I let myself in. That's . . . that's when the smell hit me."

"Dear . . . God!"

"I know. I was in shock naturally, because . . . because I thought I was going to discover her corpse upstairs, but . . . in the box-room I found . . . found the remains of the little one . . . just lying in a corner under a blanket. I . . . I couldn't even tell if it was a boy or a girl. The smell was overpowering. Even though I replaced the carpet, it had seeped through the floorboards . . . and it can still be detected, that foul odour, even . . . even after all this time."

The priest was dumbstruck. The cackling and hissing fire standing in for the words he couldn't articulate.

"I had to bury it, Father. So I . . . so I . . . I had a little casket. A beautiful piece my grandfather had made . . . the finest rosewood, inlaid with mother of pearl. A very precious piece . . . and I placed the remains in it. It was the least I could do. Then . . . under cover of darkness I interred it in the back garden of Willow Close. There's a stone cherub that marks the spot."

Father Moriarty sighed heavily. "Dear God! I had no idea . . . no idea she was in such difficulty. That's so terrible. So terrible altogether."

"But how could you know? How could anyone know?" Bram pleaded. "I couldn't tell anyone. I see with hindsight that she was banished to Killoran by her family. Cast out through no fault of her own I'm sure. The least I could do was keep her secret. Do the decent thing. That's what she'd have wanted I believe."

"You did the best you could do, given the circumstances, Bram. You can't blame yourself."

"I appreciate that, Father. I hope I did. But I think Vivian, being such a religious person, resents the fact I didn't give the little thing a Christian burial, and perhaps that's why I'm having these strange dreams about her."

"You want me to bless the grave?"

Bram nodded, grateful for the priest's understanding. "I'd much appreciate it if you could, Father."

"I'd be happy to."

The sounds of somebody dismounting from a bicycle pulled them promptly back to the present.

"Don't stir, Bram. Just the housekeeper."

Bram got up. "No, Father, I've taken up enough of your time already."

"I suppose it's best your new tenant doesn't learn any of this?"

"Absolutely."

"How is she faring by the way?"

"Very well," Bram lied.

"One wonders how we can conduct the ceremony without her knowledge."

But Bram had already taken care of that.

"She's going away to Portaluce for a few days, so I'll let you know, Father."

"Good enough. I'll await your call then."

Bram thanked him and walked away, relieved that he'd finally shared Vivian O'Meara's story.

With one disagreeable task taken care of, his next priority was getting Rita Ruttle out of Willow Close and away to Portaluce as soon as possible.

CHAPTER
THIRTY-NINE

Portaluce, Antrim Coast

Dreams.

Unsettling dreams.

So many of them so hard to countenance: scenes from the past, massing, parting, smashing, cracking, scattering far and wide, then returning to merge and fuse and meld together again and again and again into crazy murals of pain. And she, Dorinda Walsh, stuck in the paralyzed moment, having to observe the nightmare screenings through a sleep-induced coma of despair.

She sees a little girl climbing stairs.

Oh, the treads are so steep and it takes effort, slow, painstaking effort, to conquer each one! The carpet is red with daubs of yellow the colour of buttercups, the texture thin in places where boards show through. The wallpaper is yellow too, with swirls of tiny red roses riding alongside her.

The child is not alone.

Her left hand is gripped by a bigger one: a male hand coated with fine black hairs. The bigness of the man looms over her. When she looks up he's like a tree, so tall she can't see the top of him where his hair or the leaves would be.

The stairs are like a cliff-face. Three flights to the summit, going all the way up under a fall of dingy light. Up and up and up they go. And it is cold, so very cold. Icy fingers reach up the stairwell to pinch her legs between ankle-sock and hem.

The man, tugging her along, has no care that he might be hurting her. Her small arm is stretched beyond its reach, tiny hand frozen in his heavy grip. She dare not cry out.

Crying is a dangerous thing.

So she keeps her head down, focusing on the daisy motif cut-outs on the toes of her little patent shoes. And she thinks of Amy, her pet canary, asleep in her cage below, tiny beak folded inside her silky, yellow wings. Picturing Amy asleep makes her feel warm and happy and safe for now.

Finally, they gain the landing at the very top of the house.

The man halts, glares down at her.

"I hope you're not crying," he says in a voice charged with menace.

She looks up at him – the towering, tree-like man – and shakes her head from side to side.

"Good!" he barks.

With that he yanks her down a corridor to a door at the far end. It's painted bright blue, with fluffy clouds floating across it. A door into paradise.

Her little heart flutters. She imagines a wonderland beyond the door: a wonderland of sunny skies and rolling hills, where rabbits hop and children skip in meadows of the most brilliant green. Just like the images in the bedtime storybook that Mama used to read to her.

The man turns the handle and throws the door wide.

But there is no blissful world beyond the door. Only darkness, a thick curtain of black.

He shoves her in.

The door slams shut.

The little girl screams . . .

Dorrie, jolted back to semi-consciousness in her white cell, sensed that her own cries had roused her. Her head was exploding. The cacophony in her ears, like an orchestra all out of tune, banging and crashing against her skull.

She tossed from side to side and opened her eyes.

It was all right. She was safe again. She glimpsed the crucifix above the door and took it as a sign. A good sign.

Then, of a sudden in the lock, the sound of a key turning.

Someone opened the door.

Her throat constricted. She half-closed her eyes again, feigning sleep, not daring to move.

She heard the murmur of a woman's voice, the rustle of her raiment. All at once a figure, like an apparition, glided into the room. Was it an angel? Was it a ghost, a shape-shifter stealing in from some mystical realm to carry her away from this netherworld of grief?

The figure in white rested a hand on her forehead and took her pulse. The patient sensed immediately she was safe again, away from the tall man and the steep stairs and that sky-door that opened into the blackest pit.

Soon she slipped back into the tender embrace of the sleep state.

And so the dreams and nightmares came and went, as did the hours of light and dark, like pages turning in a life-sized picture book.

Sometimes the pictures were vile and ugly, thick with images of beasts and brutes. But soon the sun came out and burned them all away, so that only the brightest and best pages of the little girl's life shone through.

Mama hugging her tight.

Mama kissing her cheek.

Mama blowing out candles on a birthday cake.

Mama helping her dress.

Mama, oh dear lovely Mama! The scent of her hair, the light of her smile, the lilt of her voice. Mama, her saviour. Mama, her champion. Mama, her buffer against the cruel world.

On the fourth morning of her incarceration, F-32 awoke into the early morning light, and knew instinctively that all was well, that today she'd be leaving the white convent by the sea and going home.

The sorry episode that had propelled her behind the locked door of the cell-like room had passed. The world had righted itself again. Flawed it might still be – but she could live with that. She'd lived with such disruptions for a long time and would no doubt encounter them again in the future.

For now though, those demons – so much a part of her – had been fought and conquered: locked and chained below decks with the help of medication and the kindness of strangers in this sterile, ascetic place that was somewhere between a hospital and a cloister.

She threw back the bed-covers and went directly to the concealed closet.

It felt good to put on clothes again. There were no mirrors to reflect this small victory, but she imagined any garb an improvement on the regulation bed-shift with the embroidered monogram. Had she been a prisoner? It certainly felt like it. Dismayed, she placed the nightgown on a hanger and thrust it back into the closet for the next unfortunate addict.

She opened the bedside table and took out her handbag and effects, her mind focused on simply leaving as soon as possible.

But when all packed up and ready, a desperate sadness took hold of her, forcing her to the window. Why, she could not know, for the scene that greeted her was anything but threatening: the sky cloudless, the ocean as still as glass, so much at odds with the bruised vista she'd been expecting.

The beach shimmered golden in the morning light. The beauty of it bringing tears, and the lines of a poem:

> My tale is heard, and yet it was not told,
> My fruit is fallen, and yet my leaves are green,
> My youth is spent, and yet I am not old,
> I saw the world, and yet I was not seen . . .

"It's good to see you on your feet again."

A woman's voice had broken in on her meditation.

She turned back from the window to see a nun standing just inside the door, holding a chair.

"Sorry . . . I . . . I never heard you enter, Sister."

"Oh, there's no need to apologize." She came forward and placed the chair by the window. "We're all allowed our daydreams. How do you feel today?"

"Much better, thank you."

"Good. Please . . . won't you sit for a little?"

She drew up the other chair.

"Beautiful morning," the nun continued. "The sun is God, and He paints such arresting scenes for us, don't you think?"

"Yes. But . . . this . . . this scene makes me sad. I don't take pleasure in it. In fact I don't want to look at it any more."

"That's too bad," the nun said.

"I'd . . . I'd like very much to leave today and go home, Sister."

"Do you know where home is?" She gave her a searching look. The look a mother might give her child before setting her on the road to school.

"Yes, I do, Sister."

"Are you sure you're all right?"

"Yes, quite sure. Thank you."

"Here, take this." She passed her a small card. "The Samaritans . . . you can call them any time . . . just in case you need to talk to some-one . . . in the future. You can do so in the strictest confidence."

"Thank you. I'll remember that."

"Now, let's walk you to your car."

CHAPTER FORTY

Samaritan Centre, Killoran

"Samaritans . . . May I help you?"

It was 7 p.m. on Friday evening and Rita-Mae was on duty with a sore foot and a troubled mind.

Despite recent setbacks her important voluntary work could not be neglected. She had the dates and times marked in red on a calendar that hung in the kitchen of 8 Willow Close and she dared not miss an appointment, no matter how bad she might be feeling, or how perilous things might seem. Saving lives seemed more important than ever now, anchoring her in a rapidly changing situation she felt she had little control over.

She'd spent the previous two days and nights behind the locked doors of number 8 – all windows shut and blinded – keeping watch on the Glacken house through a crack in the curtains of her bedroom. Waiting for mother and son to reappear. But there was no sign. The curtains on both upper windows remained drawn. They'd obviously gone off somewhere. But the minute she saw those curtains pulled back she'd be over there for a showdown.

Bram Hilditch had called twice, but she hadn't answered the door. The phone had rung several times, but she'd ignored that too. Who else could it be but the landlord, with his fake sympathy and empty apologies?

His betrayal of her with the Glacken boy was simply one insult too many.

"Samaritans . . . May I help you?" she said again, into the pause.

The person on the other end didn't respond.

She waited.

Phone pressed tight to her ear, detecting only the shallowest breathing on the other end.

A woman perhaps.

Or a man holding the receiver out of range.

She studied her right foot, bandaged across the instep. One dead pigeon and a shoeless flight out of the woods – a journey of a good ten minutes – had reduced the foot to a mosaic of minor cuts and grazes. Wearing shoes was too painful so she'd resorted to sandals, even though it was not sandal weather. It might be the middle of spring, but the air was still holding on to an unseasonal chilliness.

The lull on the end of the line was getting longer. The breathing sustained and shallow, but regular. Not likely a "live" suicide, she told herself. Not like Kevin, the angry young man in the phone box whom she'd lost not so very long before.

She listened more intently for secondary sounds. Cars going by. The creak of a chair. The latter would tell her the caller was not in a public phone box.

But there was nothing. Only the faint breathing and the silence.

Someone ill in bed? Dying. Someone dying, friendless and alone, but at the very end wanting the comfort of hearing another human voice.

She'd try again.

"It's all right . . . I can wait . . . wait as long as you like," she said, tone softer, quieter. "Take your time . . . there's no rush . . . my name's Rita by the way. I'm here for you."

All at once she heard the receiver fall back on to the cradle.

The line went dead.

Well, she'd given it her best shot. If the person *had* passed away at least she'd been there for them.

She brought her mind back to the present. Blossom's booklet, *The Life of Saint Catherine of Siena*, was still in her pocket. She decided to delve into it, to pass the time between calls. Having been to the Glacken house and discovered the skylight window, she had the unnerving idea that someone was up there, watching.

Had watched Vivian-B and was now watching *her*.

Vivian-Bernadette O'Meara's writings, still in the drawer of the kitchen table along with those three intrusive photographs, had mentioned someone – a voyeur – watching her. Watching her every move.

Rita-Mae had not been able to return to that drawer since the fateful day Maud Gilhooley had bobbed up her path asking after the cake tin. So much had happened since then that she was simply too afraid to read more. But the notes she'd read about Vivian-Bernadette on file and those pages of lines she'd written were like some kind of punishment, playing in her mind like a looped recording.

I must follow in the footsteps of Catherine of Siena.

She looked at the phone. Perhaps that caller hadn't died and was summoning the courage to ring again.

Perhaps?

She turned to the first page:

CATHERINE WAS BORN DURING THE PLAGUE IN SIENA ON 25 MARCH 1347 INTO A FAMILY OF TWENTY-FIVE CHILDREN. HALF OF HER BROTHERS AND SISTERS DID NOT SURVIVE CHILDHOOD. CATHERINE WAS A TWIN, BUT HER SISTER DIED IN INFANCY.

That last made her think of her own twin sister, who'd died at birth – or so her mother claimed. What if she hadn't died?

Rita-Mae sighed. How different life might have been had her sister lived! She'd never have had to struggle through the years on her own. As time wore on and Rita-Mae grew up, her heartless mother, Hedda, point-blank refused to even discuss the dead baby. Would lash out at the mere mention of her, so Rita-Mae learned to keep her counsel with regard to the little girl she'd never known.

At sixteen, Catherine's parents wanted her to marry her brother-in-law, who'd become a widower on the death of Bonaventura, but Catherine resisted the proposal by cutting her hair and beginning a regime of extreme fasting.

Prayer and fasting would become a daily practice and end in her death at the age of thirty-three.

Brrring brrring . . . Brrring brrring . . .

The phone was ringing again.

She snatched it up.

"Samaritans . . . May I—"

"Rita . . . aye, Rita. How you?"

She caught her breath.

The stalker!

Lenny!

"I don't have to talk to you . . . y-you're not a serious case."

"I think you should listen tae me. For if you hang up on me, like you did the last time, you might . . . well, just let's say you might end up regretting it." A pause. "I mean *really* regretting it."

She palmed the mouthpiece. Took a deep breath.

"How dare you threaten me?!"

"Saw what you done to the boy, Rita."

"What boy? I don't know what you're talking about."

Sniggering. "Think you do."

She heard drink being gulped down.

"Aye . . . I think you do. See, I miss nothin', Rita. I see everything, and I'm not likin' what I'm seein' of *you* these days. In fact 'cos of what you did tae the boy I think I'll have tae take you in hand, if you get me meanin'?"

She couldn't find her voice. Her throat had turned to dust. There was a glass of water beside her, but she dared not touch it. Dared not let him hear her fear.

"See, the last crazy bitch that lived in that house . . . she started out all right, just like yerself, then she insulted the boy. That was the wrong thing tae do. Very, very wrong. Had to give her a good seein' to, in a manner of speakin'."

She heard him drag on the cigarette. Wanted to slam down the receiver. But stayed her hand, stricken by the threat.

"Maybe we could work something out, Rita. Some way you could . . . well, please me . . . put me in a better mood, if you get me meanin'. 'Cos you're a good-lookin' woman. Don't need any of that oul' make-up. And you don't drink either. Never seen you buy drink since you moved here. I like that. A good-livin' woman . . . aye, good-livin', just the way I like me women. No vices, like the rest of us. Now, why don't we start by you tellin' me what colour knickers yer wearin' under that nice blue skirt?"

"None of your business! I'm *not* wearing a blue skirt," she snapped, looking down at the skirt, which was indeed blue.

He chuckled. She heard him inhale again.

"Think you are. That foot of yours will take a bitta time tae heal up too."

"You stay the hell away from me, you hear! I won't be driven out by the likes of you. Think you're so bloody clever, intimidating women on their own. What a brave, bloody coward you are! Well, hear this, I'm not afraid of the likes of you! You're lower than the scum of the earth. Should be locked up. Or maybe you *are* locked up somewhere and this is how you get your kicks. Now, I'm going to terminate this call. Goodbye!"

She slammed the phone down, heart hammering. Head pounding. She'd broken every rule in the Samaritan handbook, but who would know? She'd had enough.

She staggered out of the cubicle, gasping for air, the weight of his threat ringing in her ears.

If you hang up on me, like you did the last time, you might . . . well, just let's say you might end up regretting it.

What had she *done*?

What would she do now?

What would *he* do now?

Oh dear God, he could be outside the Centre, waiting!

Brrring brrring . . . Brrring brrring . . .

The phone was ringing again. She knew it was *him* again. Just knew it in her bones.

She needed to leave the Centre, and fast. Never mind that she had an hour of duty still to do.

Switch the phone over to Belfast, she told herself. If volunteers felt unwell they were free to do that. And she *was* unwell.

Her hands were trembling as she went through the process, dialling the relevant numbers so the operator could make the connection.

Task completed, she found a pill and gulped it down, to stave off another attack.

There was no time to waste.

She switched off the lights.

Quietly turned the doorknob and peered outside. Two lonely street-lights showed that hers was the only car. There was no one around.

She slammed the door and made a dash for the vehicle.

CHAPTER
FORTY-ONE

Next morning she arose to a catastrophe.

The butterfly case smashed to pieces on the landing. Wings rent asunder and crushed into the mounting board.

Shards of glass scattered everywhere.

He'd been in while she slept.

The case was too high up on the wall for the boy to reach.

He knew everything about her – Lenny, the TM caller. Lenny the stalker. Had been tracking her every move from the minute she arrived in Willow Close.

Why?

She lurched to the bathroom and threw up.

He'd been in *while she slept* behind the bolted door of her bedroom. He'd invaded her space and she *hadn't heard a thing*.

She splashed cold water on her face. Wept at her reflection in the glass. The eyes of a haunted woman, glassy and vacant, stared back at her. A woman on the run, too exhausted to run any more, the finishing line too far in the distance now. Too, too far.

The little house, no longer safe.

"Why's this happening to me? Oh, dear God, *why's it happening?*"

She stood at the sink, gripping the basin; pins and needles prickling her arms, tears blinding her, thoughts spinning frantically like a conjurer's plates on sticks.

She'd fled Larne only to have her life contaminated by another monster, the like of Harry.

Her life had patterns that kept repeating. Now there was only one way left to put an end to the mayhem for good.

The sleeping pills in the cabinet were only a hand-stretch away.

Vivian-B had prayed and starved herself in order to cope. Emulating the behaviour of an ancient saint to escape her sorry life. Making *herself* suffer, as victims always do.

Had he killed her? In the box-room; had he killed her? Or had she simply retreated in there and faded away? The foul smell: the only sad reminder that she'd ever existed, along with the concealed letter in the butterfly case and a few scant notes in the Samaritan file.

An overdose? Yes, the easiest way. Just go to sleep and never wake up. How many times in her life had she come close? Perhaps it was finally time. She wept bitterly, feeling such a failure – such a fraud. How many times had she pulled people back from the brink of death, down the Samaritan helpline, only now to succumb herself?

She went downstairs. Saw there was post – a small white envelope was lying on the mat.

She picked it up. No stamp. No address.

No, it was not post. The envelope was similar to the one Vivian-Bernadette had received containing the photographs.

It was from *him*.

She carried it through to the lounge, not really caring any more. Sat down at the table by the window and boldly tore it open.

It contained three photographs. Candid shots, with her as the subject, as she'd been expecting.

The first showed her washing dishes in the kitchen sink.

The second had caught her emerging from her car at the rear of the house.

The third showed her hanging washing on the line.

Rat-a-tat-tat . . . rat-a-tat-tat.

"Rita, are you in?"

Bram Hilditch's voice, urgent, through the letterbox.

Her immediate impulse was to hide. Not answer it. His precious butterfly case lay in pieces. How would she explain that?

But she'd be gone tonight, so what did it matter? And *she* was not guilty of the offence.

She got up and admitted him.

"Thank God I've finally got you in, Rita!" He snatched off his hat and clamped it to his chest.

"Oh . . . I wasn't going anywhere, Mr Hilditch."

Her voice was calm. She was amazed at her own composure. Strange when you make up your mind about suicide, the clarity it bestows. Fear gone. She revelled in the rare feeling. Stood before him, dauntless.

"We need to get you away from here, Rita. Today, if possible."

He spotted the snapshots displayed on the table.

"What are . . . what are these?"

"You tell *me*."

"Good God, what are you saying?"

"You're a photographer after all. I naturally assumed that you—"

"You're being ridiculous . . . absolutely ridiculous."

She pulled out the drawer, drew out Vivian-Bernadette O'Meara's letter and spread the contents before him.

"Well, I had my suspicions when I found these. Your former tenant got the same."

He sat down, staring at the photos – Vivian in the box-room, combing her hair, Vivian at the line, hanging out washing, Vivian with her bag of groceries, carrying them into the house – staring at them, hand clamped to his forehead.

311

"Where . . . where did you find these? I cleaned this house thoroughly."

"Hidden behind your butterfly case."

She saw his struggle. "What!"

"Yes, that's another calamity you have to see. Come."

He followed her up the stairs. Halted halfway, realizing what she meant.

"Did you—"

"No, I did not. I got up this morning to find it smashed."

"But who . . . who . . . ?"

"The man who's been following me from the moment I set foot in this place. The stalker . . . calls himself Lenny."

"What?!"

"Yes, Lenny's been making my life hell since I moved here. I thought it was you at first. Then I thought it was Madden. But now I believe he lives over there in that house with the horrid Glacken woman and her son . . . in the attic. Did you know he was there all along?"

Bram shook his head. "I . . . I don't understand. H-How do you know his name?"

She had to be careful. Could not divulge her Samaritan work to anyone for reasons of confidentiality.

"He rings me . . . threatens me."

"You mean . . . you mean he rings *here*?"

"Yes, and last night while I was sleeping he went one step further . . . came in here and did this."

"Good God! Didn't you hear him?"

She shook her head. "No, I was asleep. I sleep very soundly when I . . ."

"When you . . . ?"

"When I have to take medication for the migraine, the epilepsy, the insomnia, the stress . . . my many ills."

They were still on the stairs. She at the top, hands spread, looking down upon him. He, the supplicant, gazing up at her, beseeching. Both striking poses like something from a religious tableau.

"Rita, you're under a lot of stress." He was looking at her gravely. "You need to leave this house right away."

"And go where exactly?"

"The seaside . . . Portaluce. Now's the time. The guesthouse I mentioned: the Ocean Spray. I know the lady who runs it. You can stay there for a few days."

"I can't afford to stay there . . . besides which, I'm not afraid of this Lenny character any more. He can go to hell as far as I'm concerned. He'll not drive *me* out."

She thought of the sleeping pills in the cabinet. When the landlord left she'd clear up her things. Ring Grace Thorne. Go to bed and never wake up.

"Glacken is a very dangerous individual. And don't worry about that. The money I mean."

"I don't want your charity!"

"Please, Rita . . . you're in a dangerous situation. Lenny Glacken is a high-up in the IRA. He's in and out of prison regularly, but when he's out he lives with his daughter over there. I tried to tell you, but you wouldn't let me in or answer the phone."

Mention of the IRA gave her a jolt. Now she understood the danger.

"And you don't have to accept my charity. You paid me in advance, remember? April's rent will cover the costs of the Ocean Spray more than adequately."

She looked down at his pleading face and knew he was making a lot of sense. Bram Hilditch was a sincere man. She could see that now. He cared enough about her to want to protect her.

"If you pack some things I'll drive you there now. It's the safest thing to do, Rita. You're too good a person to be left at the mercy of that maniac. I simply won't allow that to happen. It's imperative I take you somewhere safe."

She saw him adjust his glasses. "I . . . I care about what happens to you, Rita. Truly I do. And I'm so very sorry that these awful things have happened while you've been living here, in my hometown. You deserve better."

Had she heard him right? He said he *cared* about her. No one had ever said that to her in her whole sorry life. Not that she could recall. And he meant it too. He stood there on the stair, gazing up at her and she *knew* he meant it. His words kindling a tiny flame of hope, wavering bravely there in all the darkness.

She felt tears well up.

"You . . . you care . . . care about *me?*" she asked, amazed.

"Yes . . . yes, of course I do."

"Why?"

"Well, because . . . because, you're a very fine person and . . . and you deserve better . . . much better."

He was throwing her a lifeline. Maybe this was indeed the chance she deserved.

"Thank you, Bram," she said turning away so he wouldn't see her tears. "I'll . . . I'll just get my things."

CHAPTER
FORTY-TWO

Mid-afternoon and Gladys Millman, glamorous proprietor of the Ocean Spray, was relaxing in her drawing-room after a hectic lunch-hour with a rewarding Brandy Alexander and an *Elegant Interiors* magazine.

She was considering the merits of Laura Ashley's designer collection and checking the cost of some rather splendid curtain fabric in Aviary Garden Apple when she heard a car drawing up.

"Now, who could that be?" she muttered, not a little piqued that her "me time" was being interrupted.

Reluctant to move from her comfortable sofa, she lifted a tiny bell from the drinks table and rang it vigorously.

Seconds later, the door opened and Maureen – resident maid, waitress, cleaner and general dogsbody – appeared in the room like a well-trained puppy.

"Yes, ma'am?"

"Maureen, dear, I believe we have visitors. I have no memory of booking anyone in. Did you?"

"No, ma'am."

"Then kindly tell whoever it is" – she checked her watch – "that luncheon is over. Dinner's at five and we have no rooms left."

"But there *are* rooms—"

"That is so, but they are singles and if my eyesight is not deceiving me I see a couple arriving."

"Yes, ma'am," Maureen said, curtseying and withdrawing quietly to leave the boss in peace.

Gladys sighed and took another fortifying sip of her cocktail, happy that she'd seen off the tiresome intrusion. She returned to the Laura Ashley spread.

She was getting tired of the oceanic theme in the dining-room and was considering something more daring for summer. A page showing samples of wallpaper caught her eye. "Summer Palace Cranberry," she murmured to herself, trying to ignore the mumble of conversation emanating from reception. She really hoped Maureen would be able to deal with the pair without interrupting her *again*.

"Mmmm . . . 'with bursts of garnet and rose, and hints of millwood truffle'. Now that looks just perfect—"

A soft rapping on the door.

"Spare me," she muttered testily, removing her spectacles. "Yes, Maureen. What is it now?"

The girl entered, looking flustered, closing the door behind her.

"I really thought I could leave you to deal with matters on your own, Maureen. Is it too much to ask?"

"Sorry . . . sorry to trouble you, ma'am, but . . . but the gentleman says it's only for the lady . . . a single room. He won't be staying and . . ."

"I see, and . . ."

Maureen looked warily at the closed door.

Gladys, sensing something was wrong, cast aside the magazine and beckoned her forward.

"Yes, what is it?" she asked, cautiously.

"Well, the lady," Maureen said in a low voice, "the lady with the man looks very like the one that was here in January, Miss Gladys . . . the one that got drunk and you sent over to the drying-out convent."

"*What?*" Gladys glared at her in disbelief and rose. "But are you . . . are you sure?"

"It looks like her, b-but she's a lot thinner . . . s-so maybe it's not her."

"That's all right, Maureen dear. I'll deal with this. The cheek of her thinking she can simply walk in here after the bother she caused us last time! Tell them I'll see to them presently and then go back to your duties in the kitchen."

"Yes, ma'am."

Maureen made her exit.

Mrs Gladys Millman threw back the remains of her cocktail, reapplied her lipstick, smoothed down her Jaeger two-piece of tawny-pecan tweed, and sashayed forth to commence battle with the enemy in the lobby.

"Mrs Millman . . . Gladys, how lovely to see you again!"

Gladys halted mid-stride, disconcerted by the sight of Bram Hilditch, elegantly attired as usual in a chalk-stripe three-piece and trilby. He was clutching a pink travel case, which looked comical and much at odds with the sober suit.

What on earth, she thought, is *he* doing here, and in the company of this *reprobate*? His mother, Octavia, always grandly attired, with her posh accent and upper-crust ways – one of her more "select" customers – stayed a fortnight every summer and, even though she was competition for Gladys, could be forgiven. The Ocean Spray needed more guests of the Mrs Hilditch calibre at that time of year, inundated as it usually was by flocks of tedious farmers and their lumpen, dumpy wives, taking the sea air on the annual Twelfth of July holiday.

But it was only the beginning of April, and Abraham was *not* with his mother but this troublesome person. How very distressing! She wondered if Octavia was aware of the unsuitable liaison and made a mental note to ring her at the earliest opportunity.

"Why, Abraham!" she exclaimed, switching on the charm and trying to ignore the mousy miscreant standing behind him. "I didn't expect to see you here this time of year. I trust Octavia is keeping well?"

Bram came forward and they air-kissed briefly.

"She's very well, thank you, Gladys. And do call me Bram."

"Bram it is. My word, what happened your arm?"

She wasn't at all interested in his confounded arm, but was buying time, trying to decide how to respond to Miss Dorinda Walsh, whose introduction was imminent. She noted that the offender had turned away from them and was gazing wistfully through the window at the spectacular ocean view, as if butter wouldn't melt . . .

How *dare* she?

Images of the precious fox fur she'd lent her were threatening to blind Gladys in a red mist of fury. It had taken five specialist dry-cleanings and a hefty bill to eradicate the stains and reek of booze left by Miss Walsh's drinking spree.

She observed her now, standing in profile by the window. Thinner, definitely, as Maureen had said, and the posture seemed more erect than what Gladys recalled. But wasn't this *person* even a little embarrassed to be here again? The sheer impertinence!

"Oh, it's nothing, just a fall," Bram was saying. "I'll be taking off this blessed sling tomorrow, I'm glad to say. May I introduce my friend, Miss Ruttle?"

Ruttle? Oh, so that's what she's calling herself now, is it?

"She's one of my new tenants," Bram continued. "But unfortunately some urgent repairs need doing at her house, so I thought it best she book in with you for a few days."

No doubt she trashed your house in a drunken stupor like she did my guest-room!

But Gladys was a walking, breathing masterclass in fake sentiment and faux asides. In the hospitality trade you had to be.

"I see," she said, smiling broadly. "Miss Ruttle . . . How do you do?"

"I . . . I'm well, thank you . . . er . . . Mrs . . . ?"

"Millman."

Seen full on, the ghostly face was disconcerting. Gladys eyed her keenly, alert for signs that "Miss Ruttle" might remember her, but there wasn't the slightest flicker of recognition in the large, doe-like eyes.

She was either a very good actress or she had a doppelgänger.

"Sorry, yes . . . Mrs Millman."

She was minded to add "Don't you remember me?" but at that precise moment a family – husband, wife and two kids – returned from an outing and headed through to the lounge bar. She decided for appearance's sake not to make a scene. Besides, it was a relief to hear that this so-called Miss Ruttle was a mere tenant of Abraham's and not his consort.

Gladys slipped beautifully into the busy proprietor mode and went behind the reception desk to check the register.

"A week should be enough," Bram said. "If that's all right, Gladys, and you have the space?"

Well, it *isn't* all right actually. How on earth am I going to keep tabs on this one for a whole week? Her couple of days in January caused havoc enough.

Never mind. She'd go through the motions for the time being. Have a word with Bram in private when Maureen was showing Miss Ruttle to her room. Then, when the situation had been clarified and Bram fully understood the kind of person he was dealing with, promptly send her on her way again.

After all, there were B & Bs aplenty in the area.

"Yes, now let me see," she said, register open before her. She saw that by a happy coincidence number 5 was free. It was the room that Miss Walsh had occupied last time. *Perhaps being again in the same room might jog her memory.*

"Number five all right?" she called over Bram's shoulder, irritated that "Miss Ruttle" was hanging back, letting her landlord conduct the checking-in. "It's on the second floor."

But Miss Ruttle continued to gaze through the window, seemingly unaware that Mrs Millman had even addressed her.

"Should be fine," Bram said, a little flustered.

"Is her hearing defective?" Gladys shot back, miffed that she was being ignored. Either that or she's most likely suffering a hangover, she felt like adding.

"No, no, nothing like that," Bram confided in hushed tones, leaning in. "It's just that she's come through a lot lately and is feeling . . . how shall I say . . . a little under the weather I'm afraid. That's why I thought the sea air might do her good."

"I see," Gladys said just as quietly. "Best in that case to get her settled in, Bram. I'll get Maureen to show her up."

"Splendid, Gladys. I knew I could depend on you!"

She was surprised to see him immediately reach into his pocket and draw out a bundle of notes. "I'll pay you in advance of course."

Gladys smiled, still playing the game. Never mind, very soon she'd be putting the naive fellow right on a thing or two.

"And I hope you'll join me for an Irish coffee in private while your tenant is settling in, Bram. We've such a lot to talk about. Not least being the arrangements for your delightful mother's next stay."

"That would be a pleasure, Gladys."

Maureen was summoned and mounted the stairs ahead of the new guest.

"I'll see you before I go, Rita!" Bram called after her.

"Thank you, Bram," she said, turning. "And, thank *you*, Mrs Millman . . . it was very nice to meet you."

"The pleasure is all mine, Miss Ruttle," Gladys said, banging shut the register. "Now, Bram, let's go through to my drawing-room for that fortifying coffee I promised."

CHAPTER
FORTY-THREE

"Here you are, ma'am," Maureen said, turning the key in the door of number 5 and leading the way into the room.

Rita was pleasantly surprised. It was bright and airy with pale walls and powder-blue furnishings. The plump bed with a lacy eiderdown looked very comfortable and there were fluffy blue towels on the bed-side table the exact match of the carpet and drapes.

The word "luxury" sprang to mind. It must be very expensive, she thought, and wondered how the humble month's rent would cover a couple of nights, let alone a whole week in the grand Ocean Spray.

"Do you like it, ma'am?" the maid asked.

"Oh, it's so very lovely. Yes . . . lovely." She read her nametag. "Thank you very much, Maureen."

"You've got a nice view of the sea too," Maureen said, eager to show off the room's finer points. She crossed to the window and drew back the curtains a little more, to reveal a vista of blue ocean, which echoed the room's colour scheme beautifully.

"How very lovely!" Rita-Mae said again.

"Do you like the sea, ma'am?"

"Er . . . erm, yes, but only to look at. I . . . I can't swim, unfortunately."

The maid simpered. "I can't either, but it's lovely to look at, as you say."

Maureen stood gazing at her with interest, seemingly in no hurry to leave. Rita wondered what was detaining her.

"Well . . . thank you again, Maureen."

Then a thought struck her. She's obviously waiting for a tip.

"Where's my manners, Maureen?" she said, reaching into her handbag.

"No, ma'am, Miss Gladys doesn't allow the staff to take tips from guests. She says it's too American."

"Well, I won't tell her if you won't, Maureen."

"Thank you, ma'am," Maureen said, blushing and pocketing the fifty-pence piece.

Finally she moved towards the door.

"We serve supper at six. Do you want me to put your name down?"

"No . . . no, that's all right. I'm not really hungry. Thank you all the same."

"And breakfast's from seven to ten."

She wouldn't be having that either, but nodded just to please the pleasant young woman.

"Miss Ruttle?" Maureen's expression was unreadable.

"Yes."

"Haven't you stayed with us before?"

"No. Why do you ask?"

"It's just that . . . well, about three months ago there was a woman who stayed here that looked just like you."

"Wasn't me. This is my very first time in this lovely place. Hope it won't be my last."

"Righto," Maureen said, looking a little puzzled. "Must have been somebody else then."

"Yes . . . bye, now, Maureen, and thanks again."

The maid bowed timidly and finally withdrew.

"I must say this is absolutely delicious, Gladys," Bram enthused, taking a sip of the mightily strong Irish coffee she'd set down before him.

The proprietor had tipped a rather healthy measure of whiskey into his glass – a double in fact – in the hope that the alcohol might help him become more expansive about his odd companion.

She could see straightaway that he was overly protective of her and wondered why that might be. Well, he'd be hearing her blunt appraisal of this Ruttle/Walsh person very soon. And she was sure he wouldn't be at all impressed. That double shot of whiskey would, no doubt, help to cushion the blow.

"You always make them perfectly," Bram continued. "How on earth do you manage that flawless separation of coffee and cream?"

"Why, thank you, Bram," Gladys smiled, savouring the compliment. "One pours the cream very slowly over the back of a spoon. It's really not so complicated."

"Extraordinary!" He took another sip, an unappealing moustache of cream appearing on his upper lip. "I take it business is booming as usual."

"Yes, indeed . . . I'm happy to have Easter out of the way. It was rather hectic. The good weather brings them out in force, but who am I to complain? I trust Octavia is keeping well?"

She'd really no interest in Mrs Hilditch's well-being. The woman looked as healthy as a trout every time she turned up at the Ocean Spray. A demanding old biddy at the best of times, but her presence raised the tone somewhat and her yearly stays, in the most expensive suite with gin and Dubonnet on tap, more than covered Mrs Millman's spa treatments at a health farm in Shropshire, where she went each October for a fortnight of refreshment and rejuvenation.

"Had a little fall, but is recovering well," Bram was saying. "Would take a lot to hobble Her Grace I fear."

"And you're now a landlord?" She was steering the conversation away from idle chit-chat and in the direction of tenants and the object of her present interest, now ensconced behind the door of room number 5. "How many properties do you have now?"

"Four in all."

"My word, Bram! That's marvellous. I'm sure it's less onerous than undertaking."

He considered the remark. A doubtful little pause ensuing. Then: "Well, each occupation has its ups and downs, Gladys, I suppose. Less onerous, yes, but some tenants can be tricky. Sometimes hard to tell what you're letting in."

She couldn't but agree with him there. Time to go in for the kill.

"And your tenant, Miss Ruttle, how long has she been renting from you?"

"Oh . . . since the beginning of February. Why d'you ask?"

Gladys set down her coffee. Opened her cigarette case and offered him one. A smoke might help him come to terms with what she was about to reveal, unpleasant as it was going to be.

He shook his head.

She lit up, wondering how to phrase the next bit.

"Well, it's just that I believe I've seen her before, but she didn't go by the name of Ruttle. She called herself Walsh . . . Dorinda Walsh."

Bram frowned. "Oh . . . and where . . . where did you see her?"

"She was here at the end of January."

"Are you sure, Gladys?"

She could see he was quite discomfited. He obviously had feelings for her.

"Well, if it wasn't her I'd find it very odd. Was her spitting image."

"But she's never been to Portaluce. She said so."

"That's what she's telling *you*, Bram." She swallowed a lungful of smoke. Saw him redden.

He got up and stood by the window.

"I'm sorry, but you have to know," Gladys went on. "She caused us no end of bother here. She's an alcoholic; did you know that? We had to send her over there to the convent to dry out. Made an absolute mess of the room. I had to renew the carpet and bedding. She was sick all over the place."

"Now look here, Gladys, that's where you're totally wrong. She's teetotal. Never touches the stuff. Neither does she smoke I might add."

Gladys didn't much care for that last little jibe. She sat up more erectly. Tapped the cigarette in an ashtray. "Really? Well, I'm just telling you what I know."

"Did she sign the register?"

"Why, of course. I'll fetch it."

In seconds Gladys was back. She found the page and showed it to him.

Bram sighed with relief. "I knew you were mistaken, Gladys. That's definitely not Miss Ruttle's handwriting. Hers is very neat and precise, not like that at all."

She was about to say, "It doesn't take an Einstein to change their writing style," but decided not to cause him further upset. It was clear that Bram was quite fond of Miss Ruttle, whoever she might be.

"Oh, I see."

"Yes," he said, taking his seat again. "I can assure you, Gladys, Miss Ruttle is a lady of the utmost probity. I can vouch for that."

Gladys shut the register and sat down also, crossing her fine legs elegantly at the knee.

"A case of mistaken identity then. I *am* sorry to have brought it up, Bram," she added, thinking that it would be a shame if Octavia Hilditch were to withdraw her patronage of the Ocean Spray on the advice of her son, and the precious fortnight at Ragdale Hall spa was to disappear.

She raised her Irish coffee. "Well, here's to friendship, Bram, and the arrival of another summer."

"Yes, indeed." He smiled and raised his glass.

Then: "My goodness!" he said suddenly. "My goodness gracious me!"

"What is it, Bram?"

"I've just remembered. Miss Ruttle once told me that she had a twin sister who died at birth."

"Oh . . . and what exactly are you saying?"

He hesitated, choosing his words carefully. "Well, what I'm saying is: what if she didn't die? What if the mother gave her up for adoption because she couldn't afford to keep two children and . . . and . . . my God, sh-she's living here in Ireland and . . . and neither she nor Rita even knows of the other's existence."

"Well, it *is* possible," Gladys conceded grudgingly. "Stranger things have happened."

"Did Miss Walsh leave an address?"

"No. But I know who'll have more information about her."

"Really?"

"Yes, the convent over there. It doubles as a drying-out clinic. She stayed with them for a few days until she was well enough to drive herself home."

"I'll go over there immediately," Bram said, more animated than ever.

"But won't you finish your coffee first?"

"Of course." He lifted the glass and downed it in one gulp.

"I'll call back again, Gladys, to say cheerio to Rita."

"Are you going to tell her?"

He shook his head. "Best not for the time being. I'll do my investigations first. Wouldn't like to get her hopes up, for it all to come to nothing."

Gladys smiled. "Yes, perhaps that's wisest, Bram. We wouldn't want that. It's quite a lot to take in after all."

Hand on the doorknob, he turned. "Oh, it would be so amazing for Rita you know, to find she has a sister. She's such a very fine person, but lonely on her own. You won't breathe a word of this, will you? I mean . . . not even to Maureen?"

"Your secret is mine, Bram. Scout's honour."

She gave a mock salute and both chuckled.

"See you when you get back," she said. "I'm dying to hear what the nuns tell you. Over supper of course."

"That would be a pleasure, Gladys. An absolute pleasure."

CHAPTER FORTY-FOUR

Bram hastened along the promenade towards the convent of the Daughters of Divine Healing in a state of high excitement.

After all poor Rita had come through, something incredible was taking shape. The fates had conspired to bring her to Killoran and into his life so that *he*, Bram Hilditch, could be the agent who'd locate her long-lost sister and reunite them.

He'd always believed in destiny. Today he was experiencing it at first hand and it was an amazing feeling. "Actions are the seed of fate; deeds grow into destiny." He'd always liked the maxim. Now he was doing just that: taking action to secure a better future for Rita. He'd find her sister. And the good deed would see the flowering of a destiny that he hoped would include him as well.

He mounted the steps to the large front door of the convent – so high and towering it appeared to be nearly twice his height – and raised the weighty brass knocker. Struck the metal plate three times and waited.

The convent's elevated position on the promontory gave an imposing view over the Atlantic and to bide his time he stood in contemplation of it, conscious of the fact that he'd never before been granted such a prospect.

The remote white convent, which he'd gazed up at so often on his many visits to the little seaside town, had until now been nothing more than a splendid architectural feat lending a mysterious beauty to the coastline. He'd never thought of it as being an actual place where people lived. Perhaps that word "convent" dampened any curiosity he might have had. Until now he'd been totally ignorant of the fact it was a drying-out shelter for alcoholics.

It was a quiet, windless afternoon with just a hint of sunshine burning through the cloud. The briny smell of the ocean filled his nostrils and he took a few deep breaths of the clean, crisp air to steady himself before turning back to the door.

Nothing seemed to be stirring within, so he raised the knocker again, striking more heavily this time.

Without warning, a hatch at head height, which he hadn't noticed, was swiftly drawn back and he saw the upper half of a nun's face.

"Good afternoon," she said. "May I help you?"

Bram removed his hat. "Yes, indeed. Good day, Sister. I wish to make inquiries about a certain Dorinda Walsh, who stayed with you for a few days in January. Would it be all right if I came in?"

The nun nodded and slid the hatch home again. He heard several bolts being drawn back then the jangle of keys. Finally, a small door in the structure opened and she stood back to admit him.

"Your name is . . . ?"

"Abraham . . . Abraham Hilditch." He held out his hand, but she simply nodded, smiled demurely and directed him to a seat – a wooden bench of the penitential kind – in the cavernous hallway.

"I'm Sister Magdalena. Wait here, please." She set off down a long corridor, her feet making barely a sound on the polished tiles.

He heard a door opening and shutting, but apart from that the place was like the grave. No other sounds could be heard from within and nothing from outside could penetrate the thick, ancient walls. He wondered where all the recovering addicts might be. It was quite a sprawling building, so they were perhaps housed in a separate wing, well away from the visiting public.

He sat uneasily, wondering what he was going to learn about Miss Ruttle's twin sister.

What an amazing coincidence! His heart leaped at the very thought.

"Mr Hilditch?" The suddenness of the voice made him jump. Sister Magdalena appeared like an apparition, hands folded in front of her.

"Mother Clare will see you now, Mr Hilditch. Follow me, please."

She led him down a series of corridors and showed him into a spartan office, whose only nod to trendiness was a large palm in one corner, set in a garish ceramic pot.

Seated behind a desk was an elderly nun robed in the blue habit of her order. Late seventies, he supposed, with the pallid complexion and grim air of the dedicated ascetic.

"Mr Hilditch," Sister Magdalena announced and withdrew, pulling the door to, but not quite shutting it.

Mother Clare gave him a thin smile, but did not get up. "Please take a seat, Mr Hilditch."

There was something peculiar about her eyes.

"Thank you so much for seeing me, Mother Clare," Bram began. "I'm interested in the whereabouts of Dorinda Walsh."

"In here we don't use names. To us she was patient F-32."

"R-Right . . . I see. Well, any information you have would be greatly appreciated."

He saw now why her eyes were so unsettling. They were each of a different hue, the one much darker than the other.

"I'm sorry to disappoint you, but I can't tell you a whole lot about her. Apart from the fact that she has a periodic problem with alcohol and sometimes ends up with us. Are you a relative of hers?"

"No, just a friend," Bram said, deciding to hold back on the real reason for wanting to seek her out, for he had the feeling he wasn't going to get very far with this strange old woman who didn't seem the least bit accommodating. "An address, perhaps, anything at all that would help me find her."

She bent down to a drawer in the desk and took out an address book.

It was a hopeful sign.

"I don't have an address, unfortunately. I do, however, have the name of her doctor. He's retired now, but he helped her through many a bad patch. He could perhaps be of assistance."

"Oh . . . has the alcoholism been an ongoing problem for her then? Is she ill?"

"Yes, from time to time."

She uncapped a fountain-pen and began writing the address.

"That's why I think it best you speak to Dr Ruane. Of course he may not want to discuss F-32 with you, patient confidentiality always being a given. But he is retired now, and if your reasons for wanting to find her are honourable I see no reason why he should not. She needs all the support she can get."

She passed the paper to him.

He studied the name and address:

Dr TR Ruane, 11 Loughview Heights, Carnlough, County Antrim.

Bram heard her cap the fountain-pen and return the address book to the drawer. Took it as a sign that the meeting was at an end.

He stood up.

"Thank you, Mother Clare. You've been most helpful."

She gave him a wistful look.

"I hope you're successful," she said. "Often we do not know what burdens we place upon ourselves, sadly. Only hindsight can show us that."

It was an odd statement and he didn't know if she was talking about herself, him – or, indeed, the lost-and-soon-to-be-found Dorinda Walsh.

"Thank you again, Mother Clare," he said, eager to leave the sombre place. "You've been most kind."

"God bless you, Mr Hilditch. I wish you the Good Lord's strength and grace. Sister Magdalena will show you out."

Having sent the visitor on his way, Sister Magdalena returned to her superior's office. It was her duty to stand outside the door of Mother Clare's room when she had visitors. Sometimes she might be needed to fetch something or make tea. On this occasion she couldn't help but overhear the conversation between Mr Hilditch and her superior.

"Come and sit, Sister," Mother Clare said, indicating the chair Bram had just vacated.

"He was asking after F-32, Mother?"

Mother Clare looked towards the window. "Indeed he was."

"Do you want to tell me about her now? You said you would after she left the last time, and I would like to know, in case . . ."

"In case she comes again."

Sister Magdalena nodded.

The old nun sighed and looked towards the window again.

"There's a long history attached to her I fear. I first saw her on that beach when she was around five or six years old. Often at the weekends in late summer . . . she and her mother and . . ." Her face darkened and she got up and moved to the window.

"She and her mother and a man – or should I say *men*. Over the course of a year there were several different men . . . boyfriends one supposes, so it's fair to assume that the little girl never knew her real father."

"Are you saying she was a . . . was a fallen woman . . . her mother?"

"If that's what you want to call her then yes. On several occasions I had to intervene when I saw the child being treated badly by one of those stand-in fathers. The mother, alas, never seemed to notice. Or if she did, chose to ignore it. She was always swimming out there in the sea. Her flowered bathing-cap bobbing about on the waves . . ."

She turned back to the room and resumed her seat.

"Then one day a terrible thing happened. The mother went swimming and . . . and never came back. I still blame myself."

"That's too sad. But why blame yourself? It was an accident surely?"

"Earlier I'd seen her arguing with her paramour, you see; a tall man in a hat. He followed her into the water fully clothed, shouting at her, pushing her. I wanted to go down at that point but I was called to prayer, and when I came back . . ."

"They were gone?"

"Alas, yes. It was too late." Her eyes filled with tears. "They never found her body. I pray every day for God to forgive my negligence, that I didn't do more to save her."

She threw a glance at the window again.

"She comes to visit her mother's final resting place . . . when she has an episode. That ocean is all she has left. We do everything we can to help her back to some kind of normality, but it's best she doesn't see me. Sometimes the past is just too painful."

The young nun shook her head in dismay. "I had no idea. I thought she was just another addict."

"Addiction always has a story of grief behind it, Sister . . . some more tragic than others. The story of F-32 is one of the saddest ones

I've come across. She's still the little lost child I met on that beach all those years ago."

The sound of a bell rang out, calling them to supper.

"Yes, there are some trials simply too great to be conquered in this life," she said, getting up. "That's the cross she has to bear . . . for the sins of the mother and . . . and, alas, for the father she never knew."

CHAPTER
FORTY-FIVE

"Lord Jesus Christ, by your own three days in the tomb, you hallowed the graves of all who believe in you and so made the grave a sign of hope . . ."

Late evening, with darkness falling, Bram stood alongside Father Moriarty in the back garden of 8 Willow Close, following the words of blessing for Vivian-Bernadette's lost child.

It was a sombre scene. The two men with heads bowed, looking down on the solitary stone cherub that marked the place of interment.

". . . grant that the little one who lies here may sleep in peace until you awaken them in glory, for you are the resurrection and the life."

He reached for the aspersorium Bram was holding and sprinkled holy water.

"O God, bless this grave and send your holy angel to watch over it. We ask this through Christ our Lord. Amen."

The priest made the sign of the cross and Bram did too, realizing the ritual was at an end.

They stood in silent reverence for a little while, each thinking his own thoughts about Vivian O'Meara and the sad fate of her lost child.

"Thank you, Father . . . that was very moving," Bram said at last, relieved that the rite was over and had proceeded unnoticed. The curtains on the Glacken house were still drawn shut. Mrs Gilhooley, discharged from hospital, had gone to recuperate with her sister in Lisburn.

"Perhaps Vivian will find peace now too – wherever she is."

"God willing, Bram, God willing. I'll offer a Mass for the two of them tomorrow morning."

They returned indoors.

"I don't suppose you'll ever want to let go of this house now, Bram – with it having such a history connected with it?"

He nodded, appreciating that the priest knew only the half of what was going on. Had no idea about the Glacken family and their harassment of poor Vivian, a campaign of terror similar to the one they were now visiting on poor Rita Ruttle. What would be the end of it?

"And your new tenant," he said, as if reading Bram's mind. "Is the lovely Portaluce agreeing with her?"

"Yes, indeed. I left her off there yesterday, Father. Have a few repairs to do here, so it's best she's not around."

"Good, good . . . No better place to be than at the seaside. She's all right, is she?"

Bram was surprised by the question. "Yes . . . yes, I think so. Why do you ask, Father?"

"It's just that I saw her on a couple of occasions going into the Samaritan Centre in town. Wondered if she was depressed, that's all. They're good people, the volunteers . . . deal with potential suicides, as I'm sure you're aware."

"Yes, I know. Good people indeed."

Father Moriarty's revelation, though puzzling at first, wasn't so surprising when Bram reflected on what Rita had been going through since her move from Larne.

"I guess everyone needs a sympathetic ear from time to time," he said. "It's lonely for her being in a new town and not knowing anyone I suppose."

"Yes, and she's not a regular churchgoer either, so she misses out on the pastoral care we provide. Still, the ear of a stranger, someone who knows nothing about your background, is often a good thing."

"I agree . . . yes."

He donned his black hat again. "On the other hand she could be a volunteer herself, which is admirable. If so, it's not for us to know, since they work in the strictest confidence."

"To be sure, yes," Bram said, thinking back on how Blossom had described Rita, not so very long ago: "nice-looking and with such a good heart." He knew Blossom made tea at the Samaritan Centre. So that's perhaps what she'd meant.

The priest made to go then hesitated. "Those neighbours over there . . . the Glackens. They weren't giving her any trouble, were they?"

"Er . . . n-not that I know of, Father," Bram said, not wishing to commit himself.

"Perhaps I shouldn't be saying this," the priest continued, "but I wouldn't be too surprised if that Lenny character had something to do with Miss O'Meara's disappearance."

"Wh-Why would you say that, Father?"

"He's a reputation for the ladies . . . not a very good one from what I hear. And there were a couple of occasions when I saw him loitering by the back-gate out there."

Bram felt the colour drain from his face.

"I asked him what he was up to. Naturally he couldn't answer me, and sauntered off. But your new tenant will have nothing to worry about on that score now."

"Oh . . . ?"

"They've moved out, you know."

Bram couldn't believe his ears. "Really? I'd no idea."

"Given forty-eight hours to flee the country by IRA command a few days ago."

"You mean Lenny, the father . . . all of them, gone?"

Father Moriarty nodded. "Scotland, I believe. There were complaints of antisocial behaviour." He pulled on a pair of leather gloves and chuckled to himself. "No, the IRA don't like their *good name* being besmirched, if you'll pardon my sarcasm, Bram."

Bram smiled broadly, thinking now that Rita could return and be left in peace. "Can't say I'm sorry to see the back of them, Father. Unchristian, I know, but . . ."

The priest waved a hand in understanding.

"You're not alone in that view I'm sure." He picked up his bag. "Well, I'll be on my way then. Anything you need just call me, Bram. You know that, don't you?"

They shook hands.

"Thank you, Father. Your help is always much appreciated."

After Father Moriarty's departure, Bram sighed with relief. The fact that he'd done his duty towards Vivian-Bernadette regarding the blessing, along with the unexpected news of the Glackens' departure, renewed his faith that things were at last working to his advantage.

He went up to the landing and began clearing the remains of the ruined butterfly case into a binbag. He was saddened at the loss of the beautiful collection, but comforted himself with the thought that Rita was safe.

In the scheme of things the butterflies could always be replaced, but not Rita. He considered her now, installed at the Ocean Spray, awaiting his return.

When he'd taken his leave the evening before, she seemed very happy to be in Gladys Millman's lovely surroundings, away from the terrors of Willow Close. And who could blame her?

He sat down on the top stair, reflective. Regretting that he hadn't helped Vivian-Bernadette more. That he hadn't listened more, instead of writing her off as some pious oddity suffering delusions. He thought of the little infant lying in the cold earth just a few yards away and nearly wept at the sadness of it all. Of what the poor woman had come through on her own without the help of anyone!

But he could make amends now with Rita. Fight for her. Save her. Be her friend in her hour of need.

Tomorrow he'd be visiting Dr Ruane to learn about the whereabouts of her lost twin. He'd bring them together. Help them find joy and contentment, and take great pleasure in being the catalyst for such happiness, which seemed so sadly lacking in both their lives.

He got up and carried the bag downstairs, feeling a bit better about things.

The phone rang as he was on the verge of leaving.

"Hello, eight Willow Close."

"Hullo . . ." A woman's voice. "I . . . I want to speak to Rita Ruttle, please."

"I'm afraid Rita's not here. Who's calling, please?"

"A friend of hers . . . Grace . . . Grace Thorne . . . from the Eclips hair salon."

"I'm sorry, Mrs Thorne, but she's away for a few days. Can I take a message? I'm her landlord, Bram Hilditch."

"Yes, if you wouldn't mind. Tell her . . ." She hesitated. "Tell her I have word about Harry."

"Harry?"

"Yes . . . Harry, her husband."

Husband!

Bram nearly dropped the receiver. Had he heard her correctly?

"Husband? Oh, you must have the wrong number. The Rita who lives here isn't married."

There was a momentary pause. Then: "Rita Ruttle, Rita-Mae Ruttle . . . well, this is the number she gave me. She used to work in my salon in Larne."

He couldn't believe what he was hearing. He couldn't move. He couldn't speak. He held the earpiece to his shoulder so she wouldn't sense his shock.

"Are you still there?" Grace asked.

"Yes . . . yes, I'm still here."

"If you could ask her to ring me then . . . as soon as she can. She's got my number. It's very important. I've got word of Harry."

Before he had a chance to respond, Grace Thorne had cut the connection.

CHAPTER FORTY-SIX

"Miss Ruttle, you're not eating."

Rita, in the breakfast-room of the Ocean Spray, was sitting by the window enjoying the view when her raptness was broken in upon by the proprietor's voice.

She looked round to see Gladys Millman advancing across the room. She cut an intimidating figure in her power suit and pearls. Rita-Mae felt a little on edge at the sight of her.

She halted at her table. "You're only having tea again?" she protested. "Do you find something wrong with the food we serve here? My chef has the highest pedigree I can assure you."

"Er . . . no, I'm sure your food's lovely, Mrs Millman. It's just that . . . well, I . . . I'm not hungry, that's all."

"But you haven't eaten anything since you checked in here, from what I can see. Are you unwell? I can get you a doctor if you wish."

Mrs Millman would, no doubt, have been appalled to learn that upstairs in the bedside table was a stock of biscuits and tinned fruit, which Miss Ruttle had bought in the nearby shop the evening she'd moved in.

"N-No, that won't be necessary, thank you all the same, Mrs Millman. I'm quite fine, thank you."

The proprietor threw her a puzzled look. "As you wish, Miss Ruttle. As you wish. I'll leave you to your tea. But *do* inform Maureen if you have a change of heart, won't you?"

Interrogation over, she turned on her heel and strutted out of the room, leaving Rita-Mae to her solitary pot of tea and her thoughts.

Bram Hilditch pulled his car into a vacant spot on the High Street in Larne and cut the engine.

En route to see Dr Ruane, who lived farther up the coast, he'd decided on the detour to seek out Grace Thorne. Her phone call had stunned him. The news that Rita Ruttle was married to someone by the name of Harry seemed too incredible for words. Could it be true? And if so, why had she lied to him?

He'd tried calling Mrs Thorne back after she'd hung up, but without success. He'd tried the number several times that morning but it just rang out each time.

Well, when she came face to face with him, she could hardly run away.

He'd found the name and address of her salon, Eclips, in the *Yellow Pages*. Now all he had to do was locate it and confront her.

During the lunch-hour Rita-Mae decided on a stroll along the seafront, to avoid another clash with Gladys Millman.

She was hard to avoid, the haughty patron, always seeming to appear out of nowhere.

Why, she asked herself, is she so interested in my movements? Had Bram asked her to keep a close eye? Well, she and the landlord seemed on the best of terms, so perhaps that was the case.

She was happy that she now had a friend in Bram. At last there was someone in her life who was willing to support her, someone she could depend on. She felt bad about having suspected him as the stalker. But what was she supposed to think? He was rather eccentric after all, a hard one to fathom.

Yes, it was good to have a friend. It was an odd but very welcome feeling because for a long time there'd been no one. Her mother, now in a nursing home, had never shown her much affection – forever the critic. Little Rita-Mae was the reject who could never please, no matter how hard she tried. She never had any great urge to visit the woman. Once, when she'd got up the courage to tell her about Harry's mistreatment of her, Hedda blamed Rita for upsetting him in the first place. Men could do no wrong in her book.

The wide esplanade was a pleasant sight, stretching all the way along the shop-fronts as if keeping the ocean at bay. There were several sun-seats set at intervals, with large pots of colourful blooms here and there. The contrast of the eye-catching flowers against the backdrop of glittering blue was enchanting.

She considered crossing the road and simply sitting there for a while in appreciation of it all, but changed her mind when she saw two elderly couples, silent and contemplative, doing just that.

I'd just look out of place, she decided, sitting on my own. Besides, it's a bit breezy, and I don't particularly like the wind.

She resumed her walk. A few steps farther along she was conscious of a figure coming towards her. She'd no idea where this person had sprung from. But as Rita-Mae drew closer, she saw that it was an elderly woman – a tall, strange-looking elderly woman – dressed in long black clothes.

She felt a little uneasy at the sight of her and quickened her pace, keeping her eyes fixed firmly on the middle distance.

They drew level.

Without warning, the woman stopped and laid a hand on her wrist.

Rita-Mae let out a little cry, gazing down at the old knobbly fingers clasping her.

"Don't you remember me, Dorinda?"

"S-Sorry, I . . . I don't know who y-you are," Rita stammered, caught between being scared and angry. "Y-You must be mistaken." She was staring at the many strands of turquoise stones worn in a choker style, high on the lady's neck. Their colour matched her eyes exactly. "My name's Rita, not Dorinda."

"Rita . . . sorry if I startled you. I'm Edith LeVeck."

She smiled, loosening her hold on Rita's arm. "There must be two of you then. I said so to Dorinda when she came to my house. I sensed that there were two you see."

Rita shook her head. "Sorry, I don't know what you're talking about. I really must be going, Mrs . . . er . . . ?"

"LeVeck. But you can call me Edith."

"E-Edith . . . sorry, yes."

She backed away from her, afraid.

"Mind how you go, Rita," Edith said, giving her a melancholy look. "Be like the tree in winter. Shed your leaves. There's always time."

"What?"

But before she knew it, Edith LeVeck had walked on.

Rita was upset. She hurried after her to ask her what she'd meant. Saw her turn down a side street. But when she got there, the mysterious woman had vanished.

How could that be? Had she imagined it all? Hardly. Edith LeVeck had been as real as the paving Rita stood on.

The experience left her perplexed, and not a little shaken. She needed to sit down. Three doors along she spotted Marcella's, a cafe with large plate-glass windows. She'd go in there, sit by a window, have some tea and try to calm herself.

◆ ◆ ◆

Bram had little difficulty finding Eclips. It had a gaudy sign out front and was right there on the main street.

He entered a hot, busy salon and took up position by the reception desk. Business was booming at that early hour. He counted six customers – all female – in various stages of having their tresses styled.

A young woman spotted him, left off combing-out a client and approached him.

"I'm looking for Grace Thorne?" he asked cordially.

"Oh, Grace, she's not here at the minute. On her coffee break I'm afraid. Was it important?"

"Well, it is as a matter of fact."

"Right . . . in that case." She led him to the window. "See that cafe across the road? Burney's? You'll get her there."

"How will I know her? I've never met her I'm afraid."

"Easy to spot today," the stylist smirked. "Head full of rollers . . . she's got a big date tonight with the husband. It's their twenty-fifth wedding anniversary."

Rita-Mae entered Marcella's Cafe to find it empty. No customers and no staff either. She stood for a moment, looking about the L-shaped room with its bright decor: red banquettes with matching tables facing a long glass counter hosting some very delicious-looking cakes. The sun beaming in made it seem such a cosy and inviting place.

She took the seat by the window, glad to be having the place to herself. Could hear someone moving about in the kitchen out back. No doubt a waiter would appear soon enough.

"Mrs Thorne?" Bram said, addressing a seated blonde woman with a head full of rollers, intent on a newspaper. A cigarette was burning in an ashtray.

She looked up, startled.

"I'm so sorry to interrupt your coffee break, Mrs Thorne," he said with as much gallantry as he could muster. "I'm Bram Hilditch, Miss Ruttle's landlord. We spoke on the phone yesterday."

"Y-You came all this way . . . all this way to talk to *me*?"

"Yes . . . May I join you? It won't take long."

She glanced furtively about and nodded.

Bram manoeuvred himself into the bench seat opposite her.

"There's nothing more I can tell you about Rita, Mr Hilditch. Other than the fact I've got news of Harry."

"Harry. Her husband you mean?"

"Aye."

"So she *is* married then? I'm just wondering why she omitted telling me that."

Grace shrugged. "She's runnin' away from him y'see, 'cos he's such an awful bastard . . . pardon my French. She never wanted anyone but me to know her whereabouts. They've been married for fifteen years and he's been abusin' her all that time – and gettin' away with it."

Bram was shocked.

Grace scanned the room again, making sure no one would overhear. Leaned across to him.

"Poor Rita, he kept her a prisoner. Only allowed her the wee job with me so he could have extra money for the drink. I can't tell you how many times that poor woman's been in hospital 'cos of him. The guy should have crime-scene tape wrapped round him."

"Y-You mean he was violent towards her?"

She nodded.

He could hardly comprehend anyone hitting someone as tiny and frail as Rita.

"You don't know the half it, Mr Hilditch," Grace went on. She took a fortifying puff of her cigarette, exhaling the smoke through the open window. "Don't know how many times I told her to leave him, but she was too scared you see . . . had nowhere to go and no money – he kept everything. She ran away a few times and nobody could find her. Never said where she went. But Harry made her pay for it – if you know what I mean. I could see *that* all right."

"But . . . but wasn't there someone she could go to . . . her family maybe?"

"There's only the mother and she's in a nursin' home," Grace said, cocking a forefinger and making stirring motions at her head. "Doolally . . . away with the birds, as they say. Not that Hedda ever helped her anyway, the horrible old biddy. Was glad to get Rita off her hands when Harry came along. Talk about going from the fryin' pan into the fire."

"My God, I had no idea."

He was astonished at what he was hearing. His initial indignation on learning Rita had deceived him about being married was turning now to anguish at the tragic life Grace was describing.

"So where's . . . where's this Harry now?" he asked carefully.

"On the building sites in England, last I heard. He'd come home drunk as usual one night. They had a row. He fell and knocked himself out, y'see, and was bleeding badly. Rita was in a panic 'cos she thought she'd killed him. Pity she didn't. She took off. Think she went to the mother's house for a few days, till the heat settled. But when she came back he was gone. Said he'd left her a note saying he was going to Croydon . . . that's when Rita saw your ad and decided to make a break for it. She gave me her Killoran phone number so I could warn her when Harry showed up again. We live in the same development you see."

"I . . . I don't understand," Bram said. "If he's still over there in England then why were you calling Rita?"

In answer, she stubbed out the cigarette and checked her watch. "I need to be going now."

"Please tell me, Grace," Bram urged. "I need to know, for Rita's sake. I'm on *her* side, like you are . . . you have my word on that."

She studied him, plainly wondering if she could trust him.

"All right," she said finally, lowering her voice to a whisper.

"Don't breathe a word of this to anybody. But the police knocked my door yesterday, looking for Rita. They said it was in connection with Harry. Wouldn't say anything else. I gave them her address in Killoran so they'll be calling with her today sometime I daresay. Maybe you should tell her . . . warn her, like. God knows what it's about."

CHAPTER
FORTY-SEVEN

"Hello . . . sorry for keeping you."

In Marcella's Cafe, Portaluce, Rita-Mae's contemplation of the lovely scene was intruded upon by a female voice.

She turned to see a young waitress, notepad in hand, coming towards her.

"That's all right," she said. "I was just enjoying the view."

The waitress with the nametag JANE halted suddenly and did a double take.

"Oh . . . welcome back, miss."

"Er . . . sorry, Jane, but I haven't been here before."

"You haven't? But don't you remember having the lemon meringue pie?"

"Afraid not . . . it's my first time here."

"Gosh, miss, that's amazing. There was a woman in here a few months back that looked just like you. Same hair and everything."

"Oh, well," Rita-Mae said, making light of it, "maybe I have a double."

It was the third time she'd been mistaken for someone else since coming to Portaluce – first Maureen, the maid at the Ocean Spray, then the strange Mrs LeVeck, now this waitress. Was their eyesight defective or something?

She took up the menu and feigned interest, irritated that Jane remained standing there, openly gaping at her.

"Just a pot of tea, please."

Jane looked disappointed. "Sorry, miss . . . is that all, miss? Are you sure you don't want a slice of lemon meringue . . . like you had the last time?"

"*What?* I really don't think you heard me. I *said* I've never been in this cafe before."

"Yes, I know, miss . . . sorry, miss. I forgot."

"How could you forget? I just told you."

"Yes, miss, I know . . . I . . . I'm sorry. It's just that you're s-so like her."

"So you say, Jane, but I don't like sweet food and most especially lemon meringue pie. Never liked it in fact."

She felt bad about being so direct, but she really needed to get through to the silly girl, who continued to just stand there, gawping.

There was only one way out of the bizarre situation. She reached for her handbag and made as though she were searching in it.

"Tell you what, I'll . . . I'll have to pass on the tea. Looks like I forgot my purse anyway."

"Please, miss . . . I'm sorry, miss, I won't say anything else about . . . you know. You can have it on the house. Y-You gave me a very big tip last . . . Oh God, I'm sorry—"

But Rita was on her feet. "Sorry, Jane. Another time perhaps."

Dr Ruane's house was hard to find, set as it was in a remote spot high up on the rocky Antrim coast.

Bram had to ask directions several times and negotiate a warren of steep winding roads before finally arriving at journey's end.

He was relieved and not a little flustered when at last he pulled up in the grounds of the quaint stone cottage. Due to the difficulty of locating Loughview House he was running a good half hour late, and felt vexed about having already got off to such a bad start with the doctor.

Was it his imagination or did he get the impression that the medical man simply didn't want to be found? Was purposely hiding away, up here with the case files from his old life sealed in the attic, never to be reopened?

He recalled Ruane's hesitancy on the phone. Yes, he was being a bother to the old man; he knew that. But it was all in a good cause. Bringing Rita and Dorinda together was a goal worth pursuing, even if it meant doing a bit of digging and causing upset.

At the door he was greeted by a woman he supposed was the doctor's wife, although she didn't introduce herself: a tall, bony lady with chiselled features and the resigned air of the put-upon wife.

"I'm so sorry I'm late . . ." Bram began.

She gave a faint smile of understanding, led him into a cosy sitting-room and offered him tea, which he politely declined. He reckoned he'd inconvenienced them enough already.

"Thomas will be in shortly," she said and swayed away in her sensible brogues, leaving him with the ponderous ticking of a clock and the far-off sound of the sea.

Having vacated Marcella's Cafe, Rita-Mae lost interest in finding another snack bar to sit in. The incident with Jane had upset her. Had taken away the calm, easy mood she'd been trying to establish.

She wandered about for a bit, drifting in and out of shops – mostly of the souvenir variety, selling the usual fare of postcards, sticks of rock and seaside trophies. Bought a newspaper just for the sake of it and decided to head back to the Ocean Spray.

It was approaching tea-time, and hopefully Mrs Millman would be busy in the kitchen and not register her return.

"Mr Hilditch, how do you do?" Thomas Ruane said, coming forward to greet him. "You made it then."

Bram was surprised at the sight of the jaunty retiree, casually attired in a chunky sweater and corduroys, much at odds with the reserved, soberly dressed individual he'd been expecting.

He got up. "I'm so sorry I'm late, Doctor. Got a little lost, I'm afraid."

Ruane waved a hand. "It's understandable; most people do. You're not the first and won't be the last I'm sure. Now, you're here about a patient – or rather former patient – of mine," he added, sitting down.

"Yes, Dorinda Walsh. You see, I believe she has a twin sister whom she doesn't know exists. I'd like to know Dorinda's whereabouts. As I said on the phone, Mother Clare at the convent in Portaluce said you'd be able to help me . . . Dorinda having been a patient of yours."

Ruane looked at him steadily. Bram was expecting to hear some enlightening detail, but instead the doctor clapped his hands on the armrests and pushed himself up out of the chair.

"You'll join me in a brandy, Mr Hilditch, won't you?"

He didn't really want alcohol at that hour, but could sense that the doctor, already on his way to the drinks cabinet, would brook no refusal.

"A small one would be welcome, yes," he said. "And do call me Bram, please."

"And this sister's who, exactly?" Ruane asked, handing him the glass.

"Rita Ruttle. She's a new tenant of mine . . . in Killoran. She moved into one of my properties about three months ago."

"So you're a landlord?" He resumed his armchair and studied Bram with interest.

"Yes."

"And tell me, has Miss Ruttle been happy in your house?"

"Well, she was until . . . until she had a run-in with the neighbours, sadly. A little boy and his mother . . . you know the sort . . . common, not very nice people. They began harassing her . . . making life difficult."

"That's too bad. And what form did this harassment take? Did they break in by any chance?"

"Why, yes," Bram said, astonished at the doctor's prescience. "As a matter of fact they did."

"Mmm . . ." Ruane sighed and took a sip of his brandy. He set the glass down and leaned back in his chair. "Now, Bram," he said with a note of resignation, "in order for you to understand the lives of Dorinda – or Dorrie, as she prefers to be called – and Rita, I need to take you back to the beginning."

Safely behind the door of room number 5, Rita-Mae felt glad she'd made it up the stairs unnoticed by the proprietor.

She removed her coat and returned it to the wardrobe, but for some reason the door wouldn't shut properly. Kept springing back open every time she tried to secure it.

Maybe there was something obstructing one of the hinges.

She checked, saw nothing untoward and tried again. But when it happened a third time she realized she had to be more thorough.

Exasperated, she threw wide the doors and stood back.

Ah, there *was* something: a piece of white material stuck between the top section and the right-hand door.

Something was up there.

She pulled over a chair and climbed up to investigate. Was surprised to see a white garment neatly folded on top.

Curious, she fetched it down.

Shook it free and held it up to the light.

It took a while to figure out what exactly she was seeing.

For the white trench coat had several dark patches down the front.

Were they part of the design perhaps?

Intrigued, she took the coat over to the window to have a closer look.

Suddenly it dawned on her.

No, they were not part of a design. The random burgundy mappings were most definitely *not* designs.

They were bloodstains.

The raincoat was *covered in bloodstains.*

"Oh, my God! What is this place? Why is . . ."

She dropped it in horror, grabbed her bag and dashed from the room.

CHAPTER
FORTY-EIGHT

It was hard for Bram to drive home after finally bidding farewell to Dr Ruane.

If the outward journey was difficult then the return one was monumentally more testing. For a very different reason.

The route hadn't changed, but Bram had. The story the doctor had shared concerning Rita and Dorrie's lives was impossible to believe – and so, so desperately sad.

His heart sagged as he imagined her there in Portaluce, waiting for him. Waiting to hear the surprise he'd mentioned on leaving.

"A surprise? For me?" she'd asked in disbelief. "But what is it, Bram?"

"If I told you, it wouldn't be a surprise, now would it, Rita? So you'll just have to wait."

"Thank you," she'd said. "You've been so very kind to me."

And she'd smiled her rare and beautiful smile and turned back to the guesthouse window, lost again in her own private world – a world that he now knew something of.

The battleground that was her life.

No, there'd be no pleasant surprise for Rita.

What he had to impart to her was almost too much to bear.

He pulled the car over outside 8 Willow Close and just sat there with the engine running, fighting back tears, unable to do what he knew he had to do.

The sky was dimming, sombre clouds massing, the ocean growling balefully as Dorinda Walsh stepped out. She sped along the promenade, heading towards the beach.

She was happy, feeling the pleasant weight of the whiskey bottle in her shoulder-bag, knowing in her heart what lay ahead.

Find a nice place to sit and have a drink, Dorrie dear . . . Go with the flow . . . just go with the flow.

Dorrie stopped abruptly.

"Mama, oh dear Mama, you came back!"

Of course I'm back, Dorrie dear. I never left you, my sweetheart. Uncle Jack thought he'd got rid of me, but it takes a lot to get rid of me, darling. Now settle down and have that drink.

"Yes, Mama. I know, Mama," Dorrie trilled, happier now than ever. "I know. You always come when I need you, Mama. Always."

She picked her way down a rocky incline and went a short distance along the beach, her shoes squishing over the sand, eyes alert for the perfect place.

Not so far ahead she saw a flat rock jutting out between two bigger ones, and made towards it.

In his car outside 8 Willow Close, Bram cut the engine, wiped his tears and gazed up at the box-room window. Ryan Glacken hadn't trashed the house that time, nor had his stalker grandfather broken in and smashed the butterfly case. A little girl called Ciara had done all the damage. He knew the truth now but still found it all so very hard to take in.

Best make a move.

He dried his eyes. Time was going on. He got out of the car.

He'd stopped by Willow Close to check on things. Just to make sure that all was well.

On Portaluce beach, Dorrie put aside the half-empty bottle of whiskey and hugged her knees in the increasing cold.

"Mama, I want to see you again like last time. *Please*, Mama," she implored.

The alcohol was warming, releasing her from all the bad thoughts of the past. The loosening, the drifting away: away from the voices of rebuke, the faces of hate gathering in her head like the blackest crows, lifting her up and up into the heavens, where Mama – beautiful Mama – dwelt.

She leaned back on the rocks and began singing the song her mama loved so much.

> *I'm a single girl trying to live the single life,*
> *I'm a single girl who's got no wish to be somebody's wife,*
> *Not unless I meet the right kind of man,*
> *Who'll give me all the love that he can.*

After a quick look round Willow Close, Bram made his exit and got back in his car. He was about to move off when he saw a police car pulling in behind him.

Two officers inside.

The one in the passenger seat got out.

Fearing the worst, and remembering Grace Thorne's parting words, Bram cut his engine and stepped out. He recognized Constable Barry.

"Mr Hilditch," Barry said, casting a glance at number 8. "Would your tenant, Miss . . . er . . . *Mrs* Ruttle be at home?"

"No, I'm afraid not, Constable."

"D'you know where we can reach her?"

"Well, that's a bit problematic. She's recovering from an illness, you see . . . went to Portaluce for a few days. I'm on my way there now. Can I . . . can I take her a message perhaps?"

Barry removed his hat and hesitated.

"It's to do with her husband," he said grimly.

"Oh?"

"Bad news . . . very bad news I'm afraid."

"I . . . I'm sorry to hear that," Bram said uneasily, all kinds of thoughts racing through his head. "Maybe I'm the best one to tell her, Constable Barry, in that case. Is he ill?"

"He . . . he lost his life yesterday morning, I'm sorry to say."

Had he heard the man aright? Rita's torturer: dead. "Y-You mean . . . you mean he's . . . I mean, *Harry Ruttle's dead?*"

Barry nodded. "Afraid so. Fell to his death from the thirteenth floor of a tower block he was working on in Croydon. The scaffolding gave way under him."

"That's too bad," Bram managed to say, barely able to contain his relief at the news.

"Well, thanks for offering to tell her, Mr Hilditch."

The constable put his cap back on and adjusted the peak. He made to leave. Hesitated.

"If it's any consolation, you can assure her . . . Mrs Ruttle, I mean, that it was . . . that it was quick . . . his death I mean. He wouldn't have felt any pain. Th-That'll be some consolation I suppose."

"Yes," Bram said. "I suppose it will be."

CHAPTER FORTY-NINE

On the final leg of his journey back to Portaluce Bram drove with a lighter heart. In spite of everything, he *did* have a surprise for Rita after all. With Harry Ruttle gone she no longer had to run.

The monster was dead.

She was free.

He, Bram, would not walk away from her. He knew it with the utmost certainty. Destiny may choose who you get to meet in this life, but only your heart gets to decide who will stay. Rejection had been the theme of Rita's story from the beginning. That rejection would end with him.

He'd be there for her, no matter what it took.

On the rocks at Portaluce beach Dorrie Walsh sat gazing out at the ocean, entranced by a most beautiful display. Bands of light were playing out from the sun, which was setting behind a headland in the west. By their beams she could see her mama out there on the glittering waters, her pale arms plying the frothy breakers, perfect and true.

Not a memory. Not a dream. She was real. To Dorrie *she was real.*

There was no Uncle Jack. No sign of his car. No threat of his shadow anywhere.

Mama had returned, as Dorrie always knew she would, not in the Fatima-blue coat and white mantilla of her dream, but in the red swimsuit and beautiful flowery bathing-cap she'd seen her wearing all those years before. Lovely Mama was alive. She'd come to take her home.

"Mama!" she called out. "Mama, I'm here! I'm here!"

Bram, approaching the outskirts of Portaluce, thought back to that day in February, not so very long ago, when he'd picked up the phone and heard Rita's voice for the first time, enquiring after 8 Willow Close.

How innocent he'd been then of her reasons for wanting to move so far away from Larne! How innocent of the courage she'd needed to make that call. To finally make the break from the husband, risking her life to start over again.

Now the tyrant was finally gone.

The joy he felt on learning of Harry's demise was indecent he knew. But sometimes, whether for good or ill – and in this instance most definitely for good – bad people must die so that others can live, and live fully. Now, hopefully, with his help, Rita could do just that. They had a long road ahead of them, but together they'd make it.

Fate had handed her a second chance, and handed Bram a duty he would not shirk.

He got out of the car and hurried up the steps of the Ocean Spray, casting aside the dark picture Dr Ruane had painted of Dorinda and Rita. He'd wonderful news for Rita; her abuser was no more. That would be enough for now.

Gladys Millman, at the reception desk, was deep in conversation with a handsome young man holding a briefcase.

"Bram, there you are at last," she said. "Everything all right I hope?"

"Never better, Gladys." He moved towards the stairs, not wanting to be delayed. "Is Miss Ruttle in her room?"

"This is Victor Steenson by the way," said Gladys with a smile. "He's the current rep for Moët and Chandon, don't you know . . . the champagne people. Abraham Hilditch, a friend all the way from Killoran, Victor."

They exchanged greetings, the salesman raising a salutary hand. Bram didn't move from the stairs, annoyed with Gladys, finding her need to be in control rather irritating, especially now, when she could surely see he was anxious to get on.

"Good day to you, Mr Steenson," he said, turning back to the stairs. "You'll really have to excuse me I'm afraid."

"In answer to your question, Bram, Miss Ruttle could very well be in her room. I don't think she goes out much at all."

"Not so surprising, given that your rooms are so elegant, Mrs Millman," he heard Steenson remark, to a coquettish tittering from Gladys.

"Right. I'll just check."

He left them to it and climbed the stairs.

At room number 5 he rapped lightly.

"Rita! It's Bram."

Waited.

When she didn't answer he tried the door, not caring if he was intruding. He needed to tell her about Harry. Couldn't wait to see her face.

To his surprise the door swung open.

He looked in.

She wasn't there. At the sight of the coat on the floor he grew concerned. Went over and picked it up.

Stared aghast at the dark blotches, knowing they were bloodstains. But they were old. He could see that.

Grace Thorne's words came back to him.

He fell and knocked himself out, y'see, and was bleeding badly. She was in a panic 'cos she thought she'd killed him. Pity she didn't. She took off. I think she went to the mother's house for a few days, till the heat settled.

He searched through the pockets of the coat, fervently hoping he would not find the item that would prove beyond doubt everything the doctor had told him concerning Dorinda Walsh.

But . . .

His hand made contact with something in an inside pocket. His heart sank as he drew out a man's wallet, an empty wallet.

He thrust it back in the pocket and rushed from the room.

On Portaluce beach, Dorrie got to her feet, waving excitedly. She left the rocks and moved on to the sand.

"Mama, Mama, I'm here, I'm here!"

But Mama merely continued plying the waves, her bathing-cap of pink-and-yellow daisies bobbing up and down like the most beautiful bouquet.

"Mama, it's Dorrie! Can't you see me, Mama? Please, Mama, can't you see me?"

Dorrie headed slowly towards the ocean's edge, hearing in the distance the waves lapping on the pebbled beach.

"Mama!" she called again. "Mama!"

To her delight Mama turned and saw her, and began swimming in her direction. Dorrie heard her voice, like the most plaintive melody, coming to her over the waves.

Come, darling! Come in and join me. Go with the flow, my dear. Go with the flow. I'm here for you now.

Dorrie grew afraid. She couldn't swim. But she wanted so much to be with Mama again. So very, very much. In Mama's arms again – away from all the hurt and pain of this terrible world.

She started to cry. Stepped gingerly forward, closer now to the water's edge. The last rays of the setting sun were picking out brighter crests of the waves.

Don't be afraid, my darling! she heard her mama call out. *Come.*

The champagne rep had taken his leave and Gladys was running an eye over her order when she heard a commotion above.

She looked up, disconcerted at the sight of a very agitated Bram Hilditch rushing down the stairs.

He was carrying something.

"What on earth's the matter, Bram? Isn't Miss Ruttle in her room?"

He slung the coat on to the counter.

She saw the bloodstains.

"My God!"

"Throw it away, Gladys. *Please*, Gladys. Get rid of it."

"B-But, my God, has she . . . has she *killed* someone?"

He shook his head, ashen-faced. "No time, Gladys. No time."

CHAPTER FIFTY

"But, I'm afraid, Mama!" Dorrie wailed. "What if I can't reach you and the big waves take me away and I . . . and I never see you again?"

Oh, darling, it's a very small price to pay for us to be together. We'll be in spirit always.

Dorrie sobbed the tears of the little child she once was, torn between life and death, hope and despair.

Bram was running with a speed he never thought himself capable of. Would he make it to the beach in time? Twilight had fallen and the sky was ruddy, with dark clouds blowing in from the ocean. A shower of rain had made the rocky footpath treacherous. But he was blind to the danger. The sad refrain of Dr Ruane's words driving him on.

I first treated Rita when she was committed after trying to kill her husband, but her problems go back much further than that.

She witnessed her mother drown when she was six. The mother's boyfriend – or Uncle Jack as he was called back then, a thug of the highest order – most likely killed her. But there were no witnesses, apart from the little girl herself. He became her legal guardian, and bought the child's silence by abusing her terribly: beating her, starving her and passing her round his male associates. Violent men don't usually stop at the emotional and physical I'm afraid. She ended up with his sister when he was killed in a car accident. Hedda Mullane wasn't such an improvement on the brother, I regret to say.

All at once, Bram stumbled on the wet paving.

He fell.

So far yet to the beach.

He was facing into the darkness of all he'd heard.

Remembering, remembering.

The doctor's words pulling him back on his feet again, propelling him on.

There is no Dorinda Walsh, Bram. No Dorrie. Rita doesn't have a twin. Never had. She has a severe psychiatric disorder. Multiple personality disorder – or dissociative identity disorder, DID, to give it its more modern term. A rare condition resulting from severe and sustained childhood trauma. Few childhoods have been more miserable or heartbreaking than Rita's, alas. Dorrie is an "alter". One of several.

Halfway along the path leading towards the beach, Bram tried to run faster, breath coming in great gasps, heart hammering, shoes smacking the wet ground, loud and hollow-sounding in his ears.

When treating her I met five alters, but the two most dominant personalities were Dorinda – or Dorrie – and a little girl called Ciara. Dorrie's in her twenties: docile and eager to please, likes nice clothes and has a drink problem, like Rita's own mother. In the guise of Dorrie she can see only an idealized image of the mother. Has dreams about her being buried in prim clothes of virginal colours – blue and white. This fantasy is a necessary protection against the truth, that Florence was nothing more than a prostitute who neglected her daughter and left her at the mercy of the male visitors to her home.

Ciara, on the other hand, is an unruly little girl of seven. When you mentioned her neighbour's dead budgie I knew immediately it was the work of Ciara.

◆ ◆ ◆

Mama was drawing closer in the reddish twilight. Her voice as soothing and hypnotic as the sea itself.

There, Dorrie dear, you're not a little baby any more. Just go with the flow. Go with the flow. Just spread your arms wide and dive in.

Dorrie dried her tears, knowing in her heart of hearts she couldn't disappoint her mama. She'd be brave and obey.

"Yes, Mama, yes. I'm not afraid any more." The water was lapping at her legs. She extended her arms wide.

Now, Dorrie baby . . . oh, you're doing so well! Soon we'll be together, darling. Soon.

She was shivering uncontrollably. The ocean was making her dizzy. She hugged herself. The fear was coming back. The terrible fear.

"I'm sorry, Mama!" she cried. "I . . . I—"

Amy's here, Dorrie. You remember Amy . . . your little canary?

"She . . . she is?"

Yes, Dorrie. We're waiting . . .

Finally Bram was within sight of the beach. A wind had sprung up, coming in off the ocean in great buffeting gusts. He clambered down over the rocks.

Still no sign of Rita. Snatches of Ruane's remarkable account of her past were making him desperate.

After her mother died Uncle Jack bought her a pet, a canary . . . she called it Amy. Loved it and kept it by the bed in a little cage . . . until one day Rita committed the sin of wetting the bed. Jack's punishment was to cut the bird's head off, right in front of the child.

The incident involving the Glackens brought Ciara out. The row with the boy was the "triggering event". Rita wasn't Rita when she went to shut Mrs Gilhooley's door; she'd switched to Ciara at the sight of the bird in the cage. The symbolic trauma of that past episode took over. That part of her that was so powerless and helpless as a little girl was now the angry, boisterous Ciara, who could lash out. She killed the bird, stole the jewellery box. Returned to her own place, trashed the lounge and did the same in the box-room. The sheer exhaustion of having carried out such a spree meant that Ciara fell asleep with the extreme tiredness of a child. But it was Rita who awoke with no memory of what she'd done.

Bram, frantically scanning the beach for a sign, lost his footing. He slipped. Fell heavily on his left shoulder. A searing pain shot through the entire arm, damaging again the shoulder Lenny Glacken, the Enforcer, had dislocated. He cried out in agony.

The pain was excruciating. He crawled with difficulty to level ground and eased himself up on his right elbow.

"Oh, dear God, help me!" he cried, pushing his glasses back into place. But there was no sign of Rita.

His shoulder was throbbing. He lay down again, tired out, his mind churning with words he could barely comprehend.

Alters operate as distinct personalities, Bram. Each with their own traits, histories, and ways of relating to others and the world. Rita's amnesia is a defence mechanism. She's powerless to stop them. When an alter's out it's out. She'll have blank spells, lose time, consciousness and her dignity, will have no recollection of anything she's done or where she's been. Sometimes an alter, especially a child alter, will come forward just for a short time and play mischievous little games – displace objects, unlock doors, open windows.

Rita would have no memory at all of doing these things and believe it was the work of an intruder. She may meet people who seem to know her but whom she does not recognize or remember ever meeting. Of course marrying the abusive Harry didn't help her at all. His way of dealing with her dissociative episodes was to lock her in the garden shed. When that didn't work he'd have her committed. She'd go missing from time to time, but she'd somehow find her way back to him. The poor woman had no other choice.

"Oh dear God, I must find her!" he cried at the sky. "I'm all she's got left."

He hauled himself up again, willing the pain in his shoulder to ease.

The wind was his enemy now, battering him back. But he struggled against it, trusting his feet to guide him along the darkening beach, his eyes fixed on the shore, scanning, searching, longing desperately for a sign, the words of Ruane still playing in his head like an endless tape.

Rita's been suffering with DID all her adult life. She has no idea about the different alters. In Rita's mind she has blackouts and is simply forgetful. Recovering from such a terrible affliction is a long, painstaking process I'm afraid. In order to heal, the patient must face up to the past trauma, and for many that is too much to bear. The risk of suicide is high among people with this condition. Many prefer death than to have to go through the process of reliving the horrors of the past. Retreating into the various alters and having them carry the awful memories is the only way they can survive. That she's survived thus far without causing herself serious injury is a miracle of sorts.

Bram spotted something.

Out in the water, he spotted something. A frail white form, like a dove readying itself. Arms spread wide.

He halted.

"Rita!" he shouted.

She didn't move.

He ran.

She was less than twenty yards into the water. Still close enough to the shore to be rescued. Still near enough to be saved.

"Rita! Rita!" he yelled, vying desperately to be heard above the wind. "Don't do it, Rita!"

But she didn't hear him and continued on, her arms spread, the water rising up her legs, going deeper and deeper.

"Rita, Rita, come back! Come back!"

He stumbled and almost fell again, gritting his teeth against the returning agony in his shoulder. Cursed the pain and his impeding weight, but such things were secondary now.

"Oh dear Lord, let me get to her! Let me get to her in time!"

She was getting farther and farther out.

But she was alive. There was still a chance.

He reached the point of departure, where her discarded shoes and handbag lay.

With difficulty, he pulled off his own shoes and coat, splashed into the tide. The shock of the cold water took his breath away, the merciless wind forcing him back.

"Rita!" he cried again. "Rita, it's all right! Come back, Rita. Come back!"

But she was in another world, oblivious to his calls, drawn towards something only she could see.

He stopped.

Ruane's words sudden in his head.

When an alter's out it's out. Rita will be that personality and be it fully.

"Dorrie!" Bram yelled. "Dorrie!"

It worked.

At the sound of the name she'd stopped, turned to look at him.

"Come back, Dorrie! Come back."

She stood transfixed.

He ploughed towards her, fighting against the powerful muscles of wind and tide.

An arm's length from her, he lunged forward, his good arm outstretched.

"Dorrie! Take my hand, Dorrie!"

She screamed. Made to turn.

A wave caught her unprepared. She lost her footing – and plunged down.

"Oh, *Christ, Dorrie!*"

He reached down into the water, now turbulent with her struggles, questing desperately. His arm found a purchase about her waist. He floundered, nearly fell, but managed to keep his balance.

He tugged. She struggled. Her head broke the surface. Eyes wild with fright. She screamed again, arms windmilling frantically.

"Let go, Uncle Jack! Let go of me!"

It took all his strength to hold her.

"There's no Uncle Jack, Dorrie. You're safe now."

But she wasn't hearing his voice, only the voice of her long-dead mother calling her back home. And the pull of that voice was stronger.

"Let me go, Uncle Jack! Let me *go!*"

She lashed out, her fist smashing into his injured shoulder.

He yelled, his whole body stunned with pain, flopped down into the water, and the arm that held her loosened.

She writhed and thrashed out of his weakening hold. Vanished from sight.

"Oh God, Rita, noooo! *N-o-o-o-o-o!*"

He took a deep breath, launched himself beneath the waves, with no thought that he himself might perish. But with only the power of one arm it was useless; she was already gone, the frail body that had withstood so much pain in life sinking like a doll. Hair fanning gracefully, as if waving him goodbye.

It was over.

As the current took her down, and with a desperate will to live, he propelled himself back up, gulping and spluttering into the light.

He'd lost the fight to hold on to Rita.

But Dorrie had won the right to be free.

He crawled back to shore. Slumped down on the beach, lamenting all that was now lost to him.

Her tormentors had won. By a grim irony the stalker, Lenny Glacken, had dealt the final blow that sealed her fate.

Bram lay on the now-dark beach, crushed and desolate.

How cruel, he thought. How cruel that she never knew of the tyrant husband's death! How cruel that he, Bram, could not reach her in time to tell her that. She'd been on the brink of happiness; with the husband finally out of the way she had a chance at last.

He sat there looking out over the gloomy beach, not caring that he was soaked to the skin. Just wanting to be close to where she'd breathed her last.

Nearby lay her handbag.

There wasn't much inside: a purse, a booklet – *The Life of Saint Catherine of Siena* – and a small rectangular box.

It held a tiny silver angel.

"Bram?"

A woman's voice above him. He looked up, startled. Hadn't heard her approach.

Sister Magdalena hunkered down, put a hand on his shoulder.

"I saw you from the window. The coastguard are on their way."

He followed her gaze as she studied the ocean.

"I w-was . . . I was too late . . . too late to save her, Sister." He was weeping like he'd never done before in all his adult life.

"Don't blame yourself. You did all you could." She sighed. "Often things happen exactly as they were meant to. We may not like the outcome, but it's all part of a bigger plan. Rita had suffered enough in this life."

"Oh, God, why had I to bring her here?"

"Don't blame yourself, Bram," she said again. "How could you have known the tragedy that was Rita's life? You were trying to help her. Dwell on that. That, at the very end, you were there for her. You cared."

The tiny silver angel glinted in his hand.

"It was in her bag."

The nun studied it. Shook her head. "That's so strange. Mother Clare told me she gave her a silver angel on this very beach when she was a little girl. Not long before . . ." She stopped, tears in her eyes now. Looked away from him.

"Not long . . . not long before the mother drowned."

She nodded. "She kept the angel all this time."

"I'll . . . I'll keep it, if you don't mind, Sister."

She closed her hand over his. "Of course you must keep it, Bram . . . I'm sure Rita . . . Rita would've wanted you to have it."

She tried to smile. "Now, let's get you up. You need to get out of those wet clothes." She helped him to his feet.

"Sister, I . . . I'd . . . I'd no idea. No idea of the suffering, the terrible things she'd come through. She seemed . . . she seemed so self-reliant, so in control of things."

"I know. We look at others and think we know them, but we rarely do. The struggles, the hardships, the trials they carry inside are heavily borne and rarely spoken of."

Sister Magdalena took his hands in hers. "But out of suffering there have emerged the most beautiful souls, released from the darkness by the loving kindness of others . . . people like you."

"Thank you, Sister."

They moved down to the water's edge, the nun's blue robes flapping in the wind. Took one final look out to sea.

"God bless you, Rita," the nun said, making the sign of the cross. "May His everlasting light shine upon you. Amen."

They linked arms and slowly walked back down the lonely, wind-swept beach. Bram was overcome with grief.

"Do not grieve, Bram," she soothed, a comforting arm in his. "Rita's in a better place now. Have no doubt of that."

He nodded and in his sorrow hoped – really hoped – that Sister Magdalena spoke the truth. That there was indeed a loving deity and a better place for Rita.

A spiritual realm, a resting place, for her ever-questing soul.

EPILOGUE

Bram Hilditch hadn't reckoned on falling in love with Rita Ruttle. No, the landlord hadn't reckoned on that at all. Unrequited love was a dangerous thing; he knew that now. A very dangerous thing.

It would explain why he'd nearly lost his own life trying to save her. It would explain the uncharacteristic risk he'd taken going over to the Glacken house and sustaining an injury from a madman to protect her. Those tears he'd shed back there on the beach proved that he loved her. A woman with whom he'd shared no intimacy.

It was late evening and the landlord was in his studio above J.P. Rooney's pharmacy, pondering his great loss. The script he'd been crafting so carefully for himself – the future he'd envisioned with Rita by his side – had changed dramatically overnight.

On his desk lay a series of photographs lit by a reading lamp. Candid shots of Vivian and Rita going about their daily routines, seemingly taken without the subject's knowledge or consent. He liked that. How his telephoto lens could steal into their workaday lives, violate their privacy then withdraw like a phantom. He was not a peeping Tom. No, he was a photographer: the master behind the lens, catching beauty in the most immediate and creative way he knew.

By sending them the photos he wasn't trying to frighten them, only wanted them to appreciate how beautiful they were. What could be wrong with that? Surely it was a compliment to see oneself unposed and still looking pretty, whatever the angle. It was another kind of memorial photography, one he was infinitely more proud of.

He picked up a shot of Rita washing the dishes. He'd taken it from inside the garden shed – the shed he always kept locked and to which only he had a key – aligning his tripod with the kitchen window as dusk fell. He'd taken quite a number of shots from that vantage point. It was the ideal hideout, the darkness of evening providing the perfect cover.

And now poor, lovely Rita – whose delicate beauty and mysterious ways had entranced him from the beginning – was gone the way of her dear, departed mother, to the bottom of the deep, blue sea. He regretted now that he'd never got close to her. But Miss O'Meara's reaction to his one clumsy advance had discouraged him. Taught him the value of biding one's time.

It had happened on the day he'd driven her home from Mass. He really thought she'd have the courtesy to invite him in for tea by way of a thank you. But she didn't, and he found that disrespectful because it could only mean she didn't really trust him.

He saw himself exit the car as she turned the key in the front door.

"Er, would you mind terribly if I used the bathroom, Miss O'Meara?"

"Oh . . . well I . . ."

The wariness in those lovely green eyes again, the hesitancy.

"I won't be long . . . promise."

She had to let him in.

But in her hurry to get away from him she stumbled, catching her foot on the rug in the hallway.

He grabbed her about the waist to break her fall, and discovered he'd no wish to let her go. Wanted so much to hold on, drawing her to him in a tight embrace. Oh, the feel of that fragile body through the damp clothes, heart thudding like a captured bird, the scent of that sumptuous red hair – a body that had so much *life* coursing through it! So unlike the dead ones he'd caress in the morgue when his father was out of sight.

Vivian struggled. But he held on, breathing her in, savouring the *realness* of her. So much vitality lit by so much fear.

She screamed. Then, to his astonishment, slapped him hard across the face.

He had to let go.

"Get out!" she cried. "Or I'll call the police. I never want to see you again."

He regretted that the advance had failed so spectacularly. It ruined everything between them. She wouldn't let him into the house again. Wouldn't answer the door or return his calls. So he just had to leave it at that. Until . . . until eventually he found himself having to force the door and make that terrible discovery.

More recent events had revealed that Glacken senior had designs on her too. God knows how she ended up. Perhaps it was Lenny Glacken and not him she was running away from. That was some consolation he supposed.

Vivian had left him to deal with her secret. Was that her revenge? But he'd done the decent thing by her. His conscience was clear on that score. Now that Father Moriarty had blessed the infant's grave, those awful nightmares about her would hopefully, finally, cease.

He sighed, gathered up all the shots of Miss O'Meara, tore them into pieces and tossed them in the bin.

Rita's he would keep.

He stared at her pictures once more. Poor Rita! Life a beautiful lie. Death a painful truth: a fact that's true for all of us, not just her.

He thought back to Dr Ruane's parting words.

Most sufferers can't live in the real world, Bram. Families and friends can't cope, and abandon them. They end up in institutions or on the streets . . . lose themselves to alcohol and illegal drugs. But Rita is extraordinary. The core personality that is Rita is extraordinary. She's been a

Samaritan volunteer for several years now and never wavered in that most demanding of duties.

It's a common feature in the lives of women who've been abused. They blame themselves and try to atone for the sin by doing charitable work: volunteering, that sort of thing. Which is something of a miracle. Because by rights Rita shouldn't even be here, given what she's come through. Making the break from her abuser and fleeing to live in Killoran was a very courageous act. It shows she still has fight left. As long as she has someone looking out for her, takes her medication and avoids stressful situations – situations that might trigger a dissociative episode – then there's hope. As for a cure? In time there might well be. At present, therapy and medication is all we have, and we're succeeding to some small degree with those.

They were two of a kind, he and Rita. Unloved from the beginning. Condemned to the life of a misfit thereafter. Their childhood horror stories replaying in their heads, like freak shows. But together they could have shared those burdens, perhaps succeeded in making all that pain go away.

He'd pictured the two of them joined together in holy matrimony, living happily ever after under the roof of Lucerne House. Her Grace never part of that fancy. No, she didn't feature in those future plans at all.

Tears were threatening again and Bram, the responsible citizen and dutiful son, needed to be strong. Tears were anathema to him. He hadn't wept since way back in boyhood, imprisoned in the darkness of the freezing morgue. Nights that terrified him so much he not only wept but wet himself too, yelling out to the mother who never listened and the father who took perverse pleasure in knowing he was down there in the shadows amongst the coffins and the dead.

Oh, how he hated him! But he'd got his own back in the end. That quick injection of potassium chloride dispatched him in a heartbeat. He'd been preparing old Mrs Dobbins of Cedar Haven Mews at the time. A full vial into the jugular vein and Bram, at last, was free. How easy it was! So quick and painless. For when preparation and opportunity meet, you don't hesitate. You move in for the kill, battering down the door that's stood bolted against you for so long. Undertakers rarely come under scrutiny from the authorities. They deal with the dead, don't cause death – generally speaking.

He'd never have become a landlord or a serious photographer had he waited for nature to take its course. If Her Grace only knew the real story! But she'd never know now, would she? For we all carry our secrets sealed tightly inside. No one can glimpse the true essence of our souls unless we're careless. And Bram was *never* careless.

He pulled out a drawer and put away the pictures of his darling Rita. Saw the jar of digoxin. Drew it out and studied it. The crushed powder from the humble foxglove could be used to commit the perfect crime – given the right circumstances of course.

Her Grace's heart pills already contained a little of the deadly digitalis substance. An interesting fact that he'd gleaned from J.P., the pharmacist. And in light of that fact, adding an extra smidgen to her nightly cocktail didn't seem so wrong, the fatal dose being not so much greater than the medicinal one.

Yes, certain kinds of women could make men do terrible things.

He dried his tears.

Checked his watch. It was nearly nine o'clock.

The "magic hour" was approaching.

He threw the jar back into the drawer and turned the key. There'd be no need to doctor Her Grace's cocktails tonight.

Rita's death meant his mother could live. Better the mother than no one at all – for now at least. She'd never know how close she'd come to breathing her last. That was the tragic, brutal beauty of it all.

For we all want to live, do we not? Some of us more than others. We all go through this life dodging the bullets of happenstance, with our hopes and dreams, our obsessions and fears held tightly inside, until that is . . .

Until . . .

Bram Hilditch threw the light switch. Drew on his coat and let himself out into the crisp evening air.

Tomorrow was another day. He'd place a classified in the property pages first thing.

In his head he had the advertisement already written. Saw it on the printed page, a neat black border framing it to draw the eye.

SMALL, COMFORTABLE HOUSE IN VERY SAFE NEIGHBOURHOOD.

ONE BEDROOM, BOX ROOM, BATHROOM AND LOUNGE.

RENTAL RATES NEGOTIABLE.

SINGLE LADIES PREFERRED.

AUTHOR'S NOTES

Events in the Samaritan setting are based on details provided by former volunteers working in Northern Ireland in the 1980s. The only deviation from normal procedure was having the main character do duty alone at the Centre. This was for narrative purposes only and would not happen in real life.

SAMARITANS

The charity was founded in 1953 by Chad Varah, a Church of England vicar working in London. The idea for setting up the suicide helpline came when he officiated at the funeral of a 14-year-old girl who'd taken her own life.

As of 2016 there were 21,200 volunteers operating across 201 branches throughout the UK and Ireland.

STALKING

The National Stalking Helpline estimates that in any given year five million people experience stalking. Statistics show that the majority of victims (80.4 per cent) are female, while the majority of perpetrators (70.5 per cent) are male.

DOMESTIC VIOLENCE

One in four women will experience domestic violence at some point in her life. On average, police receive an emergency call relating to a domestic incident every thirty seconds. Two women die every week at the hands of a current or former partner.

Over a third of women will be physically assaulted by their partner for the first time during pregnancy.

Source: *Refuge Annual Report 2015–16.*

ACKNOWLEDGMENTS

Sincere thanks to all the wonderful people at Amazon who helped bring this book to fruition.

First and foremost to Editorial Director, Emilie Marneur, for commissioning the novel. Her encouragement, along with her patience – affording me the time I needed to complete the project – was paramount in driving me forward and keeping me focused throughout a rather challenging process.

To Acquisitions Editor, Sammia Hamer, for her dedication and enthusiasm from the start. Her astute insights, following her reading of the first draft, were both uplifting and inspiring. I knew I could trust her judgement fully.

To Victoria Pepe, Sammia's successor, for her fresh and practised eye in the final stages of the project.

To my Editor, Katie Green, for her excellent work. Her comprehensive understanding of the narrative and what I was trying to achieve through each successive edit was superb. She prompted me down paths I was initially hesitant to explore, and the novel has benefited greatly from her guidance and good counsel.

My heartfelt appreciation also to copyeditor Sarah Fakray and proofreader Julia Bruce.

To the lovely Catherine Mullins for reading my first draft within two days and calling me immediately to tell me how much she'd enjoyed it. Such words were a delight to hear and so much appreciated at a time of uncertainty.

Last but not least to my husband David for his keen-eyed observations and advice throughout the writing process. I would not be the writer I am today without his love, support and endless encouragement.

ABOUT THE AUTHOR

Christina McKenna grew up near the village of Draperstown, Northern Ireland. She attended the Belfast College of Art, where she obtained an honours degree in Fine Art. Having studied English as a postgraduate at the University of Ulster, she taught abroad for several years. She has lived, worked and painted pictures in Spain, Turkey, Italy, Ecuador and Mexico.

In 2004 she published a memoir, followed by two non-fiction titles on the paranormal: *The Dark Sacrament* (2006) and *Ireland's Haunted Women* (2010).

In 2011 she embarked on the Tailorstown Trilogy, a series of novels set in and around a fictional Ulster village. The books – *The Misremembered Man*, *The Disenchanted Widow* and *The Godforsaken Daughter* – were highly successful and have been translated into several languages.

68506929R00238

Made in the USA
Lexington, KY
12 October 2017